Praise for Darren O'Sullivan

'Dark, gripping and with a twist that leaves you breathless'

rrs

'Utterly brilliant . . . th
Darren O'Sullivan is p   as
an exceptional storyteller'

Lisa Hall

'I was gripped by this taut and emotional thriller'

Louise Jensen

'Engrossing, compelling and twisty from the first page to the shocking ending. This book grabbed me and didn't let go'

Michele Campbell

'Exquisitely written . . . a ripping good read'

Suzy K. Quinn

'A stellar and original concept, brilliantly executed. The final chapters had my heart in my throat! O'Sullivan is certainly one to watch'

Phoebe Morgan

'An outstandingly taut story which grabbed me and then spat me out breathless at the end'

Angela Marsons

Darren O'Sullivan is the author of psychological thrillers, *Our Little Secret*, *Close Your Eyes* and *Closer Than You Think*. He is a graduate of the Faber Academy and his debut novel, *Our Little Secret*, was a bestseller in four countries. He lives in Peterborough, Cambridgeshire where his days are spent either behind his laptop writing, in front of a group of actors directing theatre or rolling around pretending to be a dinosaur with his young son.

You can follow Darren on Twitter and Instagram @Darrensully or on Facebook/DarrenO'Sullivan-author.

Also by Darren O'Sullivan
Our Little Secret
Close Your Eyes
Closer Than You Think

Dark Corners

Darren O'Sullivan

ONE PLACE. MANY STORIES

HQ
An imprint of HarperCollins*Publishers* Ltd
1 London Bridge Street
London SE1 9GF

This edition 2020

3
First published in Great Britain by
HQ, an imprint of HarperCollins*Publishers* Ltd 2020

Copyright © Darren O'Sullivan 2020

Darren O'Sullivan asserts the moral right to be
identified as the author of this work.
A catalogue record for this book is
available from the British Library.

ISBN: 978-0-00-834201-2

MIX
Paper from
responsible sources
FSC
www.fsc.org
FSC™ C007454

This book is produced from independently certified FSC™ paper
to ensure responsible forest management.

For more information visit: www.harpercollins.co.uk/green

This book is set in 10.5/15.5 pt. Sabon

Printed and bound in Great Britain by
CPI Group (UK) Ltd, Croydon, CR0 4YY

To my boy, and my girl

15TH JULY 1998

I can't sleep thinking about what we will do tomorrow. I'm scared he will know; I'm scared he will be watching me...

CHAPTER I

August 1998
Three weeks after...

Onward they trudged. Step by step. Deeper into the woodlands, trying as best they could to maintain the straight line they had been instructed to hold. They didn't speak, they could barely look one another in the eye. They all knew just one look would confirm their worst fears, that the searching was in vain. They weaved around bushes and climbed unsteadily over fallen trees. The mud, thick and heavy, made progress even slower, and on a few occasions the sludge underfoot dragged wellington boots clean off tired feet. The summer had burnt bright and long, one of the hottest on record. But the woods were dark, cold. The air didn't move there, but hung heavily, its damp breath ancient, a thousand whispered secrets over a thousand years, clinging to everything within. And somewhere within, she might be alive. Hoping to be found. It had been three weeks since she had vanished, three long weeks. It didn't ring the bell of hope. Regardless, they didn't stop moving, they didn't stop looking.

In the middle the group walked Neve. She moved silently, helped those who were stuck and in return was helped when she became stuck herself. They had walked for long enough that the snapping of twigs and rustle of animals moving in the under-growth no longer startled them. Upon reaching a clearing, they were told by the search leader, a policeman called Thompson who had led the investigation, to stop and rest. Finding a felled tree, Neve sat and took a moment to look up through the thick canopy of summer leaves to see the sky beyond. It was beginning to morph in colour as day changed into night, a beautiful pink hue wrapped around a cloud. It looked contented, peaceful, oblivious. She assumed it would be another hour until it was too dark to continue, and that would mean another night passed with no sign of her, the twenty-second long night in the scared village. Neve caught her father watching from the small group stood in a circle, smoking hand-rolled cigarettes, discussing the next step. He smiled, trying to be reassuring, but she could see the worry in his eyes. He looked tired, older somehow. But then again, everyone in the village now looked tired and old, and afraid.

After a few minutes of rest and foot rubbing, boots were back on and they were moving again, quietly scanning the patch of ground in front of each step. Punctuating the sound of snapped twigs, heavy breathing of those less fit, wind through the treetops and bird call was one word spoken every now and then. A single name, her name.

Chloe.

Neve could hear the way that it had changed in the past few days. They used to call for Chloe as a question. As if to say, Chloe, can you hear us? Chloe, where are you? Now, the question mark had gone, the tone had deepened. Her name was now called because it was something they needed to do. If they fell silent the search would be over. With each day, each night, the hope dwindled. A few nights out alone, a person could survive. A week would be tough, but not impossible, but after three, without a sign or sound, it didn't look good. And it placed them all in the awful position of wanting to find her, but not being the one to find her. No one said it, but as Neve looked at those around her, she could see fear in their eyes – a fear of being the one to stumble across a 16-year-old girl, face down in a bog, bloated and blue. The village was used to accidents, death even. The mine that the village was built around had been a dangerous place to work, and men and women were often injured, sometimes horrifically. Pain and loss were a part of who they all were, it was part of their DNA. But no one was prepared to find Chloe. 'This sort of thing doesn't happen here,' they said to one another after she had gone missing. 'We look after our own.'

Despite the seriousness of Chloe's disappearance, gossip was rife. And being a small, ex-mining village, gossip quickly became political. The 'scabs' who'd crossed the picket line in 1984 blamed the strikers, while they in turn insisted it was one of the 'scabs'. When on the rare occasion the gossip didn't thrive on the bitter feud that ran like ice though the vein of the village, the adults whispered, in agreement, about Chloe's mother, Brenda, who everyone knew had been vile and cruel to Chloe since the day she was born. It had been noted that Brenda hadn't been on one single search, but instead holed herself up at home, curtains drawn, refusing to speak to anyone until the police banged on her door. It was widely discussed that if anyone had harmed Chloe, it would have been Brenda. There was also another name that they should have been discussing, a name that Neve and her friends had spoken to the police about, a name that was only ever mentioned by the adults in the village after a few drinks in The Miners' Arms or social club. A name that when brought up, sent a shiver down the spine of the highly superstitious community.

The Drifter.

They didn't know who he was, and apart from Neve and the rest of her friends, no one else had seen him. He had been spotted hanging around the closed mine, always at night. And, most worryingly, Chloe herself had told Neve he had been hanging around outside her house just before she vanished.

The police were looking for him, stating he was a person of interest. They speculated that whoever he was, he was indeed connected to the mine. Which meant he more than likely lived in the village itself. But so far, no one had been spoken to, no one arrested. It was as if he were a ghost.

The line of people searching came to a clearing that looked towards the mine. The small part of woodland they needed to search showed no signs of Chloe. It was time to return to The Miners' Arms, where they would either go home, or learn the next quadrants they intended to search before heading out again, light permitting. Neve was tired, and although she wanted to continue to look, as she landed on familiar territory of tarmac underfoot, her legs wobbled and failed her. Her father instinctively caught her before she hit the ground.

'Neve, you need to sleep.'

'I need to help.'

'You can't like this. You need to sleep, come back fresh.'

'Dad, I'm fine.'

'Neve, please. I know...'

'Dad, you don't know anything. Just leave me alone.'

Neve pulled herself away from her father and bounded towards the pub, her unsteadiness resolved by her defiance. As she entered, the noise of a thousand conversations swept over her. The energy inside was electric; the village determined to find the missing girl. The pub tables had maps rolled out, the corners held flat with pints of bitter. People were beginning to tie the laces on hiking boots and check torch batteries, ready to head out on the next wave. But, as the door closed behind her, the energy dipped as people noticed her entrance. Some sympathetic smiles were offered, as well as gentle nods of recognition. She knew they wanted to ask her about the Drifter, whether he was real or supernatural. She was glad they didn't. Because, although she didn't believe in ghosts, what other explanation was there?

After the brief dip with her entrance, the electricity increased as the next wave of searchers readied themselves to step into the woods, until the landlord held a radio to his ear and shouted:

'Everyone, shut up! Something's going on.'

Silence swept through the pub, everyone looking towards the landlord who turned up the radio and asked whoever was on the other end to repeat what they had said.

'We've found something, over by the old mine entrance,' a male voice returned, his desperation and sadness clear for everyone to hear.

'What – what have you found?' the landlord asked.

'A top. We've found a top. It's covered in blood.'

CHAPTER 2

19th November 2019
Morning

I roll onto my side. Open my eyes, stretch. The edge of a dream lingers for just a moment, and with it a smell. Before I can process what it is, it fades. I can't remember what was in my dream either, but as my heart is racing, I know it can't have been good. I wait for my head to begin to throb. Nothing. Maybe I've dodged a bullet this morning? Maybe I remembered to drink a pint of water and eat a teaspoon of sugar? They say it helps to stave off a hangover.

I wait to hear Oliver moving in the flat; he has always been better in the mornings than me. I expect to hear him flicking on a kettle or the news playing on the TV in the lounge. But it's quiet, and then it hits me, hard. A crippling blow to my stomach. *Of course, it's quiet, Neve, you idiot. Oliver left. Oliver left three weeks ago. I must try to not forget that. It only makes it harder.* I sigh and roll onto my other side, facing where he used to lie beside me. The corner of his pillow feels cold against my cheek. But then really, if I'm being honest with myself, it was probably cold against my cheek long before he left.

A dim morning light comes through the window. I didn't

draw my curtains, again. From where I lay, I can see the trees in Brent Lodge Park. Oliver loved that about this flat, always saying the trees and that huge expanse of grass on the park was our back garden. He loved how green it was, the birdsong that floated into our bedroom in summer.

Outside looks cold, the sun is early in the sky, I guess it's about half past six. Colder than yesterday. I think I'll just stay in bed for half an hour longer. I grab my phone; the screen is blurry. I look in the bedside unit to find my glasses. They aren't there. God knows where I've left them this time. Squinting I open my clock app and set an alarm, just twenty more minutes and I'd get up for work. But I see the time. It's 8.41 a.m. I'm late. Again. And I knew Esther was going to be pissed.

Jumping up, I make a dash for the bathroom, then as I fumble into yesterday's clothes which lay in a heap at the foot of my bed, I feel the drill in my skull start to vibrate, its intensity growing with every second until my eyes ache. I never had hangovers when I was young. Now, they were making up for lost time, hammering me harder than I felt they should. Dressed, I run for the door, grabbing my glasses which were on the radiator shelf where I keep my keys, which of course weren't there. I check the kitchen sides, moving two empty bottles of wine into the recycling bin. I check the coffee table in the living room, down the side of the sofa, coat pockets. I even check in the fridge. But I cannot find them. Deciding I'll leave and call the landlord to let me in later, I grab my bag and open the front door. Hanging on the other side is a photo fob of me and Oliver, swinging from my front door key which is sat in the lock.

'Shit, Neve.'

Closing the door behind me I pocket my cold keys and walk

as fast as my hangover, which was beginning to steam-roll over me, would allow, towards the station. It was a short walk to Hanwell station where I would hop onto the train to Ealing Broadway. A quick walk across to the Underground and then the Central line for five stops to Shepherd's Bush. On the other side, ten minutes to work. On a good day, I could do the commute in twenty-five minutes. But I could already tell it wasn't going to be a good day, and regardless, I was supposed to be at work for nine. It was now 8.52 a.m. There was no way I would be on time. Taking out my phone, I took a deep breath and called Esther.

'Good morning, The Tea Tree.'

'Esther, it's Neve.'

'Neve? Where are you?'

'Running late.'

'Again.'

'I'm so sorry.'

'You sound hungover.'

'I'm all right, just tired. I'll get an Uber.'

I could hear her sigh on the other end of the phone. 'That'll cost a fortune. Anyway, it's pretty quiet. When do you think you'll get here?

'Half past, at the very latest.'

'Right.'

'And later, why don't you go home early? I'll look after the place. How does that sound?'

'You've just dug yourself out of a hole.'

'Thought I might.' I smiled, having lightened the mood which had seemed strained between us over the past few weeks. 'I'll see you soon.'

She hesitated and I knew what was about to come; it was

the conversation she had started on several occasions in the last few weeks but stopped herself for fear of making me feel worse. I had cut her off every time with some distraction, but this time I just waited for her to continue, knowing she needed to get it off her chest.

'Neve, I get what you're going through, I really do, but we are partners in this. That means we share the work, share the responsibility.'

'I know, Esther, I know, and I'm sorry. I'm going to try harder. This isn't fair.'

'I get things are pretty shit for you right now. But they aren't easy for me either.'

'Of course.'

'My childminder costs have gone up, and I can't afford to be here all the time, both for my family, and my pocket.'

I knew what she was saying without actually saying it. She was telling me I didn't have responsibly like she did. I didn't have a two-year-old who needed my time. I didn't have the mortgage she had. My life was a mess, but it was still less complex than hers. 'I'll be there as soon as I can. I'm sorry, Esther.'

'I hate being a nag.'

'No, you're not. You're more than entitled to be pissed off. I'm just grateful you can say it.'

'Me too. See you soon.'

She hung up and I knew, despite her being kind and understanding, she had had just about enough of my apologies. As I entered the train station, I vowed to make it up to her somehow. Although I wasn't quite sure how or where I would start. Hanwell station was packed, as expected. And as I fought my way through the small gaps in the crowds, I wished I'd showered as I became conscious of my own smell of sleep and booze and regret. Ducking behind a brick pillar I opened my bag and rifled until I found a small canister of body spray, quickly coating myself in its sweet floral scent. An older person stood close by looked at me disapprovingly, but I didn't care. I still didn't smell clean, but at least I didn't smell of body odour.

A train pulled in and I jostled with the crowd on board, my shoulders pressed between two men who were much taller than me – one had his armpit perilously close to my face. Still, at least he had had a shower that morning. As the train lurched from the station, I felt my stomach lurch with it and within a minute I could feel a sweat start to break out across my top lip. I tried to remember how much I'd had to drink last night. I remembered coming home from work about seven, eating a Pot Noodle for tea and pouring my first glass of wine. From there, I know I drank more – there were two bottles on the side this morning. I had to wonder: was it OK I had become someone who drank to excess most nights? I almost let myself wonder what Oliver would say about it. Thankfully, the train announced we were pulling into West Ealing, stopping me from hearing his voice. It wasn't healthy. I wanted to convince myself that I still didn't know why he left, and that it was a complete shock, but I think deep down I saw it coming. He said we had grown apart; we had become different people. He was right, of course. He was open, honest, he had no shadows, he thought of the future, of the things that came with the future. Things I couldn't bear thinking about. I guess I had always known it, but I didn't see it, I didn't want to. I saw us having our problems, as all couples did, but I thought we would work through our differences. I knew he loved me fiercely. And I loved him the same. I really thought we would go the distance. But love isn't enough, is it?

When I found his letter three weeks ago, I assumed, right up until the moment I opened it, it would be a note saying something sweet and funny. My heart crumbled when I read that he wasn't coming back. The things I thought were little and we could work through were impossible for him.

The man beside me coughed, making my head thump. He apologised and I smiled, but judging by his reaction, I was fairly sure it looked more like a grimace. Embarrassed, I looked away and opened my bag to grab a packet of ibuprofen. I swallowed three dry, then I pressed my head against the cold glass of the train door and counted my breathing, stopping myself thinking about Oliver, until Ealing Broadway came into view.

Fighting my way off the train, I allowed myself to be swept up in the crowd heading towards the Underground and onto the Central line to finish my journey. I grab a bottle of water en route from a newsagent to stave off the claggy feeling in the back of my throat, forewarning me I would throw up, unless I was careful. As I paid, I looked through the gap in the sliding door where the cigarettes sat, wanting to be smoked. I almost asked for a pack of Marlboro but stopped myself. I was fucking up today as it was without having a cigarette after so long without one. So, I boarded the Tube with a fault sense of victory. After what felt like a lifetime crammed into the metal carriage, I made it to Shepherd's Bush, unscathed.

The Tea Tree, the coffee shop Esther and I set up three years ago, was about half a mile from the station and the walk usually took about ten minutes. However, as I stepped in the front door, the blast from the overhead heater making me feel nauseous once more, I saw it had taken me nearly twenty minutes to cover the short distance.

There were five people inside, two older couples sitting and talking, and a woman on her own stirring a cup of tea. I didn't catch a single eye as I made my way out back. As I passed the till, I couldn't even look at Esther. I knew what face she would have on – her 'I'm really pissed off but worried' look she'd perfected ever since our second year at uni. I was feeling too sensitive to deal with it. She would calm down, she always did. Then we would talk and laugh and enjoy our work together. And she would go home to her family, and I would hold the fort until closing time this evening.

Disappearing into the stockroom-cum-staffroom, I took off my coat, hung my bag on my peg and donned the floral apron that was my only uniform requirement. I hesitated before stepping back into the shop. My head was still pounding but I knew it wouldn't be long until the ibuprofen kicked in. Until then, I needed to paint on a smile, and pretend I hadn't drunk and probably cried myself into oblivion the night before. Easy, right? Just another Tuesday. Just another morning.

CHAPTER 3

19th November 2019
Evening

With the last customer gone I locked the shop door and closed the blinds, and felt exhausted. My hangover had faded by lunchtime, thankfully, but it had been replaced with an emptiness that had lasted the rest of the day, and with Esther leaving early, the final few hours of serving people, smiling politely and cleaning up the mess created by toddlers had been a slog. I hoped people didn't think I was being rude. I tried my best to be upbeat, but really, I bet it came across as just beat. And now that the day was done, I wanted nothing more than to step under a hot shower before falling into bed. But I couldn't go home, not just yet – Esther had left me a list of chores. I should have been a little annoyed she didn't trust me to undertake the jobs needed for our business. But then again, these past few weeks, I've hardly been a paragon of trust. Sometimes it felt like she was actually my boss rather than my business partner. I guess that said more about me than her.

Grabbing the list, I walked over to the speakers and connected my phone. Opening my music app, I loaded my 'classics playlist' and turned up the volume. Then, I set about cleaning the last remaining tables and loading the dishwasher. Tina Turner's 'Nutbush City Limits' came on, a song that always made me feel better. It reminded me of a time long before business and broken hearts. A time before 1998. Before that night. Before Chloe.

That song, like all the others in my playlist, took me back to being young, perhaps nine or ten. Mum and Dad were still together, still happy, and my memories were of endless summer days, the smell of rain on hot tarmac, of Refresher sweets in paper tubes, of bike rides, noisy clackers in the wheels and beads on the spokes that created an almighty din as we rode. This song reminded me of my friends. All of them.

With the tables cleaned and the cups and plates in the dishwasher, I disinfected the counters and cashed up the till. Despite how I was feeling, it hadn't been a bad day. Maybe the best mid-week takings we've had in a while. With the takings in hand, I was down to my last job. Double-checking the front door was locked, I went out back to the safe and opened it, removing the cash from Sunday and yesterday. Esther and I probably should bank every day, but it cost to deposit money, so we opted for twice a week instead. And whoever was last on Friday and Tuesday had to prepare for the bank run for the following morning. As I inputted the numbers and double-checked the amount in each denomination, I could feel a fresh headache begin to form behind my eyes. I knew I didn't have any painkillers left, so instead I grabbed a miniature bottle of Shiraz from the wine shelf and opened it. I told myself a glass of wine whilst doing the books was a normal thing to do, that I was just like everyone else. It wasn't true, of course – drinking while battling the hangover from the day before wasn't normal at all. But I pretended and doing assuaged some of the guilt.

I sat at the table nearest the till and took off my glasses.

I pinched the bridge of my nose, relieving a little of the pressure, and I let myself enjoy a few sips of the wine. Over the music, which had moved on from Tina Turner to an early Kylie Minogue, I could hear rain hitting the glass of the shop front. I used to love the sound of rain once, but not now. Outside in the street, the shapeless silhouette of a person came into view. They stopped outside the window. I couldn't see their features through the blinds, and I couldn't work out if they were looking directly towards me, or directly into the rainstorm. Regardless, I held my breath for a moment longer than I should have. My mind took me back to somewhere I didn't want to visit. Just to be safe, I reached over and put the bag of cash behind the bin. When I looked up, whoever was there had gone. And then I thought, what if it was Oliver? What if he had come back to see me, to offer an explanation as to why he took off without offering so much as an apology for his inability to do it face to face?

Jumping up, I knocked my wine over and dashed to the door. I unlocked it and stepped outside. The rain was falling so hard it hurt the top of my head. I looked left and right, but I couldn't see anyone. As I locked the door again, a shiver ran up my spine. I reasoned it was the cold rain, and nothing else, but still, I turned the music down before cleaning up the mess I made, the hairs on the back of my neck standing up on end.

When I'd finished preparing the morning bank run, I returned all of the money to the safe, grabbed my coat and locked the shop before walking as quickly as I could to the Underground. Despite it only being just after seven, it felt later, the darkness complete and all-consuming. The footpaths were littered with fallen leaves that only this morning looked beautiful; now they glistened like slugs under the streetlamps and were slippery underfoot. I walked fast, my head down, trying to see behind me until I reached the newsagent where I'd bought the water earlier today. I picked up a bottle of wine, paid, and feeling a little less uneasy I headed down the stairs into the warmer, stale air of the Underground.

CHAPTER 4

20th November 2019
Morning

I roll onto my side and try to open my eyes. I manage to open one, just a sliver and it closes again. My bedroom light is on, it's too bright, it hurts too much. And the drill is there. Hammering away.

Shit, Neve. You did it again, didn't you?

I fall out of bed, landing on my elbow, right on the knobbly bit that should have jolted pain into my hand, but instead it jolts the other way, a mainline straight into the space behind my eyes. The hammering becomes an intense throb. It hurts my head so much I think my eyes will burst. I gingerly get to my feet. I'm really hungover, more so than most days. I stagger into the kitchen, the bottle I bought on the way home is lying on its side, a small pool of red where the dregs had dripped. And there is a bottle of vodka beside it. Oliver's vodka. I must have raised a glass to him last night. The bottle is empty. I cannot remember how much was in there when I got home after being spooked at work.

I go back into my bedroom to grab my phone. No missed calls, no texts, no fiancé saying he is sorry for leaving without taking anything with him. But the consolation is, it's just before seven and I'm not late for work. I shower, wash my hair, dress. It helps. I feel less like I want to pass out. I try to find my glasses; I must have left them at work. I still have an hour before the café opens. But I want to show Esther I meant what I said, about trying harder. I can get the till ready. Warm the place up. I may even dig the Christmas decorations out of the box in the back of the storeroom and start giving The Tea Tree a more festive feel.

Despite the headache I'm feeling good about today and, grabbing a breakfast bar, I leave, locking my door behind me. It's raining. Not like last night's downpour, but the kind that feels like TV static on your skin. Stopping at the nearest shop I buy as many painkillers as I can without raising an eyebrow of suspicion, pop two and head into the station. Thankfully, the train is far less crowded than yesterday, and I find myself at Ealing Broadway in what seems much less time than usual. I even had a seat for the entire journey, a real treat.

The rain stopped as I left Shepherd's Bush station, and with my painkillers starting to kick in, I took my headphones out of my coat pocket and plugged into my playlist. As I turned onto Richmond Way, I could see our café in the distance. And even without my glasses, I knew something was terribly wrong. It was in the way people were slowing down as they passed the shop. The way they had to walk around something on the floor. I hoped I was mistaken, but as I drew closer, I could see rainwater shimmering on broken glass. A few more steps and I could see where the glass should have been. Our shop's front door had been smashed in. I could see the tables and chairs scattered on the floor within. We had been robbed. I must have let out a gasp or a cry or something because people looked at me, their quizzical expressions changing as they realised it was my shop. I fumbled in my bag for my phone. It wasn't there. I must have left it at home. Shit, Neve. Of all the days.

A woman approached, she asked if I was all right. I wanted to say no, of course I'm not bloody all right. But the words didn't come.

'Has, umm, could somebody ring the police, please?' I asked, unable to look away from the mess inside the shop.

'I have already. They'll be here soon.'

I nodded towards her and started for the door, taking my keys out of my pocket as I approached.

'Perhaps it's best if you stay outside? Until the police arrive?' the woman said. I didn't look back, just put my key in the lock, trying to jiggle it open. It was stiff as it usually was, but eventually it gave, and I opened the door. I don't know why I bothered. There was no glass in the frame. I could have stepped in without needing to unlock it. Just like the person who robbed us did.

The sound of glass crunching under my weight seemed to echo off the walls and squinting, I scanned the room. Tables had been overturned. Chairs knocked over. But, as far as I could see, nothing was missing. The glass was still intact on the serving counter but some of the cakes from the display cases were gone. With my heart pounding so hard I could feel it behind my eyes, I leant over the counter. I expected to see the till missing or smashed open but it too was untouched. My glasses sat on the top, where I left them last night. Putting them on, I looked around the café once more. It was a mess, but I couldn't see anything, besides a few cakes, missing. It confused me. Why would someone break in for a piece of cake?

It didn't take long before I could hear sirens approaching, followed by blue lights from the police car bouncing off the walls. Two officers stepped in, looked over the place, took my details,

Esther's details, and told me forensics would be out soon to dust for prints. They didn't seem bothered by it all, but, I guess, awful as it was, little had actually been taken. They speculated it was probably a bunch of kids, but I was told not to tidy yet, not until the forensics had finished. All I could do was sit and wait for Esther to turn up so we could call a window company, our insurance, post on our Facebook page that we were shut – as well as everything else I knew we had to do but couldn't yet process. I sat and waited for what felt an eternity for her to arrive, as I couldn't call her. I didn't know her number, it was stored in my phone as it had been for the past nearly two decades. Of all the days to forget your phone. I made a mental note to learn it. I bet she knew mine.

Esther arrived twenty minutes after the police left. She looked as shocked as I must have done.

'Neve? What the fuck?'

'Someone broke in last night.'

'Shit!'

'Yeah, shit.'

'Have you called the police?'

'Of course I have,' I snapped. 'Sorry. They've been and gone.'

'Shit,' she repeated as she stepped over a patch of broken glass and sat on a stool beside me. I wanted to hug her but didn't.

'I can't believe you'd think I *wouldn't* call the police!'

'Sorry.'

'Cheers, Esther.'

'Sorry, I just… is there anything missing?'

'A few cakes.'

'Cakes?'

'Yeah, a few chocolate muffins, some other bits.'

'Is that it?'

Esther stood and walked towards the display and looked in behind the glass. Then, leaning over, she looked at the till.

'They didn't even touch it,' I said.

'That's weird. Lucky, but weird,' she replied as she sat beside me once more. We both stared at the chaos of the shop, passive, like we were at the cinema. 'They just took cakes?' she asked again.

'Little shits with the munchies, no doubt.'

'Really? Are kids that bad?'

'Worse,' I said quietly, remembering how when I was a kid, it wasn't cakes but booze from the local off-licence. 'I've been told not to tidy until they come to dust for prints. Otherwise I would have started.'

She nodded and looked to the bin which had been knocked over, the contents scattered on the floor. If we'd not been robbed, she would have no doubt said something about me not emptying them, especially as it was on the list. I almost offered an apology but saw she had narrowed her gaze on something and, following her eye line, I saw her look at the empty bottle of wine.

'I only had one, while cashing up, and I paid for it.'

'Neve, you were so hungover yesterday…'

'It was only one. Just to take the edge off.'

'That sounds like something a person with a drinking problem might say.'

'I don't have a drinking problem.'

'That's another thing they would say, right?'

'Esther!' I said, my voice sounding louder and more wounded than I intended.

'Sorry, yes, now isn't the time. I just worry about you.'

'Well, don't, OK? I'm all right. I'm on the mend.'

'OK.' She smiled. 'So, I guess now all we can do is wait for the fingerprint people to come. Why didn't you call me?'

'Left my phone at home. Shall I make us a coffee?' I asked, already getting to my feet as I knew what her answer would be.

'Good idea. Neve?'

I turned and glanced back at Esther, who – for a moment – looked smaller than she usually did, her petite frame somehow swallowed by the mess around us. Although she called my name, she wasn't looking at me, not at first, her eyes were back to the small empty bottle of wine on the floor. 'Things will get better, you know that right?'

'Yep,' I responded too quickly. 'The insurance will cover it; we've got a crime reference nu—'

'That's not what I meant,' she said, bringing her eyes to mine. 'You're not keeping something from me?'

'What, no, of course not.'

'You were drinking a lot back at uni when... you know.'

'Esther. I'm fine. I'm OK.'

I tried to smile, to show her I was all right, and she didn't need to worry about me, she had enough on her plate. 'I promise.'

'OK,' she said, not convinced. 'I'll find the insurance policy so we can give them a ring.'

'I'm sorry, Esther,' I said, although I had no idea why.

'Me too,' she replied before touching me on the shoulder as she made for the stockroom at the back. As I waited for the coffee machine to warm up, I looked at the door, the glass on the floor and I knew they wouldn't find any prints. Kids were smarter than that, despite also being completely thoughtless sometimes. But, with only a few cakes missing, I knew no harm was really done. Kids just being kids.

CHAPTER 5

June 1998
Six weeks before...

'So, Baz and I were bored the other night and decided we'd go for a walk,' Michael started as he took a drag on his cigarette.

'You're always bored,' interrupted Holly without looking at him. She was keeping watch on the school, making sure none of the teachers were unexpectedly patrolling the field several hours after school had finished.

'Holly, you don't need to keep watch now, we aren't going to get into trouble.'

'My dad would kill me if he thought I was smoking.'

'But you're not. And anyway, as soon as the bell sounds at 3.15, the teachers don't give a shit what we do.'

'But...'

'Holly. They care even less just before 8 p.m.,' Chloe added, trying to reassure her twitchy friend.

'Sorry, you're right.' Holly smiled, resuming her thoughts about Michael. Most of his stories began in the same way: either he was bored, or Baz was bored, or they both were. And usually, his stories culminated in them being in trouble. That boredom had meant he had been suspended on three occasions in their secondary school career, and instead of sitting all fourteen exams, he would end up taking only nine.

'Anyway, as I was saying,' continued Michael, shooting a mean but playful look at Holly. 'We were bored, and we went for a walk, and we discovered something really cool. Wanna see it?'

'Not really,' Jamie chuckled.

'Come on, I promise, you're gonna love it. You're all gonna love it.'

Jumping to his feet, Michael urged the group to move.

'How long will it take? I've got revision to do,' Holly protested, and although Neve, Jamie and Georgia were thinking the same question, no one backed her up. It was typical of the group. Despite how closely knit they were, they still didn't want to appear any different to Baz and Michael, who cared very little for anything besides having a good time.

'I'm glad you mentioned the exams,' Michael continued, 'because what we found will help us with the stress of the bastards.'

Without waiting, Michael turned and walked away from the group towards the back corner of the school field, where a hole had been cut in the fence so they could nip out at lunch and buy cigarettes from the local corner shop. It had been there for years, before any of them started the school, and everyone knew about it. Baz joined at his side, followed by Jamie and Georgia.

Neve noticed Georgia was starting to change her look. Her usually unkempt hair was scraped back, and she could see the hint of make-up. It was subtle, and no one spoke of it, but Georgia was becoming one of the prettier girls within the group. And it changed how she walked. Instead of stomping like the tomboy she once was, she now held her head high, kept her gait light. It gave her a new air of confidence. She was blossoming, and although the boys hadn't seemed to notice, Neve knew it wouldn't be long before they did.

Chloe and Neve picked up the end of the group, curious about Michael and Baz's 'discovery'. The pair were a liability, but a lot of fun along with it. Georgia linked arms with Holly, probably making sure she didn't bail as she so often did. As they walked, Chloe and Neve chatted about how there was nothing left to discover in the village. It was too small, too samey. After only a few minutes of walking, it became clear where they were being led, and it piqued everyone's interest – even Holly's. Michael and Baz had led them to Mine Lane, and as they stepped foot on it, everyone stopped. Mine Lane, and what was at the end of it, was the place ghost stories were written about. As kids they'd told each other tales of dark shadows walking aimlessly at night, and hearing the cries of those who had died. As young children, they'd run past its entrance, too afraid to look down in case a spectre grabbed them and dragged them below. That fear was still there, still tangible.

'You do know we aren't allowed in there?' Jamie said, shifting from one foot to the other.

'Yes, we know.'

'Then where are we...'

'You'll see, have a little patience,' Michael said, smiling knowingly to Baz. 'Come on.'

Baz and Michael continued down the lane, and the group followed in silence, coming closer to the entrance of the old mine. They stood huddled together, and Neve looked back towards the main road, expecting someone to come and shout at them to leave things alone. The lane itself wasn't forbidden, and there were no fences that stopped them walking down it, no signs – not like the mine. The ground was still sacred to the people who worked the pits and shouldn't be tainted by anyone who didn't. Everyone in the group had someone in their family who had once worked there, as did every soul in the village. But unless you'd actually descended to its belly, you were silently forbidden to go anywhere near it.

The mine had only been closed less than a year, and already the road was showing the signs of neglect. Cracks lined the tarmac as seeds from hardy weeds forced their way through. Above their heads, the trees were beginning to form a canopy, turning the road into a tunnel as the branches hadn't been artificially pruned by passing lorries. And below the canopy, the few lamps that still contained a bulb didn't light up the evening sky. The electricity supply had been cut off. The place felt desolate, the atmosphere tense to everyone except Baz and Michael who continued to bounce down the lane without a care in the world. Neve could see everyone was a little jumpy at the sounds that emanated from the densely packed trees. Chloe held her best friend a little closer, and thought of ghosts. Eyes watching. Waiting to spook them. With each step, it felt like the lane was getting darker.

Baz and Michael slowed as they drew close to the old entrance barrier that was still there, its paint faded and mossy. It was pointless it being there, as twenty feet behind it was the metal fence that surrounded the entire land of the colliery – a footprint that was larger than the rest of the village.

'I'm not going in there,' said Holly shakily as they stood in front of the barrier.

'Me neither,' agreed Georgia, who for once wasn't worried about what anyone thought.

'Please, as if we'd be that stupid,' said Baz, waiting for someone to agree. No one did. 'We aren't here because of the mine.'

'Yeah, there's no way we would go down there,' Michael agreed.

'I thought you two were fearless,' Chloe teased.

'We are,' said Baz, haughtily. 'But no fucking way would we go there.'

'Then why are we here?' said Holly, checking her watch.

'Because of this.'

Baz gestured to his left at the old security hut that once checked and allowed vehicles and foot traffic onto the site. The building, roughly the size of a large shed, was made of metal and concrete, designed to be hard-wearing and functional. The hut was positioned in front of a stand of trees, probably planted to act as a sort of barrier behind the hut. Its windows and doors were boarded up with sheets of metal that had been welded to the structure, intentionally impenetrable.

'What are we doing here?' asked Chloe, exasperated with the boys for wasting time and making her walk so far.

'Well, we were thinking. You guys are so burnt out with exams and all that stuff,' said Michael, not noticing Chloe's annoyance. 'So, we figured we needed a space to unwind and de-stress.'

'Again, so why are we here?'

'Come with me, I'll show you.'

Taking Chloe by the hand, Baz led her towards the trees and guided her to squeeze between them and the hut, Michael urging the group to follow. It wasn't until they traversed between the wall and trees that the group understood why Baz and Michael were so excited. There was a small hatch that hadn't been welded shut, probably forgotten or overlooked. Baz dropped to his knees and opened the hatch inward, sliding his wide frame through the gap, disappearing from sight.

'Come on!' he bellowed from within, his voice sounding like he was shouting through a hand clamped over his mouth.

One by one the group followed and crawled through the small space until Michael, who was last, closed the hatch behind him. The darkness within was absolute, until Baz produced a small wind-up lantern, which created just enough light for the group to look around the small, claustrophobic space.

'It's not much…' started Michael.

'It's a pit,' said Georgia.

'It's technically breaking and entering. And it creeps me out, I wanna go home,' added Holly, which was greeted with a scoff from Neve and an eye-roll from Georgia. Only Chloe nodded, spooked.

'I mean, we all know the stories coming out of the mine,' she said as a way of defence when Neve caught her agreeing.

'Don't tell me you believe in ghosts?'

'No, of course not, Neve. But it's creepy here.'

'Yeah, it kinda is,' said Georgia, nodding.

Baz looked crestfallen. 'But that's part of its charm, and with a little imagination, and a little change, it could be brilliant.'

'This is what you dragged us out here for, to climb inside a concrete box?'

'Use your imagination, Holly. Picture a bean bag here,' said Baz, pointing towards the furthest corner, 'and a little table next to it.'

'Do the electrics work?' asked Jamie, with a hint of excitement in his voice.

'You know, we've not checked. Why?'

'If they do, my dad's got an old fridge, if we can get it here.'

'There you go! Jamie gets it.'

'I still don't,' said Chloe sulkily.

'Chloe, you need this place more than anyone.'

'Why would I—'

'Because you and your mum don't get on.'

'So? Our parents do all of our heads in.'

'Yeah,' agreed Georgia quietly, and instantly wished she hadn't spoken. She knew they all talked about her dad when she was out of earshot.

'Exactly,' continued Baz, oblivious to Georgia's unease. The whole group knew her dad hit her, despite her denying it on several occasions. 'And we are stuck, listening to them whinge and moan at us about not eating our dinner or doing the bins.'

'My mum gets on at me because I don't clean up the dog turd,' said Jamie.

'My dad makes shitty jokes about the music I like,' agreed Neve.

'And who is it this week?' asked Michael.

'NSYNC, of course.'

'It was Boyz II Men last week. Both crap.'

'Anyway,' interrupted Baz before a debate about musical taste ensued. 'No one cares about this place anymore. And those who might probably assume it's sealed. No one will know we are here. This could be our space. Not our parents' or Nan's,' he said, looking towards Michael who lived with his grandmother, for reasons the group still didn't know. 'There won't be anyone telling us what to do here. This can be a safe haven, to help those of us who care get through the exams.'

'And those who don't get to have some fun,' Michael added before removing his rucksack and placing it on the floor. The familiar sound of glass clinking against glass made several in the group smile.

'And on that note: I think we need to raise a toast to our independence,' he said as he unzipped his bag and pulled out a case of alcopops.

'Where the hell did you get those?' Holly asked, alarmed at the fact they were hidden from the world and armed with booze.

'I nicked them.'

'You nicked them? From where?'

'The offie,' Michael said.

'How?' Jamie asked, impressed and alarmed in equal measure.

'I do the paper round, don't I? Anyway, a truckload of stock came in last night, Mr Busby was busy doing the take and I saw my chance. He'll never know.'

'Michael!' Holly exclaimed, shocked and upset.

'Oh, chill out, he'll never know, and anyway, what does it matter, he owns the shop. He's got more than enough money.'

'It's still stealing. Baz, I can't believe you let him go through with this.'

'Hey, don't look at me, I had no idea until it was done.'

'Badass!' Georgia said, shocking Neve who expected her to be unimpressed.

'It's not a big deal. They were just sat by the door, and I took them. It's not like I shoplifted.'

'You did shoplift.'

'Not the same, Holly. I bet old Busby saw me take them and couldn't be arsed to say anything about it.'

'Michael…'

'Holly, it's done now. Chill the fuck out.'

Baz nodded, as did Jamie, while Georgia gave Holly a look as if to say 'stop being embarrassing', and the conversation was over. He was right, it was done, and there could be no way to undo it. Michael handed out the bottles and opened each one with the bottom of his clipper lighter before uncapping his last. He raised his in the air, and everyone, including Holly, joined in.

'Here's to us, our space, and the freedom to make the choices we wanna make.'

'So, what do we do now?' asked Georgia, still unimpressed as they could just drink in the park, or Baz's house when his parents were away.

'I've got an idea,' said Neve, eyeing Holly with a mischievous look that moved towards Chloe. 'How about a ghost story?'

CHAPTER 6

20th November 2019
Morning

I finished making us a coffee – for Esther, a chai latte and a strong black Americano for me – and heard Esther swear angrily. She didn't swear often, and the fact she had told me something was very wrong. Putting down the cups, I walked out back to find Esther on the floor, her face in her hands. At first, I thought she had banged her head on something and had called out in pain. I was just about to ask if she was OK, then I saw.

Beside her, the safe I had put all of our money in the night before was open, and it was empty. They hadn't just stolen a few cakes. They stole half a week's takings, a few thousand pounds. My legs felt like they were going to give way, so I stumbled to a chair and sat.

'Why didn't the police check in here?' she asked, her voice barely audible.

'I told them there was nothing missing.'

'Then why didn't you check, Neve?'

'I... I don't know.'

Esther looked up at me, and I could see anger in her eyes. I almost told her to calm down, to remember we're insured. After she'd spoken next, the words failed me.

'They didn't break into it.'

'What? I don't…'

'They didn't break into the fucking safe, Neve. Look at it. Look.'

I looked once more to the open, empty safe. And she was right, there was no sign of forced entry. No scratches, no dents. The safe was simply open.

'They either knew the code, Neve, or…'

'How would they know they code?'

'Or you didn't lock it last night.'

'No, I did, I'm sure I did.'

'Neve, either you've given the code to someone…'

'Why on earth would I do that? Are you saying I stole it?'

'. . . or you left it open. Which is it?'

I racked my brain, trying to recall if I shut the safe after returning the money. I remembered the rain, spilling my wine. Seeing the silhouette through the blinds. I remember taking the money out back, putting it in the safe. Did I shut the door? Did I lock it? Yes, I was sure I did. But I was so hungover, so tired, distracted by the person I saw outside. I couldn't be convinced.

'Neve!' Esther shouted, snapping me back into the now.

'I don't know.'

'You don't know?'

'I mean, maybe, yes. I must have left it unlocked because how else could they have got in?'

'Exactly! I go home for one evening. One evening to be with my little girl and you're drinking at work and fucking things up.'

'Esther! I wasn't drunk…'

'No, Neve, no!' she shouted, silencing me. 'I get that you're having a tough time. I do. And I'm sorry Oliver left you, it's really shit. But it has to stop affecting this place.' Her voice became softer, harder to hear. She sounded hurt. 'It has to stop affecting me and my life. I have bills to pay, a child to feed.'

'I'm sorry.'

'I'm sick of you telling me you're sorry,' she said, holding my gaze. 'I am. We've known each other a long time; we've been through it all, haven't we? I've been at your side through thick and thin, but I can't keep doing this, Neve.'

'Doing what?'

'Your life falls apart, I fix it. It was all right when we were twenty-one and at uni and you were falling in love and breaking up every ten minutes – or when you cut yourself off from the world because of what happened to that girl you used to know. It was all right that night in the club when. . .'

She didn't finish her sentence; she didn't need to. I thought of that night, and how she'd held me, soothed me, until help arrived.

'But we're adults now. *I'm* an adult now. You're still you. Living from day to day, doing what feels right in the moment. Never moving forward.'

'I was moving forward. Oliver and I...'

'Oliver despaired that you wouldn't let him in. You know that, right?'

'What, he talked to you about it?'

'He told me, more than once, that he was struggling because you wouldn't tell him about your past. He thought you were so secretive. You and he split up because you can't take responsibility for your problems.'

'Esther, that's hardly fair,' I said, choking back tears.

'What's not fair is that we're now completely skint, and I have my baby to feed, Neve – that's what's not fair.'

Her words sucked the air from my lungs.

'Go home, Neve.'

'What?'

'You look like shit, and I can't face you right now. Just go home. I'll deal with this, get the door boarded and tidied up.'

'But...'

'Seriously, just go. And if you really wanna help, perhaps think of an idea that can save this café.'

'What? The café is fine. Besides this, we're doing OK.'

'I can't keep doing "OK", Neve, I can't,' she said, getting up. 'We both know this has turned out to be a lot tougher than we thought it would be. I don't mind the long hours, I don't. But I can't afford to work for nothing.'

'Esther, it will be...'

'And we've just lost what, £2,000, £3,000?'

'Close to £3,500,' I said quietly.

'How are we going to get that back? How are we going to pay our rent on this place, let alone my mortgage? Tell me, how?'

'I don't know,' I said, tears pressing in the back of my eyes.

'Go home, Neve. Get yourself sorted out, you're a mess,' Esther said with an air of finality. I watched her get up and grab her phone. She must have dialled 111 because she asked me to get the crime reference number. I did as she asked, and when she started to talk into the phone about the stolen money, I grabbed my coat and left.

CHAPTER 7

20th November 2019
Evening

I had tried to call Esther three times during the day; each time it rang and rang before going to voicemail. I didn't leave a message. And just in case I wasn't already feeling shitty enough, I stupidly tried to call Oliver too. It rang once and then disconnected, like he had seen who was calling and hit the cancel button. Great. Despite being home for most of the day, those two small things were the sum of what I had accomplished. I was being pathetic. I knew Esther would calm down eventually. I hoped the stolen money would be insured but if the safe had been left open after all, I didn't think it would be. I also hoped that, despite my mistake, the landlord would be sympathetic, as would our customers. We would have a tough few weeks, but we would survive long enough for us to work out what to do to save our business. The way Esther looked at me today, I knew she was just about ready to give up on The Tea Tree if we didn't do something to lift our game and pay us both a proper salary. I didn't blame her; she'd been doing very well working for the marketing department of some corporate giant before we spoke of my insane idea of opening a café together. If I was her,

I probably would have given up a year ago. No, I definitely would have given up, because apparently that's what I do. I run away from my problems.

Then I thought about it properly – maybe some time apart wasn't such a bad idea. I didn't want to run away from Esther, not in a million years. She had been my first true friend since leaving my childhood home all those years ago. She was one of the few people who knew that Chloe Lambert – the girl who was once all over the news, the girl who was never found – was my best friend. She knew about the man I saw back then, the Drifter. She knew about my dad; she knew about the village I grew up in. I trusted Esther more than I trusted anyone else in the world, even Oliver. I couldn't afford to lose her from my life. But if I stepped back a little, let her run The Tree Tea on her own, just for a few weeks, she could take all of the income and pay herself properly, and I would get a break to sort my head out. It was perfect. She would make good money, and I would return fresh and sober and full of ideas of what we could do to expand our café. The more I thought about it, the better the idea became. I looked at my online banking, the joint account still in mine and Oliver's names, and saw that what was left had remained untouched. I'd half expected him to take it, but he hadn't – he was better than that.

I ran the numbers; I had enough sat in our joint account to pay my household bills for a couple of months. My personal account didn't speak the same tale, but my two credit card balances were quite low. I would be all right for a couple of months without any other income. If the stolen money wasn't covered by insurance, that would surely help, and even if it was, I'd still take leave of absence. Once I was back, I'd chip away at my credit cards until I cleared the balances. It might take a year, but that was far better than losing either my business or my best friend. Closing my banking app, I rang Esther's number again; I was going to leave a message, outlining my thoughts. But after the third ring, she picked up.

'Hey, Esther, are you all right?'

She sighed on the other end of the phone. 'Tired.'

'Yeah, I bet. Listen…'

'No, Neve, let me speak. I'm still angry, you know? I'm angry you've let yourself get into such a mess lately, I'm angry this business isn't doing what I know it could do. I'm angry some little shits robbed us. I'm really angry about that.'

'I know.'

'But that still didn't give me the right to speak like I did to you. I'm so sorry, I didn't mean to hurt you.'

'Don't be sorry, I deserved it.'

'No, Neve.'

'Esther, it's OK. I know I'm a mess.'

'Neve, you're not a mess.'

'I am, I always have been – ever since you've known me. Oliver was right, I didn't let him in, I pushed him away with my inability to let go of things, and I'm doing the same to you. I know I have to change.'

'You're not pushing me away.'

'Esther, let's be honest. You shouldn't have to scrape by.'

'What else can we do?'

'I've had an idea.'

I told her my plan, and at first she dismissed it, but the more we talked, the more receptive she became.

'Esther, I know I've not been great these past few weeks, and

I've dumped loads on you. With me taking a break, I'm making your life easier. A bit of time to sort my shit out and I'll come back with ideas, energy, and we can fix this. I'm not walking away – let's call it a sabbatical.'

'How will you survive without an income, Neve?'

'I'll be fine. I've got my credit cards.'

'But then you'll end up in a load of debt.'

'Better to have a little debt I can pay off over time, than to lose our business, and you.'

'Neve… are you sure about this?'

'We both know it's the right thing.'

'Yeah, you're probably right,' she said after a pause.

'I'll come in tomorrow and up to the weekend and help, and then we'll start afresh on Monday.'

'I doubt we'll open tomorrow.'

'Then I'll come anyway, and help.'

'Honestly, Neve, there isn't much you can do. It's mainly waiting for the glass company to fit a new door. I'll be fine. Start your break now. The sooner you go, the sooner you're back.'

'You really think it's a good idea?' I asked, suddenly doubting myself.

'I hate to say it, but yes. I think you need the space to deal with what's going on in your life and…'

She didn't finish her sentence, but we both knew what she was going to say. She needed a break from me and my misery.

'OK, my phone will stay on, and I promise I'll come back sooner if you need me to.'

'Thanks. What will you do with your time?'

'Sort myself out.'

In the background, I heard Tilly calling for help on the potty.

It felt good that, despite all this, something was still normal, still so utterly normal.

'I better go.'

'OK, Esther, I'll... I'll see you soon?'

'Yep, see you soon.'

The line went dead and for a moment I kept the phone to my ear. That was it, I had officially stepped away from my business. Now I had, it felt incredibly impulsive. But Esther didn't stop me, so it had to be right? Getting up, I walked into the kitchen and rifled around for something to eat. I found an old packet of Quavers at the back of a cupboard and opened them. What I really needed was a drink: a big, stiff, strong drink, one that hurt to swallow and tasted awful. I needed to be numbed, just for one more night, and then tomorrow, I would start to rebuild myself. But, thankfully, I didn't have anything in. It meant I had to start now.

Feeling blue, I wanted to look at Oliver's Facebook wall, to see if anything had changed since I last checked a few hours ago. But before I could stalk his profile, I saw I had a new friend request from someone I once knew and had wanted to forget. My old childhood friend, Holly. Seeing her picture made my stomach feel uneasy. I had been tagged in a post, by her, linking an article from a local paper close to where I had grown up. The headline floored me.

CONCERNS DEEPEN FOR LOCAL MISSING MAN, JAMIE HARDMAN

Jamie.

I didn't read the article but jumped onto his private Facebook page. I saw his face; one I'd not seen in a long time. He hadn't changed much. Still the same cheeky smile. Still the same mischievous glint in his eye I once found so attractive. As I read his timeline my heart sank. People had posted on his wall, lots of people, all saying similar things. They all asked him to come back, they all wondered if he was OK, and a sense of déjà vu washed over me.

Jamie, my first, had gone missing.

Just like Chloe.

CHAPTER 8

20th November 2019
Evening

He was missing. The first boy I'd ever loved was missing. I should have been concerned for him, but really, I was more concerned about what it really meant. Missing. There had to be some mistake? I tried to deduce from the messages posted on his Facebook wall in what context he could be unaccounted for, but I couldn't. It unnerved me, but the article didn't mean something terrible had happened to Jamie. He could have moved out of town without telling anyone. He could have booked a trip away, a spur of the moment thing. He was an adult, there could be a million reasons as to why he was missing. It didn't have to mean the same thing as it did back in 1998. I couldn't help but think about that shadow outside The Tea Tree. As soon as the thought landed, I dismissed it. There was no way it was connected.

Taking my phone into the kitchen, Jamie's face dominating the screen, I looked again for something to drink. I knew I shouldn't, but that seven-letter word shook me. Missing. Problem or not, I needed steadying, and a drink was the only thing that would do that. On my hands and knees, I looked into the dark corners of my booze cupboard and found an old bottle of crème de menthe that had sat in there for God knows how long. A joke gift from a friend that we drank once, despised, and put away never to drink again. I grabbed a mug from the draining board, poured a healthy measure and downed it. It made me shudder, like drinking sweet mouthwash, but I felt it warm my stomach. Pouring another I sat at the breakfast bar, transfixed by Jamie's profile picture. He hadn't aged well, becoming a fatter, greyer version of the boy I once knew. He was smiling in the photo, his teeth stained, probably through cigarettes, but he had a sadness in his eyes, a weight. And I knew why, because I carried the same weight too. Chloe.

The sadness I should have felt as soon as I discovered he was missing came. It seeped from my chest, pushed up my throat and from behind my eyes. Fuck, Jamie was missing. As my eyes glazed, I knocked back my mug of crème de menthe. Though it made me gag, I still poured a third, and the more I drank, the more I felt. Fear, sadness, curiosity even. Things I couldn't feel any more without something warming my insides.

After the fourth measure went down, I felt the alcohol wave begin to roll over me, and I needed to know Jamie was OK. I'd not wanted to know anything about him in twenty years. The summer Chloe disappeared, I ran away to live with Mum, abandoning Dad who had already been tossed aside by the mine closing the winter before. I abandoned my friends and the villagers who were grieving. I'd intended to stay with Mum for a short while, but weeks became months, which turned into years. Once I left, there was no looking back. And the village, being as small and isolated from the rest of the world as it was, never forgot. I was hated, just like my mum was, and I had made peace with that long ago.

I accepted Holly's friend request and said hello. I assumed she had added me to tell me about Jamie, but I didn't mention it. All I could do was wait, and hope she replied. I put on my coat and shoes, grabbed my keys and headed into the cold, wet night. I knew I shouldn't, I knew I should stay at home, wait for a reply, perhaps try and get an early night. But I walked to my local Tesco anyway to buy myself a bottle of wine, reasoning that I would only have one glass, just to calm my frayed nerves.

CHAPTER 9

21st November 2019
Morning

I wake with a start, like I've been holding my breath in my sleep and my body has subconsciously forced me to take air into my lungs. I'm aware of a familiar smell once again, but before I can place it, it fades. I roll onto my side; I don't even bother to try and open my eyes. They already hurt too much.

Reaching behind me I feel for Oliver. I don't know why; this time I know he isn't there. Perhaps it was just wishful thinking that the last few weeks had been a weird and incredibly vivid dream. I cough and a pain shoots through me. Then I realise I'm still fully clothed, and soaking wet – it was raining when I left last night, so I must have been so drunk that I'd not undressed. Lifting up my top, I see there is a deep purple bruise on my side.

Though the damp bedsheets are starting to make me feel clammy and cold, I don't move straight away – I need to piece together everything up to just now. It hurts to think. Slowly I recall the shop being robbed, the safe being left open by me. I remember stepping away and wanting life to be easy again, and Jamie. Oh God, Jamie. Reaching across to my bedside table, I grab my iPhone and swipe across the screen, not noticing the crack – a small shard of glass cuts my thumb. Opening Facebook, I go back to Jamie's page but notice there's a new message waiting in my inbox. It's from Holly.

> Neve, it's been a long time? Thank you for accepting my friend request. I'm shocked we weren't already connected. I'm sure we were once?

We were, as I was to the rest of my childhood friends. When I first joined Facebook about a decade after Chloe disappeared, it seemed like it would be OK to reconnect, but all it did was dig up old skeletons, things I didn't want to remember. So, over the years, one by one, I deleted them all and changed my surname on Facebook to my mother's maiden name. Holly must have really been looking for me. I read on.

> Listen, I'm just going to come out and say it. I don't know if you have seen that article I sent you about Jamie, but he disappeared three days ago. It's such a shock to us all. I know you and he were once close, so wanted you to find out from one of us before you saw it somewhere else. Yesterday, there was a news crew in the village, digging up the past, and Chloe.

I felt my heart drop. I didn't want to relive a single second of back then.

> In fact, Jamie and I spoke of her only a few weeks ago. I guess that's the most worrying thing. I want you to know, no one is angry at you for leaving, we were just

kids. If I'd had somewhere, anywhere to go, I might have done the same. Let me know if you want to come back, if you feel the pull to help. I'll make sure I'm there to meet you, if you want. It would be nice to see you, and I know everyone else feels the same way as I do. I hope you're doing well. You seem really happy in your pictures on here. Congratulations on your engagement and business success. Holly.

Until then, I'd not considered going back, but knowing Jamie was missing and I was being welcomed by Holly stirred something deep within, something akin to the feeling when you smell something that takes you back to a moment in your past. They didn't hate me. I was welcome back, and Holly was sweet for suggesting she would meet me. She was seeing it from my perspective, even with the horrible circumstance that had brought us back together. I almost messaged back telling her I would be there, but there was one other person I had to check in with before I returned to the village. I had to speak to my dad.

The phone rang seven or eight times, and I was just about to give up when the line connected. There was noise, like the microphone being dragged through a jumper, before he spoke.

'Hello.'

'Hi, Dad.'

'Who is it?'

'Dad, it's me, Neve.'

There was a pause. Longer than there should have been.

'Neve. Are you well?'

'Yes, Dad,' I lied, the smell of stale alcohol lingering on my breath, my head screaming at me to never drink again. 'I am. Are you?'

Again, another long pause.

'Yes, yes. I'm fine. Yes. All right, thank you. I wasn't expecting to hear from you.'

'Yes. Did you hear about Jamie?'

'Who?'

'Jamie, my old friend. Jamie Hardman?'

'Oh, yes, yes. Terrible news. Terrible.'

'I was thinking of coming back, to help?'

This time, the silence was so long I thought the line had disconnected. 'Hello? Dad?'

'Yes?'

'What do you think? Should I come back and help find him?'

'Well, that's up to you, isn't it? It wouldn't hurt, the poor man needs all the help he can get.'

I didn't know what he meant by that. Dad and I rarely spoke, and if we did it was always about me, London, my business and Oliver. I can't remember the last time we spoke about anyone from the village.

'So, I should come back?'

'Yes. Maybe, yes.'

I waited for him to invite me to stay with him, but he didn't.

'Dad, can I come to yours?'

'Yes, yes. That would be all right. OK. I'll see you soon. Bye, Neve.'

'OK, can I come this week…'

Dad hung up before I could ask how soon I'd be welcome. After twenty-one years of being dismissed by the man, I thought I would be used to it. But it hurt just as much as it always had.

That said, he had agreed I could stay with him, which, if I was honest, was more than I expected. It meant I had to get a few things packed, and go. If I didn't do it now, I would lose the courage.

I tried to remember the last time I went back to the village. I know Oliver and I were together, but I don't recall mentioning him to Dad, so it must have been early days – six years ago, nearer seven probably. I had to think hard as to why I was there at all. Then it came to me: I popped in to see Dad for a quick cuppa (he always made it too sweet) on my way back from seeing a friend in Sheffield, and can't have stayed for more than half an hour. My previous visit must have been when I was in my early twenties. Again, I didn't see anyone other than him, and no one knew I was coming. The time before that was the day I left. Two short visits in twenty-one years. Two too many in my opinion.

I shuddered at the thought of being in the village again, walking down the main road as I did as a child, seeing that bloody mine and its inhabitants everywhere I turned. Holly hadn't mentioned a meeting place, but I knew where I would find her. It was the same place we met back in 1998 when we began the search for Chloe. The same place every wake for every funeral was held, including Chloe's, although she was never officially found. The Miners' Arms. I wondered what the atmosphere in the old pub would be – would people be optimistic, energised even, like when Chloe disappeared, or would they be their usual sullen, grey selves? I'd be finding out soon enough. Because I was going home.

I was going back to the village.

CHAPTER 10

June 1998
Five weeks before...

It didn't take long for the forlorn security hut to feel like something the group could own. Over the past week they had smuggled in a few small beanbags, while Georgia had brought some posters from her bedroom to give the place a homey feel, and Jamie had brought his dad's old caravan fridge, only to discover the electricity didn't work after all. Still, Baz agreed that it would be a good place to store whatever booze they had as nobody would mind drinking it warm. To compensate, Jamie also took his dad's battery-operated radio, allowing the group to listen to the chart show on a Sunday night, and play cassette tapes, and despite their varying musical tastes, they didn't argue. The space was theirs, a seven-way joint custody of their own place, and they knew they needed to compromise to ensure it stayed a haven from the village. So Baz listened to his drum and bass, Chloe listened to Robbie Williams, and Jamie listened to the hip hop he currently enjoyed. The music didn't matter, only that it was their music, in their space, at a volume of their choosing.

But it wasn't quite perfect, not for everyone, even with the music and posters and alcopops. The hut made Holly feel uncomfortable. She had tried to voice it to Neve and Jamie on the walk there, stating that the place gave her the creeps, but her complaints were quickly dismissed. The lane was spooky, yes, they all agreed. But that was only because of the stories told to them as kids to stop them venturing towards the dangerous mine. They had worked, too, because no one – not even Baz – had suggested they explored the abandoned space, and tunnels below.

When Baz and Michael first introduced the group to the hut, their excitement was infectious – they all agreed it was the best idea the hopeless pair had ever had. By the time they left two hours later, they'd vowed to make it their own. The group had met most evenings that week, Wednesday being the only night they didn't because Jamie had to work for his dad. It had become an unspoken rule of the hut: if someone couldn't come, the gang shouldn't meet. This Saturday, Jamie was supposed to be at work again, but Baz and Michael insisted Jamie take the evening off.

Michael arrived first, lighting the candles to give the place some atmosphere. Flopping onto a beanbag, he sighed and watched the shadows dance on the ceiling, proud of what he and Baz had achieved. The group were due to meet at eight, but he had intentionally arrived thirty minutes early so he could take it all in. He hadn't had a space he could call his own before, a bedroom where he could shut the door and forget the world. His grandparents' place was only a one-bed, and although they converted the small dining room attached to the lounge into a bedroom, it had never quite felt like something that was his. The stud wall was thin, and his granddad often stayed up into the early hours watching the television with the volume up so loud the speakers rattled. Michael didn't complain though – he loved them dearly and was grateful to them for taking him in, for not having him become a kid in the care system when his own mother couldn't cope. He needed the hut more than anyone else, just to give himself some breathing space.

Turning on the radio, he nestled into the beanbag and put his hands behind his head. As Dave Pearce chatted with guests he hadn't ever heard of, a new boy band of some kind, he closed his eyes. Luckily for him, the chat didn't last long, and Will Smith began to rap his latest hit. He thought about skinning up a joint but didn't. He would wait for Baz who would want to share it and was better at rolling than he was. After several more songs and several more questions fired from Dave Pearce to the boy band, Baz crawled through the hatch, making Michael jump.

'Shit, Baz.'

'Thought I was the boogie man.'

'Thought you were the police more like.'

Baz scrambled up onto his feet and chuckled.

'You been here long?'

'Just got here,' Michael lied.

'I can't wait for tonight,' Baz said, rubbing his hands together.

'What are you up to?' Michael asked, noticing Baz's scheming smile.

'Nothing.'

'Bullshit.'

'Well, I was thinking…' Baz started, sitting down beside Michael and throwing his feet onto the badly damaged walnut coffee table. 'We won't be hanging out much now – the exams are nearly done, and we won't be at school. Jamie will work more, which means Neve will no doubt be in the pub more.'

'Why would she be in the pub more?'

'Oh, come on, can't you see that they have a thing going on?'

'Jamie and Neve?' Michael said, unable to hide his disappointment. 'Is something really going on with them two?'

'Not yet, I don't think. But it will. Trust me, it will,' Baz replied, raising his eyebrows and digging an elbow in Michael's side before continuing. 'Georgia will start her apprenticeship in the salon in Nottingham, Chloe won't be around as much if Neve isn't and Holly will begin to drift away from this place – we both know she's never been sold on the hut.'

'Shit, that's sad,' Michael said.

'So, with the group's imminent collapse, I thought we should have a little party.'

Baz took something from his pocket, but in the low light Michael couldn't make out what it was. He grabbed the torch and angled it towards Baz's cupped hands to see a small bag with white powder inside.

'Is that speed?' he asked.

'Yep.'

'Where the fuck did you get that from around here?'

'My skunk dealer got hold of a bit.' He smiled.

'Shit,' Michael replied, trying to match Baz's smile, but missing the mark by a long way.

'Don't worry, mate, it's gonna be a good night.'

'You done this before?'

'No, have you?'

'No.'

'Relax, Michael,' Baz said, slapping his mate on the shoulder. 'Everything'll be fine.'

Michael wasn't convinced, but didn't say anything, and instead asked Baz to roll a joint that they could enjoy while they waited for the others to arrive, a request Baz was more than happy to comply with. No sooner had the joint been rolled and lit, the rest of the group joined, apart from Jamie. In spite of the darkness in the hut, they could all see the fresh cut on Georgia's lip which she tried to cover with dark lipstick. They all saw it, but they didn't say anything.

'You think his dad has made him work?' Baz asked Neve.

'Why would I know?' she said.

'Well, cos, you and him—'

'Me and him what? Nothing is going on between Jamie and me.'

'She's telling the truth,' Chloe chipped in.

'And I don't want anything to happen between us either,' Neve added.

'Now she's lying,' Chloe said, nudging her friend and drawing a laugh from Baz and Georgia. Blushing, Neve tucked her hair behind her ear and caught Georgia's eye. She couldn't tell if she was laughing with her or enjoying her embarrassment.

'Well, he said to me earlier his dad was cool for him to have the night off work,' said Michael, unknowingly rescuing Neve. 'So, I guess we wait.' He and Baz shared a conspiratorial smile.

'What are you boys up to?' asked Holly, who until then had remained quiet.

'You'll see, when Jamie gets here.'

No sooner had Baz finished his sentence the hatch door opened and in crawled Jamie.

'Speak of the devil.'

'Sorry I'm late. Dad needed help changing a barrel, what have I missed?'

'Nothing,' said Neve a little too quickly, drawing smiles from the group and making Baz chuckle.

'What?' Jamie smiled, but with the hint of paranoia creeping across his face.

'Honestly, its nothing,' said Georgia, giving him a reassuring squeeze on the arm. Probably to piss Neve off more than anything.

'Right then, now we're all here I'd like to say something,' said Baz, moving around the coffee table to place himself against the wall where the security window used to be.

'We've been friends all the way through primary and secondary school,' he began in a clear, commanding voice. He'd obviously rehearsed his speech. 'We survived our teachers. Our lessons. We've survived the boredom of Mr Law's science class and him droning on and on. We survived our mock exams and the ball-ache of revision. And now, we're just five short days from the beginning of the end of our school journey.'

'Christ, you sound just like Mr Kessell. What was his speech about anyway?' Jamie said, changing the subject, much to Baz's annoyance.

'Just saying what he needs to, to get us out the door,' Michael said.

'You think?'

'Sure, that's all a head teacher cares about. Getting us to the finish line, and then pushing us away.'

'Well, I liked his speech today,' Chloe said. 'About how if we worked hard and did well, we could do anything we wanted. It's hopeful.'

'It's deluded,' Michael said.

'Anyway!' Baz interrupted. 'Can I continue?' He cleared his throat and picked up where he left off. 'As I said, we are just five short days from the beginning of the end of our school journey.'

'Baz, this is a bit over the top,' said Michael, prompting a punch on the arm from Georgia.

'Shut up, I'm enjoying this.'

'Thank you, Georgia.' Baz still sounded as if he was delivering a speech. 'And as much as I don't give a flying fuck about these exams, I know you all do, my friends. I know what these exams mean to you and I know that until this nightmare is over, you will be cramming in unnecessary knowledge in order to get a piece of paper telling you that you're smarter than I am.'

'Baz, do you want to…' began Holly, not enjoying the speech as much as everyone else.

'So…' he interrupted. 'I have convened this gang meeting – insisting Jamie had the night off – so we could all be together to toast our futures.'

'But we haven't finished our exams yet, Baz – what exactly is there to toast?' said Holly, looking at her watch, wishing she was at home studying.

'We're doing this now because no matter what happens with our exams, I know everyone here is going on to do great things. We're celebrating because regardless of how well you do, Holly, and how shit I do, we will all be OK.'

Holly nodded to Baz, shocked that underneath all of the practical jokes and boisterous behaviour there was someone who was thoughtful and kind. Holly didn't like Baz much, but in that moment, she warmed to him in a way she hadn't before.

'So, let's all say what we want for our lives. I'll go first. I want to be a pilot.'

'A pilot?' Michael laughed. 'Aren't you a bit fat?'

'Michael!' Holly snapped. 'Don't be a dick!'

'Yeah, Michael, don't be a dick,' Baz echoed, but smiling at his best mate. 'What do you want to be then?'

'A mechanic.'

'I want to be a barrister,' Holly said, beaming with ambition. 'What about you, Neve?'

'I don't know what kind, but I want my own business.'

'Jamie, Chloe?'

'I want to write,' said Jamie, quietly. 'Not like books or anything, but for a paper maybe?' He waited for someone to shoot a comment, laugh at him, but no one did.

'I want to be a midwife,' Chloe said. 'I've always wanted to help babies.'

They looked to Georgia who hadn't volunteered like everyone else and waited.

'I just want to get out of this place,' she said, smiling, but without a hint of mirth.

For a moment, they sat in silence. Unsure what to say or do next, Georgia looked away, uncomfortable. Baz cleared his voice again, and giving Georgia a squeeze on the arm, he spoke.

'So, this evening, we drink, we laugh, we talk of the future, and we do so safe in the knowledge that regardless of what happens this summer with our exams and our results, we will all get what we want out of our lives.'

'Nice speech, Baz,' said Jamie, as he started to give a round of applause, prompting everyone else, including Holly, to clap and cheer.

Baz took three mock bows, then took out the small bag containing the speed. 'Let's make this night one we will never forget.'

CHAPTER 11

22nd November 2019
Afternoon

Between deciding to go back to the village and actually beginning the journey, there was just less than twenty-four hours, but to me it felt like a week. I tidied my flat, removing Oliver's pictures and putting them in a box in the bottom of the wardrobe. It was tough, definitive, but I needed to do it. After, the living room felt empty, sterile. And then it was time to leave, and a sick feeling rose in my stomach. There was nothing to suggest Jamie had actually come to harm, but I couldn't shake the feeling something terrible had happened in the village, again.

I could have booked a train to go home, but instead decided to hire a car – the idea of not being able to leave the village when I wanted made me uncomfortable. As I left the flat to go collect it, I felt a growing trepidation build.

I had no idea how my return would go down. I hoped enough time had passed for me to slip in unnoticed, or if people did recognise me, they would realise I was a different person. I was no longer the scared, sad and abandoned 16-year-old girl; I hoped enough time had passed for them to understand why I left, a frightened child grieving for her best friend. But I wasn't convinced people would see it like that. The village was small, the people clung on to the past, more so than in any other place I'd been to since leaving. Perhaps it was the miner's mentality. I knew from the infrequent times I saw Dad, he still defined himself through the mine. People in the village didn't forget things – they hadn't moved on, I guess, because they didn't have anything to move on to. They were born not into the village, but into the mouth of the mine. Then, after it closed, and Chloe went missing, the village was torn apart by grief, and frozen in that moment.

I often pondered what I would be like if I'd stayed, and if my old friends would still be my friends. Would I have stayed with Jamie and now be a scared or grieving wife? I stopped myself. It was pointless wondering about a life that hadn't existed.

I took the Overground to Southall and walked half a mile to pick up the Vauxhall Corsa that would be mine for a week just before the car hire place closed for the evening. I paid the hefty deposit on my credit card and they handed over the keys. In my mind, I would stay only a few days at most.

As I drove out of West London towards the M40, I tried not to imagine those first few moments when I would step back into the village. Instead, I listened intently to what the DJ was saying on Radio 1, and the songs that she played. I soon realised I didn't know any of them, and so put on my classics playlist and settled as Savage Garden's Darren Hayes serenaded me with 'Truly Madly Deeply'. It took me back to a memory of Chloe, of us the year before we sat our exams. She loved that song and would sing it at the top of her voice, often out of tune. Once, Baz caught her doing so, and she blushed to the scarlet of our school jumpers. Thinking about that made me smile. It had been a long time since I'd smiled about Chloe. After Savage Garden, Madonna came on, followed by Texas. And I felt myself slip into a comfortable nostalgia where I remained until I saw the headstocks of the mine, the sight of them rekindling the same fear as it had when I was young, and I couldn't stop myself from shivering.

I hoped, as it had been so long, they would be smaller than I remembered. If anything, they were larger, more imposing. The dark towers loomed ahead, the headstocks' wheels like eyes, guarding the dead that resided down the mine against ever leaving. It also watched the people living above ground, spying their mistakes, learning their secrets. From up there, the villagers must look like ants, scurrying around the aged, dying colony. I turned the music off, almost as if I didn't want the mine to know I was coming. In my rear-view mirror, I saw a car approaching quickly behind me. I assumed they would see the road was clear, and then overtake, but they didn't. I sped up a little, realising I was doing about forty-five in a sixty zone, but the car behind didn't slow, it drew closer and closer until it was so close, I couldn't see it in my side mirrors.

The road we were on was narrow, and I couldn't find any-where to pull over to let whoever was behind me pass. Focusing on the road ahead, of which I could only see a hundred yards at a time, I started to panic. My foot went down and the speed-ometer crept up until I was doing just shy of 80 mph. The car behind stayed on my tail, and I was sure it was going to shunt me. Then, white marks reappeared as the road widened and the car swerved round me and carried on recklessly, careering up ahead. I took my foot off the accelerator, and the car started to slow. I was swearing under my breath, sweating under my jumper. It was obviously just some kids, doing what all kids do when they feel invincible, but for a moment, I thought they were trying to get me. To hurt me. I felt stupid for even thinking it. Paranoid and stupid. Chloe disappeared a long time ago, and life had moved on. I shouldn't assume people would still be angry with me for leaving. Why would they be? There are more pressing things at hand, like the reason I was coming back now. Jamie.

Despite this realisation, I still felt like I was going to be sick, so I pulled over and got out of the car. It was cold and the wind strong. To my right, the mine watched me curiously. I almost said something to it but stopped myself. Instead, I got back into the car and drove slowly into the village. Maybe subconsciously I thought if I moved quietly, I wouldn't be noticed. I drove past the old social club, remembering how business took a nosedive just months after the mine closed. Now, its windows were boarded up and the sign outside was paint-stripped and weather-beaten. Thick weeds grew through cracks in the tarmac of the car park. It was the first thing you saw inside the village, I guess, it summed the place up well. It looked like no one had been around for decades. I hoped the same wouldn't be said for The Miners' Arms. I needed a drink before seeing Dad. Without slowing, I continued towards the centre. It was time to let someone know I was back.

CHAPTER 12

22nd November 2019
Evening

As I made my way to the other end of the village, I could see the smaller working man's pub Jamie's father used to own ahead of me. Its sign was lit, suggesting it was still in business. I wanted nothing more than to have a peaceful drink as I familiarised myself with the place I once called home. To breathe in its smells, and deal with the inevitable memories I wouldn't want to recall.

Parking outside The Miners' Arms, I kept my head low and darted inside. It was exactly as I remembered from when I was too young to drink. The walls were still adorned with photographs throughout the years of the pits in operation. I didn't need to look, I remembered what was in each of the frames. There were smiling men in short-sleeved shirts in the dead of winter, veins bulging in their forearms from the grafting they did day in, day out. Photographs of them erecting the headstocks, which were the tallest ever erected in England. Overhead images of before and after the mine was closed in 1997. Above the bar hung postcards of the mine, their corners curled through age, the white of the paper now a nicotine-stained yellow. The pub was scruffier than back when I was young, but the smell hadn't altered at all. And for a moment I was back in the summer when Jamie and I were madly in love. The biggest difference between now and then was this place was once busy – people laughing, joking, and eventually drowning their sorrows after their livelihoods changed. Now the pub was near-empty, except for a few old men, perched on bar stools, looking into their pints.

I approached the bar and waited for the barman, who had his back to me doing something in the till. As I waited, I could hear rain start to hit the window to my right. At first it was light, gentle, but soon picked up to become a full winter deluge. It made me feel colder. On a night like this, there was nothing better than a warm whiskey and a log fire. The drink wouldn't be an issue. But the fireplace that sat in the middle of the pub looked like it hadn't been lit in a very long time. I half expected there to be weeds cracking thought the flue, much like the car park of the social club.

The barman, his back still to me, asked what I wanted, and before I could see his face, I knew who it was – to my horror, it was Jamie's dad. His 'forty a day' voice was unmistakable. I wanted to turn and leave but was frozen to the spot and, as our eyes met, there was a hint of recognition from him behind his tired, sleep-deprived expression. It quickly faded. I collected myself and ordered a whiskey and Diet Coke and he nodded. As he made my drink, I watched him. His movements were slow, deliberate, like it was taking all of his effort to complete the task, a sloth moving along the thick branch of a tree. I couldn't begin to understand how he must have been feeling. But wondered, why wasn't he out looking for his son? Then I thought about it.

Where else would he be? Jamie had been missing for four days. He obviously wasn't close by, and if I was his father, I'd want to be somewhere Jamie could find him when he decided to come home. I almost offered a kind word. I didn't. Instead, I thanked him for my drink, and sat beside the fireplace.

If anything it was colder in front of it as the wind whipped down the chimney breast. But the chill didn't last long, as the warmth of my drink soon spread through me. I took off my damp coat and slung it over the back of the Chesterfield chair to dry before walking back to the bar and ordering another from Jamie's dad. Seated again I held it in both hands, like a child with a plastic cup and I looked into the fireplace trying to picture a log burning and the sound it would make as heat cracked the wood. When I was younger, we would sometimes sit in the pub whilst Jamie worked, mocking him in his green polo neck T-shirt with 'The Miners' Arms' embroidered on it. We would laugh and tease as he cleaned tables and washed pint glasses. It was always harmless, and he would often join in. A fire was always on back then. The pub was always warm. Now, it felt so cold I wasn't sure if the seatback I leant against was damp.

Outside the rain persisted, heavy droplets thrumming against the window with such violence I waited for the glass to crack. The whiskey in my stomach buried the sick feeling I'd had all day, replacing it with a burning that I knew I'd regret tomorrow. But that was then, this was now, and I was beginning to feel less terrified. I drank it quickly and got up to ask for another. Just one more that I would sip as I prepared myself to see Dad. In that time, I hoped the rain would ease. As I approached the bar, Jamie's dad stopped busying himself and watched me.

'May I have another?' I asked quietly, almost like I was the 16-year-old girl I once was, trying her luck at the bar.

'I'll make you a double,' he replied, eyeing me once more with a curious look. 'Save you coming back so fast.'

'Thank you,' I replied, embarrassed.

He turned to face the optics and poured two measures. The whole time, he kept an eye on me in the mirror that sat behind the counter.

'You're not local,' he said, a statement rather than a question.

'No, I guess I'm not.'

'But you were once, am I right?'

'Do you recognise me?'

'I recognise your accent.'

'Oh.'

'I guess the question is, should I recognise you?' he asked as he turned towards me and handed me my drink.

I swallowed hard, unsure of how he would react.

'I'm Neve Chambers, I was once… umm, friends with Jamie.'

I waited for his gaze to harden, and his tone to either become angry or cold. But the opposite happened, and a sad smile came over his face.

'It's been a long time.'

'It has,' I said, breathing a sigh of relief. 'I'm really sorry for what's been going on.'

'Thank you, so am I.'

He poured a double vodka for himself and raised his glass.

'To Jamie coming home.'

'To Jamie coming home,' I echoed, my voice catching in my throat.

'So, what brings you back here?'

'I wanted to help, if you'll allow me to.'

'Of course, I'm very grateful you've taken the time.'

'I thought you would be upset at me wanting to be here.'

'Why?'

'Because of what happened when Chloe…' I didn't finish my sentence.

'That was a very long time ago,' he said quietly.

'Feels like yesterday.'

'Maybe. But it was a different life. How did you find out about Jamie?'

'Holly connected with me.'

'Of course,' he smiled.

There was an uncomfortable silence for the briefest of moments, and I felt his eye appraising me, either in silent judgement or wanting to ask the questions I supposed most people in this village wanted answers to, seeing as I was the last person to speak to Chloe before she vanished. He must have sensed my paranoia, and changed the subject.

'Are you staying with your father?'

'Yes,' I answered too quickly.

'Tell him Derrick says hello. I've not seen your old man in a very long time.'

'I didn't know your name; you've always been Jamie's dad,' I said smiling.

'Well, that's my name too, my more important one,' he replied, a sad smile lifting on the right side of his face once more. 'He speaks of you often. Jamie, I mean.'

'He does?'

'He said you had a business in London?'

'A café, yes.'

'He's really proud of you.'

'He was? I mean is. Sorry.' I couldn't believe I slipped up, speaking of Jamie in the past tense. This place and its ghosts had already begun seeping into my marrow.

'Yes.'

'What does he do?'

'He works here with me still, looks after the place more often than not. It's not much, but it's ours.'

'Yes.'

'Tell me about your café.'

'Well, it's not much, but it's mine,' I smiled, one he returned.

'I think my son never quite let go of you in his heart.'

I was taken aback to know Jamie had kept me in his mind. It was quickly followed by the crushing guilt that I hadn't reciprocated. I buried everything I could about the village, even those I once loved. I finished my drink and without needing to ask, Derrick turned and poured us both another. We raised our glasses again, this time without words, and drank silently. I wanted to ask how Jamie was before he vanished, if he was happy. What his life had been like in the past twenty years. I wanted to say that a part of my heart still belonged to him, my first love. But I couldn't. Instead, I went to pay for my drinks, and he told me they were on the house.

'If I can do anything…'

'I'll be fine, thank you, Neve.'

Nodding, I walked back to the chair and picked up my coat. Putting it on, I gave Derrick a smile and headed for the door. I looked over my shoulder, but Derrick had already turned his back to me, working away at cleaning glasses that looked unused. And in the furthest corner, around the side of the bar where the old pool table sat, was a man wearing a flat cap. The peak obscured his face from me, and I couldn't tell if he was looking down at his pint, which was in his hands, or if he was looking directly at me. I didn't wait to find out. Yet another shiver ran up my spine. Pretending I hadn't noticed him, I turned and left.

CHAPTER 13

22nd November 2019
Night

As soon as the cold air hit me, the alcohol that had lain warm and dormant in my stomach sprang to life, making me feel unsteady on my feet. Regardless, I thought if I got out of the rain and back into my hire car, I could still make the mile's drive to my dad's house. Reaching the driver's door, I dug into my bag to find the key, cursing myself for not doing so when I was in the dry pub. Eventually, after several rummages, a handful of swear words and one large bead of ice-cold water that escaped my mane of hair and had run down my neck, I found it. As I pulled it out, it slipped from my hand and landed by my feet. I stooped to pick it up, the image no doubt comparable to an elderly lady trying to fit a shoe, and as I stood up again, I hit my head on the wing mirror hard enough to knock it out of its casing and send a white flash across my eyes. I tried to focus so I could pop the wing mirror back in, but as I attempted to fix it, the whole thing came off in my hands.

Perhaps it was the fact it was raining, or that I was drunk again, or maybe it was being back in the village where Chloe vanished from, but I burst into tears, clutching the broken wing mirror to my chest like it was a teddy. That was how the car that approached from behind, its main beam on, found me. Embarrassed, I tried to wipe the tears from my eyes, which was pointless as I was now soaked through. I felt the car slow as it drew close to me, and I wanted to look, but didn't. Keeping my head low, I opened the Corsa's door, dropped the wing mirror on the driver's seat and closed it again. It wasn't a good idea to drive; I couldn't even get into the bloody thing without damaging it.

Stumbling to the back of the car I unlocked the boot, and watched the car pass out of the corner of my eye. I took out my bag, pulled my coat collar as high as it would go, and started to walk. I should have turned right towards Dad's, but I turned left instead and kept walking. I thought about how I used to spend the evening in or around the pub, waiting for Jamie to finish working. I thought about the two occasions when I waited on my own, before we walked hand in hand in the direction I was now heading. The ground beneath my feet was the path we had walked on twenty-one years before as a couple, before going to the place where we would spend the evening making out. My mind began to drift to one night in particular, where, after meeting near the hut, we snuck into Jamie's bedroom above the pub via the fire-exit stairs. But as I tried to recall what happened next, I was stopped by the realisation that the boy who was my first love was now missing.

Pushing the thought down, I pressed on, and after a few minutes I stood at the mouth of the lane but the darkness made it impossible to see much. However, I knew, down that lane, perhaps a quarter of a mile away, was a brick building that was once ours. A part of me, the curious part, wanted to continue walking down the lane, which felt smaller, narrower than it did back when I was young. I began but stopped after only a few paces. When we were young, all of the lights that lined the path were broken, the power disconnected, but now, far in the distance, one burnt. I guessed that was because of Chloe. A familiar and long-forgotten shudder ran up my spine. I didn't believe in ghosts, but still I felt spooked and turned to walk away. As I did, something caught the edge of my peripheral vision, a shadow moving quickly through the light cast by the only streetlamp. I spun quickly, almost losing my footing, but I couldn't see anyone.

'Hello?' My voice sounded small, the dark night swallowing it whole. I started walking backwards, uneasy on my feet, and didn't breathe until I was on the main road. As I moved in the direction of the pub, I convinced myself it was nothing, my mind playing tricks on me. It wouldn't be the first time. There was no one there, no shadow, no person, and certainly no ghosts. I needed to get back to Dad's, sleep off the booze and tomorrow, I would show my face, and then, go home. There was a reason I didn't live here anymore, and I felt stupid for thinking that it would be all right, that I would be all right if I came back.

I walked past the pub again, past the hire car that sat lonely out front. After a few minutes I drew level with Chloe's old house. It was quiet, dark. All of the curtains were drawn. Were it not for a small light on somewhere upstairs, I would think the house was empty. I kept my head down, walked on. I didn't want anyone to see me. I didn't know if Chloe's mum Brenda still lived there, but I wasn't prepared to take any chances. Up ahead, two lights from a car shone, again, the main beam on – I slowed and shielded my eyes as it passed; the driver was looking towards me. Turning, I watched their taillights as they drove past the pub and out of the village, my gut telling me that although I couldn't place them, they had recognised me.

I knew I should have gone back to Dad's and got the awkward moment of saying hello over and done with, but I wasn't quite ready. There was another place in this village I needed to visit first. Somewhere important. Somewhere I had never been before. Chloe's grave. The cemetery was a short distance behind Chloe's house. I remembered, when we were young, when her mother worked evenings, we would look out of her mum's bedroom window across the gravestones, talking of ghosts walking among them.

With Chloe's house far enough behind me, I turned and doubled back on myself. Climbing a gate, I began to search for her stone, ashamed that I didn't know where my childhood best friend had been laid to rest. Eventually, right in the middle of the cemetery, I came across it.

CHLOE LAMBERT
1982-1998

GONE BUT NOT FORGOTTEN.

I stood silently, shifting from one foot to the other, staring at the slab of granite in front of me. I expected I would feel something: sadness, regret, even fear. But there was nothing. And I didn't know why.

Behind me I heard a noise, a cough, and turning quickly, I could make out a person in the cemetery, near the gate I'd climbed over, but I couldn't make out any details. For a brief moment I thought it was him, the man from our past. They coughed again, and I heard it wasn't a him at all – it was a woman. She approached and, when she was close enough to see her features, I knew exactly who it was.

CHAPTER 14

22nd November 2019
Night

'I heard you were back,' she said, her voice deep and harsh.

Hearing her voice again after so long made me want to shiver. News travelled fast; it had to have been Derrick. Or maybe Dad expressed more interest than I thought. 'Yes,' I replied quietly.

'Because Jamie has gone missing?'

'Yes.'

Reaching in her pocket, she took out and lit a cigarette. 'Want one?'

'No, thank you, I don't smoke.'

There was nothing in the way I replied that was funny, but she smiled at me, like she knew something I didn't.

'How are you, Brenda?' I asked, filling the unbearable silence. When we were young, Brenda terrified me. It seemed time didn't change everything.

'Oh, you know,' she said, taking a drag on her cigarette, the glowing tip intensifying, throwing ugly angles on her face. 'Come to say hello to my daughter?'

'Yes,' I replied quietly.

'It's a bit weird you're here in the middle of the night, isn't it?'

'I guess so, I've just got back. Wanted to pay my respects.'

'Pay your respects.'

'Yes.'

'Well, that's nice,' she said abrasively, taking another drag on her cigarette, her eyes catching in the glow. Eyes that were hard, unblinking. 'And then are you going to see your father or run away again?'

I didn't like her tone, but she intimidated me, so I didn't challenge it. 'Yes, I'm staying with Dad for the night.'

'That surprises me, you're just like your mother.'

'I'm sorry?'

'We don't abandon our own, Neve,' she said, her eyes steely. She waited for me to reply, but the words caught in my throat. Smiling, she took another drag on her cigarette, looking from me to Chloe's grave before exhaling. 'I often come here at night. It's more peaceful. I get to talk to my daughter without any interruptions.'

'Interruptions?' I asked, regretting it instantly.

'I know some folk here think I had something to do with her disappearance.' She smiled, bitterly. Taking one more drag she stubbed it out on the top of Chloe's grave. I recoiled in shock.

'Well, it's not like she's actually buried here, is it, Neve? I'll leave you to pay your respects,' she said, turning and walking away.

I watched her scramble over the gate and head back towards the main road. Only once she was out of sight did I let out the breath I had been holding. I didn't want to be here anymore, so without speaking to Chloe, I walked away. My eye kept being drawn to the window in the row of houses that I knew was Brenda's bedroom. It was dark, but for a moment, I thought

I saw a curtain move, like someone was peering from behind it. It was impossible, there was no way Brenda had managed to get back that quickly. This place… it was already doing funny things to me.

I climbed the fence, almost breaking into a jog as I headed further away from Chloe's house, the pub, the mine behind them all. After what felt like the longest time, I was standing at the bottom of Forest Road. Up the steep hill, beyond where my eye could see, was Dad's house. I'd not walked up this hill for over twenty years, the two visits since my childhood I brought a car both times, quickly in, quickly out. When I was a teenager the walk made my calves ache, but it was now so hard I needed to stop on three occasions to ease the burn in my muscles. With laboured breathing I eventually made it to the top of the approach to Dad's door. Hesitating before stepping onto the front path, I looked at my watch, my eyes struggling to focus on the hands. It was only just after ten thirty, and yet the house was dark. I gingerly made my way to the door, after taking a deep breath.

I rang the doorbell and waited. No lights came on, no movement within, and for a while I thought he was out. But, through a gap in the living-room curtain I could make out the eerie glow of a television screen. Pressing my nose into the glass I cupped my hands and could just about make out the shape of his arm on the chair in front of the TV. I knocked on the window, but he didn't respond. I knocked louder, longer, and still nothing. A wave of heat flooded into my face – the same feeling I'd had once many, many years ago – and I rushed back to the front door, kicking over a potted plant beside it. I slammed the knocker down three times, loud enough to wake the neighbours, and still nothing. Grabbing the door handle, I turned it, I expecting it to be locked; Dad was a real stickler for locking and bolting the front door like he was sure we would be burgled if he didn't. To my surprise, it opened, and I knew something was wrong.

I held my breath and moved towards the lounge. From the doorway I could just see the top of his bald head above the high-backed chair he sat in. I listened but I couldn't hear him breathing. My hands began to shake, and I forced myself to exhale the breath I'd held at the front door, forced myself to take in another. Stepping around the chair I looked at him, his face longer than the last time I saw him, his skin ashen. I shook his shoulder gently and jumped when he sat bolt upright.

'What, what is it?' he slurred, getting to his feet and looking around at everything but me stood in front of him.

'Dad, it's me,' I said, startled but relieved.

'What time is it?' he said, squinting towards a wall where we once had a clock that was no longer there.

'It's late, Dad.'

He looked at me then, and I didn't see any happiness in his eyes. I hoped he would be delighted his little girl was home. But there was nothing.

'You woke me.'

'I'm sorry, Dad.'

'Well, make yourself at home.'

'Thank you,' I said, sounding formal, unsure of how else to behave.

'Good, good.'

He hesitated, and for a moment, we looked at each other like strangers. I wanted to know what he was thinking, as if I weren't vulnerable enough already.

'I've had a long drive, and I'm pretty tired, I'm gonna go up.'

'Yes, it's late. You should get some sleep.'

'Shall I sleep in my old room?'

'Yes, your room is your room.'

'OK, I'll see you in the morning?'

'Yes. In the morning.'

'Night, Dad.'

'Bye, Neve.'

I hoped he would get up and hug me, stroke my arm, even ask for a bloody high five. But nothing. I headed for the stairs, taking my time as I ascended. In my peripheral vision, I watched him slump back into his armchair, like I wasn't even there. When I reach the top, I flicked on a light, and waited for my eyes to adjust. Nothing had changed, nothing in twenty years. The wallpaper was the same, as were the light shades and doors. I could see into the bathroom; the loo and sink were still the same olive green that was all the rage in the Eighties.

I opened the door to the room that was once mine. The single bed was still tucked up against the wall furthest away from the window, on it an old suitcase and a few boxes. Dad had forgotten I was coming. Or he didn't care. Likely both. The wardrobe still had the corners of posters that had remained stuck with sellotape long after the rest had been torn down, and through the window, the headstocks of the mine looked in. The wheels atop it once spun 24/7 looked like two beady eyes, always watching. I dragged the case and one of the boxes from the bed. The other box was too heavy for me to move on my own, not without creating a deafening bang when I dropped it on the floor. I pushed it against the wall and lay down, curling my body around it like I used to with Oliver when he slept with his back to me. I wanted nothing more than for the alcohol that made the room spin to take me into a booze-infused sleep. But it didn't and laying there, wrapped around a huge box, I thought of Oliver, of Dad, of Jamie. I thought of Chloe. Turning to face the window I listened to the rain that had started back up, lash against the glass, while the eyes of the headstocks looked in.

CHAPTER 15

23rd November 2019
Morning

When I woke, my head throbbed and for a moment I thought I was in the wrong place – it wasn't the first time I'd woken up in a strange bed, but not something I'd done since meeting Oliver. I pieced together where I was and the previous day. I checked my phone, still hopeful that Oliver would have messaged. He hadn't. I did, however, have a Facebook message from Holly – news really had travelled fast.

> I've heard you came back last night. I'll be at the social club; they've agreed to open it as a search HQ. I'll be there from half nine. Holly.

I sat up quickly, and my head stung. Touching the back of it I felt a lump and when I pulled my hand away there was blood on it. The same applied to the pillow. For a moment I couldn't remember what had happened, then recalled breaking the wing mirror. Pressing my hand to the lump again I felt the small cut. Nothing to worry about, apart from not realising I had done it. Unsteadily rising to my feet, I looked into the mirror beside what used to be my wardrobe. My eyes were bloodshot and heavy, my skin looked desperate for some sunshine, and as I turned my head, I could just about see a matted red splodge in my hair from where I had bled.

Opening my bedroom door, I looked across the small landing to my dad's room. If I squinted I could just about make out his bed which looked like it hadn't been slept in. I took a few steps to confirm I was alone up here, and the floorboards squeaked angrily underfoot. Downstairs, I could hear the TV playing. I couldn't help but feel nervous as I made my way towards the sound. Last night I had seen my father for the first time in years, but it was late, and I was drunk. Today I would face him properly.

Knowing I couldn't see him looking as I did, I found a towel in the airing cupboard and went back up to the bathroom, I had a quick shower that dribbled lukewarm water over me. I had forgotten how shit the shower was here, and how Dad only put the hot water on for an hour a day. The tepid water was yet another thing I didn't miss about this place. Stepping out of the shower I dashed back to my old bedroom and shut the door to get dressed. Feeling slighter better as each layer of clean clothes went onto my body, I pulled my hair into a messy bun, and grabbed my glasses which had somehow survived unscathed. I appraised myself one more time before going down to see him. I looked OK, which in the circumstances was better than I could have wished for. Would he even notice, anyway?

I was shocked to see the lounge was empty, and grabbing the remote I turned down the TV. I expected him to be in his armchair, where he was last night. After Mum left, he'd often fall asleep in front of the telly. From the lounge I went into the kitchen, having to fold my arms over my chest as the room was freezing. The back door was wide open, and outside, standing in the middle of the lawn was my dad, wrapped in his dressing gown. He was looking at the old tree at the end of the garden that once had a rope swing attached. For a moment, I could hear my giggles, asking him to push me higher.

'Dad?' I called out, but he mustn't have heard me. 'Dad!' I said louder, and he turned, startled to see me stood in the kitchen doorway. 'What are you doing? It's freezing out here!'

'Oh, I'm umm, just getting some air,' he said, half smiling.

'Come back in here, you'll catch a cold,' I said, waving him towards me. He did as I asked, and I closed the door behind me. I expected him to perhaps offer a cup of tea, but by the time I locked the back door, he had shuffled back into the living room.

'I'll put the kettle on?' I called out.

'OK,' he replied, turning up the TV.

'OK,' I echoed, defeated.

I watched Dad as I waited for the kettle to boil. He looked frail, too frail, and although he was dismissive as ever, there was something else. He wasn't one to step outside and get fresh air, and he wasn't one to forget to make someone a cup of tea. He may not be the most emotionally connected person in the world, but he'd always used tea to bridge the gap.

The kettle boiled and I opened the fridge door looking for milk. Where the milk should have been sat a bag of sugar. I looked in the cupboard where the sugar was kept, and sure enough, there was the milk. That in itself wasn't alarming, but combined with everything else... what was going on?

I made our drinks and sat on the sofa, where we sipped in silence.

'I'm going to the social to meet Holly, and see if I can help.'

'The social is shut.'

'I know. It's open just as a base for people to meet and help.'

'Help with what?' he asked, his eyes still on the screen.

'Finding Jamie.'

'Oh, yes. Well, I'm sure he will turn up,' he said, dismissing the seriousness of it.

Putting on my coat I called goodbye, and waited – perhaps longer than I should have – for him to say something back, but my farewell was unanswered. Quietly, I closed the door behind me. As I stepped onto the footpath that led to town I looked up, heavy dark clouds above me moved apace. The wind was strong up there, adding to my sense of disorientation. A horn blared behind me and I spun around to see a white van, half on the footpath, half on the road. I thought it was someone trying to run me down, but the driver had slammed on the brakes. Instinctively, I covered myself, waiting to be hit. Thankfully, it came to a halt inches before that happened. I stumbled backward, looked up at the van. A sign said it was for GM Cleaning Services. I mumbled an apology, even though I wasn't in the wrong. I expected the driver to say something, offer a sorry like I had, or perhaps even shout at me, but she just stared towards me. As I began to walk away again, I looked over my shoulder and saw the woman, who was probably in her late forties, get out. She would have been too old to know who I was back then. But still, as she looked at me, I couldn't help but think she was judging me silently, it was like she was trying to scare me. Perhaps Derrick had told more people than Brenda and Holly I was back, and she was letting me know the village knew. And that I should be careful.

I turned, put my head down, and walked on.

It wasn't until I was halfway down my dad's road and heading towards the village centre did I stop to think about where I was going. I was walking to meet Holly, someone who I had not seen since the summer Chloe vanished, to help her look for Jamie. I suspected there would be lots of people there; people who had known me before. My heart began to race.

CHAPTER 16

23rd November 2019
Morning

Jamie's face was everywhere, his sad smile, the same one I saw on Facebook, was photocopied in black and white and stuck on every other lamppost on the main road of the village. The posters didn't say much, just listed a number to call if he was spotted. His tired expression watched me all the way to the furthest edge of the village.

Once the social club was in sight, I tried to make out if I could see Holly amongst the few gathered outside in the car park. I checked my phone, tempted to try and call her through Facebook messenger. It was like she knew I would want to spot her before approaching, as she had messaged ten minutes earlier, telling me she would be wearing a bright red coat, just in case I couldn't work out who she was. Casting my eye back towards the social I could see a handful of people milling around. They mostly consisted of well-meaning elderly folk who probably had little else to do but make cups of tea for those out looking. But I couldn't see a red coat anywhere. Checking the time, I saw it was 10.15 a.m. She probably waited for me for a while, but then gave up. As I drew ever closer, an older lady by the door greeted me with a warm, but serious smile. Did she know who I was?

'Good morning, I'm looking for Holly?' I asked quietly, guarded.

'Good morning, dear, are you here to help?'

'If I can.'

'Bless you, yes, we need all the help we can get.'

Dad had said something similar, but I didn't ask her to elaborate.

'Do you know him?' I asked, hoping I could learn something about the boy I once knew so well.

'Yes, he's very popular in the village, poor man. Holly is just inside, you've timed it well, the group are about to head out into the woods.' Before I could respond, the lady took me by the arm and guided me in.

As I was dragged into the bar area, and eyes met mine, I knew I couldn't back out. I was expecting to see people in hi-vis jackets with walkie talkies. I expected mountain rescue to be leading the search, as the woods around the village are dense and it's easy to lose your way. I expected police, just like in 1998. But what I saw didn't even come close to my assumption. There were four people standing around a table, one of them in a red coat. Holly. I could hear her talking about how they were about to search the woods. Just like they did with Chloe. I never wanted to step foot into that forest again.

As I approached, Holly looked up at me and smiled. I tried to smile back. But those two words swam around my head. The woods. She walked towards me, her arms outstretched, ready to embrace, and in acquiescence I stepped inside the space she created for me and hugged her back.

'Neve, it's so good to see you.'

'You too, Holly.'

Pulling away she looked at me; I wanted to look away. Time had been good to her, she seemed young, stress-free, fit.

'You look fantastic,' I said, stepping away.

'Thank you. So do you,' she lied. 'It's been so long.'

'I know, over twenty years,' I mused tentatively, and she smiled, us both knowing full well how long it had been.

'I just wish it was under better circumstances,' she continued, before any thoughts of the past could take hold. 'Thank you for coming back to help. Let's meet the others who are helping this morning.'

Holly introduced me to the three other people she was with. I nodded politely, but failed to retain their names. After the solemn introductions were complete, Holly's tone changed, her mind back on the business of finding Jamie. Her eyes fixed on the map that had been pinned flat on the table with mugs of tea.

'So, today we are sweeping west of the mine and then north towards the lake. It's a small search area, but the woodland is dense. So we move slow, take our time. The forecast isn't good and it'll likely get wet out there, so I don't want anyone getting hurt.' The group nodded, and I couldn't help but feel that, given their advanced ages, we would be moving slow regardless of the terrain. 'We should come out around here,' she said, pointing to a spot on the map, close to the lane. 'As always, thank you for taking the time to help. If you see anything at all, no matter how small, please tell me. I'd rather us be wrong several times than miss something that might tell us where he is.'

The group nodded and began to move, putting on rucksacks and zipping up coats. I felt fear begin to creep into my bones. We were about to go back into those woods. Next to the others, all wearing expensive-looking hiking kit, I felt entirely underdressed in my thin Topshop coat and ankle boots. I wanted to say something about being unprepared, trying to find a way to get out of the search, but as I began to open my mouth, Holly spoke.

'OK, let's go,' Holly said decisively as she headed towards the door. Breaking into a jog, I caught up as she headed out into the murky winter air.

'Holly, where are the police?'

'There are no police, it's just us.'

'But I thought Jamie was a missing person?'

'He is.'

'So then why…'

'This isn't the first time Jamie has gone missing.'

'What do you mean?'

'For many years now, Jamie has struggled with his mental health; he has down times. Understandably,' she added quietly, but loud enough for us both to know I had heard her and understood. 'He always comes back, sometimes it's a day or two, sometimes it's a week. In 2008, he disappeared for nearly a month.'

'2008,' I said, a statement rather than a question.

'Yep, July 2008. Of course, the police are looking for him, as they always do when someone calls. He's vulnerable, so they do take it seriously.'

'So why aren't they here?'

'Because Jamie leaves the village, usually. So, the police use what resources they have to search through CCTV at train and bus stations to identify where he is. Normally, he comes home before they find him anyway.'

'So, if he has done this before…' I didn't finish my sentence. I couldn't – it was insensitive, unkind.

'Why was it mentioned in the paper, why did I message you to tell you he had disappeared?' she finished.

'Yes,' I said, ashamed. 'Sorry.'

'It's OK, I guess there's a lot going on in your head being back here.'

'You could say that.' I tried to smile, but the woods were drawing ever closer.

'Jamie usually leaves a note, saying he needs time out. Saying that it's all too much. The village, the mine, the past. If I'm honest, we can usually see it coming. He goes quiet, he starts to disengage, doesn't turn up for work, barely leaves the house, that sort of thing. But he was in good spirits the day before. He was like the old Jamie you remember when you think of him.' She stopped walking and turned to face me, a graveness in her eyes. 'There was no note, no explanation. Jamie's just vanished.'

I let her go ahead of me, the three others followed closely, putting me at the back of the small search party. They walked in unison, unafraid of being in the woods. Above them, the clouds grew darker still, threatening to burst at any moment.

'Are you OK, Neve?' Holly called back when she saw I had stopped.

'Yes, fine.' I began to walk again. She didn't say it, she didn't need to, but I could see in her eyes that she was worried that what was happening now was a part of something linked to the ghosts from our past.

CHAPTER 17

June 1998
Three weeks before...

The exams were over, the stress had been lifted, and with the freedom that came with being sixteen and temporarily out of education, life was good. The group had drifted apart during that stressful exam time. But now it was over, they were as close as ever. They knocked on one another's doors and wandered the nearly deserted streets in the hot summer evenings. And they came to their hut every night. Just to hang out, smoke cigarettes, stave off boredom with silly games. Then, they went home at the time stated by the grown-ups and woke late the next day to begin the process again.

This night was different, though. If anyone asked whose idea it was to have an impromptu post-exam party at the hut, no one would know the answer; it had just happened. The evening started tame. A few drinks, and conversations about the future. It felt like old times, more innocent times. But as the evening progressed, the conversations quietened to intimate exchanges in smaller groups. Baz and Michael were chatting with Georgia about their misadventures when stoned, and she giggled between them, enjoying the attention they were giving her. Georgia wore her hair down, which was something she rarely did. At first, Neve thought it was for attention, but when she swished it, exposing her neck, there were small finger-shaped bruises close to her ear. Neve didn't mention them to Chloe as they chatted, over a cigarette. Instead their topic was boys, and Neve was trying to steer the conversation in the direction of Jamie. Jamie himself sat on the other side of the small hut, closest to the entrance hatch with Holly. They were making small talk about next year. Holly was telling Jamie about how she wanted to study to be a barrister; he was genuinely interested in what it took to become one, and enjoyed their light, easy conversation. But still he kept an eye on Neve across the room, wondering if she and Chloe were talking about *him*.

Outside, the warm summer day had finally given way to night and the wind, which was calm when the sun was up, began to stir. It moaned as it whipped around the mine. They all heard it, but Baz, Michael and Georgia didn't seem to pay it any attention. As it howled, it almost sounded like a person calling out. The hatch door blew open, hitting Jamie on the arm, making him jump.

'That's freaky,' Jamie whispered to Holly, not wanting to be heard.

'I hate this place; it gives me the creeps.'

'Me too,' he admitted, making her smile; she wasn't alone in her thoughts.

The wind moaned again, louder, like it was directly overhead, like the crying voices were above them, and this time, everyone stopped talking, Neve turned down the radio. For a moment, they all looked up, listening.

Waiting.

There was a thud from outside the hut – a bang, like a clenched fist, on the sheet of metal that was once the security hut window. Everyone jumped, Chloe let out a little squeal. Baz placed a finger to his lips to silence the group.

'Someone is outside. No one move,' he whispered.

They all nodded, afraid that if he was right, they would all be in a lot of trouble for trespassing.

'Check outside,' Baz mouthed, pointing animatedly towards the boys. Jamie and Michael crawled to either side of the hut, pressed their faces to the holes that Michael had cut with a penknife, to see outside. The group looked on silence. Above them, the wind howled again, breathing over them, moaning. Holly had tears in her eyes, and as Jamie had moved, she was isolated in one corner of the hut, trying not to let the panic that was rising inside her take over.

'I can't see anything,' Jamie whispered, moving away from the hole in the wall, and closer to Neve, making Holly feel even more exposed.

'Me neither,' Michael said, also moving away. The group was now in the centre of the hut, as if at any moment the walls would fall, and someone would grab them. 'Someone should check.'

Everyone agreed, but no one volunteered to crawl out of the hut to look around. Finally, Baz exhaled and said he would go. He made a point of saying it directly to Chloe, and she nodded appreciatively. He crept past Holly, who was doing her best to hide the fact she was now crying, and crawled out of the hatch. Inside the group waited, listening as a twig snapped under his foot, and Michael saw his shadow pass the hole in the wall. And then, silence. The group looked from one to the other, straining to hear anything.

'Baz?' Michael whispered towards the wall where he last heard his friend. 'Baz?'

The group all looked the same way, towards what was once the security hut window. Neve felt herself leaning in, dragging everyone with her until the whole group were huddled close together, inches from the sheet of metal. Then, another huge bang close to their faces, followed by a deafening scream – Baz's scream. The group panicked, Holly began to sob, Michael started yelling incoherently, and Jamie shouted for everyone to get out as fast as they could. The group scrambled over one another to leave the hut, terrified that they would be boxed in if they didn't.

As Chloe opened the hatch, there was the shape of a person. She screamed and stumbled backwards into Michael – and in crawled Baz, laughing at his own wickedness.

'Fucking hell, Baz, you prick!'

'You should have seen your faces,' he laughed.

'Not funny, Baz, I nearly had a heart attack,' Chloe said.

'I'm sorry, I couldn't help myself,' he chuckled.

'Knob,' Neve laughed, with a playful punch in the arm.

Jamie didn't say anything, he smiled, but even in the low light they could see his skin was washed out white. Holly wiped tears from her eyes. She couldn't bring herself to find it funny.

'Michael, you shit your pants,' Baz said, brushing past Holly.

'Piss off,' he laughed. 'I'm stoned.'

'What was it? The bang?' Georgia asked, her breathing surprisingly calm, considering. Neve noticed it, and wondered what was really going on in Georgia's life that made her so unafraid at that moment.

'A branch. It must have fallen from a tree in the wind. Fuck, that was too funny. You lot are so jumpy.'

'Can you blame us? This place…' was all Holly could say before choking on a sob.

'What, the ghosts of the mine?' Baz said, dismissively. 'They're just stories told to us as kids to wind us up. None of it's true.'

'My dad used to tell me one from when my granddad worked down there,' Jamie started, not looking at anyone in particular. 'He said that when my granddad was young, back in the Fifties, a man he worked with was trapped under a fallen rock in one of the deepest tunnels. His leg was pinned, he couldn't move. He had his pick-axe, and near him, a sheet of iron that was the collapsed support beam. He banged and banged on it until they found him. They could see him through a small gap in the fallen boulders, but they couldn't reach him. He tried to hammer the rock, dig himself out, but it was no use. It took them two weeks to dig through, and by that time he was dead.'

'That's messed up,' Michael said. 'Imagine dying like that.'

'That's not the end of the story,' Jamie continued, his pale face captured in the low candlelight, making him look ghostly. 'They couldn't free him from the rubble, so they blocked his body in, laying him to rest hundreds of feet down the mine.'

The group didn't speak but waited for Jamie to continue. 'My granddad said after that day, when they worked in the dark corners of the mine, they could hear tapping, like a hand pick chipping into the rock. And on the night shifts, he swore he could hear his work friend calling through the narrow tunnels, begging to be freed.'

'Bullshit,' Baz said, dismissing Jamie's story.

'Shut up, Baz,' Neve said. 'Did that really happen?'

'I didn't believe it, at first, I thought it was my dad trying to spook me, but I looked it up – it happened. My granddad was one of the men who buried him.'

'Fuck!'

'The day he retired, my granddad went down, as close as he could to where he lay, and called out to him, asking if he was still there.'

'Did he hear a voice?' Chloe hung on every word.

'No, but he did hear the sound of metal hitting metal, the same sound he made when alive and begging for help.'

'You think he's still down there? Wanting to be freed?'

'I don't know,' he continued, unable to hold anyone's eye. 'What I do know is that once my granddad retired, he would walk around the mine – probably missing the place, like most do – and at night, he would hear that sound of metal on metal. He heard it until the day he died.' Looking up he smiled at the group, their faces full of uncertainty. 'Still, probably all bullshit, right?'

His question was greeted by silence. Baz then declared that they all needed a drink to calm their nerves and insisted everyone grab another bottle. Everyone agreed, and turned the radio back on. After a while the adrenaline of Baz's prank and talk of ghosts was replaced with normal conversation. But Holly, who hadn't been able to shake off her feeling of dread, said she wanted to leave and asked if someone would walk her back. Jamie said he would, which made Neve feel jealous and proud all at once.

As she said her goodbyes, Baz was pulling out a bag of white powder, just like he had done two weeks before. Holly didn't like drugs and could just about tolerate that Baz and Michael smoked weed. Baz offered it around the table. Jamie stated he wouldn't do it, and she found comfort in that some of her friends wouldn't change. The most troubling thing for her wasn't that Baz and Michael had taken it and would do so again tonight;

what truly worried her was Georgia. She had shown interest, asked questions, and as Holly made her excuses and ducked under the hatch door to leave, she saw her friend bend down over the coffee table with a rolled-up fiver and snort the white powder.

Jamie returned after ten minutes, announcing himself before crawling through the hut.

'Did she get home OK?' Neve asked, but only because she felt someone should.

'Yeah, she was freaked out. I kinda get it. Walking back down the lane on my own… well, let's just say, I'll not be doing that again,' he joked, but Neve could see he was really quite afraid.

'She's always freaking out about something; I wonder why we hang out with her,' Georgia said – a question no one seemed keen to answer. She turned up the music, a mix tape of all of the hits from the previous summer. The music wasn't to everyone's taste but they all bopped along happily enough. Chloe, Neve and Jamie sat on the beanbags drinking quietly, talking about nothing and everything, whilst Michael tidied around them frantically, the speed he had snorted just after Georgia pumping though his veins and causing him to sweat profusely.

'Michael, you don't have to tidy around us,' said Chloe, laughing at him.

'Gotta keep this place tip top,' he said, as he began to crawl through the hatch to empty the full ashtrays. 'Gotta look after it.'

Georgia and Baz were not much better; they stood either side of the coffee table, shifting from one foot to the other, talking a thousand miles an hour. Even in the low light, Neve could see their pupils were dilated. She couldn't help but feel disappointed in Georgia; they weren't best friends, not like herself and Chloe, but in primary school they had been very close. And Neve knew more than most about how bad things had been in her household back then. Georgia had a brother called Martin who was fifteen years older than she was. When they were in year three at school, Martin was arrested for possession with intent to supply, and was sent to prison. Neve remembered how it broke Georgia's heart to not see her brother, and yet here she was, trying to impress Baz.

'Guys,' said Michael as he crept back in from outside. No one paid any attention to him. 'Guys!' he said, louder, panic on his face.

'What? Is someone coming?' asked Jamie, jumping up, the night's events still fresh.

'No.'

'Then what is it?'

'It's nothing, he's high,' said Baz quickly.

'I've just seen someone. I've just seen someone near the mine.'

'What?' said Georgia. 'No, we can't be found, my dad will kill me.'

'We won't be found, he's just high,' reiterated Baz.

'I swear, someone is moving around outside the mine entrance.'

'Maybe it's Jamie's ghost,' mocked Baz.

'Stop fucking around. Both of you,' said Jamie.

'I'm not messing here,' continued Michael. 'I really did see someone.'

'Just chill out, Michael.'

'I'll take a look,' said Chloe getting to her feet – if anything, just to calm down Michael who looked like he was about to hyperventilate.

Crawling outside the hut, Chloe moved to the corner and stood with her back pressed against the old granite wall, looking towards the mine. Michael came to join her, pointing to the entrance, its wide opening like a mouth, dark and terrifying.

'Michael, I can't see anyone.'

'I promise you, there is someone there.'

'Maybe, Michael, you've just overdone it.'

'Chloe, I know I'm high, but I promise you someone is there.'

'Michael, drugs do funny things to your—'

She didn't finish her sentence, for she saw movement coming from the direction of the mine. A solitary figure limped out from the dark, a small torch shining onto the ground. And despite the mine being hundreds of metres away, and the night making it impossible for Chloe to be seen, she ducked down and held her breath.

'Shit. There is someone there.'

'I told you.'

'Who is it? How'd they get in?'

'They can't.'

'What?'

'Everywhere is boarded up. There's barbed wire fence all around it. Whoever that is has come from the mine itself.'

'Don't be stupid, Michael, they couldn't come from the mine.'

'Exactly.'

'So what are you saying?'

'I'm saying, loads of people died down there, didn't they?'

'Nonsense.' Chloe shivered involuntarily at what Michael was saying. The torch spun towards them. Chloe knew there was no way anyone could see them. But the light hovered in their direction for longer than either of them liked. Eventually, it snapped down and the figure moved towards the entrance again. Then, quite suddenly, the light went out and the figure was gone.

'Fuck, that was weird,' Chloe whispered.

'Yeah, really weird,' Michael echoed as he slowly backed towards the hatch and inside the hut once more. Chloe followed and the group waited for her to say something. But she couldn't find the words.

Baz impatiently had to ask, 'So, is Michael tripping out?'

'No,' she whispered, feeling sick.

'No? There *was* someone there?'

'Yes.'

'Who?'

'I don't know.'

'I think it's haunted,' said Michael.

'Michael, shut up, you're high. Who was it, Chloe?'

'I don't know.'

'You're not agreeing with Mike, are you?' asked Georgia unblinking.

Chloe hesitated; she didn't know what else to say.

CHAPTER 18

23rd November 2019
Afternoon

Despite being at least twenty years younger than most of the small search party, I was by far the most unfit. My breathing was laboured, my legs felt like lead and the boots I had owned for only six weeks were now completely ruined. Mud covered all of us from the knees down, and the air in the woods had thickened to a hanging rain that seeped through the seams of my coat, through my jumper, and onto my skin. We had combed the area Holly laid out for over three hours, our breath suspended above our heads like small clouds, and had found nothing. No signs of Jamie, no sign of anything. We had only walked about half a mile away from the social club, but with the woodland being so dense, we could have been anywhere. It would have been disorientating if the mine hadn't loomed over us, acting as a compass, watching our every move.

We walked in silence, listening to our surroundings, hoping for him to call out, or appear. But it had been eerily quiet. Too quiet, as if the woods were holding their breath, watching us, watching me. It was just like that summer. With the weak sun barely breaking through, it was eerily dark. Long shadows and shrouded spaces surrounded us on either side, making me feel claustrophobic. As I had fallen to the back of the group, I felt vulnerable; despite not wanting to, I kept looking over my shoulder to make sure no one was there. My imagination kept playing tricks on me, and on a few occasions, I was convinced I could see a silhouette of a man just behind the tree line.

Thankfully, before my haunted thoughts could take hold, Holly announced we were stopping for a break. We didn't pause for long, maybe five minutes, but it was much needed. Then we set off again, quietly moving though bush and bog in search of *something*.

I allowed myself to think about when Jamie and I were young; the way he used to make me smile. I thought about the day I left, without saying goodbye or offering an explanation or apology. I had to wonder whether Jamie's current problems were because of me, or what happened to us all in the summer of 1998. Jamie was really good to me when we were young, he had done more for me than anyone should. I owed it to him to help. I suppose that's why I came back – though I'm not sure I would have done for the others.

We returned to the social club, having spotted nothing unusual. As I quietly sipped my tea with three sugars, in a vain attempt to relieve my hangover, I watched as Holly embraced her fellow search party members one by one. She thanked them, told them not to give up hope. I watched her, mesmerised by the woman she had become. That quiet, insecure girl I'd once known had changed: she was now a leader, a fearless one at that. I wondered, when we were kids, was I kind enough to her? As the last of her helpers left, she turned and smiled towards me.

'How are you feeling?' she asked.

'I'm OK, it was harder out there than I thought it would be.'

'Yeah, it's impossible to keep searching, hoping you *don't* find anything, wishing you *would*. Plays heavily on the emotions.' She plonked herself beside me and took her tea from the table. 'He'll turn up, he just forgot to write a note this time. Anyway, tell me about you. What's new? How's life been?'

'Oh, you know, ups and downs, like anyone's, I guess.'

'Yeah, I guess,' she replied, and I could tell there was a hint of something else in her voice. 'How long are you staying for?' she continued, brighter.

'A few days maybe? I don't feel like I should be here.'

'Nonsense, of course you should be here, it's your home.'

'It doesn't *feel* like my home, it hasn't for a very long time. It's weird being back with Dad...' I trailed off.

'How is he?'

'Yeah, you know, he's the same old Dad. He's OK.'

She smiled, knowing how hard things were with him after my mum left.

'Thank you for agreeing to come out today, it really helps.'

'I don't feel like I'm helping much.'

'You've given up time from your life in London to be here. Trust me, it helps.'

I smiled, not wanting to tell her I came back from London because my life was a complete mess and I was fucking up things left, right and centre. I was only back because I had nowhere else to be. Instead, I promised Holly I would go out again.

'Really?'

'Of course. Will it be today?'

'I think it'll be later this afternoon.'

'Have I got time to nip back and change? I promise to try wear something slightly more appropriate.'

'Yeah, we'll go out in a few hours.' I got up, dredged my cup of tea, then put it on the dusty bar counter. Behind me I heard the door open but didn't think much of it. When I turned, I saw Holly walking towards it, opening her arms and wrapping them around someone, hugging them close. Quietly, I made my way to the door, hoping I could slip past and not interrupt. I couldn't see who it was, but assumed it was someone very close to Jamie. As I drew level, Holly let go and the woman lifted her gaze, locking onto mine. Before I could say anything, the woman slapped me so hard across the face I stumbled backward.

'How dare you come here!' she screamed, rage and pain pushing their way through her words. 'How *dare* you come back!'

I opened my mouth to defend myself but choked on my words. I could taste blood where I had bitten down on the inside of my cheek. The woman advanced towards me and I prepared for her to hit me again. Thankfully, Holly came to my rescue, stepping between us. 'Julie, calm down.'

Julie burst into tears and stormed towards the door. Flinging it open she turned back, and if looks could kill, I was sure I would have died on the spot.

'This is *your* fault, *all* of it. I wish you hadn't got your claws into my son. You're cursed.' She turned and left, and I stood shocked, trying to process what just happened.

'Are you OK?' Holly asked, and all I could do was nod. 'I'll go to her; you go back to your dad's. I'll message you later?'

Again, all I could do was nod.

Holly turned on her heel and chased after Jamie's mum, leaving me in the social club on my own, unable to work out what the fuck just happened. I put my fingers inside my mouth, the inside of my cheek sore to the touch, and I could feel a slight tear in the skin. Retracting my fingers, there was a little blood on them, not enough to justify the amount of pain I was in. Did I deserve what just happened?

That summer had been hard on us all, but would Jamie have managed better if I had stayed? I didn't want to think about the answer. Clearing away the final few mugs from the table, I looked at the map where Holly and her party had searched. She was methodical, clear in her direction. The shaded areas followed searches. A few areas were still to be covered: one was around the hut, and the other around the place where Jamie and I had our first kiss.

As I left to walk back to Dad's house, I was torn: I wanted nothing more than to leave and never return. I also felt Jamie's mum was right: it was my fault that he was missing, that he had struggled with life because of me. And I owed it to him to stay, even if it was just for one more search. I just hoped of the two places left, the hut wouldn't be the last place I would ever see.

CHAPTER 19

23rd November 2019
Afternoon

I retrieved the hire car from outside of The Miners' Arms and drove it back to Dad's house. The adrenaline was still coursing through my body from where Jamie's mum had slapped me, making my legs shake. By the time I got back to Dad's, the inside of my mouth had numbed a little, but the ache in the back of my head from last night's booze had intensified. I was cold, wet and miserable. All I wanted to do was have a shower, get into something comfy and flake in front of the telly. Instead, I would change into my other pair of jeans – ready to go out again and search the woods – and I would have to deal with the awkwardness of spending time with Dad. I told myself it was just for one more night. This time tomorrow, I would be on my way back to London.

As I stepped out of the car, I could hear an alarm sounding from his house. Running towards the door I tried the handle, but it was locked. I started banging, calling for Dad. After a few attempts I heard him coughing, and the door opened. He stepped outside, smoke bellowing out into the street.

'Dad, are you OK?'

'Yes. What's happening?'

'There's a fire.'

Looking into the hallway I could see the kitchen door open, smoke billowing from within. Taking a deep breath, I ran into the house and saw dark smoke seeping through the small gap where the old metal door didn't sit flush against the rest of the oven. I turned it off at the wall and unlatched the windows and back door to let the smoke escape, before tentatively opening the oven. Inside was something black, so badly burnt I couldn't tell what it was. Using two tea towels I picked it up and took it outside, before setting the hose on it, just in case it decided to re-ignite. The cold water made the charred food crumble like a bath bomb. Satisfied that the pan had cooled, I moved it from the grass to Dad's patio table. A scorch mark remained on the lawn, but apart from that and the residual smoke, there didn't seem to be any damage. Within a few minutes the kitchen had cleared enough for me to be able to breathe, although I knew that the smell would linger all day. Standing by the back door I coughed a little, the last of the smoke tickling the back of my throat as Dad joined me in the kitchen.

'Dad, you left something in the oven.'

'What?'

'You put something in the oven and forgot about it.'

'I…' he started, unable to finish, and I saw the same look on his face I noticed this morning when I caught him in the garden.

'Dad, where were you?'

'I was asleep, I think.'

'Did you not hear the smoke alarm? Did you not smell it burning? What were you even cooking?'

'I – I don't know.'

'What do you mean, you don't know?' I asked, fearing what he would next say.

'I don't know,' he repeated, quieter this time.

I pressed him again, but he was unable to look me in the eye and walked away. I followed him back into the living room, where he sat down like nothing had happened.

'Dad, you need to talk to me.'

'What about?'

'About what just happened. This isn't the first time you've forgotten something.'

He looked at me, as if to ask, *how could you tell?*

'I found the milk in the cupboard and the sugar in the fridge. And this morning, in the garden, I could see something was wrong.'

'I've, umm…' he paused.

'Dad, just talk to me, for once just bloody talk to me. Your house could have burned down, or worse. Dad, what if I didn't bang on the door, waking you? What then?'

'I've been forgetting things lately,' he said quietly, his tone even. It confirmed my fears.

'OK, have you spoken to anyone about it?' I tried to sound calm but inside my heart began to thump. It was the first time he had ever opened up to me about anything.

'What? No, no, it's fine, I've just been distracted, that's all,' he said, turning up the TV. I took the remote from him, switching it off.

'Dad. You need to talk to someone about this.'

'We just have.'

'I mean a professional. I'm going to ring the doctor's surgery, see if they can fit you in.'

'I have.'

'When?'

'A few weeks ago.'

'And what did the doctor say?'

'He said it was nothing.'

'We need to go again, don't you think?'

'No, he said it was nothing.'

I ignored Dad's protests and googled the doctor's number. It rang four times before an automated message stated that the surgery was closed, and if it was an emergency, I had to call another number. It wasn't an emergency, but it was troubling. Before I went home tomorrow, I knew I needed to get him in front of his GP, otherwise he would never go back. I just hoped when I did get him in, we would be told it was nothing to worry about – just a bored, absent mind and nothing more sinister. Of course, I didn't want anything to happen to Dad – we had our differences, a lifetime of things unsaid, but I still loved him dearly. I needed to know he was all right, I needed to know as soon as possible, because I didn't want to stay here any longer than I absolutely needed to.

CHAPTER 20

23rd November 2019
Afternoon

The smell of smoke hadn't lifted, a constant reminder of our dilemma. Dad and I had barely spoken since I tried to call the doctor. Regardless, I stayed close and tried to watch him discreetly. Was he bored, or was his forgetfulness something more? Despite us not actually talking, the tension between us seemed to have lifted, at least. I made us cups of tea and curled up on the sofa – TV on, shoes off. Every now and then, Dad took his eye off the screen and looked at me. I tried not to notice it, to keep my eye on the daytime talk show we were watching, but I wondered what he was thinking. Was he noticing the woman I had become, or was he seeing the girl he once knew?

At just before 3.30 p.m. there was a knock at the door, and Dad started to get up.

'It's OK, Dad, I'll go.'

Opening the front door, I smiled, possibly for the first time since arriving at the village. 'Holly.'

'Hey, Neve, I tried to message but you've not seen them, so I thought I'd pop by. I hope you don't mind?'

'No, of course not, sorry, I've been with Dad all afternoon.'

'It's fine, I just thought for a moment you'd…'

She didn't finish her sentence; she didn't need to. I knew exactly what she couldn't say. She thought I had left, again.

'We're about to go out, before it gets dark – do you still want to help?'

'Yes, of course.'

'Great, here—' Holly handed me a bright blue North Face coat, identical except in colour to the red one she was wearing.

'Oh no, you don't have to.'

'Please, Neve, you must have been freezing earlier. This will keep the damp out.'

'Thanks, Holly. Will you give me a second, just so I can tell Dad where I'm going.'

'Of course.'

Popping my head into the lounge I called, 'Dad,' and he turned to look at me. I wasn't expecting it, so for a moment I lost my words.

'I'm, umm, I'm going out with Holly. I'll be back in a couple of hours. Shall I stop at the chippy on the way back? Get us something?'

'It's shut.'

'What, since when?'

'About ten years ago.'

'Oh, well, I'll order a takeaway then. Saves you having to put the oven on,' I said, jokingly, regretting it straight away – although Dad smiled, I could see that look again, that worry. 'I'll be back soon, OK?' He nodded and turned back to the TV. 'I love you, Dad.'

He didn't reply.

I offered to drive down in the car, but Holly said it would be better to walk. The stroll would help us mentally prepare. The sun was beginning to sit heavy in the sky and we had about an hour before it would be pitch black. As we drew close to the social club, Holly told me – or warned me – that Michael was helping with the search. It didn't help quell my anxiety.

'Don't worry, Neve,' Holly said, reading my thoughts. 'He knows you're helping. He's looking forward to seeing you.'

'OK,' was all I could say in response. I wondered what kind of man he had become. The last time I saw him, he was a reckless teenager, experimenting with drugs, always wanting a laugh, the class clown.

I was shocked when I saw him. Unlike Holly, I could still tell it was him, although ageing suited him. His gangly frame was more solid, and the chaos in his eyes had been replaced with a steadiness. I was shocked to see that so far, my old friends all looked well. Perhaps I was wrong to assume those who hadn't left the village would be fated to a life in the shadow of the mine.

The search party was just as small as this morning's pitiful group. Just four in total. Holly, me, Michael and surprisingly, Jamie's dad, Derrick. As Holly and I approached the table where the map lay open, Michael said a quiet hello, his smile warm, forgiving perhaps. I said hello back and Derrick gave a nod. We didn't get chance to chat, as Holly stated we needed to move, to use what light we had left. She was right, as she probably was when we were young. The difference was this time we listened.

She handed Derrick a radio, telling him to stay on channel two; then she and Michael headed out of the social and left, while Derrick and I turned right. We would descend into the woods and then sweep towards one another. It was a short route, one that was close to the main road. Despite barely knowing

Derrick, I felt reassured and more settled than before. As we walked towards the woods, we made small talk. He spoke about the trees, their history and how the large bank of earth that lined the road we were hidden behind was man-made. He spoke of the mine itself, how he never worked down there, but had visited a few times on open days with his father who was a miner. He mentioned the darkness, the heat coming from the rock.

I knew how warm it was down there but didn't say.

He rambled on as we walked into ever-thickening undergrowth, and I knew why – he was scared of finding something. I wondered if he was also scared of what it meant if he *didn't* find anything. He didn't mention anything to do with the summer of 1998, and I thought maybe what happened back then was really something confined to the pages of a history book. Holly had changed, Michael too. Maybe things had finally moved on.

The small talk stopped as soon as we hit the woods. We needed to listen, to hear anything that didn't belong in nature, in the hope we would find Jamie. If I was honest, I didn't know why they wanted to search for him in the woods. If he had decided to take time away, wouldn't he be away from the village itself? I couldn't help thinking I was missing something. We walked slowly, methodically, for about half an hour, climbing over fallen trees and fighting through thick bushes that had refused to die back with winter, and despite the woods being dense, we kept parallel to the main road, meaning I could see the street lights at all times, and could hear when a car drove by. The bank of earth was too high to see much else. I guess the idea was that trees would create a wall that would stretch higher than the mine headstocks, hiding it from sight. It didn't work. The mine would always dominate this place.

Derrick stopped walking and awkwardly stated he needed to make a call of nature, so I stepped away, as he nipped behind a tree.

I looked towards the street lights, noticing one was flickering, its old filament bulb ready to burn out. To my right the headlights of a car bled over the bank, catching the shape of something standing on its brow. The car sped past, hiding whatever was there from plain sight. I only saw it for a spilt second, and although I couldn't be sure, I felt like I'd seen the shape of a person. And I couldn't help feeling he was watching.

'Sorry about that,' Derrick said behind me, making me jump.

'No, it's fine. Shall we carry on?' I said, moving quickly towards him.

I kept as close as I could to him. The trees around us started to leak darkness. It felt like things were hiding within – if I believed in ghosts, I might have felt more afraid.

'Derrick, are you there?' the radio squawked, Holly on the other end.

'Yes, we're here.'

'We need you on the main footpath in Vicar Water Country Park,' she said, and I could tell she was panicked.

'OK, we're on our way.'

'Be quick, Michael – I – we think we've found something.'

Derrick and I ran towards the country park. Despite him being a lot older than me, he was considerably fitter as he jumped over fallen trees and ploughed his way through thick bushes. Eventually, we cleared a gravel footpath that – if we walked left – would have taken us back to the exact point we'd stepped into the woods. To our right – far off in the distance – two torch lights shone. I knew exactly where they stood, I knew the place very well indeed. It was the spot where Jamie and I first kissed in the summer of 1998.

I nearly said something to Derrick, who looked desperate as we ran towards Holly and Michael. Holly lifted the torch to see us, the beam temporarily blinding me. She apologised, and lowered it, catching Michael in her beam before it went back to the floor. In that split second of seeing Michael's face, I thought he had seen a ghost.

'What is it? What have you found?' Derrick asked, not even trying to hide the fear from his voice.

Without saying anything, Michael lowered his torch to the floor. It caught the edge of the seat where I could see JH & NC 4 EVA carved into the wood. Under a bench lay a light grey hooded jumper, covered in blood. Derrick stumbled backwards, covering his mouth.

I looked back at Holly, and then to Michael for an explanation, but they returned my questioning blankly. It wasn't just that we had found Jamie's jumper covered in blood. Chloe's had been found in exactly the same way.

'I'll call the police,' Holly said quietly, not for the first time in her life.

CHAPTER 21

24th November 2019
Morning

Last night, when we found the top, Holly, Michael and I shared a knowing look, that people's worst fears – my worst fears – had been confirmed. Jamie was dead. Now, I wasn't so convinced – it wasn't even confirmed we had found Jamie's top. Really, we had jumped to that conclusion based on what we had experienced before. It had to be a coincidence, it had to, because there is no way what we found last night has anything to do with Chloe. She vanished a lifetime ago.

Getting out of bed, I looked out of the window to see the sun trying but failing to break through the dark, fast-moving clouds. It looked like one of those days where it was always just about to get dark. I needed to move, ring the doctor and then plan my escape. My phone had died sometime in the night, so I plugged it in to charge, then I concentrated on my muddy memories and tried to put yesterday together coherently.

Holly radioed to say she and Michael had found a top. The police were called, we waited, they took statements then told us to go home, they would be in touch. Instead Holly said she needed a drink – no, wait, I said that. Derrick took us back to

The Miners' Arms, and we had a few drinks. I must have drunk too much, as the rest is foggy. I recall others there, not just Holly, Michael and Derrick. I can't remember who. I can't remember how I got back to Dad's either. It seemed, halfway through the night, my memories just vanished.

Beside me, the phone screen lit up as it came to life. A few more seconds and I'd be able to see the time, and check if Holly had messaged any update.

Eventually, the home screen appeared and a text message came through. My heart skipped a beat when I saw it was from Oliver. Hovering my thumb over the screen I hestitated before tapping it. I didn't know what to expect. What I saw confused me:

Neve, I don't appreciate you calling me over and over in the night. Take the hint, please, just leave me alone.

I didn't understand, I'd not contacted him, had I? Checking my call log, I choked on my own breath. At the very top was Oliver, and I had called him eighteen times. Tapping the information symbol, I learnt I had called him that many times in an eleven-minute window between 1.18 a.m.–1.29 a.m.

'Oh Neve, for fuck's sake,' I said out loud, too hungover to scream, too drained to sound anything other than numb.

I couldn't believe I had rung him. OK, that wasn't true. I could believe it, but eighteen times in eleven minutes? It didn't exactly scream, 'Let's talk it through, maybe we do have a future.' Looking at the message again, I tried to find something hidden within its words. But there was just a coldness I'd not heard from Oliver before. Then again, people change, I knew that more than most. I went to close my messages, but there was another message under Oliver's, one from Esther.

Hey, how is everything? Are you enjoying the time off?

She didn't ask how I was, and more importantly, she said nothing about the village. Which meant that news of what had happened hadn't broken out yet. But I knew it would soon. I almost texted her back, but in that moment, I knew I needed to hear her voice. She was the closest thing to family. Closer than my own blood – my dad – and I pined for that safe feeling. Her mobile ran three times before she picked up.

'Hey, Neve! How are you?'

'I'm all right.' My voice was dry and cracking.

'You sound rough,' she said, and I couldn't tell if she was smiling or concerned.

'It's been a weird couple of days,' I said honestly. 'How is everything? Is Tilly OK? How's The Tea Tree?'

Esther updated me on her life, and said the shop was reopening today, a grand unveiling at noon. Esther told me how the local community had gathered round her in support. She had friends, their relatives and their friends help with the clean-up and restocking. And apparently the grand reopening was going to be busy, with everyone involved coming to support. Despite my hangover, I beamed. It was the best possible news. Esther would do well, and the guilt of my messing up and running away started to fade.

'So, have you been anywhere nice?' she asked.

'You could say that.'

'OK?'

'I'm home.'

'So, just chilling in the flat a bit, it sounds lush...'

'No, Esther, I'm home. I'm back in the village.'

There was a pause. Esther knew more than most about my life in this place. She knew about Chloe, and on a night when she visited me in hospital after I dropped out of uni, she knew about the Drifter.

'Neve, why are you back there?'

'One of my old friends, he's gone missing.'

I heard her take a short, sharp breath.

'I think I'm losing it again,' I said quietly.

'You're not, and anyway, you never lost it before.'

'Since coming back, I keep seeing him.'

'Who?'

'The Drifter.'

There was a silence after I spoke those two familiar, haunting words. Saying it out loud felt strangely settling. The words had been lifted from a dark corner in my head and were out in the world. And I'm glad it was Esther I said them to. I knew she wouldn't judge, belittle, think I was making it up. I knew she would believe me.

'Have you told anyone?'

'Only you.'

'OK, keep it that way.'

'Because I'm mad?'

'Because it will scare people there. You always said how the Drifter caused so much tension. Don't speak of him yet, it will only do the same again, and then they'll... Have they found your friend?'

'They found a top, a bloodstained top, just like...' I didn't finish my sentence; I didn't need to.

'Neve, I think you should leave.'

'I can't. I *want* to, I really do, but I can't. Not yet.'

'Neve…'

'But I promise, as soon as I've sorted a few more things. I'm leaving. I promise.'

'OK, listen, but please can you touch base with me?'

'I will.'

'Every day.'

'OK.'

'Promise.'

'I promise, I'll ring or message.'

'Every day.'

'Yes, Esther, every day.'

'All right.'

'I should go,' I said, not wanting to, but knowing I should. Esther's concern made me feel guilty for taking up yet more of her time. 'And no doubt you have lots to do today?'

'Yeah,' she agreed with a laugh. 'Call me if you need me.'

'I will, thanks, Esther.'

Esther reassured me it was OK, and hung up. I cradled the phone to my ear for a little longer, sucking in the last of her kindness and understanding. As soon as I did what I needed to do here, I would go home, buy a nice bottle of wine and go to Esther's. I would drink moderately and be honest with how I'm feeling about everything – about life, about Oliver and home. I would tell her I was scared I was regressing back to that girl she visited in hospital once before.

First, I had to resolve what was happening here. Going into the Facebook messenger app I saw Holly had been in touch. Her message made my blood run cold. All of that warmth and security I had rushing though me, thanks to Esther, drained out of my body. Holly's message said that the police were confident it was Jamie's blood that we found last night. And that, as of an hour ago, they still hadn't found him. She also asked if I would meet with everyone later. She didn't say who she meant by 'everyone'. But I knew.

Grabbing a quick shower, I tried to wash away the unease I had felt since arriving back in the village. An unease that was growing with each passing minute. As the tepid water ran over my scalp, making the cut from the wing mirror sting, I planned my day. I needed to get Dad to the doctor, that was my priority, then I needed to see Holly and 'everyone' and once we'd raked over the past once more, I would leave. I didn't care how much pressure would be put on me to stay: I did it once, I could do it again.

Once dressed, I made my way downstairs, the thumping in my head intensifying with each heavy, clumsy footstep. Reaching the bottom, I looked into the lounge: Dad's chair was empty. Walking through into the kitchen I looked into the garden, in case there as a repeat of the previous morning, but there was no sign of him there either. There was, however, a scribbled note next to the kettle. Dad's handwriting, saying the doctor called this morning, and asked him to come in for 8.30 a.m. Maybe Dad had managed to get through yesterday when I was out? It was only 8.44 a.m. I must have only just missed him – perhaps him closing the front door on his way out was what startled me awake. I felt I needed to be with Dad when the doctor was talking to him, for support, but also, because I knew if I didn't hear what he or she had to say with my own ears, I'd never know what was going on. I grabbed my coat and headed out.

As I made my way down towards the village, I couldn't help

noticing the roads seemed busier. The quiet, stagnant feel of the place was gone, replaced with something I recalled from years ago. As I turned onto the main road, I could see people milling around, strangers waiting to find out more details about what we discovered last night, or locals waiting for their fifteen minutes of fame. There was a constant ebb and flow, a sense of the place coming back to life again. Seeing people this way – excited, speculative, quick to spread rumours – renewed my resolve.

I had no intention of staying a second longer than I absolutely needed to. I didn't want to be dragged back in speculation from two decades before. I wanted to be in my bed in London tonight, putting all of this behind me. I would delete Holly from Facebook, change my number if I needed to, focus only on helping Esther with our business, which was hopefully turning a corner. I knew it was awful to think that way, I knew it was shallow and I was being a coward. Something had happened to Jamie, but I didn't know who he was anymore. I didn't know who anyone was anymore.

I opened the doctor's surgery door and made my way to the desk. I tried to smile, but wasn't fooling anyone, least of all the receptionist who removed her glasses to hold my gaze.

'May I help you?' she asked, her tone clipped.

'Yes, could you tell me which doctor Sean Chambers is with, please.'

'Oh, I'm afraid I can't, it's doctor – patient confidentiality. If you would like to take a seat, I'm sure he will be out soon.' She smiled.

'No, you see, I should be in there with him. He gets confused.'

'I'm really sorry. I can't,' she said, still smiling.

'Please,' I tried again, raising my voice a little, causing the few waiting patients to turn in their chairs and look disapprovingly at me.

'Neve.'

I turned to see a wide man standing in the doorway of the nearest doctor's office. He smiled and gestured for me to come in. Only when I was close could I tell it was someone I knew.

'Baz?'

He looked around, embarrassed, hoping other patients hadn't heard him being referred to by his teenage name. 'It's Barry now. Come in, Neve, your dad is in here.' He waved back to the receptionist who dropped her smile and replaced her glasses.

'You're his doctor?"

'Yes,' he said with a laugh.

'I had no idea,' I said, stepping past him into his office. 'Hi, Dad,' I smiled.

'Hello, love,' he replied, and I couldn't help but feel the warmth of it. He had not called me love in a very long time.

'Please, sit down. I was just talking with your dad about the concerns you raised with me last night.'

'Concerns I raised?'

'We met, in the pub after...' he hesitated.

'Did we?'

He looked at me, a small smile, as if to say, 'Yes, we did and yes, Neve, you were very drunk.' Thankfully, he didn't articulate it, but continued in his professional manner. 'You spoke of your concern, and that's why we are here. So, Mr Chambers, let's continue. You said you've been noticing things for the last few months, what sort of things?'

'Well,' Dad started quietly, uneasy with what he needed to

say. 'Things like what happened yesterday, you know, with the cooker,' he said, looking at me.

'What happened with the cooker?'

'Dad put some food in the oven and forgot about it. I came home and the house was filled with smoke.'

'I see. Have there been any other instances?'

'Well.' Dad shifted in his seat, cleared his throat. Balled his hands into a fist on his lap. 'Sometimes, I'll wake up in the morning and the back door is open, but I was sure I closed it and locked it the day before. And I keep misplacing things like keys. They always turn up, just not where I remember leaving them.'

'And how are you sleeping?'

'Well, I sleep at night, but I'm sleeping more in the day too. And sometimes, I'll swear it's early in the day, but it's later, and I lose track of where the time has gone.'

'I think what we need to do is run some tests.'

'What kind of tests?' I asked.

'They vary, we need to take some bloods to check liver function, kidney function, that sort of thing. We will also schedule you a mental ability test.'

'I see,' said Dad, defeated.

'Mr Chambers, I know you're assuming the worst. Co-ordination and memory issues aren't just confined to what we automatically think of.'

He didn't say dementia. He didn't need to. My father's father had it in the last few years of his life.

'There could be one of a hundred things that could cause your symptoms. Let's not get too disheartened, let's do the tests and then go from there. All right?'

'Yes, all right. Thank you, doctor,' Dad said, getting to his feet and shaking Baz's hand. He opened the door and showed Dad out. 'Just down the corridor is the nurse's office. Go and sit down there, I'll ring across now and they will call you in. Is that OK, Mr Chambers?'

Dad nodded. 'Thank you, doctor.'

'Not at all. Neve, have you got a second?' he asked, as I began to follow Dad.

'Sure. Dad, I'll be quick, do you want me to come in with you?'

'No, it's just a blood test.'

'OK, well, I'll be at reception when you're done.'

He nodded at me, and I couldn't help but feel he looked lost as he walked down the corridor that led to the nurse's room; so alone. I watched him until the door was closed again.

'Hi, Neve.'

'Hi. So, you're a doctor, and I should know that because we talked about it last night. Sorry,' I said, embarrassed.

'Don't be, I would have had a few drinks too if I found what you found. How are you holding up, you know, being back here?'

'Weird.'

'I bet. Listen, I know you might not want to hear this, but, until we've established what's going on with your dad, he will need someone nearby. I'm not saying you have to be a full-time carer or anything like that, but he's alone, and he needs someone to keep an eye on him. Make sure he doesn't get into any trouble. Keep his spirits up.'

'Yes, yes of course. So, what do you think is wrong?'

'It's hard to say categorically,' he replied, pulling on his earlobe, unable to hold my eye. He almost looked apologetic at what he wasn't telling me.

'I see.'

'Are you OK?'

'Yes, sorry, yes, I'm fine. I should go, see he's all right with the nurse, then get him home.'

'OK, and Neve – has Holly messaged yet, about meeting?' I nodded. 'So, I'll see you there?' he asked, his eyes firing an intensity into me.

'I'll be there. See you later.'

I opened the door to leave, but turned back as I was about to step out. 'Baz, Jamie's top, do you think…' I couldn't finish my sentence. 'Nothing, it doesn't matter.'

'Yes, Neve, I do,' he said emphatically. 'Do you?'

'I wished I didn't, but how can I not?'

'Let's talk about it later?'

'OK.'

The door to the office closed and composing myself, I waited for Dad to return.

'Everything all right?' he asked once he rounded the corner and could see me.

'Yes, just catching up,' I lied. 'I've not seen Baz in years. Shall we go home? Have a bit of cake or something.'

If anything, there were more people, talking, waiting, milling about, as we made our way home. We crossed the road, heading for Dad's, and on the other side a man who was approaching from the opposite direction, stopped. His eye on us. His sudden halt rippled through me, and I stopped too, just for a beat, before forcing my step back in unison with Dad's. I didn't know who he was, but it seemed he knew me. Two words shot into my mind: the Drifter. But it couldn't be him, could it? Before I could turn away or lower my head, he whipped out a camera and took a photo and I knew he was a journalist, trying to make a story. I wanted to challenge him on it, tell him to delete it, but my words were caught. Besides, Dad hadn't noticed, and I didn't want to upset him or cause him alarm. The man opposite smiled at me, an unkind smile. I kept my head down for the rest of the walk.

Opening the front door to Dad's, I went straight to flick the kettle on as he sank into his chair. He looked fragile, vulnerable, and despite being desperate to get out of this place, I knew I couldn't leave him. He needed someone to keep an eye on him, make sure he was safe, and as I thought about it, I realised what else would I be doing that could be more important? My dad needed me, and despite our challenges, I loved him with all my heart.

I was here, I was needed. Baz said Dad needed me, not anyone else, me.

I was stuck in the village.

CHAPTER 22

July 1998
Two weeks before...

It was too risky to go to the hut in the day. Despite the village not caring about what they did or where they went, if it was discovered the group of seven were getting drunk in the security hut that led to the mine, their mine, there would surely be outrage, adults saying and doing things to make their lives hell. But with the village being so small the number of other places they could go was limited. The park was too close to Chloe's home, within earshot of her mother who would yell at her for something. And when they hung around the chippy or offie, they were moved along by the owners, who no doubt assumed, correctly, that they were up to no good. Neve couldn't work out why they kept coming back to school, but they did. There were other places, fields, bus shelters, but weeks after the exams had finished, they still drifted to the old field they once shared their lunch breaks. Neve wondered if it was because, just like the hut, it was a safe space to enjoy the sun, and space, with no interruptions. It got her thinking: could you say the same of anywhere else around here?

'Right, it's gone five, shall we go back to my house?' said Baz, who was rolling a cigarette indiscreetly.

'You're gonna get caught!' said Holly, looking towards the school, waiting for a teacher to run towards them.

'So, what can they do? We don't go to this school anymore,' he replied as he lit his cigarette and blew smoke high into the air.

'Then we're trespassing.'

'No, we're still technically students until September. And anyway, trespassing is kind of our thing,' he continued, laughing. 'So, are we going back to my house or what? My parents will be long gone by now. I wanna get pissed.'

'I'm there,' said Michael.

'Shouldn't you be doing your paper round about now?' Chloe asked.

'I got sacked. Old Busby found out about the missing hooch. Said he'd have me arrested if I did it again,' he replied, finding it funnier than it was.

'So, Michael's coming, anyone else?' Baz asked, laughing at Michael.

'I'm coming,' said Jamie, who wasn't looking at Baz when he spoke, but at Neve, who smiled nervously, and confirmed she would be there as well.

'Brilliant. Georgia, Chloe?'

'Yes,' they replied in unison, their eyes closed as they looked towards the sun, working on their tans.

'So, we're not going to the hut?' asked Holly, a hint of relief in her tone that no one except Neve picked up on.

'Not yet. The sun is shining, and we can't sunbathe in there.'

'Aren't you worried about your parents coming home?' asked Holly, who hadn't said if she was going or not.

'Honestly, it's fine. Friday night is their night, now I'm sixteen they sometimes don't come home at all.'

'Why not?'

'They stay in a hotel to shag,' Michael chipped in, making himself laugh more than anyone else.

'Fuck off mate, I don't wanna think about my parents like that, twat. And even if they do come back, it won't be until late. We won't be there because as soon as the sun goes down, we'll move on to the hut.'

'Do we have to? That place weirds me out,' said Chloe.

'We've all talked about it. That man you saw was probably squatting in the mine – I bet he worked there once and like everyone else, missed it and wanted to see it one more time.'

'I know, but…'

'But nothing. It wasn't a ghost, just some person who shouldn't have been there.'

'I guess,' Chloe replied. But since that night when she and Michael had seen a man near the mine entrance, she was sure she had seen him again. She didn't tell anyone, but she was sure the same man had stood outside her house a few nights ago. When she approached, he walked away quickly.

'He's right, Chloe,' said Neve reassuringly. 'We freaked out because we were drunk. It wasn't anyone.'

'But…'

'It wasn't anyone, OK.'

'OK. Sorry.'

'Right, shall we go?' Baz rose to his feet and turned to walk away from the school.

The gang, as always, followed when Baz made a move and headed in the direction of hole in the fence. As they walked, Baz talked to Michael about how this might well be the last time they would ever crawl through the hole – when they were on their apprenticeships, they would be able to have a fag break whenever they wanted, no sneaking or hiding or worrying about being caught.

Neve and Jamie tagged onto the rear of the group, walking side by side, so close their hands almost touched. Their friendship had deepened under the stress of the exams. Neve had had feelings for Jamie for a long time, but assumed, because of his aloof nature, he wasn't interested. His aloofness took a turn as the first wave of exams began. Jamie started calling Neve to talk about how each one went. He made her laugh and they would talk until either Jamie's dad or Neve's mum told them to get off the landline. They didn't speak now, they just walked silently, in perfect unison.

As they took turns to duck through the gap in the fence, Neve hesitated and turned to look back at the other huge building in the village, one that was younger than the mine, one that wouldn't ever close. It had been her reluctant home for the past five years. She would miss school. It was the place she met her friends, the place she had her first kiss, her first fight. School was where she learnt she wanted to be a businesswoman and perhaps own a company. It was a part of her, and, for the first time, Neve understood why her dad was so sad about the mine closing.

'Come on, Neve, let's go,' Jamie said quietly, offering his hand to help her through the gap, although they both knew she was more than capable of climbing out unaided.

It only took ten minutes for them to get back to Baz's house. There was an air of anticipation about the evening. They had all made their excuses: Neve and Chloe said they were staying at Georgia's; Georgia said she was staying at Holly's; Holly was…

well, Neve didn't know what excuse Holly gave, but they all had their lies set which meant they could stay in Baz's garden in tents, like they had been planning for weeks. The boys didn't need to spin familiar lies. It was easy for them to stay with Baz, they often did. However, Michael and Jamie's parents didn't know that Baz's mum and dad wouldn't be there.

Arriving at his house Baz led them towards the side gate, and reaching over the top, he loosened a squeaking bolt until the gate reluctantly opened. '*Me casa es su casa.*' He gestured grandly to his friends as he led them to the side door which went straight into the kitchen. They had all been there before, but Michael couldn't help appearing wide-eyed as they stepped in. The kitchen was something out of a show home. The space was so big it had an island in the middle, and hanging above it were saucepans that looked like they had never been used. The floorspace was almost the same size as Michael's grandparents' whole flat, with twin sofas facing each other, separated by a large television in the far corner. Despite the sofa technically being in the same room, the open-plan space was so long, it felt like an entirely different room. Michael used to feel jealous of Baz's life, his wealth and good fortune. Now, he drank it all in. He would picture it being his kitchen, his island in the middle, his sofas and TV. One day he would have a place just like it. Baz took his environment in his stride. He had grown up in abundance, as his dad was a partner in the business that owned the mine, drawing a fortune out of others' hard graft. He was one of the very few adults who wasn't sad it was gone. He had made enough money to not need to work a second longer than its official close the previous winter.

Baz wasn't embarrassed, nor did he show off about his dad's

wealth. He didn't offer explanation or apologise for it. To him, it was just one of those things. Some were rich, some were poor, and either way it didn't really matter. As the group moved into the kitchen, he told them to make themselves at home before opening a pantry door, retrieving three bottles of spirits. One vodka, one 20/20 and a bottle of peach schnapps. He poured out the drinks into plastic glasses from a cupboard and handed them out, depending on everyone's tastes.

'To the night ahead,' he said, knocking back the entire contents of his neat vodka.

'The night ahead,' the group echoed as they followed suit and drained their glasses.

'Tastes like hairspray,' Georgia said as she shivered. Beside her, Chloe was pulling a face that made Michael laugh. Without hesitation, Baz refilled their cups, except for Holly's, who only sipped her drink, and they knocked them back in one go. Again, Holly only managed a sip.

'Don't tell me you're gonna puke?' Baz asked when he noticed her cup.

'No, I'll just not keep up, that's fine.'

'Come on, let's get in the sun,' Neve said, rolling her eyes.

Baz walked across the open-plan space and opened the back door, leading directly onto a large patio area. He didn't wait to hold the door open for anyone and it swung back into Michael, who didn't seem to notice, or if he did, he wasn't bothered. As the group followed, Neve hung back with Holly.

'Don't worry, Baz is just being Baz. He's like a bulldog, charging about. You don't have to keep up, Holly, drink at your own pace, but let yourself get drunk with us for a change.'

'I'm just not much of a drinker.'

'So, go slow.'

'I just…'

'Baz will keep offering drinks, but he won't make you drink it. Besides, if you don't drink much, he'll be able to drink more.'

'Great.'

'You know what I mean, Holly. He doesn't pressure his friends.'

'Am I, though?'

'What?'

'Am I his friend?'

'You wouldn't be here if you weren't. Just chill out. Enjoy yourself. Now we've left school, we're practically adults.'

'I guess?'

'You guess. Holly, what's your problem?'

'Nothing.'

'Let's just enjoy today all right? Get drunk, have a laugh.'

'You know I worry.'

'There's nothing to worry about.'

'Baz and Michael tend to get stupid.'

Neve looked at Holly. She knew she didn't like drugs, that was fine. Neve didn't like them either, and if she was honest, she was glad there would be nothing more than a little pot tonight. Holly looked desperate for reassurance. So, Neve took a breath and touched her friend on the arm. 'Holly, it's just us, some booze and a bit of pot. A bit boring really, when you think about it.'

'You're right. I just… do I have to get drunk?'

'I know I'm right and no, not if you don't want to, just drink enough to loosen up. Now go work on your tan, chill, I'll get you a Coke or something.'

'OK.'

'Holly, *smile*.'

'OK. Thanks, Neve.'

Holly walked into the garden while Neve hung back to grab the vodka Baz couldn't carry. She looked through the back door at her friends who were setting up blankets on the ground to sunbathe on. Georgia sat with Michael as he skinned up a joint, learning how to crumble the resin into the Rizla. Baz was busying himself filling up drinks again; Neve could see he acted differently when he approached Chloe, who was sitting on the edge of the blanket, facing away, her head back, working on her tan. Holly approached and sat beside her; Chloe smiled at her before they both looked towards the sun.

Neve took a can of cherry Coke from the fridge and cracked it open, pouring half the contents into a glass. Satisfied she wasn't being watched; she filled the rest of the glass with vodka. If Holly noticed, Neve would say she added a drop, just in case anyone tasted it and teased her for not drinking. Holly would thank her, and before she knew it, she'd be hammered.

Neve knew it would be a great night, but ever since Chloe and Michael had seen that man by the mine, it felt different. They had explained him away – a squatter, a drifter, someone who was harmless, someone who had no idea they were there. Still, thinking of him, and thinking of the story Jamie told about the man who was trapped down there, sent a shiver down her spine. She shook it off and stepped outside, smiling to Holly with the drink in her hand, feeling silly for letting herself, for the briefest of moments, believe in the stories they spoke of.

CHAPTER 23

24th November 2019
Evening

Dad slept for most of the day in his armchair. I spent a large portion of that time tiptoeing around, tidying his house, watering the plants in the bathroom that were in desperate need of saving. I don't know why, but I wanted my dad to wake and the world around him be a little brighter, happier – something new, even. Then, when I had run out of things to do that wouldn't disturb him, I found myself sitting on the sofa opposite just watching him sleep. I couldn't help but stare at the sagging skin and deep wrinkles that marred his once strong, and dare I say, handsome face. I thought about my dad when I was young. He wasn't around much; the world here consisted of the shift patterns down the mine, and that meant he would often be having breakfast as I was getting ready for bed. Our lives, like most lives in the village, were just passing ships. And when I woke up each morning, he was there, covered in coal dust, tired, smelling like an unused fireplace, proud. He would kiss me, kiss Mum, eat a hot meal whilst I got ready for school and then go to bed.

But as I drifted back to those times, I remembered another side to our family – during the rare times when Dad took his holiday. I thought of a summer when I was around ten or eleven, Dad gently shaking me awake, a smile on his face. 'Wake up, love, we're going out.' Sleepy and confused, I climbed into the back of the car, still in my pyjamas and we drove away from the village until, several hours later, Mum pointed to a stretch of blue that was the sea. Dad allowed me to bury him neck deep in the sand and Mum drew a funny body over him, making him look like he was wearing a bikini. She got out the video camera and filmed him. He feigned being embarrassed, but really, I could see he loved being someone who could laugh and play in the sunshine with his family. He fake-protested, begging my mum to stop filming him, but she didn't, she told him to smile, say hello to the camera, and said that this moment would be something we could laugh about in years to come. We stayed in a tent, on a campsite close to the coast, the sound of the sea breathing at night matching the gentle breathing of Mum and Dad as they slept. Back then, life was clean, bright. It made sense. Then the mine shut, and overnight he became the aged, battered thing that slept in an armchair and only spoke of the small things. And that recording, I have no idea what happened to it.

When I was young, I couldn't comprehend how sad Dad must have been to lose his purpose. And, as I watched him gently snore, I realised that I didn't blame him for Mum leaving anymore. It wasn't his fault; it wasn't hers either. The fault lay with the mine. I understood why he was cold towards me, distant, because, like the mine, like Mum, I left him too.

Beside me, my phone lit up with an incoming Facebook message. It was Holly, asking if I was OK, and if I was still coming to meet the others. I said I was fine, and I would be there. She messaged back instantly, saying she'd be at The Miners' Arms in half an hour. Derrick had put a sign out saying the pub would be closed for the next few days, understandably, but Holly was allowed to use it if she needed to. I guess it was the least he could do after all her efforts to try find his troubled son, even if they were in vain. I didn't wake Dad and instead left a note saying I wouldn't be long and that there was a sandwich in the fridge, in case he was hungry before I got back. As I set off to leave, I hoped he would just sleep until I was home. That way, he wouldn't be alone.

I was shocked at how cold the air felt on my skin. My exhaled breath seemed to freeze above me. The walk towards the village felt tense, and as hard as I tried, I couldn't help but want to look behind me with each step, to make sure I wasn't being followed. Frost had begun to form on car windows and the patches of the footpath that hadn't seen any sun during the day crunched underfoot. I walked quickly and held my breath until I drew level with the pub.

Ironically, the one day Derrick didn't open would have been his biggest opportunity for business, since over the hours the village had slowly filled with people from neighbouring communities, or media outlets, tying to understand what had happened. I hadn't watched the news, because I knew they would link this new mystery with one from a long time ago, trying to connect dots. I knew, because I was doing exactly the same thing in my head, and as Holly wanted to meet, I knew she had too.

'Hello?' I called out, unable to see anyone else in the pub.

'Over here,' Holly called, emerging from the corner where I had seen the man watching me two nights earlier. I walked towards Holly's voice, trying to appear in control, my nerves in check. I didn't want to seem spooked – after all, I was the one who didn't believe in ghosts.

Holly stood and greeted me with a warm hug before turning to the group, suddenly revealed in the dim light. Michael, Baz – and Georgia. It took a moment, but I released it had been her in the van, nearly hitting me, as it mounted the kerb. I hadn't placed her yesterday, assuming she was older than I was. Of all of my old friends, Georgia looked like the one who had struggled the most with the past; besides Jamie, of course.

'Well, here she is,' Georgia said quietly.

'Hi, Georgia. Nice to see you again,' I said, indicating I knew it was her who'd scared me. She smiled enigmatically.

Holly gestured for me to take a seat as she sat back at hers. Picking up her cup of tea she blew on it.

'That's one's yours,' she said, pointing at a second steaming cup in front of me.

'Thank you,' I replied, but really, I wanted something much stronger. Having the group back together – well, most of it – made me feel uncomfortable. The last time we were all in the same place, at the same time, was after Chloe went missing. And even though I knew that I was transferring old feelings to the present, I couldn't stop it.

Above me, I was sure the ceiling had cracked, like it did when I was at university. But I daren't look.

'Now we're all here, we need to talk about what's happened,' Holly began.

'Jamie has hurt himself,' Michael said quietly.

'But, the top on the ground, it's just like…'

'He's done it as a cry for help. We all know he's not coped well since Chloe died. He's replicated what was found when we were kids, he wants us to know.'

'But don't you think…' Georgia started.

'No, don't, I don't want to hear it,' Michael butted in. 'I don't want anyone to speak about ghosts and the past. I want to leave it well alone. Jamie is ill, and he needs our help. We need to find him.'

'He'll come back when he is ready,' Baz agreed.

'But what if he's...'

'This is going to sound awful, and I'm sorry. But if Jamie is dead, then there would have been a body, wouldn't there? Besides, who would have hurt him? One of us?'

'I agree, Jamie is calling for help, but you know the press are starting to dig up the past,' said Georgia. 'It won't be long before they make the connection.'

I knew I should have said something about the man I'd seen, the man who reminded me of the Drifter, but I didn't. What was being said made sense, as sad as it was. Jamie hadn't recovered from the summer of 1998. I remember it hitting him hard. He questioned life, mortality. He panicked that the Drifter would come for him.

'So, what do we do now?' Baz asked no one in particular. 'What do we say if they start to bring up what happened here in 1998?'

'Well, Neve will run away again.'

'Georgia!' Holly said, standing up in my defence.

'What, am I not allowed to voice my opinion?'

'Yes, but you don't need to be a bitch about it.'

'I'm the bitch? I didn't fuck off when Chloe went missing, leaving the rest of us to pick up the pieces, did I, Holly?'

'Georgia, just calm down.'

'I didn't leave us all high and dry when Chloe's top turned up, covered in her blood. Did I? And I bet, Holly, you've not told her how much it hurt you for her to go like that.'

'Georgia, please calm down.'

'No, I will not fucking calm down. She hasn't been here; she hasn't had to deal with everything since.'

'Enough!' Michael said, his voice booming above Holly and Georgia's. 'Come out for a fag, calm down, this isn't going to help anything, is it?'

Georgia didn't respond. Instead she grabbed her coat and bag and stormed out, followed closely behind by Michael; in their wake, a heavy silence.

'Neve…' Holly broke it. 'Georgia had it rougher than the rest of us when Chloe… her dad was arrested.'

'What, why?'

'After we told the police about the Drifter, they started to look at who he might be, they went door to door, and Georgia's dad… Well, he lived alone, isolated, and remember how we all suspected he mistreated Georgia?'

'Yes, I remember…'

'Well, they discovered it was true. Then they found Chloe's diary. She had written a few times about how Georgia's dad creeped her out. They got a warrant to search his house and found pictures.'

My throat was dry. 'Pictures. Of what?'

'Of Chloe.'

'What the fuck?'

'Nothing like what you might be thinking. They were mostly copies of Georgia's pictures of us all hanging out. But we had been coloured over with a biro.'

'God.'

'Obviously, he was arrested.'

'Oh shit.'

'They tried to make him the Drifter, but he didn't fit. He was awful to Georgia, and perhaps he had a thing for Chloe, but he was never near the mine. He was never charged, there was nothing to actually link him to Chloe going missing. But for a few days, all the village spoke of was how strange he was, how it must have been him. Some think it was him, even now.'

I didn't reply but nodded my head. I was back there in darkness, the silence and then that terrifying din, metal banging against metal. It was that which made us split up, lose sight of each other. And then I never saw Chloe again.

'I can see why they thought it was him,' I said quietly.

'It's been rough on her, the questions about her dad. They tried to get her to press charges for how he treated her, but she wouldn't.'

'Why?'

'Who else has she got, Neve?'

'So, she stayed with him?'

'No, social services got involved. She had to live away with her aunt and uncle until she was eighteen, and, then she came back.'

'Shit.'

'She's had it rough. It doesn't excuse her lashing out like that but...'

'No wonder she hates me.'

'That still doesn't...'

'I didn't know her dad had been dragged into it,' I just managed to say before my words choked on a sob.

Holly rubbed my shoulder and got up, walking towards the bar. Baz sat unblinking, like he was facing a patient who he had given bad news.

'I still can't believe you're a GP,' I said, laughing through my tears.

'I know, right.'

'I'd never have called it.'

'Well, after Chloe, I wanted to help.'

'I'm really pleased you're doing what you're doing. It gives you hope, you know?'

Before Baz could answer, Holly was back, holding a tray with a few glasses of red wine and some beers.

'Holly, are you stealing from the bar?'

She grinned. 'No, of course not, Baz. I've left some money on the till.'

Holly sat down beside me and took a glass of red, Baz joined her, and I went for a pint and we quietly drank. After a minute I heard the pub door open and close and over my shoulder I saw Michael and Georgia return. They sat down and picked up their drinks.

'Georgia, I...' I began.

'Leave it, Neve,' she replied, but without the anger I heard before. This was more of a defeated, tired sound.

'So, now we have calmed down...' began Baz quietly. 'What do we do?'

'Nothing,' said Holly. 'We keep looking for him, we keep trying to find him. We find Jamie, this all stops.'

'And if we don't find him, what then?' Michael asked the group.

'I don't know,' Holly replied.

'I might sound stupid – this probably is – but have we considered, what if Jamie hasn't done this to himself?'

'What are you saying, Georgia?'

'I mean, we're assuming because it seems obvious it can't be true, but what if it's *him*? What if it's the one from when we were young?'

She couldn't say the Drifter, and I didn't blame her.

'I don't want to hear about ghosts,' Michael said, punctuating each word.

'I think I've seen him,' I blurted out, before I could stop myself.

'Who?' asked Holly, even though she knew.

'Him. I think I've seen the Drifter.'

'What? When?' asked Baz, his calm demeanour gone.

'Are you sure?' Holly said, her voice high and panicked.

'Yes, no. I don't know. I thought it was just my imagination, but with the top and...'

'When did you last see him?'

Until that moment I hadn't considered the importance of that question.

'I think I saw him last night, just before you radioed.'

'Impossible.'

'I wanted to think that too. It's been too long. But I'm sure it was him. What if he is back?'

CHAPTER 24

24th November 2019
Night

As a group, we decided that if anyone from the local papers asked questions about Jamie's disappearance and the similarities to Chloe's, we were going to talk about how Jamie needs our help, and nothing more. We also agreed I should call the police, tell them what I'd seen, just in case. So, before leaving the pub, I stepped away from the others and called the local police station. I told them about the figure I saw up high on the bank, just moments before Jamie's top was found. I had expected them to want to speak to me right away, I'd mentally prepared for them to invite me to the station. But the policeman I spoke with – someone called Hastings – said that I should come down and make a statement in the morning. It felt like before, like when I was a kid; the police weren't taking me seriously.

We finished our drinks and said our farewells. Georgia had warmed a little to me and although she didn't apologise for her outburst, she smiled as she said goodbye. The walk home felt longer than it had the previous few trips to and from the village. The night darker and with each turn of a corner, each bend in the road, I expected to see the shape of the Drifter. As I passed Chloe's house, Brenda was smoking from Chloe's bedroom.

'Cold one tonight,' she said. I pretended I'd not heard her.

When I got back Dad wasn't in his chair and I saw from the kitchen the back door was closed. Quietly I moved upstairs to see if he was there and to my surprise and delight, I could see the shape of him on his bed, asleep. Walking into his room, a space I rarely stepped foot in, even as a kid, I lifted the covers and tucked him in. I kissed him on the head and whispered that I loved him. Twice in one night, twice more than in twenty years and despite him being asleep, I waited a moment for him to whisper it back. But of course, he didn't.

I went downstairs to make myself a cup of tea and saw Dad had left a note.

Thanks for the sandwich. Dad.

Despite it all, I caught myself smiling.

When I went to my room and reached to draw the curtains, I saw something out of the corner of my eye. Movement from the opposite side of the street, close to a row of garages. At first, I dismissed it, but as I looked again, I had to cover my hand with my mouth to stop myself from screaming. A man walked out from that dark space. He was wearing the same long black coat, the same heavy boots from back then. I couldn't see his face, it was hidden under the hood of the coat, but I knew he was looking directly at me. Turning, I grabbed my phone from the bed to ring the police, and by the time I was back at the window, he was gone.

I looked down the road and couldn't see anything. I looked the other way, nothing. It was like the air hadn't been disturbed, like he was never there. It was like the ceiling was falling in again. My finger hovered over the keypad, and I hesitated. If I called the police, what would I say? I've just seen a man outside my dad's house, but he vanished, and I'm not sure if he was real or just my imagination.

Instead of dialling, I logged into Facebook and began to type a message to Holly; it took several attempts as I couldn't stop my hands from shaking. Eventually, I managed to send it.

I've just seen him again. Outside my dad's house. What do we do, Holly?

Checking once more, the night was quiet, and not knowing what else to do, I sat on the edge of the bed, and waited for daylight.

CHAPTER 25

25th November 2019
Morning

Dad was still in bed after I had showered, and assuming he hadn't slept properly in a decade, I didn't disturb him. I took a little comfort in knowing he had slept deeply; it compensated for my tentative slumber whilst perched on the narrow seat in my old room's bay window. He lay motionless, still tucked in from the night before, my kiss still upon his head.

Downstairs, I put out a bowl and some cereal for Dad for when he woke, wrote a note telling him I would be back later – saying maybe we could watch a film together – and left. Closing the front door quietly behind me, I shivered. Last night had been a cold one, so cold frost glistened off the front lawn, and the windscreen of the hire car parked on the road looked like it was made of a sheet of white plastic. I didn't have an ice scraper, so using my maxed-out credit card from the car hire deposit I'd likely lose, I went to work on clearing the glass, without any gloves. My hands burned by the time I climbed behind the steering wheel and fired up the engine.

After a tough, careful drive, I found the station that looked more like a community centre than an institute designed to protect the public. I stepped inside and was met by a gloomy officer at the front desk.

'Can I help you?'

'Hello, yes, I need to talk to someone about, umm, an incident yesterday?' I said, noticing that the officer looked young – too young to be wearing a uniform, in my opinion. His narrow shoulders were lost under his shirt which hung over him like a tent. The tie around his neck was almost as wide as his frame. I almost asked if he was on work experience but stopped myself. I had a habit of saying the wrong things.

'I see, can I ask what incident?' he said, whilst scratching the fluff on his chin that resembled something like a beard. He tried to appear interested, despite his voice sounding flat.

'Yes, it's about that top they found, over near the mine. The one with blood on it.'

'I see,' he repeated, although this time the boredom in his voice was gone. 'Please take a seat, someone will be out shortly.'

Before I could respond, he upped and left through a set of doors directly behind him, unable to hide his excitement, and a few moments later, an older officer stepped through. Heavy steps, a tired face.

'Good morning.'

'Good morning,' I replied; it was the same voice I had spoken to on the phone. Hastings. I offered my hand, which he shook, although I could see he wasn't keen.

'You have some information,' he said, a statement more than a question.

'Yes, I called yesterday.'

'Would you like to follow me, Ms—?'

'I'm Neve Chambers,' I said.

He turned and walked through the double doors and I followed closely behind, the younger officer holding the door open for me. I was expecting to see a cell or something on the other side, but there was a small kitchen area, an office and some toilets. He led me into the office and offered a chair in front of a desk. Again, watching police programmes, I expected paperwork to be everywhere. Perhaps a whiteboard on a wall, covered in words and pictures of suspects. The desk was tidy: one laptop, a stack of Post-its and a Harlan Coben book, open and face down so he didn't lose his page.

'What would you like to tell me?' he asked, sitting down in his chair, which squeaked angrily under his weight.

'Do I need a pen or something to write it all down?'

'Let's talk first, shall we?'

'Sorry, yes. I was one of the people who found that top yesterday whilst looking for Jamie.'

'Go on.'

'Do you know if it's definitely his blood?'

'It's being investigated. Please, continue, Ms Chambers.'

'I don't know if you remember, a long time ago a girl went miss—'

'Chloe Lambert,' he interrupted. 'I remember.'

'Yes, Chloe.'

'You were one of her friends.'

'Yes, I was.'

'And you're here to tell me again about the man you called the Drifter?' He paused, allowing a moment for the name to register with me. 'I was a lot younger back then, but yes, you told me all about the shadowy man who you and your friends saw hanging around the mine. A man who we never found, who no one else ever saw, despite the village being so small.'

'I know what I saw back then,' I said quietly.

'Maybe.' He paused again, eyeing me, and I remembered him, I remember him eyeing me the same way when I was young.

'PC Hastings—' I knew I needed to take a different tack; Hastings didn't like me, he hadn't liked any of us when we were young. 'I remember you now and, oh, what was his name. Your boss.'

'DCI Thompson.'

'Yes, Thompson. I remember how much you did when trying to find Chloe, it meant a lot to everyone. How is he?'

'Retired.'

'Well, it has been a long time.'

'Your Drifter haunted him.'

'What do you mean?'

'He didn't stop looking for that person until the day he left the force. He was never the same after that case. He couldn't let go.'

'Could anyone?' I asked with all sincerity.

'No, I guess not,' he replied, kissing his teeth, and again he looked at me in a way which was unnerving. 'The Drifter seems to live forever,' he added in an accusatory way. The small talk was over.

'I know what I saw, PC Hastings,' I repeated.

'But he was never found. We searched and searched, but he was like smoke. Don't get me wrong, I was desperate to find him, we all were, because we wanted closure. But he wasn't found, was he, and nor was Chloe.'

'I...'

'Ms Chambers, we spent a long time – long after the papers stopped talking about it – chasing your ghost. And since then, the Drifter has never even been mentioned, not outside the usual chats in the local pubs.'

'I know it sounds crazy, but I know what I saw.'

'Do you?' he said. He *knew* something, and I felt my heart rate jump.

'What about the top? The fact that it's so similar to what happened with Chloe. Don't you think there could be a link?'

He looked at me for a moment, and I couldn't work out what he was thinking, but it felt like I was a person of interest to him, rather than a witness. He seemed to ponder his next move and then sighed.

'Jamie Hardman is an unwell person. He has a history of self-harm, and of disappearing. He is a well-loved man here. We are taking this incident seriously. But we all know Jamie, Ms Chambers. This is nothing more than what it presents itself to be: an unwell man calling for help.'

'But the top, don't you agree—'

'Jamie has always struggled with what happened when you were all young. Everyone knows that. He has never spoken of that summer and how losing his friend affected him. He is calling to us to help him. He's ready to heal.'

What he said echoed what had been said in the pub the night before. Maybe I had been seeing things.

'Ms Chambers, I have a small force here, I cannot afford the time or manpower chasing someone you only think you saw.'

'I saw him.'

'In the same way you saw the roof of that club fall down?' he asked, enjoying himself. 'I've read up on you, I know about why you had to leave university. A brief psychotic episode, I think, is the technical term. Am I right?'

'Yes,' I said quietly, thinking of that night. It was just another evening out, nothing to suggest I was about to have an episode. We drank, laughed, flirted with boys, and just after midnight, I saw a crack form in the ceiling. It spread in all directions, just before it caved in. I was sure I was going to die. Esther held me, shielded my eyes until help arrived. They said it was stress, exam pressure. But I knew it wasn't. It was Chloe.

'Seems you have a history of seeing things that aren't really happening. I don't have time for ghosts. I just want to find that boy. If you want to help...'

'Yes, yes I do.'

'I don't mean this disrespectfully – but if you want to help, you'll not talk about the Drifter. People are superstitious, and I don't want scaremongering to ruin our search.'

'But...'

'Back when Chloe went missing, it ended up being a circus. I'd like to avoid that.'

'I understand,' I said, defeated.

'Thank you. Now, if you'll excuse me, I've got work to do,' he said, dismissing me.

In shock I stood and backed out of his office. Passing through the double doors, the younger officer said something, but I didn't hear. I left the station, climbed into my car and burst into tears. Everyone thought Jamie had just left. It seemed to be the logical explanation to this, but I couldn't shake the feeling in my gut telling me otherwise. I *know* what I saw back then. I *know* what I have seen since coming back. The Drifter *wasn't* a ghost or a figment of my imagination. He was real. He had done something to Jamie, and he had left his bloodstained top to make sure we were listening. I wanted to be wrong, I almost begged it to be me losing my sense of reality again, but I knew he was back.

CHAPTER 26

25th November 2019
Morning

Returning to the village, the headstocks guiding me home, I pulled up outside the social club, hoping that Holly was there, organising her small team of well-meaning volunteers to comb the woods. But the door was closed. I opened my Facebook and saw she had replied to my panicked message last night. She said that she was free if I wanted to come over. I was touched by her kindness. Again, I considered how I could have been kinder when we were young. As I messaged back, I made a silent vow to be a better friend than I thought possible. And I knew I wouldn't run like last time. I would be present; I would help in any way to find Jamie and protect those who'd shouldered the grief for Chloe back then.

In the message I told her I had been to the police and was around and if she was still free, I'd like to see her. She responded straight away with an address, and punching it into my phone, I drove the short distance. As I rang the doorbell, I could hear the sound of a little voice screaming and playing. Holly was a mum? I hadn't asked, and assumed because I was childless, everyone was. She opened the door, wrapped in her dressing gown.

'Don't worry, I'm dressed underneath, it's just cold in this house. Come on in.'

Turning away, she sidestepped a large toy dinosaur and then caught a charging little one who was about to crash into a doorframe, moving with such fluidity, like it was all utterly natural behaviour. I thought how if that was me, I would have fallen over the toy and helplessly watched my child smash face first into the frame. This was why I wouldn't have kids; it wouldn't be fair on anyone.

'Harry, please, slow down.'

Harry said something I couldn't quite make out and then ran back towards the sound of the TV coming from what I assumed was the lounge.

'That was Harry, and Finn is asleep upstairs.'

'Two boys. Wow, you have your hands full,' I replied, a strange feeling beginning to push its way from deep in my gut.

'I do and wouldn't change it for the world. Coffee?'

'I'd love one.'

Following Holly, we walked into a small, tidy kitchen-cum-dining space. Modest, yet I could tell Holly was incredibly house-proud. I thought about my silent vow this morning. I sat at a bar stool as she grabbed a couple of mugs and flicked the kettle on.

'I didn't know you had children.'

'You weren't to know.'

'I'm sorry I've not asked. And the dad?'

Holly paused for a moment before replying. 'He's not here.'

'Sorry. Sorry, what a stupid question.'

'It's OK. Neve? Are you all right?'

'Yeah, I'm fine. Didn't sleep well.'

'Did you definitely see someone last night?'

'Yes, I'm one hundred per cent sure.' The ceiling moved above me. 'Well, ninety-five per cent.'

'Shit.'

'Holly, I've just been thinking about what happened when we were young.'

'Try not to, it's not healthy.'

'Do you not think about it?'

'Yes, of course, every day,' she said with a sad smile. 'But like I said, it's not healthy.'

'I'm sorry I left you and everyone to pick up the pieces after Chloe.'

'If I could have, I might have done the same.'

'Really?'

'Yes.'

'You have no idea how good it feels to hear that.'

'Neve, we were young, we weren't built to cope with it all.'

I looked at Holly, the strength she now owned that wasn't present as a kid. And then I looked around her kitchen, the pictures on the walls of her and her boys. Smiling, hugging. I didn't know how she could do it. There were a few spaces on the wall where it looked like other pictures once hung – no doubt, images of the father that had not been replaced.

'I'm not sure I am coping now,' I said before I descended into thoughts about the life I might have had. 'I'm freaking out, Holly. I spoke to the police; they aren't interested in exploring it. Hastings, a copper from back then, practically told me I was making it up. What do we do?'

'I think we need to meet with the others again. Talk through what we know. Let me see if the pub is free, so we can meet without people seeing us.'

'Why would that matter?'

'Because it's us. Because people haven't forgotten the past. Because if people see us talking, they will think the worst.'

From the baby monitor I'd not noticed came the sound of a crying; apologising, Holly left to go to Finn upstairs. The kettle finished boiling so I made us both a cup of coffee and sat back down to listen to Holly talking to Finn through the monitor. Her words, soft and loving, and whatever actions she was undertaking, were clearly well received as every now and then I heard baby Finn giggle.

And for a moment, I felt something akin to a pang of loss.

I shook it off, it was hardly the time. As I took my first sip of the hot coffee, Harry bounded into the kitchen.

'Hello,' I said, forcing a smile onto my face.

He didn't respond, he just looked at me, accusingly. He knew, children always know.

'My name is Neve, I'm a friend of your mummy's. What's your name?'

'I'm Harry.'

'Hello Harry, and how old are you, do you know?'

'Yep, I'm four.'

'Wow, Harry, you're such a big boy.' He seemed to like my response, as a smile replaced the accusatory look.

'Do you want to see my dinosaurs?'

'Yes, please.'

Harry ran out of the kitchen and back into the living room. For a moment I waited for him to return, but it didn't take long to realise he wasn't coming back, and I was supposed to follow. When I stepped into the living room, I was taken aback at the chaos – whereas the kitchen/diner was immaculate, the lounge was anything but. Toys were strewn over the floor, covering all available floor space. The TV played one of the Pixar films in the background and in the middle of it all sat Harry with a large scary-looking dinosaur and a smaller one.

'This is my T-Rex, he's my favourite.'

'I see, and why is he your favourite?'

'Because he's the baddie and he eats everyone.'

'Wow, he is pretty scary.'

'Here, you hold this one,' he said, handing me the smaller dinosaur, and without giving me any time to realise what was happening, he began to talk with what I guessed was a dinosaur voice. I almost made an excuse and scuttled back into the kitchen, but decided instead it would do me good to try and forget the shit going on outside in the real world. So, jumping up I began to run away, drawing a circle into the carpet as Harry and his dinosaur chased me. Once he caught me and ate me, I became Batman, and he became the Joker, who of course had a T-Rex as a minion. And we continued to play. I made a laser out of a small slinky and pinged Joker from a motorbike he had acquired somehow, much to Harry's delight.

'You two having fun?' came a voice from behind me, and turning I saw Holly standing with Finn in her arms. I laughed and tucked my hair behind my ear, embarrassed.

'Harry, Mummy and Neve need to chat for a bit, are you OK to play on your own?'

'But Mummy, I want her to play.'

'She can't, darling. I'll tell you what, after Mummy and Neve have talked for a while, we could go to the park.'

'Yes!'

'OK darling, we'll be in the kitchen.'

I followed Holly and sat back at the breakfast bar, my coffee cool enough to drink now.

'You're good with kids. Have you thought about having any of your own?' Her words hit me harder than I thought possible.

'Yes, I've thought about it, just never seemed the right time,' I lied.

'Oh, Neve, trust me, there is no such thing as the right time. Are you married?'

'Engaged.'

'How exciting! Have you two set a date?'

I thought of Oliver's message yesterday morning, his coldness, and I wanted to cry.

'No, not yet.'

'Sorry, I'm prying.'

'No, it's OK.' I took a deep breath and watched as Holly turned slightly so she could feed Finn.

'You don't mind?' she said after he latched, and she turned back to face me.

'No, of course not.'

'Tell me about him.'

I thought of my silent vow. I didn't want to break it by lying. 'Holly, I'm not being totally honest. My fiancé, Oliver, he left me a few weeks ago.'

'Oh, Neve, I'm so sorry.'

'We both wanted different things,' I said. Again, being truthful, but I omitted that he wanted a future, a family, and I wanted to stay hidden as I had done my whole life.

'What about you?' I asked.

'I'm still married, but as I've said, he's gone.'

'I'm so sorry.'

'Don't be, it's just one of those things. We talk and still get on, for the sake of the kids.'

'Must be tough.'

'It is. But you and I, we're survivors, aren't we?'

'Yes, we are,' I agreed.

'And right now, we've got more pressing things to survive than our love lives.'

'Yes, we have. What are we going to do?'

'Let me message the others, get a place to meet, and we will go from there. How does that sound?'

'Sounds good. Thank you, Holly. I promise, I'm not making it up, about the man.'

'I know. We all saw him when we were kids. All of us.'

'But none of you have seen him since.'

'True, but that doesn't mean you haven't. If you say you've seen him, you've seen him, and as a group we need to work out what we do next. We have to find Jamie, and I think we need to find the Drifter too.'

She was right, we needed to find Jamie, but with each passing moment, I was more and more convinced that we never would. Or if we did, he would be dead.

'Can we go into the woods again?'

'No. The police have said we need to stand down and let them do their jobs.'

'All we're trying to do is help.'

'I know, and I said that to them. But since it's gone beyond Jamie wandering off to him potentially being hurt, or worse…'

I didn't know what to say, instead I smiled at Holly. 'I better go, spend some time with my dad.'

'Yes, of course, let me message the others and let you know. Can I grab your number? I'll add you to the WhatsApp chat.'

'Of course.'

Holly took my number in her phone and then, as Finn had finished feeding, she burped him over her shoulder as she walked me to the door. Outside, the crisp morning was being replaced with clouds that had blown overhead, dulling everything to a grey. I quickly gave her a kiss on the cheek and stepped outside, not wanting the cold air to sweep into her house.

'See you later,' I said, aware I wasn't worried about doing so.

As I walked back to the car, I had a notification ping on my phone, quickly followed by another, and another. Holly was organised, motivated and had already created a WhatsApp group, added me and posted about needing to meet. I quickly learnt that the pub was off limits. Derrick had opened it to the police and local media, who were beginning to appear in larger numbers. It was good for business. Baz's place was out of action, whatever that meant. Georgia's dad would have a fit if we met there. He was the last person any of us wanted to see. With my dad's pending tests, I didn't think it was a good idea to go to his, besides, it wasn't my house to offer. And then Michael messaged, his words sent a shiver up my spine.

Think about it, guys, we need to meet, and we need to meet somewhere where people won't know we are meeting. Somewhere off the beaten track. Somewhere quiet. As much as it makes me nervous, isn't it obvious?

It was obvious and terrifying in equal measure, and as no one replied, it meant it was happening.

We were going to the only place where we could hang out as kids.

We were going back to the hut.

CHAPTER 27

25th November 2019
Night

As the day dragged on, a thick fog descended over the village, reducing visibility so much that, looking out of the living-room window, I could just about see the shape of the lamppost on the footpath in front – the light it emitted was a shrouded glow, something belonging in a Sherlock Holmes story rather than a mining village in the Midlands. I messaged Esther, telling her I was OK, and that, if she had time, we could chat. She messaged saying she'd call once Tilly was down. I found myself watching the black screen of my phone, desperate for it to light up with the picture of us, smiling and giving a thumbs up, the Tea Tree sign behind us moments before we opened our café's doors for the first time. I had only left London, and Esther, a few days ago, but it felt like a lifetime. I missed her.

Dad had been in good spirits and actually managed to take my mind off the Drifter, Jamie and Oliver. We didn't talk about much, nothing of any consequence. I guess that was why it felt so nice. For the first time in as long as I could remember, Dad and I were just talking. No agenda, no hidden meaning or thoughts left unsaid. It felt normal. Remembering I loved the Agatha Christie books, Dad found the new *Murder on the Orient Express* movie and we spent the afternoon watching it, and he cooked me his world-famous toad in the hole. Replete and content, I washed up, and as I began to dry the dishes my phone screen lit up. Closing the kitchen door so Dad wouldn't have to listen to me chatting, I picked up.

'Hey.'

'Hey. How are you?'

'You first. How is everything? How was the reopening yesterday?'

'Well, good news or bad?'

Before I could choose, Esther told me that because the safe was unlocked, the money inside wouldn't be insured.

'Esther, I'm so sorry.'

She didn't forgive me, or say it was OK, but continued by telling me that the reopening was a success. Lots of people, lots of income. If it could be sustained, they would be doing better than ever. The news was wonderful – it didn't let me off the hook, but it helped me feel less like I might throw up.

'What about you? Tell me what's going on.'

I started by telling her about the lovely afternoon spent with my dad, how it was becoming easier to be around him, and before I knew it, I'd slipped into a detailed account of seeing Holly's children; even saying how I wished I could turn back time.

'Neve, stop. You can't keep berating yourself about Oliver leaving.'

'But that was our problem, wasn't it? He wanted those things. And I couldn't tell him why I didn't.'

'You have your reasons,' she said, not agreeing or disagreeing with me.

'Yeah, but were they right?'

She didn't reply.

'I just wish I'd let him in more, I guess.'

'Well, this might sound crass, and I'm sorry. But one day, you'll meet someone else and know not to make the same mistake.'

'I guess.'

To move the conversation on, I told her about Georgia's dad.

'So, it could have been him?'

'That's what they thought. But there was no proof.'

'Shit. That's really messed up. You need to get out of there. That place sounds too weird.'

'It is weird. But I can't.'

'What on earth have you got to stay for?'

I was about to answer, but the phone pinged in my ear, an incoming message. Holding the phone away I looked at the screen: it was Holly saying she was about to leave.

'I gotta go, Esther.'

'OK. Let's touch base tomorrow, even if it's a text. I'm worried about you.'

'Don't be,' I said, not even half believing it. 'Give Tilly a squeeze for me,' I added, aware I'd never said anything like it before. Esther noticed.

'I will.'

I hung up the phone and catching my reflection in the kitchen window, I stood taller. I made Dad one final cup of tea, and then I got ready to leave.

'Where are you going?'

'Just off to meet up with my friends,' I said, noticing how it felt like I had stepped back into my teenage years. 'I won't be late, and have my mobile, so call me if you need me OK?'

'Don't get into any trouble,' he said on autopilot, like he had every time I'd gone anywhere as a kid. I wanted to kiss him again, like I had when he slept. Closing the door behind me I almost got into the car, but instead I started to walk back towards the village. The walk I felt I'd done a thousand times in the last few days. As I passed the pub, I could hear voices coming from within. Not many, but a few. The events of the past forty-eight hours seemed to have brought people out of hiding. I wanted to believe people were talking about how they could help find Jamie, but really, they were likely gossiping about who might have killed him, despite there being no proof he was actually dead. I could almost hear their comments – one side of the miners' union blaming the other. Jamie was the son of the landlord of the pub that had been the central hub for those who refused to strike in the Eighties. The 'scabs'. I had no doubt the pub was full of the same folk, accusing those who did strike of being murderers. Michael was right, we couldn't meet in The Miners' Arms, the gossip would be rife, and all eyes would fall on us.

As I walked past the pub, a few people stood outside smoking. They were talking about something in hushed tones, and as I drew close, they stopped. Like I was a stranger in a Western, an unknown face who had just stepped into the tavern. I should have felt horrified; instead, I quietly laughed at their desperation for drama. It was pathetic, and once I was several paces past them, I could hear the quiet mutterings once more.

As the headstocks drew ever closer, it felt like the temperature dropped, and turning onto the lane that led down to the hut, I could see frost on the ground from the previous day. The thick conifers that lined the lane blocked out all daylight, holding this small corner of the world at ransom to the night. The deeper I walked, the less I could hear until the only thing left was the humming of the one working street light as the bulb inside flickered. No wind, no cars. No murmurs carrying on a breeze. Just the hum, and my shallow breathing. Then, from behind me I heard a snap, the sound of a twig breaking underfoot.

'Who's there?'

I could see no one on the path, no one in the woods that lined either side. It didn't offer any solace – I knew you only needed to be back a few feet from the tree line at this time of day, and no one would know you were there. Walking backwards, I moved as quickly as I could, and turning, I broke into a jog. As I approached the hut, I could hear Holly talking quietly from within, and my panic eased. Baz was there too, and I think I made out Michael's voice. I took a moment to compose myself. I looked towards the mine, the lifeless shell that had been dead for decades, and wouldn't rest. Walking behind the hut I called out.

'Guys, it's me, it's Neve.'

Dropping low I opened the hatch and fought to get inside, much harder now as an adult. Thankfully, Michael offered out a hand, which I was more than willing to take, unashamed that I was struggling.

'Here. Let me help you up,' he said as he grasped my arm and aided me to my feet.

'Thank you.'

'Did anyone see you coming?' Holly asked.

'No, a few people outside the pub were a bit weird, but no one followed.'

'Good. That's good,' she replied but I was no longer looking at her. My eyes instead were drawn to the room. The place that once was a retreat for us, a place that now haunted my dreams. The coffee table Michael crafted joints on was still there, now on its side by a wall instead of in the middle of the room. And the walls were still adorned with graffiti, as well as a few posters that were aged and lifeless. The beanbags and candles were long gone, cleared out when the search for Chloe begun. We were warned to never come back, a warning I heeded, as had everyone else by the looks of it, until tonight.

'Neve?' Baz asked, bringing me back into the room.

'Sorry. It's just weird being back.'

'Take your time,' Michael started. 'Georgia isn't here yet, and don't really want to start until she is. We need to be united in our plans to sort this mess out.'

'And find Jamie,' Holly added.

'Yes, sorry, and find Jamie.'

'So, how long is Georgia going to be?' I asked, the anxiety within the walls of the hut rubbing itself against me.

'I spoke to her this morning. She said after work she was going home, and that she would walk down once she had made sure her dad had something to eat.'

'What time did she finish?'

'Half past five.'

I looked at my phone, it was quarter past seven; Georgia had had plenty of time to get home, eat and make her way. As I caught Baz's eye, I could see an anxiety in him also. 'I'll give her a ring,' he said.

Baz unlocked his mobile and I glanced at the screen. Georgia's number was the first one on his call list. We all waited, quietly as the phone connected and rang several times before clicking to voicemail.

'Maybe her dad has asked her to help out with something.'

'Yes, I bet that's it.'

'Do you have her home number?' Holly asked Baz, and I wondered why he would, since we lived in an age where landlines were almost obsolete. Unless something was going on between Baz and Georgia perhaps? Nodding, Baz rang her home number and after three rings a gruff-sounding man answered.

'Mr Clements. It's Doctor McBride… No, no, nothing to worry about, I was just wondering if Georgia was at home.'

I couldn't hear what Georgia's dad was saying, so I watched Baz intently, and saw the colour drain from his face.

'I see, no, I'm sure all is fine, thank you, Mr Clements.'

Baz lowered the phone.

'Well, where is she?' asked Holly.

'I don't know,' he said quietly, so quiet it was almost missed.

'Baz, where is she? What did her dad say?' Holly asked again, her upbeat tone grave with worry.

'He said she left the house at just before nine this morning, and she hasn't come home.'

'Shit, you don't think—'

'Michael, calm down. It could mean anything; we shouldn't jump to conclusions.'

'Yes but, I mean, you have to agree,' said Michael, his voice rising in panic.

'Michael,' Baz said firmly, subduing Michael and likely preventing a panic attack. 'We don't know anything; she could just be having a really busy day at work. Let's try and calm down a little.'

'Neve, how sure are you that you saw the Drifter?' Michael asked, quieter, but no less panicked.

'Pretty sure,' I replied.

'How sure. Be specific.'

Baz clapped his hands decisively, snapped everyone away from dark thoughts of dark times in dark places. 'Right, I refuse to accept this. Come on.'

'Where are we going?'

'We're going to get Georgia. Sorry, Neve, I just don't believe that after twenty-odd years of silence he is back. I refuse to believe this is anything more than Jamie needing help for himself and Georgia being held up at work. Let's find her and then focus on finding him.'

'What about the Drifter?' asked Michael.

'Let's stop thinking about fucking ghosts like we did when we were kids and find our friends, shall we?'

Baz brushed past me and dropping low he disappeared though the hatch, followed closely by Michael.

'What was that about?' I asked Holly quietly.

'Barry and Georgia kind of have a thing going on. He's worried, that's all. Don't take it personally.'

'OK.'

Holly touched my arm, offered a meek smile and disappeared through the hatch, leaving me alone. I looked at the coffee table tucked up against the wall and couldn't help thinking of that last night when Chloe and I sat around it. Shaking off the memory, I scurried though the gap and ran to catch up with the others as they walked back towards the village. Everyone struggled to keep up with Baz as he stormed ahead.

CHAPTER 28

July 1998
One week before...

It had been a week since their party at Baz's house, and despite several of the group thinking the night would conclude with them in the hut, it hadn't. Holly got really drunk and ended up in a lot of trouble. Her dad, a stern and traditional man, was horrified when Baz reluctantly rang him as Holly started to throw up in a bush. Holly had been grounded for a month for it. And the group rule was almost broken, but Chloe insisted: if they couldn't all go, no one should.

Despite Holly's punishment, when the mine closed, tough parenting seemed to fall short, and it was just six days before her house arrest was over. With Jamie not needed at work, and apprenticeships yet to begin, they found themselves back at Baz's, his parents out again. They drank and sunbathed and listened to Madonna's *Ray of Light* album which Georgia, dressed in a pair of incredibly short shorts, insisted on. Michael protested, as did Jamie. In the heat of the evening, and with Georgia's flesh on display, the boys didn't really have any power. It got under Neve's skin, as she watched Jamie trying not to look, but then again, they all noticed her. In just one short year,

Georgia's shape had changed from that of a young girl to that of a woman.

As the sun began to dip behind a low bank of clouds on the horizon, it was time to think about going home. Last week, when Holly was picked up, all of their parents learnt that their children had been lying to them. They had got away with it but knew they wouldn't again. Neve, however, wasn't ready for the night to end. She knew if they were caught, her parents wouldn't care. They seldom seemed to notice her at all lately. Dad was still miserable because of the mine and Mum seemed distracted elsewhere. And besides, even if she were to get into the worst trouble when she got home, she and Jamie had been exchanging looks all afternoon, and on more than one occasion he made a point of touching her hand whilst passing a drink or holding her gaze longer than a friend should. She wanted to enjoy that for a little longer, perhaps even step it up a notch – maybe she would even steal a kiss from him.

'I thought we were going to go back to the hut?' she said, trying to stir her sleepy, drunk friends. The boys smiled, mischief in their eyes. Chloe sat bolt upright, but Neve sensed there was something nervous under the excitement.

'Yeah, but I can't be bothered now.' Holly sounded a little annoyed that Neve had suggested their evening should do anything but end. 'Besides. We were in so much shit last week.'

Michael broke into a laugh, quickly joined by Baz.

'It's not funny. I told you I didn't want to drink, guys.'

'It's pretty funny.'

'I think we should go back,' said Jamie, eager not to let the evening end. Neve was hoping it wouldn't for the same reason. 'We could stop and get drinks on the way, maybe some Red Bull to wake us up?'

'I said I'd be home before dark.'

'Come on, Holly, we've not been there in like, forever!'

'Since we saw that weird man,' Chloe added quietly.

'I've told you. He was just some lonely old soul, probably worked down there. He's long gone now, and if not, he's harmless anyway,' Baz continued. 'The real issue with your plan, Jamie, is who is going to serve us? No one has got any ID.'

'Well, we could try?'

'Or we could just stay here?' said Georgia, her eyes pink and heavy from smoking some of Michael's joint.

'Georgia, we've stayed here for all our lives, haven't we? We should be having an adventure.'

'Fuck, yeah!' Baz shouted, liking the idea of doing something reckless.

'I'm in,' nodded Michael. 'What shall we do?'

'Well, if we are doing this, Neve is right, we start by getting more booze,' said Chloe, who was putting her shoes back on, preparing to leave, the nervousness gone.

'But we don't have ID,' repeated Georgia with waning objection.

'Or money,' Jamie said, realising his own idea was horribly flawed, making Georgia smile, much to the annoyance of Neve, as she felt he should be on her side, not Georgia's.

'Shit, yeah. Well, that idea's bollocksed. Still, Neve is right, we *have* to go to the hut, it's ours. And we should be there tonight,' said Baz, determined not to give up on the recklessness stirring inside. 'Come on, let's go,' he continued decisively and as always, the group followed suit.

'What about the booze?' Holly said, hoping it would delay them.

'If we are going to the hut, we'll pass mine. I reckon I could steal some from my dad,' said Georgia, her attention towards Baz. 'But it won't be much. Chloe, come with me?'

'Sure,' she said.

'It's a start. And then we can work out how to get some more,' said Baz, a smile on his face.

The group left and made their way up the village, towards the entrance for the mine. They moved as quietly as a mob of drunk teenagers could, worried they would be seen by someone who would tell their parents they were out and up to no good. The village was more insular, more claustrophobic than other places because everyone was connected. More than just knowing everyone's business, the mine meant they *were* each other's business. Baz seemed to care less about being caught and was singing 'Football's Coming Home' at the top of his voice, despite England losing to Romania the night before in the World Cup. Baz was right not to worry, for even with him singing out of tune and at the top of his voice, no one silenced him, no one asked any questions of the seven teenagers. No one cared.

As they turned onto the abandoned lane that led to the mine, the tension lifted. This was their lane now, leading to their hut. And standing in the middle of it, they waited for Georgia and Chloe to nip back to Georgia's and come back with some of her dad's alcohol. Neve stood a little distance from the others, trying to light a cigarette, the total darkness only illuminated for the length of a flint spark. Jamie joined her, lighter in hand.

'Here,' he said as he sparked it, allowing Neve to ignite the tip of her cigarette.

'Thanks,' she said quietly between puffs.

'No problem.' He smiled at her.

In the low light Neve watched him take a breath, like he was about to saying something to her, but before he could, Baz interrupted.

'Here they come.'

Ahead, two dark silhouettes wandered towards them. Michael saw them and knew it was Georgia and Chloe, but he couldn't stop the hairs on his forearms standing on end.

'I'm sorry, guys,' Georgia said, disappointed. 'Dad was up, seemed really keen to talk to Chloe about college. I couldn't get anything.'

The group wandered further into the canopy of trees, deeper into the darkness until they reached their hut. One by one they crawled inside, where they lit candles and turned on the radio. It had been over a week since they were there and there was a warm, damp feeling in the air. The heat of the summer evaporated the remnants of empty hooch bottles and lager cans that lay around the place, leeching the vapour into the air. With no ventilation besides two small spy holes, the air became thick. Michael began to tidy, as he often did, as the others settled into their space.

'So, here we are, and there is nothing to drink. Great,' sighed Neve, who was slumped into a beanbag.

'Yeah, some "night to remember",' complained Holly, out of character. 'I'm just gonna go home.' She moved towards the hatch to leave.

'No, don't go,' Baz said, stopping her in her tracks. 'Come on. Let's celebrate our freedom from school.'

'How long can we possibly celebrate leaving school? It's been weeks now,' Holly asked.

'Until we start something new, come on, it's a big deal. We are free of that place.'

'Not really, I'm going back for sixth form.'

'We are all free besides Chloe then,' Baz laughed. 'My point is, we finished, together, which is shocking because I would have put money on Michael being expelled.'

'Yeah right, if anyone was gonna get kicked out it was you,' chuckled Michael.

'And,' Baz continued, 'I know I keep banging on about it, but this is our last summer together.'

'You're so pessimistic,' Georgia said. 'Surely it will be like this every summer?'

She looked around for confirmation, but no one was able to do so. Baz was right: after this summer, everything would change. And in the silence, the room felt sullen. A light bulb went off in Baz's head and grabbing an empty bottle of 20/20 he told the group to sit around the coffee table.

'Baz, if you think I'm playing spin the bottle with you, you're dreaming. I'm drunk, but I'm not that drunk,' said Georgia.

'We're not playing spin the bottle, and anyway – rude!'

'So, what are we playing?' asked Michael, rolling a joint.

'We…' continued Baz, proud of himself for having the idea, 'are going to have a game of truth or dare.'

The group reacted, the idea exciting them. Truth or dare would mean that Neve would undoubtedly get to kiss Jamie, especially if she went for a dare. She exchanged a glance with Chloe, who knew exactly what she was thinking. The gang moved into a circle, apart from Holly who was still by the hatch entrance, watching. Baz placed the bottle on the floor in the middle of the group who shuffled into place around it, ensuring they were equidistant to one another. Neve and Jamie caught each other's eye. As Baz had proposed the game, he got to spin the bottle first; he twisted it hard, and the bottle somersaulted. The group held their breath, waiting to see where it would stop. The top finally rested, facing Chloe.

'Truth or dare?' he asked.

'Umm, dare. No, truth.'

'OK, truth,' interjected Georgia. 'Chloe, who do you fancy from school. A teacher, I mean.'

Chloe shot Georgia a look; she knew full well who Chloe fancied from school, and she was annoyed that Georgia had indirectly betrayed her trust by asking her. The rules were the rules. So Chloe told her friends she had always liked Mr Hawes, the school's drama teacher who was probably close to fifty, and far too old for a 16-year-old to like.

'But he's so old!' protested Baz.

'Yeah, but he's mature and wise.'

'Oh God, Chloe, that's kinda gross,' said Neve. 'And anyway, why didn't I know about this?'

'Because you can't keep secrets, Neve. Shall we move on?' Neve knew Chloe was right, but it didn't take the sting out of her words.

Chloe spun the bottle, it wobbled and stopped on Jamie. 'Truth or dare.'

'Truth,' he said quietly.

'Oh, let me have this one!' said Michael, grinning from ear to ear. 'So, Jamie, in keeping with the previous question, who do you fancy from school?'

'I don't fancy any of the teachers.'

'I mean students, which student do you fancy from school?'

Jamie opened his mouth to speak and closed it again as the colour rushed to his face.

'So, who is it?'

'Can I change it to a dare?' he asked, barely able to look up in case he caught Neve's eye.

'Nope, rules are rules,' said Baz, enjoying watching his friend squirm.

'Baz, Michael. We all know the answer. Does he really need to say?' said Chloe, trying to help out Neve who was blushing so intensely, her cheeks were the same shade of pink as Michael's stoned eyes.

'Yes,' the boys replied simultaneously. 'Jamie! You have to answer!'

'Neve,' he said quietly under his breath.

'Sorry, mate, didn't quite catch that, could you speak up?'

'I said…' he paused and looked over to Neve sat opposite before looking back at his feet. 'I said Neve.'

The boys exploded into applause, whooping and cheering their friend, slapping him on the back and tousling his hair. 'Finally, he's bloody said it!' Baz applauded. The girls smiled sympathetically at both Jamie and Neve, who couldn't look at one another.

'OK, we've tormented the lad enough,' Georgia said. 'Let's carry on. Lover boy, your turn to spin.'

Jamie leant forward and spun the bottle. It landed on Michael.

'Truth or dare?' he asked, his voice still quiet, his embarrassment still raw.

'Let's mix this up a bit. Dare.'

'OK, I've got one,' Neve interjected, wanting to make Michael pay for embarrassing Jamie. 'As we've run out of booze, go into the village and get some from the offie.'

'Neve, we've been through this. We've got no money or ID.'

'Exactly. I dare you to steal some.'

CHAPTER 29

26th November 2019
Night

It had been over twenty-four hours since Georgia failed to show at the hut, and still no one knew where she was. Rumours had started to spread around the village – another missing. Georgia, like Jamie, had disappeared without a trace. We had been out, searching half the night for her, and all I managed to find was a chill that crept into my bones and the niggling tingle in the back of my throat which threatened to become a cold. Baz called the police late last night to report her missing, and because of Jamie, they took it seriously and began to widen their search, starting by asking us what we knew about her last movements. It was good that they were being proactive in finding both Jamie and now Georgia. But bad news travels fast, and just after dawn, more people descended onto the village. I hadn't seen it myself, but there were whisperings of the BBC being here. This wasn't local news anymore. This was beginning to capture the nation.

Baz understandably seemed to struggle more than the rest with Georgia going missing. He hadn't slept and refused to, because he'd been the last to see her as she had been to his house the evening before, where they had dinner together. It meant that the police asked a few more questions of him than the rest of us. I wasn't sure if they were trying to get a picture of her mental state or seeking to establish if he was someone they should be watching. The police also asked Georgia's dad to come in. It was likely he'd confirm she was home the time Baz stated, and then got up for work as per usual yesterday morning. They would probably ascertain his mental wellbeing as well as hers. I could only imagine how it must have felt to be speaking with the police again. When she hadn't come home for lunch, Georgia's dad hadn't thought much of it, and it wasn't until just before six that he began to wonder where she was – and in that time that none of us had seen her, Georgia had vanished.

Just like Jamie.

Just like Chloe.

I'd only come back to help find Jamie, but the combination of seeing the Drifter, the stuff with Dad and now this, made me unsure if I would ever get out. I knew how selfish I was being. I had become that person who was stuck in a traffic jam, complaining about the accident ahead rather than being grateful that I wasn't involved in it. I couldn't stop myself feeling frustrated.

The problem was, with the place being so small, so claustrophobic, I wasn't just *figuratively* a prisoner. When dawn arrived and people began to discover what was going on, I became effectively housebound, as I had no intention of talking to anyone about what was going on, locals or media alike. Even if I *did* want to leave my dad's house – go to the shop to get a bottle of wine or escape to the pub for a few much-needed drinks – I couldn't. Gossip was ripe, sweet and sticky, a fruit that was falling apart, making an awful mess, and we were all in the middle of it.

So I stayed inside, chatting to the group intermittently on WhatsApp through the day, and waited for something. Esther rang around 3 p.m. waking me from a fitful sleep, as I'd not called the night before. She told me she had just seen the village on the mid-afternoon report on Sky News. She begged me again to leave, come back, but I couldn't.

From the safety of my dad's living room, I watched the streets outside get busier with the quiet ramblings of people, nipping to the village centre. They came back with pints of milk, loaves of bread, but really, I knew most were just being nosy, finding an excuse to go out so they could pass the pub to see what was happening. I didn't judge them for their curious nature, or wanting their fifteen minutes of fame, but did wonder if anyone would care if the same thing happened in London. Probably not; definitely not.

Besides curtain-twitching, and speaking to Esther, the day dragged endlessly as we waited for something. Even the group chat with the others, which seemed fervent earlier in the day, had silenced. We were all holding our breath.

As evening descended, I made Dad and me a pasta bake for tea. Thankfully, he seemed less tense than I felt, and making sure he was comfortable, and the doors were locked, I told him that if anyone knocked, he shouldn't answer. He agreed, but didn't question why. I took myself to bed, just after nine. I wasn't tired, just anxious, and I needed time to process the past few days quietly, alone. As I lay there, staring at the ceiling, my phone pinged. My first thought, even with everything that was happening, was that it might be Oliver. He knew very little about my childhood, but he knew I was from here. I quickly dismissed it and then wished I'd told him more when I'd had the chance. Knowing it would be from the group chat, or, possibly Esther who wanted to make sure I was still all right, I reached for it. To my surprise, I saw it was a text message from Michael, sent directly to me.

How are you holding up?

I looked at the message, confused. I couldn't help but feel a little guarded. I'm OK. The waiting is tough.

Yeah, I know what you mean.

Already, three dots appeared as he wrote another. I waited to see what he had to say before offering anymore.

Hey, Neve. I need to get out for an hour or so. Do you fancy going for a beer or something?

Won't people talk?

I don't mean here, I'll come pick you up. We can get out, go to Nottingham?

I hesitated; what if we were needed here? What if Georgia was found? What if Jamie turned up? More importantly – what did Michael want from me? Even though I wanted nothing more than to get out of the village, I wasn't sure I should. Michael, perhaps sensing my hesitation, messaged again.

I'll tell Baz to call me if we're needed back. What do you say?

It might help if I filled you in properly on what's happened in the past 20 years.

He was right, of course. We wouldn't be disappearing; we were easy to reach. Besides, having time to ask questions and fill in the gaps of the past twenty years I'd not pieced together would probably help, and I knew a few drinks would definitely help.

OK.

Great, I'll pop over and get you in about 10 minutes?

See you soon.

Rolling out of bed I opened my bag and pulled out the last clean top I had packed. Dressing, I didn't give myself a second look before heading downstairs. Dad was in his chair, dozing. When I gently touched his shoulder, he stirred.

'You all right?' he asked, concern on his face. The man who was cold and uninterested when I first arrived had been transformed.

'Yes, Dad, I'm just popping out for a bit.'

'OK, love. I'll be here,' he smiled, and in that moment, I felt the need to kiss my father again, the urge was too strong. Leaning in, I kissed him on the cheek, and as I pulled back, I could see something soft in the way he looked at me. The man who was once so tender, so kind, was coming back.

'See you later, Dad.'

'Don't get into any trouble.'

Outside I heard a car pull up, and looking through the curtain, I could see Michael in the driver's seat. Putting on my shoes and coat, I stepped into the freezing cold air and climbed into the passenger seat.

'Hi,' he said.

'Hi. God, it's cold.'

'Miserable.'

'So, where are we going?'

'I thought we'd head to a pub I like on the outskirts of Nottingham. No one will care about what's going on here.'

'But it's all over the news.'

'It is, and those who care are here.'

He smiled; he was likely right. 'Sounds perfect, I need a drink.'

'Me too, but only one, obviously.'

Michael pulled away and as we drove, we chatted aimlessly. We didn't talk of the village, the mine, of Jamie or Georgia. They were all there, hidden behind our words and the pauses between breaths. I spoke of the café, of Esther. Told him about where I lived in London, and my flat, for which I was beginning to feel homesick, and he told me about his car garage on the outskirts of the village. I didn't realise quite how well he was doing. He had taken over his uncle's dilapidated old shed and turned it into the best car mechanic's in the area. I could tell it was something he loved; just like my little café with Esther, before everything went wrong.

We arrived and Michael pulled into a large pub car park besides a grand old Tudor building. As I climbed out, I looked at the sign. A picture of Robin Hood stood under its name, The Archer's Inn. Once inside, heat warmed my cheeks from the fire blazing away. I felt the tension in my shoulders melt like butter on freshly made toast. Finding a small table, nestled between two high-backed chairs I told Michael to sit as I went to the bar to buy the first round. I went for a JD and Diet Coke, something to warm me, and Michael asked for a pint. Returning, I handed him his drink, which he took, then turned his phone over, so the screen was face down. For a moment, sitting opposite each other, neither of us spoke. I guess we had to make sure his theory was correct, and no one cared about us – no eyes cast our way, asking questions.

It didn't take long for me to ask the one thing I wanted to know above all others. 'Michael, do people hate me?'

He considered my question for a moment, which told me what came out of his mouth would be the truth. One I so desperately needed.

'Not now,' he said. 'Yes, when Holly told us you were coming back, it wasn't well received, and if I'm honest I said I didn't want to know. But you did come back, and you're different.'

'We're all different,' I added.

'We are, but you seem to understand what you did back then. I don't hate you anymore.'

'I shouldn't have run away from it all.'

'No, you shouldn't have.'

'I've regretted it ever since.'

'Have you?' he asked.

'Yes, of course. I was scared, Michael.'

'Well, the rest of us, we couldn't run away, we stuck together. We helped each other through it.'

'How was it, after I went?'

'Baz cried for weeks. Georgia barely spoke. Even though her dad was never charged, it ruined them both. Holly tried to keep our spirits up, she obsessed over it, every detail. It really affected her.'

'I didn't know...'

'No, you didn't. I developed a little drug problem, and Jamie... well, Jamie was never the same.'

'I'm so sorry. It probably doesn't mean anything, but I struggled too.'

'Did you?' he said sceptically.

'Yes, I had bad dreams, night terrors really. I still get them now. Not every day, like when I was young, a few times a month, maybe?'

'Dreams, that's hardly—'

I cut him off, I don't know why, but I needed him to know that I suffered with the group.

'I tried uni, I studied business management. I wanted to be a CEO of a big firm, you know. But in second year I had what they called an "episode". It came from nothing really, I don't even remember most of it...' I hesitated as I was transported back to the busy university bar: the screaming, kicking, biting. My friends trying to hold me down. The roof was coming in, or so I thought. And then hospital.

'A brief psychotic episode, they called it,' I said quietly, before looking to Michael who smiled back sympathetically.

'Sounds rough.'

'We've all had it rough, haven't we? And now two of us are missing.'

'And the Drifter is back,' he said, but I wasn't sure if it was a statement or a question.

'I'm so sure I've seen him again, but I'm also aware I might just be imagining it as way of coping being back here. Or perhaps

I'm having another episode. I don't know. I didn't heal from it; I didn't have anyone to talk to about it. It doesn't excuse leaving, but I suffered too, Michael. I still do.'

Standing up, I went to the bar and got myself another drink. Looking back to gesture to Michael to join me, he shook his head, telling me he was fine. He and I watched each other from across the bar, as they poured me a double shot this time, our looks conveying all of the things unsaid over the past two decades. When I rejoined him, he held my eye and we both took a large mouthful of our drinks.

From there, the conversation moved on to more positive things. Michael spoke of both Georgia and Jamie turning up, saying there had to be a rational explanation for what was going on – and for a while, I bought into it. The Drifter was a manifestation of my own guilt, Georgia was still pissed off that I was back and had left the village to clear her head, and Jamie would return, ashamed of his absence and worrying people. And I let myself imagine it would all happen soon, and then life would go back to normal.

As Michael got up to order my third JD and his second pint, I looked around the room. I watched the people who looked calm, happy, oblivious to what was going on. At the bar was a couple, probably a few years younger than me. I watched as the man leant in and whispered something in his partner's ear. She giggled at his comment and swept her long, dark hair out of the way so she could feel his touch as he leant in to say more. She laughed again, louder this time and lifted her head up, exposing a small tattoo near her shoulder, three small waves. I wondered what they meant, if anything at all. Then, she looked at me and it was like she knew. Her expression became serious, penetrating.

She gave me a smile that was full of empathy. One that told me she was *like* me somehow. I thought that maybe she recognised me, but it wasn't that. It was something else, something that connected us. I smiled back, and she turned her attention to her partner beside her once more. I considered the couple a little while longer. Had they experienced trauma, grief, loss? It was hard to believe; they looked content in one another's world. They looked happy. And then I thought of Oliver.

Michael came back with our drinks and I drank mine a little too quickly, the alcohol beginning to make my head swim.

'I missed you after you left,' he said, snapping me from my thoughts.

'Did you? I missed you too.'

'Bullshit,' he said, smiling a sad smile. 'I used to have such a thing for you.'

His comment caught me off guard. 'What?'

'Don't make me say it again,' he said, his cheeks reddening.

'Why didn't you say?'

'Because I was shy I guess; besides, you and Jamie were…'

He stopped himself and took three big sips of his pint. The silence that hung between us wasn't a comfortable one, but I didn't know what to say. Thankfully, before I had a chance to speak, he moved on from his revelation.

'It was a shit time back then,' he eventually said, his eyes focusing on the space just above the top of his pint glass. 'It brought out the worst in everyone. The village was a community, and despite the differences, people got on, people helped each other. But that place died when Chloe did.'

I took a breath to say something but stopped myself.

He continued, 'Everyone was so angry.'

'At who?'

'At us.'

'Why?'

'Once it was clear Georgia's dad wasn't a killer, and when they couldn't find out who the Drifter really was, they needed someone to blame, and as they started to think we were lying they blamed us. We made up a killer, we gave hope when it wasn't there to give.'

'But the Drifter was real.'

'I know that, we all know that. But no one saw him but us, did they?'

I couldn't help but feel he was accusing me of something.

'You know the rest, the media lost interest, moved on to other stories in other places. But we couldn't move on, we had nowhere to go. You know how weird it was to watch Chloe's coffin be carried towards the cemetery, knowing there was no body inside?'

'No, I don't,' I said quietly, ashamed I wasn't there.

He held my eye for a little longer than perhaps he should. 'Jamie really struggled with that aspect of it all. The empty coffin. It haunted him more than the Drifter ever could. More than that night down the mine ever could.'

There it was again: the darkness, the banging, blind panic separating us. The Drifter separating us. I fidgeted in my chair; Michael was talking of things we promised never to say out loud. I was about to open my mouth and stop him talking when his phone rang, breaking his stare. He turned over his phone, looked at the caller ID, and then back to me. 'It's Baz.'

I watched his face, reading the fine lines and micro expressions as Baz said something I couldn't hear. I didn't need to. The colour drained from Michael's face.

'We've got to go back.'

'Why, what's happened?'

'They've found something.'

Getting up he put on his coat as he walked quickly to the exit and the car. I struggled to keep up and, stepping outside, I was stunned to see it had started raining. Dashing across the car park, using my coat as an umbrella, I climbed in beside Michael who had fired up the engine before I had even closed the door. Shifting it into reverse he aggressively navigated the car into the middle of the car park, before wheel spinning in the gravel to get his car moving forward.

'Michael, what did Baz say? What's going on?'

Focusing on the road ahead, the window wipers barely making any difference in the deluge, he replied, his voice shaking, afraid.

'Georgia's top... they found Georgia's top, and it's covered in blood.'

CHAPTER 30

26th November 2019
Night

As we drove back, the rain pounding against the windscreen was so loud Michael and I didn't speak. Just before we entered the village, I could see blue lights ahead, their unmistakable hue cutting through the rain that hung like heavy mist in the night air. I was expecting Michael to stop as we approached the three police cars and ambulance which were parked in the entrance of the cemetery, but he didn't. He slowed, looked at the commotion, just like anyone would, and continued.

'Michael? Why?'

'It won't do us any good to stop.'

He was right – if we started to snoop around, the gossip would no doubt cast us in an unfavourable light. And we needed time to think, time to work out what we were going to do before the police started to look to us for answers we couldn't give. As the cemetery disappeared behind us, we drew level with Chloe's house. There was no light, no movement. But still, I couldn't help but think Brenda was there watching.

'Where are the others?' he asked. I unlocked my phone and went to the group chat and posted the question. They were waiting for us, waiting to work out a good place to meet. Baz suggested we met at Holly's, but she was adamant she didn't want that kind of energy around her kids.

Besides, we don't want people seeing us together, do we? Holly added.

She was right, we didn't.
This place. This fucking place.

I guess there is only one place we can go really, isn't there? added Baz in the chat.

Both Holly and I agreed.
'Well, where are they?' Michael asked impatiently, his eyes focused on the road ahead.
'They're going to the hut.'
He nodded, as if he knew that would be where we ended up. We passed the pub and turned right onto a residential road a few hundred yards from the lane that led towards it. Then, grabbing an umbrella from his boot, we walked onto the main road, turned right, and right again down the lane, making sure no one saw us.
Once inside the hut we used our phones to light the space and waited. There were a million thoughts going on in my head, and with it, a thousand more questions, but I didn't speak, and neither did he. I watched him, his gaze barely lifting from the floor, completely lost in his thoughts. He must have felt my eyes on him as he finally flicked a glance at me. I saw a heaviness there, the same heaviness I felt.

Holly arrived first, calling out before she entered so we weren't spooked, and shortly after that, Baz crawled through the hatch, his face pained, struggling to not crack and spill whatever he was thinking. And that was it. Just four of us.

'Tell us what you know?' Michael said to Baz, who slumped onto the coffee table. He didn't respond. Instead he cradled his head in his hands, fighting a war inside his own head. 'Baz!'

Baz snapped to attention, his expression confused – he was so deep in his own thoughts he hadn't registered Michael's question. 'Tell us what you know.'

'Where did you find it?' Holly asked, and I couldn't help noting how 'it' sounded so impersonal.

'I went to Chloe's grave. Earlier.'

'Why?' Holly questioned.

'This whole thing about Jamie's top and then Georgia... I thought about Chloe, and I realised I'd not been in so long. When I got there, it was on her gravestone.'

'Shit!' Holly whispered.

'Fuck,' Michael agreed. I didn't say anything, but stood with my mouth agape, trying to understand exactly what this meant.

'Baz, what do we do?' Holly asked, her question greeted by silence. 'What does this mean?' she said, trying to force a conversation, a dialogue, a solution.

'Neve,' Baz said quietly. 'Can I ask you again, how sure are you that you saw the Drifter?'

I had asked myself the same question. And now I knew a definitive answer. 'Now, one hundred per cent.'

He nodded gravely.

'Baz, what are you thinking?' asked Holly, sounding startled by panic.

'First Jamie, and now Georgia. He's real, he's back, and he's picking us off one by one – and we all know why, don't we?'

'It can't be…?' said Holly, who hadn't managed to catch up.

'Holly,' I started quietly, touching her arm, 'he was there that night. He was there when Chloe went missing.'

Holly looked at me, shock and realisation setting in. She turned to Baz for reassurance, but he only exhaled loudly, his head back in the comfort of his hands once more. Next she snapped to Michael – I could almost *hear* her begging for us to be wrong – and Michael simply nodded towards her.

There could be no denying it now, no confusing what I had seen with something conjured from the back of my mind. The Drifter was back, and he was coming for us one by one.

CHAPTER 31

30th November 2019
Morning

News left the village quickly after Georgia's top was found. And by the following morning, the media swarm had descended. There was no longer gossip of the BBC being here, no longer the wait for reporters to be banging on people's door – they were here en mass. Part of me understood why. One bloodied top belonging to a man with well-known mental health issues was hardly noteworthy. But two within a week, in the same village where the infamous Chloe Lambert disappeared decades before – that's a story. Four days had passed since Baz had found Georgia's top. I had stayed inside Dad's house the entire time. Still a prisoner of sorts. Nothing happened, nothing of note. Dad slept a lot; I wanted to drink but didn't let myself. It was all a little bleak. Today was different. There was hope, light. He had a doctor's appointment this morning. He wanted to go alone. I hoped that there would be good news.

True to my word, I kept Esther in the loop. She said that the village had been mentioned a few times on the news. This morning, she messaged saying that *we* had been mentioned; the connection had been made. Because of that connection, there were now live reports coming from the village centre, interviews with locals. Esther didn't say either way, but I wondered if those interviews were about what was happening now, or the events of 1998. She told me about The Tea Tree and found it strange that the thing that was so important to me seemed an afterthought. Still, it was nice to hear that business was picking up. She begged me to come home, and I wanted to, I missed her and the business, and London, which was so big I could hide in plain sight. But I knew I needed to stay, for Holly, for Chloe. Before hanging up, I told Esther I loved her.

I turned on the TV to see the report she spoke of. Sure enough, a reporter was outside The Miners' Arms talking to someone I had seen walking to and from the village only days before. It made me nervous. There were more eyes watching, more questions being asked not just of Jamie and Georgia, but of the past too.

I wanted to keep a low profile, wait for it to blow over. But the group chat had sprung to life. Michael speculated that now our names and connections were out, it would raise more questions if we all continued to hide away than if we were seen in public. If we didn't act, they would hate all over again, like they did back in 1998. So, it was agreed we would meet in the pub, make sure we were actively involved, as a group, in the search for our friends. That made me nervous. Then, the TV screen filled with PC Hastings' face, and my heart began to beat harder still.

Thankfully, the front door opened, Dad was home and his presence forced me to switch the TV off. He walked into the living room, slumped into his chair and turned it back on again, changing from the news to a documentary.

'Dad? What did they say?' I asked tenderly.

'It's fine, Neve. It's all fine.'

'What do you mean it's fine?'

'Well, they said my blood tests came back and it's not, you know… that.'

'Well, what is it then?'

'Oh, I can't remember these fancy names for things. All that matters is it will get better.'

Grabbing my phone, I googled what else could be causing his symptoms and saw that an underactive thyroid could be to blame. I asked if that was it. He nodded.

'Sounds about right.'

I read more: apparently, an underactive thyroid could cause memory loss, confusion and sleep deprivation. All of Dad's symptoms. I gave him a long hug and as I did so, I could feel myself start to cry. I expected him to push me away, but he didn't – he held me, stroked the back of my hair, and as I cried into his jumper, he told me it was all right. Everything was all right. I cried because of Chloe, of being here, I cried because of the others going missing. But mainly, I was crying tears of relief.

Dad fell asleep in his chair shortly after, and I tiptoed upstairs to grab the car keys. I knew I wasn't going to leave; I had known since we understood categorically that the Drifter was back, but I kept the car for as long as possible anyway. Because, if I was honest, despite knowing I would stay, I also knew I might still run. I looked at my travel bag at the foot of the bed – it would be so easy to pack it, throw it in the boot of the car and not look back. I could even ask Dad to come with me, but I already knew what his answer would be. I forced myself to leave my clothes untouched and close the bedroom door. Resting my head on it, I took a deep breath, forced down my need to run, and walked downstairs with just a key in my hand. As I approached the lounge, I heard Dad crying from within. It was clear what he'd been told wasn't good news and he had lied to protect me. I announced myself, giving him a chance to wipe his tears and pull himself together.

'Fancy a tea, Dad?'

'That would be lovely, thank you.'

'I've got to pop out soon; the car I hired needs to be returned today.'

'Oh, do you need to go back to London with it?'

I hesitated. 'No, I can change my drop-off point online. There'll be somewhere close by.'

'Oh, that's good.'

'Yes, so, I'll be off soon. And I'll get an Uber back.'

'Uber?'

'A taxi. Do you need me to do anything?'

'No, no, I'm fine.'

I googled the car rental company and saw there was a depot about ten miles away. One quick call, and the drop-off point was changed. To get to the car rental place, I needed to drive through the village and out east of it. And as I did, I had to move slowly. The roads were busy: vans and cars parked in the usually quiet parking spaces that lined either side of the street. I passed the cemetery, the white tent pitched over Chloe's grave, bunches of flowers beside it. Then I passed Chloe's house: Brenda stood on the front doorstep, wrapped in a dressing gown, smoking. I drove past the pub, its doors wide open despite it being only 10 a.m. and three degrees outside. Then past the lane, and despite not wanting to, I couldn't help but look down towards the hut, towards the mine.

That was when I saw the shape of a person standing right near the bend in the road that led to the hut. I slammed on my brakes, the car behind having to do the same, and as she overtook, the driver flipped her middle finger at me. Reversing, I looked down the lane, expecting to see nothing, but he was there, in the distance, and I was sure he was looking towards me. I felt like a rabbit in headlights, unable to move, or even blink – until he started advancing. Panicking, I started to drive off, forgetting I had put on the handbrake, and removing it, I stalled the car. I fired up the engine again, too frightened to look, as I expected to see him charging towards me, and drove away quickly, nearly hitting a car coming in the other direction. I kept checking my rear-view mirror until I was a few miles away from the village. And only then did I slow down enough to catch my breath, and release the tears that pressed against the back of my eyes, desperate to escape. Pulling over at the next layby I took my phone and messaged the group.

I've seen him again; he was near the hut. He looked right at me.

CHAPTER 32

30th November 2019
Evening

With the car dropped off, and my tattered nerves back in check, I climbed into the back of a cab and began the journey home, where I would wait for the agreed time of seven to meet in the pub. I got out of the taxi and stepped inside, to see Dad still in front of the TV watching an old episode of *Top Gear*. I expected him to be asleep, but as the door closed, he called out.

'That you, Neve?'

'Yeah, Dad, it's me.' I walked into the living room and sat down on the sofa. 'You all right?'

'Oh, I'm fine. Just fine,' he said, not taking his eyes from the TV, and my heart sank a little. I was expecting that answer, of course; I silently hoped that, with the warmth we had shared, he would be honest and say things weren't fine. 'Someone knocked for you earlier.'

'Sorry?'

'A man, he knocked on the door, and asked if he could talk to you.'

'A man? What man?'

'I don't know – I didn't ask – just a man.'

'Did he say he was a reporter?'

'No, nothing like that.'

That was strange, didn't the media have to announce who they were?

'What did he look like?'

'Old.'

'Can you describe anything else, what was he wearing?'

'I don't know, I didn't pay attention.'

'Was he wearing a long, dark coat?' I asked, my hands beginning to sweat.

'Yes, maybe,' he said, uninterested.

'Did he say what he wanted?'

'No, just that he would get you later.'

'*Get me?* He said those exact words?'

'Get you. Find you. I can't remember.'

I looked out of the window, wondering if he was out there, watching, waiting for me to come back. The wind blew through the trees outside, throwing their branches in the path of the streetlamps, making it look like the shadows were crawling towards me. I couldn't see anyone. After locking the doors, I tried to pretend to Dad everything was OK – and walking into the kitchen to check the back, I had to close the fridge door that was wide open.

I messaged the others, my hands shaking as I did, telling them about the man coming to my dad's door. Michael said he didn't want anyone walking alone, especially me, so suggested he picked us all up for our very public meet-up at seven. True to his word, at three minutes to, he knocked on my father's door, but despite knowing it was him, I still felt my nerves twitch. He smiled awkwardly and we walked to his car to drive to Holly's house. By the time we got to hers, I felt better for Michael being close, and said I would get her. She answered the door looking noticeably drained.

'Holly?'

'It's weird not having the kids here. I didn't sleep well without them.'

I hadn't considered how hard it must be for her to have to ask her mum to look after the kids for a few days. Holly was worried, and rightly so – she could be next, after all. She wanted to protect her children, and I didn't consider the cost of doing it. Without giving myself a moment to reconsider, I stepped into her doorway and hugged her. She squeezed me tightly, a little too tight, and when she eventually stepped back, she smiled.

'Thanks, Neve.'

'For what?'

'Being a friend.'

Her words broke my heart.

'Shall we go?' she said, lifting her smile. Baz was working the late clinic, so our next stop was the doctor's surgery, and once he was collected, we would go to The Miners' Arms together.

As we stepped out of the wind and into the pub, I was struck by just how busy it was; catching Baz's eyes – which were bloodshot and dilated – I could see he too was in shock at the same thing. Mostly locals, some not. I expected everyone to stop talking and stare, like the smokers had done only a few days ago. But they didn't. People gave knowing looks, polite nods or sympathetic smiles. The only person who eyed us with any suspicion was PC Hastings, but I reasoned it was because he felt like he had to more than anyone else. The boys approached the bar whilst Holly and I found a table.

'Here you are, guys,' Baz said, placing a tray of drinks down, his hand instantly going to his ear to pull on his lobe the moment he could.

'Thanks, Baz,' I said.

'I need this,' Holly sighed, and for a moment we didn't speak, each one of us focused on our glass, the occasional glance to one another, unsure of what to do or say.

'I can't believe how busy it is here tonight. It's not been this rammed since...'

Michael didn't finish. He didn't need to. I noticed Baz looking intently around the pub, like he was trying to work something out.

'Baz?'

'I was just thinking. He might be in this pub right now, having a beer.'

I shifted in my chair, trying to take a look around the room. It was pointless, everyone could be the Drifter. And no one. He could stand right next to me and I would have no idea who he was; none of us would.

'Baz, Neve, stop looking for him,' Michael said quietly. 'All that's going to happen is you're going to start thinking everyone is him. It's a slippery slope to somewhere none of us want to go if we let our paranoia take hold.'

'Michael's right, we need to calm down. Has anyone heard anything new?' Holly asked, trying to sound calm but the tremor in her voice giving her away.

'Nothing yet,' Baz said.

Just then, Derrick came over to our table. 'What are you lot doing here?' he said. He didn't sound confrontational; if anything he sounded frightened.

'We just needed a drink,' Michael said, honestly. 'How are you?'

'I'm surviving.'

'Place is busy.'

'Yeah. People enjoying the fact that two of their own are missing.'

I wanted to say something, but what could I say that would make any impact?

'Something weird is going on here,' he continued. 'I don't know what, but I do know it's something to do with you.'

I felt heat rush into my face. 'How do you mean?' I said, taking a sip of my drink and trying to appear cool.

'People are talking a lot about Chloe, about what might have happened to her. They think what's happening now is connected.'

'What makes people think that?'

'The tops, mainly. And Hastings said you saw the Drifter, Neve – is that true?'

I couldn't believe it; that little weasel took information I confided in him as a police officer and turned it into gossip. Looking past Derrick to the bar, I saw Hastings looking my way. Wanker.

'Maybe, I don't know.'

'You didn't believe us about the Drifter then, Derrick, why now?'

'You were kids, and the whole village knew you were mixed up in things: drink, drugs. And when the police found nothing but a bloody top, it was hard to trust your version of events.'

'Why would we make it up, Derrick?'

'I don't know. We were in shock over Chloe. Scared. No one was thinking right and by the time we were, the Drifter had become a ghost story, like most of the bloody stories around here. I believe you now.'

'And the police?' I asked, gesturing towards the bar.

'That little shit. Who knows what he's thinking?'

'I think I want to go home,' Holly said, her face washed out.

'I'll take you back.'

'Thanks, Michael.'

'I think we should all go home,' Baz agreed. I could sense he was pleased as much as he was frightened. We had appeared in the world again, and the world suggested it would be best we hid. There would be no rumours about us, no speculation as to why we were hiding. No questions of guilt. People were connecting now to what happened in 1998, and the warning rang true that we could be next. Frighteningly, the Drifter was out there somewhere. Waiting to punish us for reasons only he knew. We finished our drinks quickly and headed out.

We didn't talk much as Michael drove us all home, all of us trying to process what was going on, the lies we had told, and how they had come back to haunt us. Michael dropped me off last, and before getting out of his car I asked for a cigarette.

'I thought you didn't smoke?'

'I don't, but can I have one?'

'Sure, here take the packet, there's only a few in there but...'

'Thank you,' I said, kissing him on the cheek.

I got out of the car and went towards the front door. The wind was still strong and blew my hair across my face, into my eyes. I unlocked the door and nipped to get a lighter from the kitchen. The oven was on again, but nothing was in it this time, thankfully. Back on the doorstep I pulled the door to and tried to light the cigarette. It took several attempts, the wind kept snuffing the flame and I was out of practice. Four attempts, and it was lit. As I inhaled, I coughed, the smoke tickling down into my lungs, making them feel heavy. But the taste – that was something I had missed dearly without even knowing it. I took a few more drags, enjoying the light-headed feeling as the rush of nicotine hit my blood stream. Blowing the smoke up into the sky I watched the wind push mackerel clouds in front of the moon, which was bright and full. I'd not seen a sky like it since moving to London. And for a moment, I let myself enjoy it. I shook off my guilt and stress and worry and floated with the clouds as I smoked my cigarette. And it was wonderful.

Bending down to stub out the burning ambers the moment passed, and the tension flooded back. As I stood, I gasped, fear shooting through me causing my whole body to prickle with pins and needles. My muscles ready to fight or flight. Because standing at the end of my footpath was a man in a long, dark coat.

CHAPTER 33

July 1998
That same night. One week before…

After Neve suggested Michael steal some alcohol, there was a brief silence.

'What?' Holly said gasping.

'I dare you to steal some booze from the offie,' Neve said again.

'That's a stupid idea,' Holly said in protest. But no one was listening. Baz clapped approvingly, and Neve went on to remind him that he stole a case of hooch when they first found the hut.

'That was different,' Michael said, 'and besides, I got caught, remember? Old Busby threated to call the police. I lost my shitty job. Don't any of you care?' He laughed, but behind it there was a nervousness.

'It'll be fine,' Neve said.

'Michael, you can't back out of this,' Baz said, slapping his friend on the back. Michael nodded, said he'd do it, and puffed out his chest, trying to fake confidence. He joked that Mr Busby, the shopkeeper, was old and dithery. 'It would be like taking candy from a drunk baby,' he said as the group mobilised, blowing out candles before heading towards the hatch.

The gang walked up the lane, quiet whispers between each other as they made plans. Jamie and Neve, now too embarrassed to walk together, kept apart. Jamie was up front with Baz and Michael, bounding with the boys who didn't believe in consequences, Georgia in the centre of them all, soaking in their male energy. Chloe stopped to sort out the shoelace that had come undone and watched as Neve and Holly walked on. Neve had linked arms with Holly, but not in the same way she linked arms with Chloe. She could tell, Neve was just hanging onto Holly, forcing her to move. She almost called out for someone to wait, but worried she would look foolish, so didn't. With her shoelace tucked back in its place she stood and felt a shudder up her spine, and the sensation of being watched. She looked to her right, into the thick line of trees, unable to see anything beyond the first few feet. Looking over her shoulder back at the hut she swore, for a split second, there was someone walking past it, towards the mine. She almost mentioned it to the others, but knew it was more than likely her drunk, tired eyes seeing things. Speeding up, she linked arms with Neve on the other side of Holly and didn't dare to look back again.

'Chloe, you OK?' Neve asked, feeling the tension transfer to her.

'Yeah, yeah, I'm fine.' Chloe smiled. But even in the near pitch black, Neve could see her friend's eyes looked hollow.

The group turned onto the main road that ran through the village, designed to connect most of the homes to the mine, and in the distance, they could see the lights of the Victoria Wine shop where Michael would attempt to complete his dare.

'How are you going to do it?' Baz asked as they walked, rubbing his mate's shoulders like a trainer before his boxer stepped into the ring.

'I need a distraction. Someone to keep Mr Busby busy.'

'I can do it,' Georgia said. 'I've got about 30p. I'll buy a bar of chocolate.'

'Brilliant. While you do that, Michael, you go to the fridge at the back and grab a bottle of something.'

'Any preference?' Michael replied, trying to sound braver than he actually felt.

The group walked past the shop, looking back in. There were no other customers inside. Then, as Baz, Jamie, Neve, Holly and Chloe waited around the side of the building, Michael and Georgia went in. The group seemed to be waiting for what felt like way too long before the front door crashed open, Georgia running out first and heading away from the group. The deep, gravelly voice of Mr Busby followed from inside the shop. 'Come back here, you little shits!'

Michael staggered into the road, and he too ran, followed by a large, red-faced, heavy-breathing man with a manic look in his eye. 'I'll kill ya, you little bugger!' he yelled as he turned and saw the others hiding down the side of his shop.

'Shit, run!' Baz yelled as he bolted away.

Neve turned and darted behind the shop, heading in the other direction to where she saw Georgia, Michael and Baz run. Behind her was Jamie. As she ran, she heard Mr Busby call out that he was ringing the police, and fear shot into her veins. If she was caught, if her dad found out... He was a hard man; a proud man and she knew he would go ballistic at her. Putting her head down, she ran faster and harder than she ever had until the main strip of the village was far behind, and the streetlamps less regular. She paused beside the social club, the sound of a few men jeering and laughing coming from within, her dad no doubt inside, assuming she was with her friends at a girly sleepover.

She fought to catch her breath. She couldn't see Jamie, or anyone else, and feeling insecure she started to move again. As she did, sirens whirled towards her. As the sounds of the police drew closer, she increased her walking speed and knowing she needed to hide, turned onto the single-track lane that led to the country park that sat in the shadow of the old mine headstocks. Although she wanted to move fast, the lack of light meant she had to be careful – the deeper she walked into the country park, the darker it became, as if the night was swallowing the last of the light from the day. The tarmac soon became loose gravel but she could see a line of grass in the middle of the lane, guiding her deeper in. On her right, the trees were so densely packed it may as well have been a solid wall, and she thought to herself she was stupid for coming this way. To her right she heard a twig break. The suddenness of it snapping punctuated the silence. She stood up, held her breath. There was another twig. Somewhere in the darkness, something was moving. Then she heard a voice, quiet, ghostly.

'Hello,' it said, and for a moment Neve thought it was one of the lost souls from the stories. 'Hello,' it called again, and her skin prickled with fear. A shape, an outline of a person, came towards her from the gloom. She stumbled away from the bench and was about to bolt, when the voice spoke again.

'Neve, is that you?' Hearing her name placed the voice and she exhaled loudly, relieved.

'Jamie?'

'Yes. It's me,' he said as he stepped close enough for her to make out his features.

'Shit, I thought you were… you know, him.'

'Sorry, I didn't mean to scare you. Are you all right?'

'Yes, I'm fine. Where are the others?' Neve asked.

'I don't know. The police are looking.'

'What do we do?'

'I don't think the police will look down here, I think we wait it out.'

'Yeah, good idea.'

Neve sat on the bench and Jamie sat beside her. She felt exhausted from the roller-coaster of adrenaline, excitement and fear. Without asking, she placed her head on his shoulder.

'I just want to go home,' she said quietly, closing her eyes, surprised she felt so safe with Jamie. He wrapped his arm round her, and the haunted, frightening place that existed only a moment before became something else, a haven for the two of them. She lifted her head, turned to face him, and his eyes stayed on hers. For a moment, she thought they might kiss, she moved to initiate it, but just as she did, he looked away, over her head, towards the old mine.

'Feels like it's always watching, doesn't it?' he said, and Neve looked too, grateful he hadn't noticed her attempt to kiss him.

'I don't know why they don't just knock it down.'

'Because it's still important,' he said.

'To who?'

'You know, my dad, your dad. Every other family in the village. We're all connected to it.'

'Yeah, I guess. How are we gonna move on and be something else if it's always there,' she asked, and Jamie could sense an anger or resentment at it, although he didn't know why. 'Can I tell you a secret?' she continued playfully, lifting the mood.

'I love secrets.'

'The mine, it's always creeped me out.'

'What? Why?'

'The stories, you know, people dying down there. It's spooky.'

'Neve, do you believe in ghosts?'

'No, not at all, it's just creepy, isn't it?'

'I do… believe.'

'Really?'

'Yep, I mean, my granddad's story, about that poor man. I think he's still down there, somewhere.'

'But he's dead.'

'Yes, but something must happen to us when we are dead. Mum tells me that Einstein proved energy cannot die, it just changes into another form of energy. And that's what we are, isn't it? Energy. *His* energy still exists. And if his is trapped…' he trailed off, and I knew what he was saying. If his energy was still trapped, he might well be wandering the mine still.

'I like the mine,' he continued. 'I think it holds a lot of secrets. I'd love to go inside, walk through its tunnels. Feel the energy that's there.'

Neve didn't reply; she was stunned into silence by what Jamie had said. The boy she had a crush on was good-looking, athletic, popular, and until that moment she hadn't realised he had a depth to him as well. It made him even more attractive to her.

'Do you think the police have given up yet?' he asked quietly.

Before she could answer, torchlight shone into their faces. They were so caught up in one another they didn't hear the advancing person. Neve felt her heart begin to race, thinking it was the man she had seen outside the mine a few weeks ago; the Drifter, the ghost. But, as soon as they were blinded, the torch was lowered.

'Good evening,' the voice said.

'Hello?' Jamie replied, his voice quivering a little.

'What are you doing down here?'

'We...' I hesitated, heat burning into my cheeks.

'We're just, you know, hanging out,' Jamie said, feigning embarrassment.

'Oh, I see,' said the man. 'Have you seen any other kids down here?' he asked. His form came into view, revealing him to be a police officer.

'No, just us,' Jamie said.

'Sorry to disturb you.' With that he turned and walked away. Neve mused he probably thought they were a couple making out, and not one of the group who had just robbed Mr Busby.

'Shit, that was close,' Jamie said after he was out of sight.

'Yeah, lucky we look like an item,' Neve replied.

Perhaps it was the adrenaline. Perhaps it was the fact she knew he liked her, Neve wasn't sure, what she did know is that she wanted him to kiss her more than anything in the world. And she also knew, if it didn't happen then, in that moment, it probably wouldn't ever happen.

'Jamie?'

'Yes?'

'Truth or dare,' she smiled.

'Dare,' he said, his expression serious.

'I dare you to...'

Neve didn't finish her sentence, as Jamie leant in and kissed her on the lips.

CHAPTER 34

30th November 2019
Night

'I think it's time we spoke,' the man said. I recognised the voice, but I couldn't place him.

'Who are you?'

'I think you know who I am,' he said. He started to move towards me, and I instinctively stepped back. He halted his advance. 'I don't mean you any harm.'

'Have you been following me?'

'Yes.'

'Were you in the pub, the night I came back? Were you the man sat in the corner, watching me?'

'Yes.'

'And down the lane three days ago, was that you coming towards me?'

'Yes, Miss Chambers, it was.'

'How do you know my name?'

'Oh, I know a lot about you.'

'Did you knock on this door earlier? Speak to my father?'

'I did.'

'Are you the Drifter?' I asked, terrified.

He laughed, a throaty rasp, making me wonder if he was sick. 'I thought you didn't believe in ghosts.'

I didn't know how to respond.

'You don't remember me, do you? I'm not surprised. It's been a very long time.'

The man took off his flat cap, and the streetlamp caught his aged and worn-out face. Thick stubble lined his cheeks and chin. His eyes sat dark and heavy with the weight of the world resting on the lower lids. And, finally, I knew his face.

'Thompson?'

'Hello Miss Chambers.'

DCI Thompson was the lead investigator into Chloe's disappearance. He was the one who interviewed everyone I knew, including me. He was there when Chloe's top was found – the man who prepared me to see it, to confirm it was hers. I didn't doubt he would have been the man who arrested Georgia's dad. And from what Hastings told me about him, Chloe Lambert's disappearance had stayed with him.

'I heard you retired.' I tried to sound calm, but heard my voice crack.

'I did, a very long time ago.'

'Why have you been following me?'

'I'm just trying to work things out.'

'Work things out?'

'Yep. And keep an eye on you.'

'What do you want?'

'The same thing I've wanted for over twenty years. I want to find out what happened to Chloe.'

'DCI Thompson...'

'I'm retired. Now I'm just Robert.'

'Have you been here the whole time?'

'What, since Chloe?' he laughed again, one that turned into a cough. 'No, no, I've been far away from this place.'

'Then why did you come back?'

'I heard from PC Hastings that Jamie has gone missing.'

'Jamie has a history of going missing,' I interrupted, sounding much more knowledgeable about Jamie's comings and goings than I was.

'Yes, and each time, I have come back to make sure he gets home safely.'

'Why would you care?'

'Because I think he knows more about what happened to Chloe than he lets on, perhaps. Or perhaps, I just care.'

'And why are you here, outside my house?'

'Miss Chambers, did you really see the Drifter again?'

'Yes, but now I'm thinking it was you.'

'How do you come to that conclusion?'

'You were in the pub, down the lane. You were in the woods watching me just before we found Jamie's top. You were there, by those garages watching my window.'

'Miss Chambers...'

Listening to my words made me feel indignant. He wasn't making sure I was OK; he was stalking me. 'You scared me. You've been scaring me ever since I came back. I'll call the real police if I see you round...'

'Miss Chambers.'

'In fact, I'm in my right mind to call the police right now.'

'Neve,' he said, and hearing him call me by my first name stunned me into silence. 'I assure you, that wasn't me.'

'What?'

'I saw you in the pub, I was keeping warm, having a drink, and was surprised as all hell to see you of all people step in. And when I was down the lane, I was looking around the old hut you used to hang out in when you were kids. Those other places, I assure you, that wasn't me.'

'It wasn't you?'

'No, I promise. And I'm assuming, if I've read your face properly, you have really seen him?'

I nodded. 'I think he is behind Jamie and Georgia going missing. I think he is going after us one by one.'

'I think so too,' he said, and his words brought a lot of comfort. 'I'll find him, Miss Chambers, but in return I'll need your help.'

'Why? How can I help?'

'Every copper has one case that haunts them, and Chloe is mine. I didn't think I would ever solve it, but I almost made peace with it. But then you found Jamie's top.'

'I didn't find it,' I said defensively.

'The collective "you". The you from back then. Then, the top at the cemetery. Well, let's just say, my gut tells me I might solve this thing after all.'

'And how am I supposed to help with that?'

'You were with Chloe hours before she went missing.'

'Are you accusing me...'

'Should I be?' he asked, a glint in his eye. Like he was trying to work me out.

'No, of course not.'

'I've watched you, Miss Chambers; you seem bright, and my gut also tells me that you will help me unravel the truth. Will you help me put this case to bed?'

'Shouldn't we leave that to the real police?'

'What, leave it with PC Hastings? Believe me, you'll be far happier if I'm trying to work it out.'

'Why?'

'Because Hastings was convinced you had something to do with Chloe all those years ago.'

'What?' I knew why he seemed so angry at me in the police station a few days ago. Hastings thought I killed Chloe.

'He wouldn't let it go either, even when we had nothing connecting you to her going missing.'

'Why would he think it was me?'

'Sometimes a copper's gut fails him, and his head gets in the way. Besides, he was young, too young for such a big case. And then you left town and...'

'I was scared. My mum offered me a place to get away from here for a while.'

'I know, Miss Chambers, I know. I spoke with your father a lot about what else was going on in the family home. I understand why you left. Hastings wouldn't let it go. He was convinced, nearly got himself suspended for digging when he was told to stop. Needless to say, I don't think he is a fan of yours. And between you and me, PC Hastings isn't the brightest bulb.'

'I went to him about the Drifter the other day. He didn't believe me, and now you've told me all this, he probably thinks I have something to do with it all.'

'Probably.'

'I don't have *anything* to do with this.'

'I know, and I know you also didn't have anything to do with Chloe.'

'Thank you,' I said, meaning it.

'Hastings wasn't with us the night we found Chloe's top. He wasn't there when I took you to it. I saw the look on your face. It wasn't a look of someone who knew what they were about to see. I saw it shake you to your core.'

I had a flash of that night, the silence in the pub after someone squawked into the radio a top had been found. The smell of wet mud and coal dust as we ran through the woods, the taste of blood as I bit the inside of my cheek to stifle my cries when I saw Chloe's jumper.

'It did.'

'I'd give Hastings a wide berth if you can. Miss Chambers, take my number, in case he gives you any hassle.'

He gave me his mobile number and I saved it under DCI Thompson, despite him telling me again he wasn't a DCI anymore.

'Thanks for this,' I said. It was nice to have someone believe me.

'No problem. So, will you help me find Chloe?'

'Yes, of course I'll help,' I lied.

CHAPTER 35

1st December 2019
Morning

My subconscious mind quickly switched off after speaking with DCI Thompson, and I fell fast asleep, my mind thankfully knowing I needed to shut down and process what was going on. It didn't last long, and just after three, I was wide awake again, staring at the ceiling. Focusing on the shadows created by the small rivets in the aertex. The brief conversation with Thompson played on a loop in my head, over and over, and I struggled to order the pictures. He had been there in the pub and down the lane but not in the woods or outside my house, and I believed him. He had no reason to lie. It weirdly confirmed what I already knew – the Drifter was back, but so was DCI Thompson, and I had merged the two in my mind.

We weren't just facing one problem anymore. There were two ghosts from 1998 roaming the village, two people who were connected to that night. One of them knew what happened, one didn't, both wanted to end it. And then, in the middle, there was me.

By the time dawn began to splinter the night sky, I had run and rerun the past ten days, since that message from Holly telling me Jamie was missing. I wanted to help rid the village of the Drifter somehow, I wanted him to be found. I just didn't know how to go about it.

By the time Dad was up and moving I had been awake for nearly five hours, and needy for some company, I came downstairs shortly after he did. Walking into the kitchen he stood with his back to me, his hands clamped on the draining board, staring out of the window. I thought for a moment he was enjoying the sunshine which, although weak, was out, trying its best to warm the winter ground. But he wasn't. The shed door was wide open, the lawn mower in the middle of the garden. Its cable had been unravelled and the plug was resting on the outside window ledge. By the back door were muddy footprints.

'Dad?'

'I don't remember waking up,' he said, his back still to me. I didn't know what to say – what can you say to someone who knows they are beginning to lose who they were? How do I talk about it when he had lied, telling me everything was OK? I took a tentative step towards him, joined his side, placed my hand on top of his and squeezed. And for a while, we didn't move. I just held his hand and we looked outside.

'Neve, what do I do?'

'Well,' I said, fighting to keep my emotions under control. Dad had never asked for help before. 'How about you put the kettle on while I tidy up?'

I smiled at him and gave his hand another squeeze, and he smiled back before moving towards the cupboard to grab a couple of mugs. Stepping into his large shoes to go into the garden, I couldn't help but remember when I was a kid. I used to walk around in his old boots, pretending I worked down the mine. When I was little, I didn't want to be a ballet dancer or a pop star like most of the girls in my class, girls like Chloe. I wanted to be a miner, just like my dad. And I would often put on his boots and helmet and pretend I was. I would dig holes in the garden, looking for coal, and Mum would despair when I came in, covered in soil and leaving the garden looking like we had a problem with foxes. She would tell me off, say I wasn't being a proper lady. Dad wouldn't say anything, he would just smile, catch my eye and give me a wink. Those moments made my heart burst. I hated myself for so easily forgetting them.

Through the open door, I looked through at him in the kitchen: small and sad and lost as he made us both tea. The weight of the world pressing down on him, like he had become the coal he once mined. Putting away the lawnmower, I came back inside and sat with him at the kitchen table.

'What are you thinking Dad?'

'Why on God's earth did I think it was a good idea to mow the lawn last night?'

'I don't know,' I said, taking a sip of my tea.

'I mean, I can barely be arsed to do it in the middle of the day,' he said with a wink, and I laughed tea out of my nose. He was there – buried under the worry and forgetfulness was my dad who made light of things. He laughed with me, just for a moment until the weight shifted back onto him.

'I don't want to go into a home.'

'Dad?'

'I've been thinking, and I don't want to go into a home, it would kill me.'

'You're not going into a home,' I said, hoping I sounded convincing.

'Doctor McBride didn't say I have a… what did you say it could be?'

'A thyroid issue.'

'That's it, he didn't say it was a thyroid issue. I just hoped when I said I couldn't remember the name, you'd find something on the internet to explain it. I'm sorry I lied.'

'Don't be, I know you were trying to protect us both.'

He nodded, his eyes brimming.

'Have the blood tests come back yet?'

'I didn't do them.'

'Dad…' I said, exasperated, but not at all shocked. 'I watched you walk towards the nurse's office?'

'I did, but I didn't go in. I just said I was waiting for someone. Before you came into that first appointment, he told me he was convinced it is… well, he didn't say the words. It was like he couldn't, but you know. What's weird is, even with the lawnmower thing, I don't feel like I have Alzheimer's. I just can't remember doing things. Does that make sense?'

'I think so. Can I be honest, Dad?'

'Yes, sure.'

'This is the most you've ever told me about how you feel. Ever.'

'Yes, I guess it is,' he said, trying to smile again, but falling short. 'I'm sorry, love.'

'I always thought that after Mum left, you stopped caring.'

'About what, about you? Of course not. Neve, you are now, and have always been my girl.'

It was my turn to well up; two decades of things unsaid sat just behind my eyes, desperate to come out. 'So, why don't you ever call? Why don't you ever want to visit?'

'When you grew up, I felt like I was a burden, I was an embarrassment.'

'What, why?'

'I lost my job, your mother. I was ashamed. And then you wanted to leave too.'

'Oh, Dad!' Reaching over, I hugged my dad and felt tears escape. I had been so selfish in assuming his distance from me was because of him not caring, not because of how vulnerable he was. I understood what DCI Thompson meant when he said he'd spoken with Dad and understood why I had gone. Dad thought I didn't want to be with him anymore. I vowed would never let him feel like that again.

'Shall we go back and see Doctor McBride? Both of us. Get those tests done.'

'What? So, he can confirm I'm losing my mind?'

'It might not be what you, I, or even Dr McBride thinks. We won't know for sure until we do the tests. What do you say? I can call him right now.'

He offered a small nod and rubbing his arm I got up to make the call. After three rings a receptionist picked up.

'Sherwood Practice.'

'Hello, it's Neve Chambers, my father Sean Chambers has been seeing Dr McBride about an ongoing health concern. I was wondering if I could make an appointment this morning for us to come and see him.'

'I'm afraid Dr McBride isn't in today.'

'Oh, when will he be back in?'

'I'm afraid we don't know.'

'What? Why not?' My heart skipped, and I forced myself to be rational.

'Miss Chambers, you are friends with Dr McBride, aren't you?'

'Yes, we are friends.'

'I shouldn't really say but...'

'But what?'

'Barry hasn't turned up for work today. No one can find him.'

CHAPTER 36

1st December 2019
Afternoon

'Ms Chambers, thank you for taking the time to come in today,' PC Hastings said, his smile designed to be disarming, though it was anything but. He looked at me like he wanted to hurt me. He'd scared me a little last time I was at the station and unnerved me further in the way he looked at me in the pub. But things had changed. I could feel he was no longer the 'big man' on the case. I caught the news. There was a new face in front of the cameras; a new DCI from a larger force who had stepped in to lead the investigation, one designed to handle cases like this. A woman, and Hastings seemed the type to hate that his new boss was female, and that made him dangerous now, unpredictable.

'Not at all,' I smiled back. 'I want to help in any way I can.'

'Well, we appreciate that. Please, make yourself comfortable.'

I knew it wasn't standard practice for a police officer to ask you to come to the station for 'a chat'. He should have come to my dad's house instead. I suspected he wanted the formality of it, flexing the little power he now held. He needed to be on his own turf.

'I suspect you're wondering why I wanted to talk?'

'Because Baz is missing.'

'You mean Dr Barry McBride. Yes, partly.'

'Do you know anything about what is going on?' I countered.

'Why don't you tell me what you know,' he said. Our little game of chess was well underway.

'I know my friends are going missing. I know that with both Jamie and Georgia, it looks like foul play. And Baz, let's just hope...'

'Hope what, Ms Chambers?'

'Hope he decided to leave, rather than anything else.'

'What, like you did?'

'Yes, like I did.' I felt indignant. 'Are we here to talk about what's happening now, or what happened over twenty years ago?'

'In my mind, Ms Chambers, I think they are part of the same question.' He smiled again before standing. 'I think it's curious that more people are going missing since you have returned. I asked your friends about this earlier, Michael and Holly, they found it curious too.' His tone had shifted, and his words felt rehearsed. I started to wonder if he had ever questioned anyone before, because everything he was doing felt like it came from some TV cop show.

'Are you implying...'

'I'm implying nothing, just curious. And I'm wondering how to interpret the curiosity.'

He's trying to use my friends against me. Fucking. Wanker.

'Perhaps you could start by looking into the Drifter?'

'Ah yes, I wondered how long it would take for him to come up. Neve – may I call you Neve?'

'Sure.'

'Tell me more about him.'

'Well, as I've said, I've seen him in the woods...'

'I'm sorry, let me be clear, tell me about him from 1998.'

'Why?'

'I'm trying to get a picture of who this man is.'

'So, you believe me now?'

He didn't answer but watched me from behind his desk.

'I don't know what I can say that's not been documented already.'

'Yes, I've looked at your statements from back then.'

'They're probably more helpful than me trying to remember.'

He ignored my comment and turned his back to me, realigning a picture on the wall. 'There was a lot of myth surrounding what happened to Chloe, and it was fuelled by this idea of the Drifter being a ghost from the mine.'

'I never said it was a ghost.'

'Not directly, no. You spoke of a man shrouded in shadow, moving only at night. And then Chloe went missing. And this Drifter – who you and your friends independently say you saw – vanishes without a trace, and Chloe is never found.'

'I don't know what to say.'

'I thought that she was down the mine, that whoever took her left her down there. There was no evidence to suggest anything of the sort. And as you know, the tunnels were searched. But we couldn't search everywhere, too many unsafe places. Too many unfinished tunnels. Still. I've always wondered.'

'How can I help you, PC Hastings?' I said, my thoughts on what Thompson said the night before.

'Where did you see this man – this Drifter – back then?'

'I saw him near the mine mostly. Sometimes in the woods nearby. You know this.'

'And now, where have you *claimed* to see him?'

I didn't like the way he stressed the word 'claimed'. 'In the woods and outside my father's house.'

'And you're confident, this is different to your "episode" in 2003 when—'

'I know what happened to me in 2003. And yes, I am.'

'So, a few more places then. I mean, different places to back then.'

'Yes, a few more places.'

'It's just you're the only one to have seen him?'

'Yes, I am.'

'Curious. What I don't understand is, why would he return after twenty-one years? Why *now*?'

'I'm hoping you will find that out.'

'That's the plan.' He smiled again, the same fox-like grin. It was wiped off his face quickly when someone entered the room without knocking.

'Hastings,' a voice said behind me, a female voice. I turned to see a middle-aged woman, high cheekbones and strong green eyes, hands in her pockets. She smiled towards me, and then looked back at Hastings, who I could tell was squirming.

'This is Neve Chambers,' he said.

She offered her hand and introduced herself – I didn't catch her name, but knew it was the same woman I briefly caught on TV this morning after Hastings' five minutes of fame. The DCI from elsewhere.

'I was just asking her about when she last saw Dr McBride,' he offered without being asked, and I had to hide my smile at how pathetic he really was.

'I see, and when was that?' the DCI asked.

'Last night, we met for a drink,' I replied.

'We?'

'Dr McBride, Michael, Holly and me.'

'Could anyone corroborate this?'

'Yes, the pub was busy. Heaving. PC Hastings was even there,' I added, knowing I might regret it.

'I see,' she said, looking over me at him. Her expression said more than words could.

'Well, Ms Chambers, thank you for coming down. Sorry to take up your time,' she said, offering her hand. I stood and took it; it was firm, commanding. She oozed confidence and control and I wished I could be a fly on the wall after I left.

'If I can do anything else to help?' I said.

'Thank you. We have your number?' She looked again at Hastings who must have nodded. 'Good. Keep your phone on, so I can get hold of you when I have any news, or have any more questions?'

'Of course.'

'And if you can think of anything, please don't hesitate to call the station.'

'I won't,' I lied, for the second time in under twenty-four hours.

I dismissed myself without saying goodbye and walked

towards the bus stop to catch the bus back to the village. As I waited, I messaged Holly and Michael.

I don't know what Hastings has said to you, but please, will you meet me? Something happened last night I really need to talk to you about. But not in the pub, Hastings has made it quite clear he is watching, and the new DCI in the village is smart. Can we meet at the hut? Around 8? Please.

CHAPTER 37

1st December 2019
Evening

Dad had gone to bed early, and I could hear him muttering to himself from his room. I thought about our chat and his haunting words, that he would rather die than go into a home. I left a note in the kitchen, telling him I'd be back soon. I placed it next to a sandwich wrapped in clingfilm, next to a cup, teabags, sugar and a small jug of milk. I hoped he would see I wanted to help, I was being thoughtful, rather than taking away his independence. Messaging Esther to tell her I was OK, despite the latest development, I grabbed a torch and a few candles from his emergency power cut box, stuffed them into my coat pockets and left the safety of his house to walk, in the dark, to the hut where I was to meet the others. Or what was left of us. As I walked, my phone pinged and pulling it out of my coat pocket I saw it was from Esther.

Free to talk?

I wanted to speak to her, hear her voice, tell her what was happening and have her help me make sense of it. But I didn't.

Can't, with Dad. Call you tomorrow?

Sure. Xxx

Putting the phone in my pocket, I continued on towards the lane. Above me the trees moved like a stormy sea, moaning, surging. And beyond it, the mine watched me approach.

Finishing my cigarette, I prepared myself, then turned the corner to the hut. I don't know why I came so early. The hut, the place that once was synonymous with fun and a carefree life, now felt haunted. Walking around the back, I dropped low and crawled through the hatch. I lit the candles, warming the darkness to trick myself it was somewhere comfortable. One eye towards the hole in the wall that looked towards the mine. All I could do now was wait for the others.

'Neve?'

Michael's voice made me jump and I stumbled, catching my calf on the corner of the coffee table. 'I'm here.'

After a shuffle, and a groan, Michael crawled into the hut and stood, dusting his jeans down. 'I swear, that hole gets smaller and smaller,' he said, smiling, but I could tell he was rattled.

'I thought the same,' I said, trying to appear in control. I offered him a cigarette, which he took, lighting up before me. I looked to the ceiling. There was a new crack.

'How are you holding up?' Michael asked. I smiled back and took a drag. 'I know, silly question, right. This is a fucking mess,' he finished, rubbing his eyes.

'Are you OK, Michael?'

He looked at me, half scoffed and lowered his head. It was a stupid question. Of course, he wasn't OK.

'Neve, when we were kids, I wish…'

Before he could finish the hatch moved, and in crawled Holly, who looked as we all felt: tired, drained, afraid. I didn't waste time with frivolities and told them about DCI Thompson's visit last night. They didn't comment, but fresh panic rose. I said he had been to the hut, and that we shouldn't stay long.

'Why did he come here?' Michael asked. 'I thought he was retired?'

'He is, Michael, but he's searching regardless.'

'And making things twice as complicated. You know, Hastings asked to talk to me today,' Michael added, his eyes wide, and wild and fearful.

'Me too,' Holly added.

'And me,' I said. 'I also spoke with the new DCI on the case. She's sharp.'

'Fuck!' said Michael, turning his back to me and Holly. 'Fuck! I thought all this shit was over. I thought we could get on with our fucking lives.'

'Michael, calm down.'

'Calm down? It's like you've forgotten what actually happened back then.'

'No, Michael, I haven't forgotten.'

'Are you sure, because from here it looks like you've convinced yourself Chloe really was taken by the Drifter.'

'Michael, please, we need to calm down,' Holly reiterated, her voice cracking.

'Let's say it out loud, for once – let's actually say out loud what actually happened to Chloe.'

CHAPTER 38

1st December 2019
Evening

Michael didn't hold back as he spoke of the night. He didn't omit any details. Much of the story I couldn't remember; perhaps my own subconscious forced it back, trying to protect me. But he didn't have that luxury. For Michael, it seemed every minute detail had been playing on a loop over and over for the past twenty-one years. He remembered exactly what we wore, exactly when the rain started to fall. He recounted everything up to the moment we walked into the mine, and as he spoke, he didn't pause for breath. I couldn't take it anymore.

'Michael. Stop.'

'No, Neve, isn't it time we said it? Isn't it time we took some fucking responsibility?'

'I don't want to go back there, Michael, I can't.'

'It's too late for that. We were a group of seven, and now we are three. It's pretty fucking clear we've been forced back, isn't it?' He pressed on, needing so say it out loud. Part of me understood, but I knew I wasn't ready to hear it, even after all this time. 'We went down the mine, to fuck about, and Chloe…'

'Michael. Enough!' I shouted.

'No, Neve, *no*. I need to say it; for so long I have needed to say it. Aren't you haunted by it?'

'Yes. I think about it all the time.'

'Don't you still see her?'

'All the time,' I echoed, this time quieter.

'So then why can't you talk about it?'

'I just can't.'

'Because you don't want to feel responsible?'

'Michael, stop,' Holly said. 'We were kids, we were scared.'

'Yes, we were scared. We were all scared. Fucking hell, Holly, we've been scared ever since. And I've never directed that fear at anyone; I've swallowed it, smiled through it. I've mended cars; and drank in The Miners' Arms through it, and when I've seen Chloe's mum, I've nodded my head and offered a kind word, and you know what? I've been angry this whole time. Anger and fear, the only things I've really felt in twenty-one years.'

'I know you're angry, Michael, I am too...' he cut me off. His words were hard and cold like the dirty floor we stood on. 'Whose idea was it to go down the mine in the first place? Neve! Whose idea was it?'

'It was my idea.'

'And whose idea was it to do that stupid fucking ouija board?'

'Mine. But Baz brought it.'

'But it was *your* idea, Neve. In fact, who was behind every decision we made that night?'

'Michael, that's not...' Holly started in my defence. He slammed his hand on the upturned table, silencing us. In the candlelight, I watched his eyes film over. When he blinked, a tear rolled down.

'And then he came. Banging, do you remember? We panicked.

And Chloe fell, do you remember, Neve?' Michael rubbed his eyes, stepped away and faced the opposite wall, his head resting on it.

'Yes, I remember.'

'Michael, it's OK,' Holly said, going over to comfort him. It looked like it was something she had done many times before. 'It's OK, it's all right. Take a deep breath,' she whispered, and I could see his shoulders relax a little. I didn't know what to do, or say, so I said nothing at all.

'I wanted to go to get help.' His voice sounded, broken, defeated. 'I wanted to call the police. Who stopped us, Neve? Who told us to keep quiet?'

'I did,' I whispered.

'I can't hear you.'

'It was me,' I said, again much too loud for the small space. My words echoed off the wall above Michael's head, and landed back in my ears. It was me.

Michael turned, faced me, and seeing him so sad, so broken, I began to cry.

'Do you remember what happened next?' he said. I nodded. I begged. 'Please, Michael. No more.'

'When we found her.'

'Please.'

'You didn't look, did you? Over the edge. You didn't see her down there.'

'I couldn't.'

'Nor could the rest of us, but we had to. And then you used Jamie to bury her. You made us all responsible for her disappearance. Chloe has been down there ever since.'

'It wasn't just me, was it, Michael? It was your idea to take her top and put it somewhere else to draw people away from the mine. And it was Baz who said we should blame the Drifter. It wasn't all me,' I said, tears filling my eyes.

'It's your fault we had to all lie like we did. What happened to Chloe was a tragic accident, and you made us hide it from everyone. You made it a crime.'

'I was scared.'

'We were all scared. We wanted to get help. You stopped us. You did that, Neve. And then you fucked off and left us to clean up the mess.'

He waited for me to reply, to fuel the argument he had been clearly dying to have for so long. But I didn't. I couldn't. He was right about it all. If we'd gone to the police, explained what had happened, we wouldn't have got into trouble. It was an accident. And although we were trespassing, I don't think we would have been punished too severely. What happened to Chloe was punishment enough. Michael turned away from me, unable to look at me anymore and lit another cigarette. I didn't blame him either. I wanted to turn away from me too.

'I refuse to go to jail for something I didn't do,' he said.

'You did, Michael. You did, we all did,' Holly said quietly. Sympathetically.

'Holly, you've got more to lose than us. What about your kids? What happens if the truth comes out?'

'Michael, don't you think I've thought about my kids?'

'And now, that copper from back then is snooping around, there is a new hotshot DCI in the village, and we are going missing one by one. People are going to find out what happened...'

'The truth won't come out. Don't you see, Michael? What's

going on now has nothing to do with Chloe; this is about crimes that are happening now.'

'Yes, but they are happening *because* of Chloe. And the Drifter is back to punish us.'

'It doesn't make sense to me,' I said, shocked I was speaking at all.

'What?'

'The Drifter. Why is he after us?'

'It wasn't just our lives you ruined that night. It was his too.'

'I don't understand.'

'For fuck's sake, Neve.'

'Michael,' Holly comforted, her arm reaching out to hold him once more.

'Have you not thought about this?' he persisted.

'No.'

'No, you just moved to London, brushed us all under an old carpet.' His words stung, but I didn't correct him. 'The Drifter, whoever he was, was just a man, he wasn't a ghost, he wasn't Georgia's dad, he wasn't a kid killer. He was just someone who missed the mine. Someone who wanted to care for it. That's why we saw him there. That's why he chased us out that night. He was trying to scare us from hurting ourselves. He wasn't in the wrong, we were. And then he got the blame. We'll never know who he was, but I know one thing. We ruined the chance for him to have anything like a normal life.'

'You don't know that, Michael, you're speculating.'

'Am I? The Drifter was all over the news. And he knew it was him they were referring to. Imagine always looking over your shoulder, Neve, always waiting to be caught.' I knew exactly how that felt. 'Always waiting to be caught for something *you didn't do,*' he said, as if reading my mind. 'We ruined his life, and now he is doing to us what we claimed he did back then.'

'Fine, let's say that's what's happening. But why now, Michael? It doesn't make sense.'

'I don't know, Holly, because we are getting on with our lives? I don't know why he's waited this long, but if I were him, if any of us were him, wouldn't we do the same? Wouldn't we want revenge?'

We fell silent. I hadn't thought about the consequences of having the world look for the Drifter. I didn't think what it must have done to that person, whoever they were. I had ruined not only our lives, but I had ruined his too. And now he was back to make us all pay.

'So, what do we do now?' Holly asked.

'I guess, we find him, before he finds us.'

'And what about Hastings, and the DCI?'

'We need them to stay focused on the now.'

'How do we do that?' asked Holly.

'Lie,' I said.

'What?'

'Lie,' I repeated quietly. 'Holly, you need to tell them you have seen the Drifter too.'

'Neve, I can't do that.'

'You've lied before. And this isn't really a lie at all. He is out there.'

'Like we lied in ninety-eight – like *that*, Neve,' Michael hissed. 'Look how well that's worked out for us.'

'This will make it go away. Tell them about the Drifter, tell them you've seen him around the mine or outside your house. Even better, say you've seen him outside Baz's house. It will make him focus on what he should be seeing, not looking for anything else.'

'Fine.'

'Holly?!' Michael said.

'She's right. It makes sense,' Holly said, defeated but knowing it was the only thing we could do. 'I'll call it in first thing.'

'Do it tonight, late, say midnight.'

Holly didn't respond but nodded.

'And Thompson?' Michael added.

'I don't know. I'm hoping he and Hastings will talk, share information, but I doubt it. Thompson didn't seem keen on Hastings,' I said with a pause. 'But he seemed to trust me.'

'So, what are you going to do?'

'I guess I'll keep him sweet. Keep him focused on what's happening right now to us.'

I took out my phone and unlocked it.

'Who are you messaging?' Holly asked.

'Him. I'll meet, keep him looking the wrong way Thompson.' I messaged him. My hands shook as I did. I needed to make this go away, I owed it to them all.

Are you free for a drink this evening? I feel like I need someone to talk to.

CHAPTER 39

July 1998
Five days before...

The heat of the day held deep into the night, and at nearly 11 p.m., it showed no signs of letting go. The air was hot and thick in Neve's bedroom despite her windows being wide open. Each time the warm breeze picked up, the wooden frame groaned under the strain, threatening to split. But it made little difference. There was no respite from the ground-cracking heat that had sucked the moisture from the air.

Neve lay on her bed. Her covers were scrunched into a ball at the end of it. On the wall beside her a poster of The Backstreet Boys smiled back. Beside them, one of NSYNC, who they all had a huge crush on. Perfect smiles on the faces of perfect boys with perfect teeth. On the floor next to the bed sat Chloe and beside her, the hem of her top pushed high up her midriff, exposing her stomach, lay Georgia. She was too hot to care that a deep bruise on her ribs was visible. Holly wasn't there. She had been caught by the police when Michael stole the booze from Mr Busby's off-licence, and despite them not arresting her, they insisted – as it was late, and she had been drinking – they needed to take her home. Michael, who made it home unscathed, said he could hear her parents shouting at her from his house in the next street. They'd not seen her since, and no one had mentioned it beyond Michael's testimony of how much shit she was in.

In the background Georgia's mixtape played, and they all succumbed to the sounds of Boyz II Men serenading them. Chloe and Georgia hadn't intended to stay so late. The boys were away with Baz's dad in Nottingham, so it gave the girls the perfect excuse to gossip, and before they knew it the strong summer sun had slipped behind the horizon and night staked its claim. They spoke idly of leaving school, their prospects for their exams results and, in their absence, the boys. Georgia was called out for liking Baz, making her blush. Neve knew Georgia wouldn't stand a chance, for Baz – for all of his bravado and pranks – was secretly a bit of a romantic, and his affections were directed towards Chloe. Content they had teased Georgia enough, Chloe thought it would be fair to turn the attention towards Neve, asking for juicy details about Jamie. Neve resisted, only reiterating what they all knew. They kissed two days ago on the bench near the country park.

'Aw, come on, Neve. You must have more!' teased Georgia, happy the topic of conversation had moved away from herself and Baz.

'Honestly, there isn't anything to tell,' Neve said defensively.

'There must be!' pushed Georgia.

'I promise.'

'Come on, Neve,' Chloe said exasperatedly, rising to her knees. 'You have to tell us something, it's killing me not knowing.'

'There is nothing left to tell.'

'You can't hold out on us. We don't have secrets from each

other. And besides, you and Jamie is the only thing happening in this crappy village.'

'I'm not holding out, Chloe, honestly. I just don't know what's going on with me and him. I haven't seen him since.'

Since their kiss, Jamie had disappeared. It had only been two days. But after weeks of speaking every day, it felt longer. He was working with his dad at the pub, that was normal. Neve hoped she'd not seen him for that reason alone and not because he'd realised he didn't like her. It had played on her mind since he hadn't kissed her goodnight after walking her home.

'Do you think he's gone off me?' she asked quietly.

'No,' said Chloe. 'Of course not. He's just shy, and busy helping his dad. From what I gather, since the mine closed, the pub's been quieter than usual.'

'So why does he have to be there so much?' Neve asked, desperately.

'Jamie's dad had to let go of most of his staff. Jamie is working instead. Probably costs his dad less to employ a 16-year-old. It's a bit shit really, isn't it? I mean, the mine closing has really fucked things up for us,' Chloe said quietly to no one in particular. 'I heard my dad saying they are probably going to fill it in soon.'

'What?'

'That's what they've done with all the other mines. Once they're closed, they throw a load of dirt down there and fill it.'

'Oh,' said Neve, thinking about what Jamie had said about one day going down into the mine. Perhaps he wouldn't get the chance. 'It's kinda sad.'

'No way, it's a good thing,' said Georgia. 'Fucking place is creepy.'

'Yeah, but still. It would have been good to go down it, see for ourselves. I bet the boys would be up for it,' Neve said, motivated by the assumption that Jamie would approve of the idea.

'Are you saying we should break in?' Georgia smiled.

'Why not? By the sounds of it, it might be our only chance.'

Outside, the breeze picked up again, snapping the window open, the wooden frame cracking under the strain, making Chloe jump. Worried it would snap entirely, Neve got up to put the latch on, and as she did, she saw the shape of someone walking away from her house, in the direction of the mine. Their form was only defined when it was directly under one of the working streetlights. Even still, Neve knew it was him.

'Shit, guys. Look.'

Chloe and Georgia sprang up to the window to peer outside.

'Fuck, is that him?' Georgia asked. 'So creepy, what is he doing?'

'I don't know,' Neve said quietly.

The Drifter stopped under a streetlight and looked up at it. Neve gave the others a confused glance, and a shiver ran up her spine as she saw the mild panic in their faces. He stood, unmoving, just looking at the light. It was weird, unnerving, but they couldn't take their eyes off him.

'He must be bloody boiling,' continued Georgia, noticing his dark trousers and long workman's coat. 'This is so creepy. He looks like he's from a different time.'

Chloe didn't comment, she just watched while the colour slowly drained from her face.

'Chloe, is that is the same man you saw near the mine?' Georgia asked. Chloe didn't respond but nodded, unable to look away.

As Neve and Georgia turned back to look at him, he was no

longer fixated on the light above him, and instead had turned his attention in the direction of her house. He had seen them at Neve's window. Neve panicked, pulling the curtains closed, and Georgia dropped to the floor to hide under the windowsill. Chloe stood frozen to the spot. Neve dragged Chloe down with her, and the three of them pressed their backs against the wall directly under the window.

'What the fuck?' Neve asked, rhetorically, not noticing Chloe's terrified expression. 'How did he know we were there?'

'What if he comes to the house?' said Georgia, her words snagging in her throat.

'Hang on, I'll look.'

Neve slowly turned and shuffled onto the balls of her feet. Hiding behind the window ledge, she slowly raised herself behind so her eye line came above the window frame. She looked from outside her house and traced the road down towards the light where he stood. But he had gone. She looked further down the road; he wasn't there. He had vanished, just like smoke.

She told them he had disappeared, and Georgia breathed a sigh of relief. Chloe, however, remained quiet, her face ashen.

'Chloe? Are you all right?' Neve asked, and all Chloe could do was nod.

'Chloe? What's wrong?'

Chloe took a deep breath and told them she was fine.

CHAPTER 40

1st December 2019
Night

We left the hut separately: first Holly, then a few minutes later Michael, and after a cigarette, I crawled out of the hatch. I hoped I would never come back. The hut wasn't the place it once was for me, for us. And being inside only brought pain and sadness. I began to walk back towards the village in the pouring rain and by the time I reached the pub, the damp that was confined to my toes had climbed up my socks, making my whole body feel cold.

As I closed the door behind me, I felt the room quieten, just for a beat, before the noise returned.

Taking off my coat, I shook excess water off and scanned the room to see if Thompson was there. I couldn't see him. That didn't mean much. Approaching the bar, Derrick had his head down, pouring a Coke; he looked tired and I couldn't remember if the last time I saw him, I asked how he was. It seemed with Georgia, and now Baz, going missing, and what that meant, Jamie had been forgotten. He was still a part of the gossip, but now he was more of a secondary character. As I drew closer, he looked up. He shook his head and then flicked a glance to the right. I followed, and saw Hastings at the end of the bar, his back to me, talking into his phone. Looking back to Derrick, he flicked his head to the left and understanding, I walked around the bar, towards the darkest corner and sat at the same table I'd seen Thompson on my first night.

Derrick approached, a large drink in his hand, and he put it down in front of me.

'I got you a JD, I hope that's all right?'

'It's perfect, thank you. And thank you for giving me the heads-up.'

'Hastings is always here; I don't know why he isn't out finding the three of them.'

'I think that new DCI has put his nose out of joint.'

'He's a spoilt little shit. More concerned with theories and speculation than doing any actual work. Like he's that investigator fella from the old books. You know, the Agatha Christie ones.'

'Poirot,' I smiled; Derrick and I had the same assumption of the weaselly little man in the police uniform.

'Yes, that's the fella. And, I want you to know, he doesn't much like you.'

'I know. What's he said?'

'He keeps on about how what's happening is connected to Chloe. And that you know more than you let on about it.'

He waited for me to reply – intently watching, trying to see if there was any truth in what Hastings was saying.

'He was the same back in 1998. He was part of the reason I left. Derrick, he scares me a bit.'

His look softened. 'Well, don't worry. He'll not bother you while you're in here.'

'Thank you.'

'Don't mention it.'

Derrick affectionately tapped me on the forearm twice and headed back to the bar. As he did, Thompson passed him coming the other way, towards me. Derrick paused, turned and caught my eye. I smiled, telling him I was all right. He smiled back but didn't look convinced as he rounded the corner to serve another customer. Thompson approached the table, nodded, removed his heavy coat and sat himself down opposite me with a heave.

'Thanks for coming out, DCI…'

'Robert.'

'Robert.'

'Is everything all right, Miss Chambers?'

'Yes, I think,' I said, clipped, knowing he was trying to pry beyond my wellbeing. 'If I've got to call you Robert, will you call me Neve?'

'Seems like a fair request. So, how are you doing, Neve?'

I don't know why, but it was in this moment the walls crashed down and my emotions flooded over me. I wasn't all right, I was far from it. With Oliver, the café robbery and Dad's health all existing underneath the horror of me and my friends being picked off one by one, I was shocked I'd made it so far without falling into pieces. I didn't cry, I just buried my head into my hands and held my breath until I was sure I wouldn't pass out. Thankfully, the moment passed.

'Let me get us a couple of drinks,' he said, giving me a little space to get my thoughts back in order. I knew what he was doing; he was playing the classic good cop thing he'd done back in 1998. I didn't mind. After a few minutes he returned with a pint for him, and another JD for me. I wasn't sure if he asked Derrick, or if he knew what I drank. I hoped the former. I didn't like him being that observant. He may be older, but his mind was still keen. I needed to be careful of what I said, and how I said it.

'Thank you,' I said as I took the drink from his broad, ageing hand. It would be easy to drink several drinks tonight, but I knew this would be my last this evening, just enough booze floating around to take off the edge. But nothing more.

'So, I'm assuming we aren't here for a social drink. Neve, what's on your mind?'

'I guess I'm just having a hard time with it all.'

'Specifically?' he said, clearly in no mood for small talk.

'That no one in this village believes me about the Drifter.'

'Well, you can't blame them, can you? He is a person you and your friends claimed to have seen the night Chloe disappeared.'

'Not just that night. We saw him for weeks leading up to…' I hesitated; I didn't want to say 'the night Chloe disappeared'.

'Yes, I remember, he was hanging around. She even wrote in her diary about how he had seen her outside her house on a few occasions.' I nodded and looked down, my fingernails were dirty. I couldn't remember the last time I painted them.

'I'm assuming you know about what happened to me in 2003?' I said quietly, forcing myself to hold his gaze when he looked towards me.

'Yes. Hastings told me. He said it made you unreliable.'

I thought as much. 'Robert, yes, I did have an episode when I was young, I'm not going to deny that to anyone, but I *have* seen him here. I promise you, this isn't the same thing.'

He continued to hold my gaze for a moment, considering

me; I couldn't get a read of what he was thinking. Eventually, he leant back, took a few mouthfuls of his pint and nodded.

'As I've said, I believe you.'

'Robert, who is he?'

Looking over my head he observed the other patrons in the pub, assessing them with his smoky eyes. Content we were not being watched or listened to, he leant in slightly and spoke in a hushed tone.

'Back then, the future of the mine wasn't set. We didn't know that it would become a place of historical interest and protected, like it is now. In fact, the word was it would be filled and bulldozed. Probably turned into a block of flats. The company that owned the mine employed people to salvage what they could from down there – tools, materials, things that could be sold on abroad. We always believed your "Drifter" was one of these employees. It explains why he was around the mine. It also explains why no one knew who he was. These employees usually came from outside the village. You know, cash-in-hand types.'

'Why would they employ people from outside? Wasn't most of the village out of work?'

'It was too soon, too raw.'

It made sense. Dad was so sad after the mine closed, if someone had asked him to go down and bring up things to sell on, he would have said no. It might have broken him.

'So, where did he go?'

'After Chloe, he must have left. We tried to trace him through the employer. Their staff turnover was high and paying people cash in hand meant there wasn't a proper employment register. Although there was no recession in the nineties, there was a spike in interest rates around 1998, and it meant lots of working-class people lost their homes. It made it almost impossible to trace everyone who was employed by the colliery for the clean-up operation. People worked and moved onto the next quick fix. It was just as it was. Whoever he was, he's kept a low profile for a very long time.'

'And now he is back.'

'So it appears.'

Robert took another long sip of his pint and as he placed it down, I watched him lose himself to thoughts. I didn't want to interrupt. The more he was thinking about the Drifter being here now, the less he was thinking about anything else, which was exactly what we needed.

'The only thing that still isn't making any sense,' he said looking at his pint, his eyebrows knitted in concentration, 'is why now – why has he come back after all this time?'

'Robert, what if he's been waiting for me to come home?'

'I don't understand.'

'What if he has always been here, and he's doing this now, because I am back?'

'Have you not been back until now?'

'Fleeting visits. Never for more than an hour.'

'I see, that's interesting,' he said, as he looked up and away, thinking, visualising.

'So, you think it's one of the villagers?'

'I'm not accusing anyone, but for years there has been nothing, and then the second I'm back, we are going missing.'

'Jamie went missing before you came home.'

'He did, but what if Jamie was taken to get me to come back?'

Thompson nodded, sipped his pint. 'That would make sense, but why is he doing this?' he asked.

'I wish I knew.'

'It's been two decades, why now?' he questioned himself. 'What is his motivation now?' he asked, this time directly at me.

'I don't know,' I lied. Of course, I knew: he wanted to punish us for ruining his life when we lied about Chloe.

'I know I missed something in 1998, I just can't think what that could be,' Thompson said intensely, and I swallowed, my mouth becoming dry suddenly. I was glad I'd only had two JDs.

'Robert, what do we do?' I managed to say, my voice even, hiding the sudden spike of fear.

'Well, I'm going to lean on Hastings a bit, see if the kid can give me anything.'

'Like what?' I asked, glad the conversation was moving on.

'Forensics from the tops. Any other abnormalities or clues from the crime scenes. My first concern is your friends. We need to find them.'

'What if…'

'We don't work in "what's ifs", Neve. Let's keep to the assumption they are alive, until we have to think of anything else. We did the same with Chloe, even long after she was "buried" we kept looking for her.'

'Yes, sorry. I'm just freaking out.'

'Well, try to calm yourself because I need you to keep me posted, see if you can remember anything from back then that might help us now. Can you do that?'

'Yes.'

Lie.

'Good. Is there anything else you want to say to me?'

His question made my skin prickle. It was an odd way of wording it, like he was testing me.

'Hastings called me into his office.'

'Yes, I heard. What did he want?'

'To try to intimidate me – it doesn't help that I'm the only one to have seen the Drifter.'

'That we know about.'

'How do you mean?'

'If what's suggested is going on, Jamie, Georgia and Baz saw the Drifter too.'

I thought about that for a moment – he was right. They would have seen the Drifter, right before he did whatever he did to them. It made me wonder, why hasn't he attacked me in the same way? Why is he taunting me by hanging around in the shadows?

'I think you need to keep a low profile,' Robert said, as if reading my mind. 'You, Holly and Michael. I don't think any of you are safe. Whoever has taken your friends, I think they are close. He could be any one of us.' His attention drifted away from me.

Robert's stark warning was amplified by him looking over my head towards the others in the pub. Thanking him again I got up, put on my coat and headed for the door. As I did, Hastings watched me from the bar, a curious expression on his face, one that almost looked like a smile.

CHAPTER 41

2nd December 2019
Morning

Waking up, I stretched and waited for the inevitable throb to begin behind my eyes, then, remembering I only let myself have two drinks, the throb didn't come. I wasn't hung over. Going into the bathroom I splashed cold water on my face. The shock invigorated my skin, and snapped me into focus. Downstairs I saw Dad wasn't in the chair. Fearing he was outside again, in the freezing cold, I hurried to the kitchen. The door was locked, and on the side was a note:

> Didn't want to wake you, nipped to doctor's for that memory test thingy. I'll get those bloods done too. I promise. Won't be long.
> Dad.

Fuck. Running back upstairs I threw on some clothes and started quickly towards the surgery. I passed Chloe's old house, my eye drawn up to her bedroom window, and I jumped when staring back, a cigarette in her hand, was Brenda. She didn't say anything, didn't move, but stared at me. It was like she knew. She took a drag on her cigarette, the embers glowing brighter, throwing shadows over her bony face. I could swear for a moment that there was someone behind her, also watching. She exhaled, stepped back from the window, and there was no one else there. I thought for a second she might be coming to her front door, so jogged away, towards the village, only slowing when I was sure Brenda wasn't pursuing.

Just before I got to the main road, I could see three police cars. It looked like they were outside Holly's house. I tried not to panic as I headed towards her front door. Before I could turn onto her garden path, the arms of Hastings reached out and stopped me.

'Where is Holly? Is she OK?'

'Ms Chambers, please…' Hastings replied, his grip tightening on my arm.

'Just tell me, is she all right?' I said, looking over his shoulder into Holly's house. I could see something hanging on the coat rack inside her front door. A top. One that was covered in blood. And beside it was the DCI talking to someone in forensic clothing. 'What's going on?'

'Ms Chambers. Please.'

'Neve—' A voice came from behind me, and turning I saw it was Thompson. Hands in his pockets, his demeanour calm, in control. 'PC Hastings, I'll escort Ms Chambers away.' Even though he was retired and had no authority, he still commanded respect, and Hastings let go.

'What's going on?' I pleaded again.

'Come with me,' Thompson said quietly, as he took my arm and yanked me away. Knowing I would get nowhere with Hastings, I acquiesced.

'She isn't allowed to know anything,' Hastings called as we walked away. Thompson didn't reply but shot a glance that made Hastings turn towards the house and pretend to be busy instructing people.

It wasn't until we turned the corner, far enough away to not be heard or seen did he stop walking.

'Holly is missing.'

'Shit. Shit,' I said, my hands going up to my mouth, covering it so I didn't say something I would regret. I felt dizzy and sat on the edge of a garden wall. Lowering my head between my legs, I took several deep breathes. Thompson sat beside me, rubbed my back until I felt calmer.

'Sorry,' I said.

'Don't be.'

'When did it happen?'

'I'm not sure yet. She rang in late last night, saying she had seen a man dressed in a dark coat outside her house.'

I knew as much but didn't let it show. 'What was that I saw on her coat rack? Was that her top?'

'Again, unconfirmed. I believe it belongs to Dr McBride.'

'Baz,' I said quietly. He was taunting us again, showing us we could do nothing to stop him. 'I've got to go, do you mind?'

'To Michael.'

'Yes,' I said, shocked at how well he could read the situation.

'I'll update you if I come across anything.'

'Thank you, Robert.'

'Hey,' came a voice, booming in our direction. Turning, I saw Hastings bound towards us. 'Hey, what are you two discussing?'

'Go, Neve. I'll deal with him.'

'Are you sure?'

'Yes, go.'

I stood and walked away quickly. Hastings shouted for me to stop, but I didn't. Looking over my shoulder, Thompson held out his hands to slow Hastings' march and they began to talk. I couldn't hear much of what was being said, apart from two words 'the Drifter'. Hastings would have no choice but to investigate it properly because Holly kept her word and reported she had seen him. And now she was missing.

Taking my phone out of my pocket, I rang Michael who picked up on the first ring.

'Neve?'

'She's gone. Holly has been taken.'

'Fuck. I saw on Facebook there were police on her road.'

'And it looks like Baz's top has been left inside her house.'

'Inside her house?'

'Yes.'

'He's playing games with us.'

'Yes,' I repeated, fear trying to strangle my words.

'Where are you?'

'I'm in the village.'

'Go to the pub, I'm coming to get you.'

'I can't, I've got to go and get Dad from the doctor.'

'Neve, your dad will be fine. He's not being targeted, we are. Go to the pub. I'll be there in ten minutes.'

I didn't respond.

'Neve!'

'Yes, OK, yes, I'll go to the pub.

Hanging up, I turned around and began walking back towards Holly's. The most direct way to the pub was past her house, but I wouldn't tempt Hastings to do or say something to me. So,

I turned onto the road that ran behind her house and made my way towards The Miners' Arms. When I arrived, I waited in the car park, smoking a cigarette to keep myself calm. Behind me, the pub doors were open, revealing people inside. Their voices overlapped so I was unable to pick out a single conversation thread. I didn't need to. I knew what they were talking about. Holly. More gossip, more drama.

And hearing their voices, I remembered why I ran away all those years ago.

CHAPTER 42

2nd December 2019
Morning

Michael pulled up, but the car had barely stopped when he reached over and opened the passenger door. I climbed in and he smiled at me before putting the car in gear. I didn't know what to say to him. So I sat quietly, inhaling the smell of old cigarettes masked by a pine-scented car freshener which hung from his rear-view mirror. Leaving the pub car park, he turned right, in the direction of Holly's.

'Michael?'

'I just need to see for myself.'

'Why?'

'I don't know, Neve. I just need to.'

'I don't think that's a good idea. Hastings—'

'I don't care about that little shit. I need to see, OK.'

I nodded, understanding. He shouldn't want to see his best friend's top covered in blood. And yet, I'd done exactly the same thing all those years ago when they had found Chloe's. There was something that drew us into the tragedy. We needed it, we needed it much more than anyone would like to think.

We turned into Holly's road and Michael slowed as we passed

her house. I kept low, so he could see through my window clearly; I was hiding too. I didn't want to fall under Hastings' beady watch again. Or worse, I didn't want the new DCI to see me – she was bright, and that was far scarier than anything Hastings could ever be. Keeping low in my seat, my head turned towards Michael, I watched him, and I knew when he saw the top; there was a slight flicker of his eyelid as he suppressed his reaction, and then he sped up, and sensing we were clear, I sat upright once more. I lit a cigarette for him and handed it over. Lighting another, we smoked in silence as he took a wide loop to head back in the other direction, past Holly's road and towards his house. As he drove, I smoked and looked at the mine – no matter where we were, it was always watching. I thought about how I could get me and Dad out of this place. This wasn't me running away from a problem anymore, this was trying to survive. I wanted to go now, but I couldn't, not yet. Tonight, I would grab Dad, a few of his things and we would leave. I would tell Michael to do the same, because we were powerless. If the Drifter could take Holly from her own house, leaving Baz's bloody top to taunt us, he could do anything. The village was small, no one had seen him, no one could find our friends. He could move in and around us like a ghost, and we couldn't win. Michael might protest, he might stay, that was his choice. I needed to go.

I was relieved when we pulled into Michael's drive on the westernmost outskirt of the village. The mine's omnipresence was interrupted by a dip in the road and a line of mature birch trees. Michael's house was tucked on a small lane fifty feet from the main road. It looked like it had once been a farmhouse that had seen better days. The roof had missing tiles and the window frames were of old, cracked wood that were once painted white but had faded with time. In the drive were four cars, all damaged in some way, no doubt linked to his business. They were projects for him to fix, or stock for spare parts perhaps.

I took a breath to ask something about the house – it was a far cry from the one-bed flat he grew up in with his grandparents – but before I could, Michael got out of the car and walked hastily towards his house. I grabbed the handle to follow but stopped when I heard him cry out like a wounded animal. His head was thrown back, screaming to the clouds above. Michael screamed for a few more seconds before his head dropped impossibly low. The weight of it seemed to force him to the ground. I quietly climbed out of the car and approached, unsure of how I should act, what I should say. I tentatively placed my hand on his back, and he didn't move, didn't flinch. I gently rubbed it.

'Michael?'

'Sorry. I just needed to do that.'

'Don't be. Shall we go inside?'

He didn't reply but nodded and fumbled with his house keys. I took his hand in mine and slid down to take control of the keys, guiding them into the lock. He looked at me, a strange, sorry expression. I turned and opened his front door, and we stepped inside.

Leading him into the front room, I sat him on the sofa and went to find his kitchen. I flicked the kettle on to make a tea and opened the fridge to grab the milk. There were four beers. It was tempting, but I closed the fridge door. As I made the tea, I tried to keep an ear on Michael. But the house was silent. Going back into the living room, Michael hadn't moved from where I'd sat him down.

'Here,' I said, handing him his tea.

'Thanks.'

'This place is huge,' I said.

'It's a work in progress. When Granddad died, I was left with a little money and their flat. I bought this last year to renovate and then move into.'

'So, no one will know we are here?'

'It wouldn't be hard to find us; this place isn't a secret. But it is more discreet.'

I nodded.

'Neve, I'm scared.'

'Me too,' I said, my hand reaching up and rubbing his back once more.

'I thought you were gonna leave long before this point. I'm glad I'm not alone right now.'

I felt myself move in closer to Michael, my head resting upon his shoulder. I needed to tell him I was in fact going to leave, but I needed to pick my moment. I could tell he wouldn't follow, he would stay. He reached over and put his arm around me, and I felt myself drawing closer. Michael was one of the few men to hug me since Oliver and I didn't know how much I needed to feel comfort. Perhaps it was the adrenaline, the fear, but I wanted to be closer still. Turning to face him, I leant in and kissed him, and at first, he embraced it, but quickly pulled away and stood.

'Neve, stop.'

'I'm sorry, Michael, I thought...'

'What?'

'Nothing. I'm sorry. I shouldn't have.'

'Just, you and I – we can't, Neve.'

'No, you're right. I'm sorry.'

'It's OK,' he said quietly, before he sighed and flopped against the backrest of the sofa. I should have felt more embarrassed for throwing myself at him, but strangely I didn't. 'So, what do we do, Michael? Do you think we should leave?' I asked tentatively, testing the waters.

'No.'

'But…'

'If we leave, it would look like we are running; we would look guilty of doing something to our friends.'

'But we haven't done anything wrong.'

'This time, no,' he said, looking at me to say something that contradicted him. We had gone way beyond that.

Maybe that night, after he banged and shouted, and we fled. Maybe he stayed down there, maybe he found Chloe and saw what happened next? Maybe this wasn't about us ruining his life. Maybe he has been waiting all this time for us to be together once more, so he could make us pay. And because that wasn't ever going to happen, he contrived our coming together again by taking Jamie. And maybe, if I did run, he would just follow. Maybe he would hurt my dad to get to me. I wanted to survive; maybe running wasn't the answer at all?

'So, we just sit here?' I asked, the walls feeling closer.

'Yes, we stick together, we wait for the police to find him.'

'Or him to find us.'

CHAPTER 43

July 1998
Three days before…

Neve couldn't help looking back at Jamie. The security light outside the fire-exit door shone just enough to illuminate his body. And as they had fooled around in total darkness, it was the first time she had seen a boy semi-naked. He didn't try to cover himself, but smiled at her, content, without a care in the world. It wasn't often she saw him so at peace; it made him even more attractive to her. She mouthed a goodbye and he waved before rolling onto his side and grabbing a cigarette to light.

'Want one?' he asked, and nodding, Neve stepped back into his bedroom, glad for the excuse not to leave. She wanted to get back into bed with him, take her clothes off and kiss him, her skin pressing into his until they both fell asleep. But she didn't do anything about it, she felt too nervous. So, taking the lit cigarette from his hand, she walked to his bedroom window and leant outside, enjoying the sound of crickets that chirped in the long grass opposite. She took one long drag, blowing the smoke up into the clear night sky – and then he was by her side, his shoulder touching hers, their bare arms in contact from the shoulder to the elbow. And they smoked together, looking out into the darkness, hearing the sound of a summer night. It reminded her of when she was young, the evenings when they went on bike rides as the sun set, Chloe perched on her handlebars screaming as Neve peddled faster and faster. Jamie was there too, riding side by side. Almost as close as they were now. Neve turned and watched him smoke, oblivious of her. She could see his features without him knowing. Only a few nights before, she sat in her bedroom looking at the mine, wondering if Jamie had gone off her. Upon his return that night from Nottingham, he showed more interest. Neve found herself in the pub, when the others were elsewhere, waiting for him to finish his shift so they could walk to the hut together and join them, the lane providing the perfect, secretive place to kiss. She didn't know why he had gone from being so distant to so close but suspected that the boys adding a little pressure had something to do with it. She was grateful for it.

Just as she started to wonder what might happen next, and when they might do more than just kiss and fool around, Jamie spoke, his eyes looking towards the headstocks.

'There is something about that building, isn't there?'

'It's spooky.'

'It's more than that. It's like it was once alive, and now it's dead.'

Neve nodded, taking another drag on her cigarette. 'Georgia thinks they will likely fill it in.'

'Yeah, she's probably right,' he said, downbeat. 'Shame. I've always felt drawn to it; I was sure I'd end up working down there. I know my dad has the pub, and he'll probably want me to take over it when he's older, but I felt I'd be a miner. Like my granddad. It's kinda sad I'll never know what it's like to be that far underground. People say it's closer to hell. But I don't see it like that.'

'No?'

'No, it's closer to the centre of the earth. Closer to life than anything else.'

Neve looked at Jamie; he didn't look back, his attention fixed on the mine and Neve could see something in his gaze, a sadness, a longing perhaps. The future for Jamie wasn't set, anything could happen, and he knew it. She couldn't help feeling attracted to him even more.

'Jamie, do you really want to go down the mine?'

'I just always assumed I would,' he said, still looking out towards it.

'Then let's do it. Let's go down, all of us.'

Jamie turned, and as he spoke his caution, she could see he was excited by the idea. 'We could get into a lot of trouble.'

'Only if we get caught. And no one will care. No one has found us at the hut, have they?'

'No, they haven't,' he smiled.

'It will be the same. And it will be good for us. What do you think?'

'Are you sure? It seems risky?'

'Maybe, but aren't the best things a little risky? I mean, wouldn't it be cool to go and find your granddad's ghost?' she smiled.

'Yeah, it would.'

'In that case, Jamie, truth or dare.'

Jamie didn't reply, instead he flicked his cigarette out of the window, stepped into her space and kissed her before guiding her back to bed.

She didn't expect the first time she had sex to feel so good.

It hurt, like she knew it would, but it wasn't just sex; she and Jamie connected. He was gentle, reassuring. She was too, it was the first time for both of them. Neve wanted to stay all night, sleep in his arms, but she needed to leave. So, after she dressed, she kissed him on the cheek as he drifted to sleep, and snuck down the fire escape. Just before she closed the door, Jamie spoke, his voice sleepy.

'Goodnight, Buttercup.'

Buttercup. Her first-ever pet name. She loved it.

After carefully making her way down the metal stairs of the pub's fire escape, Neve turned onto the main road and started her quiet walk home. The pub had long kicked out the final few hardy patrons, and with the mine being shut, she knew she wouldn't bump into anyone just starting or ending one of the weird shift patterns the whole village revolved around. It was strange, she had grown up in a place that never fell silent. As she got close to Chloe's she could see the lights on in most of the windows, and from Chloe's bedroom window Neve could see a small red glow wax and wane in intensity as Chloe smoked.

'So?' came a voice from behind. Neve pretended she didn't hear, and hoped it was too dark for Chloe to see she was both smiling uncontrollably, and blushing. It wasn't until Neve was directly under the window she could see her friend.

'Have you been at your window all evening, waiting for me to come past?'

'Of course I haven't,' Chloe replied a little unconvincingly. 'Well, what else am I gonna do in the shitty place? You and Jamie are the only bit of excitement lately.'

'That's sad,' Neve whispered back.

'It's shit,' Chloe replied. 'Anyway, so, did you...'

'Chloe, I'm not saying.'

'That's a yes then.'

'I better go, Mum and Dad will go ballistic if they find out I'm not in bed.'

'Aww come on, I want all the juicy details!'

'Chloe, I really have to go. What time should I come over tomorrow?'

'Anytime. Mum goes to work at eight so the house is ours.'

'OK, great, I'll be over tomorrow.'

'And you promise to tell all?' she teased.

'Yes, I promise.' Neve paused. She could sense there was some other reason for Chloe being at her window. Something more than just to gossip about her and Jamie. 'Are you all right? It's really late.'

Even in the low light, Neve watched the smile drop from her face. 'Yeah, just have a hard time sleeping these days.'

'Chloe – have you seen him tonight?'

Chloe didn't need Neve to explain who the 'him' was. 'No, not tonight.'

'Last night?'

'Yep. About where you're stood now.'

Neve shuddered and took an involuntary step to her right. She didn't like the idea of standing in the same space as the Drifter.

'Fucking weirdo.'

'Yeah, fucking weirdo,' she smiled, but Neve could see she was freaking out. From behind Chloe there came a shout from her mother.

'Are you smoking out of that fucking window?'

'No, Mum,' Chloe shouted back over her shoulder before

rolling her eyes towards Neve. 'Shit, I better go. See you tomorrow, you little slut.'

'Piss off,' Neve replied, again blushing. Chloe smiled, dropped her cigarette into the bushes below and closed her window, leaving Neve to walk the rest of her way home, the silence wrapping around her once more. Chloe's unease transferred to her, making her aware of that silence. It had taken the shine off her perfect evening.

At the top of the hill, Neve expected her house to be silent and still, so she was shocked to see the front door wide open, light from within spilling out onto the footpath. She thought she had been caught, and her heart thumped in her ears. They would ask her where she had been, and she would try to lie. But she knew she was a terrible liar. It wouldn't take long for them to know she was with Jamie, in his room, alone. Instead, the shape of her mum filled the doorway, a large suitcase beside her. She had her head low until she was only a few feet away from Neve. When she looked up, she jumped, unable to hide her shock.

'Neve?'

Neve looked from Mum – who clearly had no idea she was out late – towards the suitcase, the side bulging from being so full.

'Mum. What are you doing?'

'I…' She hesitated, looking around as if trying to pull an answer out of thin air. 'I could ask you the same thing. I thought you were in bed?'

'No.'

'Where have you been?'

'Out. Where are you going?' she said, gesturing to the suitcase.

'I umm – I'm going to see my sister.'

'Why?'

'Because. I just am.'

'When are you coming back?'

Neve's mum didn't answer but looked down at the suitcase, fiddling with the zips.

'Mum, you are coming back, right?'

She didn't respond.

'Mum?'

'I'm sorry, Neve. I can't stay here anymore, I just can't.'

'What do you mean, you can't stay here?'

'This place, it has nothing left for anyone anymore. I just can't…'

'But what about Dad?' Neve asked, tears beginning to fill her eyes. 'Mum, were you going to go without saying goodbye?'

Neve waited for her mum to say something of comfort, to offer an excuse, but she couldn't. She thought Neve was asleep upstairs. Neve knew she had no intention of saying goodbye to her daughter.

'Neve, come with me?'

'You were just gonna leave without saying goodbye?'

'I didn't want to wake you. Come with me?'

'Have you said goodbye to Dad?'

Again, she didn't reply. Her words caught somewhere in her stomach.

'I'll wake him. He needs to know.'

'No, Neve.'

'You just can't… Dad!' Neve called and was shocked when her mum came and placed a hand over her mouth, trapping her voice.

'Neve, please, don't,' she begged. 'Please. I need to go, if I talk to your dad, he'll stop me.'

'So, let him stop you.'

'I can't, Neve, I just can't.'

'Do you not love us anymore?' Neve cried, stepping back, waiting for the blow of learning she didn't.

'Of course I do, I love you both.'

'Then why…'

'This place is killing me, just like it's killing your dad. I'm sorry, I really am. Come with me. We can go to London, there's so much to do there.'

'No, Mum, my friends are here. I'm starting college in September.'

'You can start college there.'

'No, Mum, I can't,' she cried. A sob that felt different to anything she had experienced before. The second part of her childhood dying on one evening. 'Who will look after Dad?'

Neve's mum opened her mouth to say something but stopped herself. Instead, she offered an apologetic smile, grabbed the strap of her suitcase, half lifting, half dragging it down the path.

Neve stepped into the house and as her mum turned off the path to be hidden by bushes that lined the front garden, she shut the door. Quietly taking off her shoes, she moved towards the stairs and jumped when she saw her dad in the living-room armchair. He was facing the TV, although the TV wasn't on. She opened her mouth to say something – an apology for sneaking out of the house – but no words would come.

Going upstairs and into her bedroom, she opened her window and watched her mum battle her way downhill towards a taxi which was waiting at the bottom of the road. Neve watched until her mum loaded her case into the boot of it, climbed into the back seat and drove away. She didn't look back, she didn't reconsider, or have a moment where she doubted what she was doing. She just left. Neve's eye was drawn up towards the mine and a shiver ran down her spine as one of the headstock wheels was gently turning, inviting her. She realised that nobody gave a shit about her besides Jamie; nobody gave a shit about her friends either. They could do what they wanted, including going down into the forbidden mine because nobody gave a fuck about anything other than themselves. Sitting on her bed, she felt the need to cry. But now, no tears would come.

CHAPTER 44

2nd December 2019
Afternoon

I knew Michael was right when he told me that the Drifter was after us – only us – but still, I couldn't help but worry for my dad. So, we drove back home. When we arrived, the house was empty. It probably meant nothing, and yet I couldn't stop myself from feeling a dread wash over me. We left and spent the next hour driving around the village, trying to find him. I wanted to stay out all afternoon. Hastings saw us from outside the pub on two occasions as we passed, and I knew he would be suspicious, so we headed back to Michael's and waited. I tried ringing Dad's landline every twenty minutes or so and felt relieved when I managed to get hold of him just after 4 p.m.. The relief I felt was like nothing I had felt before. My dad was OK. He was home. When I asked where he had been, he said he'd been in the pub. It surprised me. He mentioned Holly, asked if I knew. I said I did and offered no more information. I asked about the memory test, he told me it went well. I could sense a lightness in his voice, which made me believe him. And if it went well, then things weren't as bad as we thought.

As the evening drew on, Michael and I sat on opposite sides

of the sofa in his living room. In spite of everything, I knew I couldn't outrun this thing anymore. Twenty-one years of careering away from that night, twenty-one years of outsmarting everyone had come back on us. I refused to accept that we just had to wait for him to arrive and pick us off. There was another alternative. One I'd refused to consider.

'Michael, what if we came clean?'

'What!?'

'What if we went to the police, told them everything, told them about that night, what happened, what we did.'

'Neve. We'll go to jail!'

'Yes, we probably would. We deserve to, don't we?'

He sighed. 'Yes, we do. How will it help if we came clean now?'

'We can lead them to Chloe. We can take ownership of what happened. And then, maybe the Drifter will stop? Or maybe, if we lead them to Chloe, we will find him.'

'I don't think he will stop, and I don't think the police will find him either. He's taken... he's hurt four of us.'

'I guess.'

'We can't go to the police – we've missed our window, we've missed it by twenty-one years. We have to stick to the plan. Keep them focused on the crimes now, find the Drifter now and then they will charge him for Chloe too, and we can get on with our lives.'

'I'm not sure how we can just get on...'

'We managed to before, didn't we? We have to do it again.'

'So, what do we do?'

'We wait.'

'What if he doesn't come here? What if he doesn't know about this place?'

'Everyone in the village knows about this place. He'll come. I can feel it. And then we make him take us to our friends.'

He nodded solemnly at me. It was important to be hopeful, I guess. So, we had to stick it out, we had to wait for the Drifter to come for us, like he had the others. We had to be ready, ambush the man who was ambushing us.

Hour after hour ticked by slowly as we holed up and prepared for the Drifter to come, and just after 8 o'clock my mobile rang, the number display showing me it was Thompson.

'Shit, what should I say?'

'Ignore it.'

'If I ignore it, he'll come looking for me.'

'Then say something about us being scared, gone into hiding. Don't know who to trust.'

I nodded and answered the phone.

'Neve, where are you? Are you OK?'

'Yes, I'm fine. I'm with Michael.'

'Thank God. I was worried. I went to your dad's and you weren't there.'

'Sorry, I should have said something. I got spooked. Is there any sign of Holly?'

'No, not yet. They've deployed more officers from Nottingham to help with the search. Hastings is pissed off.'

'Can you tell me anything?'

'There was no sign of a forced entry into Holly's, which means she let him in. It's someone she feels she can trust.'

I looked over to Michael, who looked back, nervously. And I wondered why. 'Hastings won't talk to me, but I suspect the same could be said for Dr McBride, possibly the others too. And although it's not confirmed, the police strongly believe the top does belong to the doctor.'

'And the village?'

'Busy. More reporters from major stations. More people in the streets being interviewed, sharing their speculations. Where are you both?'

'I'd rather not say.'

'Why?'

'Because…' I looked to Michael for reassurance, he bit his lower lip, his right eye showed the signs of a stress twitch. 'Because the Drifter is able to take people without leaving any traces of his presence. And you said yourself, the Drifter could be anyone. I don't know who to trust.'

'You trust Michael?'

Michael got up, walked away, lit a cigarette. 'I do, yes. He and I are in the same situation, aren't we?' I didn't know why I added a question mark.

'Yes, I guess you are. You're right to not trust me.'

'Am I?'

'I'd not trust me if I were you. Sit tight. I'll find him.' Thompson hung up and I kept the phone to my ear for a while longer than I should.

'What did he say?'

'Whoever took Holly, she let them in, it's someone she knows. Someone close.'

'That could be anyone,' he said too quickly. 'Holly was popular with her yoga friends, Mum friends, pub friends. It hardly gives us a list of people we could look at.'

'Thompson said Baz was likely to have done the same.'

'What? So, it's someone known to both?'

'Likely known to all of us.'

'Who the bloody hell can it be?' He was sweating.

'It's gotta be someone connected to Chloe also.'

'Her mum?' Michael asked.

'I don't think so. She's mental, but I don't think she can see past her own grief.'

'Then who?'

We speculated over more names in the village, ruling them out one after the other. As before, it seemed everyone could be the Drifter, and no one at all. It even seemed it could be one of us. When I said that, I tried to sound like I was being flippant. But I watched his response. He was worried… but then, so was I.

As the day wore on, a headache began to develop behind my eyes that increased with each passing minute, the sleep deprivation starting to take its toll. I knew if I didn't close my eyes soon, a migraine would begin to rage. I needed to doze, just for a moment, on the sofa. Michael insisted we went upstairs, as there was only one way in which he could come for us. So, we sat in his bedroom and waited. In any other context, being in his room would have been weird, especially given my horrendous pass at him. But he didn't seem to care. Michael made me a cup of tea, and we sat on the edge of the bed and smoked cigarettes. As the night wore on, I felt my limbs begin to feel heavy. It was only just 10 p.m. I put it down to exhaustion, at first.

'It's OK, Neve, lie down, close your eyes. I'll stay up.'

'Are you sure?' I asked, already beginning to shuffle up the bed so my head would hit the pillow. I didn't want to sleep, but I couldn't help it. It was almost like I didn't have a choice. My body was shutting down regardless.

'Neve, you look shattered.'

'It's come over me so quickly. Don't let me sleep more than a couple of hours.'

'I won't.'

Michael got off the bed and sat himself in a chair in the corner of the room. From where I lay, I watched him looking out of the window, squinting to see shapes in the low light outside. He appeared tense, scared. I was too, and yet, I couldn't keep my eyes open. My blinks were long and heavy, my vision struggled to focus on the solid mass of my friend only ten feet away. He looked towards me and offered a smile designed to reassure me, calm me, but it didn't.

'Michael?' I tried to say, but my words slurred.

'Shhhhh, see you in a few hours,' he said quietly. 'Get some sleep.'

CHAPTER 45

2nd December 2019
Night

Chloe visited my dreams. She probably did most nights, but I remembered it this time, which was rare. She was in a cage, begging me to find the key. As I stepped away to search, her shape changed to that of the Drifter. The cage door unlocked, and a mist, like dry ice, flooded from inside, consuming my feet, creeping up my body, numbing it until it seeped into my mouth and down my throat, freezing my screams. Then I woke with a gasp, and for a moment I couldn't focus on anything other than trying to catch my breath. As my eyes adjusted, I could see the air from my lungs turn to condensation, and sitting up quickly, the covers fell from my body, exposing me to the cold air inside the room. My head pounded, and my mouth was so dry that it hurt to swallow.

I searched for Michael; he was gone. His chair was empty, and beside it, the window was wide open, the curtains blowing in the cold wind. Outside, the night held strong, and I didn't know if I'd been out for five minutes or five hours. Rolling out of the bed I grabbed my phone to see the time – ten something, I couldn't make out the numbers without my glasses. I found them on the pillow, one of the arms bent. I put them on awkwardly, 10.47. I had been out for under an hour.

I walked to the window. I could see no movement, no light. The lane that led to this house was as deserted as when we arrived hours before. I quietly closed the window and locked it. I wanted to call out to Michael, but thought better of it. Moving to the bedroom door I looked out into the wide upstairs hallway. I wished a light was on, so I could see into the dark corners, but I didn't dare to flick the switch. Moving towards the stairs, I began to descend, cursing when the third from top squeezed angrily underfoot. As I reached the bottom step, I slowly looked around the banister in the direction of the kitchen, hoping I would see the light spilling under the crack in the door. It was dark. It felt like the house was empty. I couldn't help myself and called out quietly.

'Michael? Michael – where are you?'

There was no response. But I knew there wouldn't be one. Resting my hand on the closed kitchen door, I pushed my ear to the wood and listened. There was no sign of anyone on the other side, so I gently opened it. I could see a little better in the kitchen as a glow spilled from a small security light in the garden. As the door opened wider, I could see the back door. A shape blocked it: a long, dark coat.

I gasped and fell backwards, landing hard on the wooden floor. The shock didn't last long and as I fell, I assessed the coat was too high up to be worn by a person, and so it must have been hanging on the door. Scrabbling to my feet, I switched on the kitchen light. The fluorescent lamp hummed as it flickered to life. And in the light, I could see the coat I thought for moment was the Drifter. Gingerly, I moved towards it, half expecting something to happen. Placing my hands on it I pulled it down from the coat hanger. It was heavy, thick, and covered in what I could only assume was coal dust. He had been here, in this house.

My thoughts went to Michael. Dropping the coat, I moved quickly into the hallway, switching on the lights as I did so. I wanted every light in the house on, I wanted it to feel like day. I checked downstairs, then back upstairs; the last room I entered was the one I started in. Sitting on the bed I put my hand down under the folded cover. I felt something cold, tacky, and when I pulled my hand out, there was blood on it. Flipping the cover back over, I found a top. Holly's top.

'Michael,' I shouted. 'Michael, where are you?' I don't know why I called out. He wasn't there. The Drifter had come when I was asleep.

I had slept and Michael had been taken. And Holly's top... Holly's blood, it was on my hands. I could see something poking out from under the top. Carefully, I pulled it out and turned it over. The Drifter had left me a note.

If you ever want to see your friends again, you will come back to where this all began.

CHAPTER 46

July 1998
Ninety minutes before...

Wiping her wet hair out of her eyes, Neve dropped low and ducked under the barbed wire. It was harder than she thought it would be not to catch her skin, and she had to drop further, fully prone, to crawl through. The rain started only fifteen minutes before, but it was torrential, and the ground was already completely sodden. Confident she was far enough past the razor-sharp wire to not get caught, she stood and wiped her muddy hands on her jeans. She noticed the air on the other side of the fence felt different, charged.

She turned to look at the rest of the group who all stood on the other side of the crude fence, wet through, with excitement and fear in their eyes. Behind them, she could just make out the lights coming from the village. She couldn't help but feel a shiver run up and down her spine. She hoped that as she spoke, her own fear didn't show. It was because of her that they were all here.

'Come on, guys, it's easy. Just do what I did, you'll be fine.' She waited for someone to say something in protest. No one did. The silence acted as her cue, and she turned and walked away from the six friends who stood frozen, her steps taking her towards the entrance of the old mine.

'Wait, Neve—' called Holly from the other side of the fence. 'Are you sure we should be doing this?'

'If we don't go down and have a look now, we never will.'

'Yes, maybe we have gone too far?' chirped in Georgia.

'Georgia,' replied Neve, 'you agreed it would be fun.'

'I know, it's just…'

'Just what? Don't you want to know what's down there?'

'Yeah, I guess.'

'So, let's do it. Chloe? Are you coming?'

Chloe nodded, but didn't move. She was struggling to pluck up the courage to take the first step.

Neve turned and looked towards the mine. Her friends' fear was contagious and had crawled under her skin. She thought of Jamie's story – the trapped miner – and swore she could hear tapping. She stared at the entrance to the mine, its mouth agape, dark, cold. She felt herself hesitate, and jumped when Jamie, who had crawled under the fence, came and stood beside her, touching her arm.

'Fuck it, let's do it,' he said quietly.

Looking back, Neve saw Georgia helping Holly, whose top had snagged on the wire as she crawled under the fence.

'Shit. My mum is gonna kill me.'

'Don't worry, I can fix it with a bit of thread,' replied Georgia.

Then, Baz and Michael dropped to the floor, giggling, and as Neve turned a torch onto their faces to tell them to shut up, she could see their eyes were bright pink.

'Hey, you promised you weren't gonna get too stoned before doing this?' she hissed.

'Chill out, Neve,' said Michael. 'We've only had one spliff between us.'

'Yeah, Neve, we're good,' chirped Baz, still giggling.

Neve rolled her eyes but couldn't stop herself from smiling as the pair crawled, pretending to be commandos. Baz had even taken it upon himself to cover his face in mud, and when Chloe looked at him quizzically, he responded.

'Camouflage, innit.'

'Shut up, you two,' Jamie snapped. 'You're making enough noise for the whole village to hear.'

They ignored Jamie and continued to pretend they were in the army, rolling towards the shadow of the old colliery. Their silliness broke the tension, and everyone smiled. That's why everyone loved them. As Jamie ushered them towards the entrance and told them to sit, Neve looked to see Chloe wasn't smiling, and she hadn't crawled under the fence either. Her best friend pleaded with her with her eyes, *begged* her, and Neve knew Chloe really didn't want to do this. So as not to embarrass her, Neve walked back towards the fence.

'Come on, Chloe, it'll be fine.'

'Neve, is this all because of your mum leaving?'

Chloe's question took Neve aback; she hadn't expected her friend to understand, and yet, she did.

'I'm just trying to make memories,' she replied, deflecting the truth.

'I'm shitting myself; you know I don't like things like this.'

'Nothing is going to happen, Chloe.'

'Yeah, but people died down there.'

'People die in their houses. I bet someone has died in yours once.'

'Oh, great! Thanks, Neve, I'm not going to be able to sleep ever again now.'

'What I mean is, nothing happens in your house, does it?'

'There are no stories about my house.'

'Chloe, they're just ghost stories, they aren't real.'

'What if he is down there?'

'He won't be.'

'How do you know?'

'Trust me, OK.'

'Neve, what if he is a ghost? What if the Drifter is haunting us?'

'Chloe, there is no such thing as ghosts.'

Behind them, there was a smash as Baz threw a stone through one of the old windows. Jamie dashed across to stop him throwing another. Neve turned back to Chloe who was still on the other side.

'Chloe, nothing will happen here. I promise. Besides. Once we have had a few drinks, we'll be fine.'

'Are you scared too?'

'Yeah, just don't tell the others, especially Jamie.'

With a knowing smile, Chloe lowered herself to the ground and crawled under the fence, just like everyone else had. The wire snagged her shoe and pulled, catching her ankle and making it bleed.

'Ouch, shit.'

Neve helped Chloe to her feet and the pair joined the rest of the group who were hiding in the shadows of the colliery tower. Chloe sat down and looked at her leg. A thin line of blood could be seen running into her shoe.

'Are you OK?' Baz called, his stupid games momentarily halted.

'Yeah, I'm fine.'

'Right, guys, are we ready?' asked Neve. Georgia and Chloe nodded. Jamie offered her a wink. Michael grinned at her. 'Don't be a prick down there. All right? You too, Baz?'

'Yes, boss,' Baz replied as Michael gave a salute.

Neve shook her head and laughed before stepping into the mouth of the colliery. Although she didn't believe in ghosts, she couldn't help feeling the hairs on her arms stand on end. Slowly, she began to walk, her friends following closely behind as they entered the abandoned mine.

And as she disappeared into the darkness, she thought about the Drifter.

CHAPTER 47

2nd December 2019
Night

Running downstairs, I fumbled my shoes on, barely able to tie my laces as I couldn't stop my hands from shaking. Finding Michael's keys, I let myself into his car and fired up the engine. I knew exactly where to go. I knew where the Drifter wanted me. If I let myself be hopeful, if I let myself believe his note, then my childhood friends would be there, still alive. What choice did I have? If I ran, like I did all those years ago, he would hurt the people whose lives I'd already ruined. I had a chance to do something right for the first time in my life – I had to do it.

The drive seemed to take forever, the headstocks glaring at me as I struggled to keep control of the car. I kept my foot to the floor until I reached the edge of the village. Then I slowed to the speed limit, hoping I would pass through without being seen by anyone. As I came close to The Miners' Arms, I tried to keep myself low in my seat, but still able to watch the road, and look at the pub to try establishing the mood. It seemed to be busier than ever. Scores of people stood outside, smoking, drinking and talking despite it being so cold. There was nothing to suggest any one of them knew what was happening right now, and I didn't know if I was relieved or not. Close to the group of drinkers, I could make out the shape of who I thought was Thompson. He sat on his own, a pint beside him. Far enough away from the group to not be involved, but I suspected, close enough to listen. As I passed, I saw in my rear-view mirror him looking at my taillights before he took out a note pad and considered something. I was confident he didn't know it was me. I didn't know if that was reassuring or not. No, it was a good thing. The Drifter told me to come alone, and I would, and I hoped by doing so, he would let go of my friends.

Half a mile away from the pub, I turned into a cul-de-sac, pulled over and stopped the engine. I was close to the lane and didn't want to leave Michael's car anywhere suspicious. Then, climbing out, I quietly walked towards the lane, towards the hut. Towards the mine.

CHAPTER 48

2nd December 2019
Night

Each step I took on the dark and forgotten tarmac felt like another step towards my last. The trees that lined the lane watched with curiosity as I put one foot in front of the other. I wanted to look to my left and right, look at the trees that sat passively watching, as they had done for a hundred years. I knew I had to press on, walking a route I knew all too well.

I walked towards the ten-foot-tall fence lined with barbed wire that enclosed the entire site. Once, when I was young, I could duck under it without maiming myself, but not now. Luckily, I didn't need to. There was a gap, the metal fence cut away from the post and pulled out. Keeping low, I moved as fast as I could across a field towards the mine. I would plead with the Drifter, tell him the truth: it was all me. All of it. I would beg for him to let them go. They have suffered enough. Now it was my turn to pay the price for what happened.

The uneven ground was hard to move across, and on a few occasions my ankle turned as my foot slipped into an unseen crevice. I ploughed on, moving fast, drawing closer to the mine until its huge headstocks leant over me. I wanted to look up, see its ever-present eyes staring down, but knew if I did my head would spin. When I was only a matter of feet from the entrance, I lost my footing as the uneven ground became the tarmac car park and fell hard, my elbow jammed into my ribcage, temporarily robbing me of my ability to breath. Rolling onto my back, I fought to get air into my lungs. After a few moments, the ache in my chest began to ease and fumbling to my feet, I pressed on until my hands touched the walls of the colliery. Cold air seeped out from the shallow entrance. It wouldn't stay cold. I knew, the further down I went, the hotter it would get. Taking a final moment to steady myself, I stepped into the entrance, the dark cavernous mouth swallowing me whole.

CHAPTER 49

July 1998
Sixty minutes before...

None of the group had expected it to be so dark. They had of course heard from friends and family about the 'blackness' of the mine. But, despite the descriptions given, it hadn't prepared them for it. Neve led the group, slowly moving down, and it became clear very quickly that they would become lost if they were not very careful.

'Neve, don't you think we've explored enough?' Holly asked, shuffling along somewhere near the back of the group.

'You're not scared, are you?' Georgia replied.

'Yes! I'm freaking out, I can't even see my hand in front of my face.'

'Hang on.'

Baz pulled out his Zippo lighter, sparked it and a small flame began to flicker. It caught the angles of his face, and the rivets in the rock, creating sharp lines that made both he and the mine itself appear menacing. Jamie followed, igniting his disposable lighter. Michael pulled out a small wind-up torch that barely held its charge, so every few steps he had to turn the handle to generate more light. Its dull beam reflected off exposed metal rods that supported the tunnel and chains that still hung from the ceiling. Being able to see was somehow *more* unnerving.

'There, is that better, Holly?' Neve asked.

'Not really, no,' she replied honestly.

Neve pressed on, Jamie by her side, holding her hand in the darkness. They turned left, and then right, each step taking further down.

'Neve, do you have any idea where we're heading?'

'Dad often speaks of this place. I think I know where we are.'

'We're gonna get lost unless we leave a trail,' said Baz.

The group agreed and knew they needed to act like Hansel and Gretel and leave a trail of breadcrumbs to guide them back. But they didn't have bread, so at each junction, each turn in the narrow passages, a member of the group removed an item of soaking wet, superfluous clothing. Michael's hat, Neve's hoody, Jamie even left his shoes, claiming he wanted to be more connected to the moment. With the intermittent illumination from the lighters and wind-up torch, and the trail to guide them back, the group began to relax. Michael took it upon himself to try and scare the others by running ahead and jumping out of dark corners, making the group laugh when Baz screamed like he was a five-year-old girl.

'Stop it, you bastard!'

'Mate, you crack me up.'

'Fuck off!'

They all began to shout down the tunnels, their voices bouncing back in perfect echoes. Everyone but Jamie, who walked quietly, barefoot, absorbing the life he felt he should have had.

Before long, they came across a turning that veered to the right, tracks laid in the rock, which coal would have been shunted along. An upturned coal cart lay close by, now all rusted through.

'The water is flowing, that's good,' said Jamie, looking at the small channel of water running close to where they walked.

'What?'

'My granddad used to tell me, flowing water was OK; water that was stagnant wasn't.'

They moved slowly, the ground underfoot slippery. Georgia complained that her new trainers were getting ruined. But no one else passed comment, they were too busy concentrating on the next step. Above them, chains hung lifelessly every few metres. Chloe half expected one to begin to swing at any moment.

'I think he died down there.' Jamie pointed to his left, where a dark cavern extended away. Somewhere down there lay the corpse of a buried miner. But his was not the only story that came from these depths. Tales of rail carts moving on their own and whispers in people's ears. Men's screams. As they turned down it, Neve felt the air move around her, sweeping through her hair, and her cocksure attitude was swept away with it.

Michael stopped messing around and walked towards the tracks. 'Right, let's do this,' he said, his tone serious, which was more nerve-wracking than when he was trying to scare the others.

Nodding, Baz took off his rucksack and unzipped it, pulling out a solid wooden board.

'What is that?' Holly asked.

'What do you think it is?' Michael replied.

'No. No, you didn't say anything about a ouija board. No, I want to go – I want to go now!'

'Come on, Holly, you don't actually believe in this stuff?' Neve asked quietly, trying to reassure her, but she wasn't kidding anyone; the board made her feel afraid also, despite her suggesting they brought one down.

'All I know is there are things we don't know. I don't wanna start pissing around with it.'

'Fine. Go if you want.'

'Are you coming?'

'No way! I'm staying here,' Neve said, trying to sound sure of herself.

'Is *anyone* coming?' Holly asked, her voice bouncing off the cavern walls, and once it faded, it was greeted with the return of silence.

'We all wanna stay,' Baz said. 'Come on, Holly. Nothing will happen. It'll be fun.'

Reluctantly, Holly nodded and walked into the narrow shaft to join the others who had placed themselves around the ouija board, a glass from Baz's kitchen upside down on the top. One at a time, they placed a finger on the glass.

'So, what do we do?' he asked.

'I guess we ask questions?'

'OK, who's gonna go first?'

The group looked at one another, waiting for someone to speak. Rolling his eyes, Jamie began.

'If there is anyone down here, let us know. Make the glass move. Make a noise. Something.'

They all held their breaths, staring at the top of the glass, waiting for something to happen. After a few moments Jamie looked up, and the group caught his eye. He looked like he heard something.

'If there is anyone here, move the glass, spell out your name. Bang something,' he called again. And again, they waited in silence.

'I don't think…' Michael began his sentence before being cut off by a distant noise.

'Did you hear that?'

'What the fuck was that?' Georgia asked.

'I'm freaking out,' Holly said, letting go of the glass.

'Guys, shut up,' Jamie interrupted. 'If that was you, can you do it again, so, we can hear it clearer.'

Another tap came from somewhere down the mine.

'Fuck!' Baz said, covering his mouth.

'Jamie, say something else,' Michael said excitedly.

'Can you do it again? This time, tap twice.'

A pause, and then, just as the group began to breathe once more, two taps quietly returned, the sound of hammer on rock, sending the group into a frenzy. Michael and Georgia were grinning, afraid, but enjoying the fear. Neve found herself clutching onto Jamie, and Chloe held onto her. Holly began to cry, and Baz tried to comfort her.

'Could you do it again?' Jamie called out, stepping away from Neve and Chloe who held each other tighter. 'Make a clearer noise. So, we know for sure you're definitely listen…'

The bangs picked up again, more than they could count. Louder than a tap. Much louder. It sounded like a metal pipe hitting something else metal. Like the ghost was hitting the steel arteries that reinforced the tunnels with a hammer. It came from in front of them, a place deeper into the mine, further into the bowels of hell. Then, just as the group began to panic, it stopped.

'Michael, wind up the torch,' Jamie said quietly, his breathing jagged and shallow. Nodding, Michael did as Jamie asked and once it had a bit of power, he flicked it on in the direction of the sound.

'What the fuck…'

Down the mine, just on the edge of what they could see, something stood in the middle of the passage. 'What is that?'

'Some sort of machine?' Georgia queried; the smile wiped from her face.

Michael advanced, and after three steps the torch went out.

'Shit,' he said, quickly winding it again. When he held it up, the thing was moving towards them. The Drifter.

The group descended into hysteria, screaming, crying, running. Baz dropped his lighter and Michael's torch failed again as the group tried to run the way they came, back to the entrance of the mine.

CHAPTER 50

2nd December 2019
Night

Only a few steps into the mine was all it took to rob me of my ability to see. But I couldn't stop. I walked with my arms outstretched, like something out of a zombie movie, trying to feel my way until I found the first corner that swept the tunnel towards the left. Keeping one hand on the wall to not lose my way, the texture of it was abrasive and damp. I tentatively moved further into the dark, the ground beneath my feet sloping as I descended. My other hand was still in front, feeling thin air – hoping not to grab anything, or anyone. And the smell was the one that had permeated my entire adult life in that place between being asleep and awake. Coal air.

My hand brushed something unfamiliar, and I let out a yelp. It was just a chain hanging from the ceiling. I took a deep breath, the air already feeling thick. Each step away from the world – away from its open spaces and phone reception – compounded my anxiety, which continued to build, a sea that was bracing for an approaching storm. I tried to keep myself calm, but panic set in, the walls beginning to close in around me. The ceiling looked like it might crack at any moment.

I stopped, closed my eyes. I told myself to slow down. I thought of my dad, of one night in particular when I was young and woke up as my night light flickered. The filament inside fighting to survive and failing, leaving me in total darkness for the first time I could recall. It was so dark I couldn't see, and as I began to cry, Dad came in and calmed me. I thought I had gone blind. He held me in his arms, his smell, the one I loved that was part sweat, part coal dust, calmed me, and when my sobs became jagged little sniffles, he told me our eyes were actually those of superheroes and when I didn't understand, he told me to close them, count to thirty and then open them again, and when I did, I could see the objects in my bedroom.

'It's a little trick we all know down the mine,' he said. 'We all just pause, close our eyes and let our vision find us.'

Closing my eyes helped, for when I opened them, I could just about make out the wall I was touching, and the wall on the other side of the tunnel. I could see the chains hanging limp from the ceiling and the slight tonal change where the metal structures ran in the rock. It was still too dark to see if a person stood in the dark corners, pressed into the crevices, but I could just about see enough of the grainy dark world to know if I was about to trip or fall over something. Still, it didn't offer much comfort. The dread in my gut hadn't lifted.

I had to continue further into the belly of the monster that had watched my every move since coming back. The more I walked, the warmer it began to feel, the earth itself radiating heat. I unfastened and then took off my coat and decided to leave it at the next corner I approached before turning left. At the next turn I placed my scarf, then my jumper at the next. Then I approached a fork in the tunnel, one I remembered vividly:

turning left would take me further down into the heat and dust, closer to where we found Chloe. And right was another long tunnel that gradually descended. It was in that tunnel that we'd set up our ouija board and tried to scare one another, before the Drifter started banging and shouting, terrifying us all.

If I had – if any of us had – remembered to follow our trail that night, we would have all made it out together. But we didn't. We were young, petrified, and in our world, we hadn't heard of consequences, until that moment.

Walking past the tunnel where our foolish game began, my shoes wet from the running water, I heard something, a voice, a whimper. I held my breath, waiting to hear it again. Nothing. Despite being hot, a shudder ran up my spine, and I had to remind myself that I didn't believe in ghosts.

I pushed the whimper I heard out of my head and continued. I was sure I knew the way – and would then know the way out – but with each step, my confidence wavered, and with no more items of clothing to leave, I had to rely on my memory of back then, which was tainted, damaged. And then, ahead of me, I saw it, a void where the narrow tunnel became a larger room, the ceiling of it higher than I could touch. The space as wide as a church, and in the middle of it, a hole eight feet wide that descended around twenty more.

I was where the Drifter wanted me; I was back in the place it all began.

And I was alone.

Quietly, I made my way towards the middle of the cavernous room, wondering if I had misinterpreted the note. No, I was here, the place where it all began. That night when Chloe fell, the night the blame fell upon *him*. It had to be. I hoped that

I would find Holly and the others, and I would help them get out before facing the Drifter. It was just me in a dark, vast space with the remains of my best friend in a hole directly in front of me.

I wanted to look down, I wanted to see. But I couldn't. Even now, even after all this time, I was still unable to face what had happened that night, and Michael was right. Compared to the others, I had it easy, because I didn't look back then.

I thought again about the noise I heard when I was walking past the tunnel where we set up the ouija board. Maybe I did actually hear a whimper; Holly perhaps, or Georgia. Turning, I began to make my way back towards it, one single step, and then I was blinded by a torch which shone directly into my face. A deep voice spoke from behind it.

'It's been a long time, Neve.'

CHAPTER 51

2nd December 2019
Night

I couldn't see who had spoken, my eyes burning from the light in my face. But that voice, I knew it, though I couldn't quite place it.

'Take out your phone and throw it towards me,' he commanded and, doing as I was told, I took my mobile from my back pocket and threw it on the ground, near his feet.

'It doesn't work down here,' I said as a way of telling him I couldn't call the police.

'On your knees,' he instructed and again I did as I was told. Awkwardly, I lowered myself to the ground, my hands up, shielding my eyes from the light, trying to see the man behind it.

'You haven't changed in all these years,' he said, the torch dancing a little as he spoke, revealing more of his frame behind. But the voice, I knew who he was, I was sure of it.

'I can see you really trying to work this out, Buttercup. You were never much good at problem-solving,' he said, enjoying himself.

That name, *Buttercup*. I had been called it before, a very long time ago, and I knew who he was. Seeing my shock, my confusion, he lowered the torch and waited for my eyes to recover and for me to be able to see his face and confirm it was him.

'Hello, Neve,' he said, waiting for me to reply. I couldn't, because I didn't understand why the man standing in front of me wearing a long, dark coat, the man who I thought was the Drifter, was in fact the person I had come back to find.

'Jamie?' I said, trying to get to my feet.

'Just stay on the floor, Neve,' he snapped, frightening me into doing as I was told. I felt my head swim. Jamie was the Drifter? It didn't make sense. People were looking for him, the whole village, someone would have seen him, and yet, as my eyes adjusted further, I could clearly see that the man in the Drifter's coat was my first love.

'I – I don't understand.'

'I knew you wouldn't.'

'Why am I here?'

'Now, come on, Neve, surely even you can work that out.'

'Where are the others?' I asked, to which he laughed. 'Jamie, where are the others?'

'Oh, Buttercup, you are hopeless.'

There was something in the way he spoke that told me he wasn't the same boy I'd fallen in love with all those years ago; there was something different, something dangerous, and in that moment, I knew the others were likely dead, and I would be next. It was him all along. He had faked being hurt; he had faked the Drifter back into existence. And he had come for the rest of us, one by one. I needed to buy time. No one was coming to help, I was alone, I didn't tell anyone I was coming. I had stepped into his trap. I had made it easy for him.

'Jamie, why are you doing this?'

'Have you said hello to Chloe yet?' he laughed. 'Of course you haven't, because you're still a coward. You can pretend all you want, Neve, but she is there, behind you, in the bottom of that hole. She is still in the place we found her. The place where you couldn't look and pleaded with me to help. Do you remember? You begged me to go down, take off her top, so we could plant it elsewhere. It was Michael's idea, but you begged *me* to do it.'

'You didn't have to!'

'Of course I did! You were hysterical, you were my girlfriend, and I wanted to make you happy, I wanted to help make it all go away for you. And I did, didn't I?'

'Jamie...'

'But it didn't go away for me. Every day since, I remember removing her top from her dead body, her glazed eyes staring at me. I remember her blood on my hands. Blood that should have been on yours.'

'I didn't kill Chloe; it was an accident.'

'But you made sure we didn't go to the police and tell them what happened. You were the one that said it would ruin us all.'

'I was scared.'

'So was I. I wanted to go to the police. You stopped me. You did this to me.'

Jamie began to cry, and I had to do something or else I knew he would kill me. The room was wide, and although it was pitch black either side of the small pool of light created by his torch, I knew the exit was to my right. If I acted quickly, I could bolt for it and run back to the real world and get help, and then, once I found Thompson or Hastings or the new DCI, I would come clean about it all. I would go back to 1998, say word for word what happened and what I did. Because Jamie was right,

Chloe was behind me, and it was time she was laid to rest. There would no longer be an empty grave.

Taking a breath, I sprang up and I ran. Jamie didn't have time to react, his sobs were uninterrupted, his torch stayed low. As I skimmed past him, I knew I could get away, lose him in the tunnels until I found my way out. Jamie was three paces behind and still hadn't reacted when another torch blinded me coming from where I was trying to exit. I raised my hands to protect my eyes, and in doing so lost my footing and stumbled, coming to a halt, a rabbit in headlights.

Spinning around I saw Jamie, his torch low, still crying. Behind him, another torch shone towards me – the person advancing until they reached Jamie. To my right another torch shone, another to my left. Then a final torch lit. I was completely surrounded. I called out asking who it was, but no one replied. I heard only Jamie's sobs, the sound bouncing off the mine walls coming back to me like the ground itself was weeping, and then the quiet whispers of a soft voice trying to comfort him.

'It's OK, Jay, everything is going to be OK, it's over.'

'Who is that? What's going on?' I asked, desperately trying not to cry. Jamie's torch was raised to point at me, and I turned away from it, back towards the entrance, hoping there was a gap, a space for me to run to. Who I saw stunned me. Caught in the light from Jamie's torch opposite was someone standing in a long, dark coat like the one Jamie was in.

I looked to my right, behind the torch that was pointed at me, and could make out the shape of another person, another coat, another Drifter. I couldn't see their faces, but I knew at that moment who they were.

CHAPTER 52

July 1998
Thirty minutes before...

Neve had run so hard from the mine that by the time she reached the hut, she was sure she would throw up. She was the first one back, the first one to crawl through the hatch. Despite it only being an hour since she'd been in that space with all of her friends, drinking and laughing and daring each other on, it felt a lot longer. Still reeling from what happened, all she could hope was that everyone was all right. She took a moment to try to calm her breathing, rationalise her mind. Her body was soaked and cold, her muscles aching. She couldn't get over how dark it was down there. The field she ran across had been permanently lit, and that light shrouded the whole village, giving a sense that the place didn't really have a night, just two variations of day. One artificial, one real. But the lights had been out for nearly a year, and the night was catching up on lost time. On her run, she couldn't see the ground beneath her feet, and on several occasions, she fell in the wet mud.

As the minutes ticked by, Neve began to fear the worst. It was supposed to be a bit of fun, a final hurrah before they all went in their different directions. For a moment she feared something terrible had happened. The scream that came from Chloe's mouth when she saw him down there was enough to make anyone's blood run cold. But she pushed it back; Chloe was just panicking, like they all were. Her scream would be something they would laugh at in time to come.

As if on cue, Neve heard the sound of a body slamming into the wall beside their entrance, and then she saw the shape of Baz slip through the gap. As he rose to his knees, Neve could see blood on the side of his head.

'Shit, Baz, are you OK?'

'Yeah, I'm fine.'

'What happened?"

'I fell over an old wheelbarrow or something. It's so bloody dark down there I couldn't see.'

'Me neither.'

'Are you hurt?'

'No, a bit shaken up, but fine.'

'Is no one else back yet?'

'Not yet, just you and me.'

'I'm sure everyone is OK,' he said quietly, and Neve could tell it was a question more than a statement. The panic began to rise again, and it felt like if she didn't talk it would take over.

'I can't believe he was down there.'

'Me neither. Fucking weirdo.'

'You think he'll call the police?'

'And say what, he was trespassing like us? No, he was just as wrong to be there.'

'Do you think…'

Before Neve could finish her sentence, Georgia crawled through the hatch and joined them, her mascara streaked down her face from sobbing. She was trying to say something, each word snagging on a breath she couldn't draw. Reaching over, Baz took her firmly in his grasp and told her to take deep, measured breaths. Neve fell silent as she witnessed a side to Baz she'd not seen before. The class clown had a tenderness, a kindness. As Baz calmed Georgia, bringing her back from the brink of a panic attack, Neve crept to the hole in the wall. She knew she wouldn't be able to see anyone running towards her, but she looked anyway, desperate for the rest of them to arrive. After a few minutes – or an hour, she wasn't sure – Jamie and Michael crawled into the hut. Michael was pale and quiet. As soon as he cleared the entrance he slumped up against a wall, his head in his hands. Neve barely gave him a glance, her attention focused solely on Jamie. He was covered in dirt, out of breath, but otherwise unharmed.

'You OK, Neve?' he asked calmly.

'Yes, are you?'

'Yes,' Jamie said as he gave Neve a kiss on the lips. 'Baz, Georgia, are you all right?'

Baz said he was fine, and Georgia nodded, calmer but still unable to form words.

'Where are Chloe and Holly?' he asked, looking around at their group of five that should have been seven.

'We don't know,' Baz said, his attention still on Georgia.

'Shit. We have to go back,' Jamie said.

'I don't want to go back down there,' Georgia said, her words still catching on shallow breaths.

'You can stay here, we don't all need to go.'

'I can't either,' said Michael, unable to lift his head from his hands, prompting Baz to walk over and rub his shoulder, reassuring his friend it was all right to not want to go either. 'Jamie, are you coming?'

'Yes.'

'Neve.'

'Yes.'

'Neve, no.'

'Jamie, yes.'

'Neve, I don't want you to. I don't want anything to happen to you.'

'Jamie, I'm going. Chloe might be stuck, Holly too. I want to help.'

'Baz, please, talk sense to her.'

'Jamie, if she wants to go, she wants to go.'

'But…'

'I get you want to protect me,' interrupted Neve. 'It's sweet, but I am capable, and I don't need your protection.'

'She's right, mate. Come on, we're wasting time.'

Neve held Jamie's eye, not prepared to blink first. He nodded, defeated, and moved towards the hole to crawl back out into the field. She followed and Baz brought up the rear. Georgia and Michael exchanged looks; they didn't want to go back. But they knew they had to, so they joined their friends. Quietly, they made their way towards the barbed wire fence, hoping at any moment both Chloe and Holly would dash towards them. With each step, Neve panicked, praying that she wouldn't have to go back down the mine again.

CHAPTER 53

2nd December 2019
Night

'Neve, there's no point trying to run.' Another familiar voice came out of the darkness, deep and calming. Just like he would be if he was talking to a patient of his in the village practice. 'There is nowhere to go.'

'I don't understand. Why are you doing this?'

'Because we have to,' Baz said calmly.

'You don't, you don't have to do anything.'

'We've waited a long time for this,' another voice called out. One that was as harsh and cold as when I first saw her in the village.

'Neve, over to the hole,' a third ordered.

'Please,' I begged.

'Neve, don't make this any more difficult than it already is.'

I didn't move, I couldn't. Fear had frozen me to the spot and sensing it, one of them grabbed my arm. I didn't want to believe it was him, but as soon as he held me – as soon as he was close enough for me to see into Michael's eyes – I had no choice but to accept I had been tricked.

Michael led me towards the hole, his torch pointing towards

the opening, and forced me to look. Below was just dirt and rocks. Nothing to suggest there was a person buried underneath. I closed my eyes because I still couldn't look.

'Open your eyes, Neve,' Georgia said, her harsh tone bouncing around and into my ear.

'I can't,' I managed to say between sobs. Georgia moved quickly over to me, grabbed my face and forced my eyes open, urging me to look down.

'That's enough,' another voice called out; one I didn't want to believe I'd heard. She was the one person who had been the kindest to me since coming back, she was the one person who had invited me into her home to play with her children. Obeying her instruction, Michael and Georgia let go and I fell to the floor.

'Holly, no,' I begged. 'Please, no. Please. You have to stop.'

'Do you know how long we have waited for this, Neve?' she began, ignoring my plea. 'Do you know how much work it's taken to get you here, to keep you here?'

'Please,' I said again.

'We tried once before, back in 2008. We tried to get you back to help find Jamie. We just needed you back so we could tell you how fucked up we all are, because of you. We wanted you to help us find a way to be OK, like you were. But, despite our best efforts, you were too busy to care, too important for those of us stuck in the village.'

I wracked my brain but couldn't place when they had asked.

'Look at her, she doesn't have a clue what you're talking about,' Georgia barked. 'Let's just get on with this and go.'

'No, I want her to understand,' Holly said.

'Me too,' Baz added. Jamie had stopped crying and I could just make him out in the dim light nodding, as was Michael.

'Fine,' Georgia said, defeated.

'You faked Jamie going missing to get me back?'

'Finally, she gets it.'

'Georgia, enough,' Holly said. 'Yes, we did.'

'And when you said he had a history of going missing, you were lying?'

'No, I have disappeared a few times,' Jamie said quietly. 'I always came down here, to find Chloe. I couldn't ever remember the way.'

'The last time we found him, he'd not eaten in three days.'

'I just wanted to find her, to say I was sorry,' he said, before breaking into fresh sobs on Holly's shoulder.

'Jamie...' I said, my voice trailing off. I couldn't find the words to beg him for forgiveness. If I hadn't insisted we came down here to celebrate the end of the summer, our last summer as kids, maybe, he would have been all right. Maybe he would have married and settled and been happy, like he wanted to be.

'It's not just me,' Jamie said. 'We've all struggled.'

'So have I, I promise, I have these dreams...'

'Dreams! You wanna talk about dreams, Neve? We all had dreams, to get away from this place, to have a happy life. You took all that from us.'

'Then we see you on Facebook, your new business and your new London life and we think: how is it fair that we are here, we can never leave, and she gets to do what she wants?' Georgia said, her voice tight.

'The final nail was you announcing your engagement. Not only did you manage to escape this place, but you managed to find someone to love,' Baz said, his voice less commanding, less in control of his emotions.

'Baz, I didn't make you do anything.'

'We were so scared, we looked to you and you told us it would be OK. You said you had a plan. And we would all be OK.'

'I was just a kid!' I said again, my voice bouncing off the walls, coming back to me sounding less honest.

'You still don't get it, do you?' Michael said. 'You still don't see. None of us got away with it. No one.'

'Georgia's dad knew something was wrong, and, after he was released, she confided in him.'

'And he will never let me leave his house, not until the day he dies. I've tried to leave, but each time he threatened to talk to the police. It ruined his life. So, he keeps mine.'

'Baz… was in love with Chloe.'

'I still am,' he said quietly.

'I've gone the other way,' Michael said. 'I can't be intimate with anyone. Because when I try to let myself be open to the idea – when I try let the walls down – I see her, and I remember how you made me bury her body down here,' Michael said, pointing to the dark hole near my feet.

'And I… well, I have to watch my husband battle every day. The man who fathered my children, who struggles to let go of that night, and what you made him do, because he thought he loved you.'

I looked at Jamie, and then at Holly. It made sense why everyone comforted her when we were looking for Jamie. How his mother embraced her. She was Jamie's wife. And her little one, I now saw the resemblance. The same dark hair, the same pale complexion.

'You ruined us all, Neve. Tonight has been a long time coming.'

A new voice spoke from the darkness behind my childhood friends. Raspy, tired. When she stepped closer, I gasped. It was Brenda. I didn't understand, this was our secret, our mistake, how did she know? How long has she known?

'I don't understand.'

'They told me.'

'When?'

'Six months ago.'

'Brenda, I...'

'For twenty years I didn't know what happened to my girl. Twenty years of visiting a gravestone that had an empty coffin underneath. And I always knew you had something to do with it. I did. When Jamie told me, I knew we had to get you back.'

'This was your idea?' I asked, knowing the answer.

'I wanted to know everything, everything about that night and what happened to my daughter. I wanted to know her last words, if it was quick. I wanted to know where she was. So, they brought me here. Until then, I didn't care where you had gone. You were the girl who led my daughter astray. People here think I hated her, but they were wrong. I loved my girl. I wanted her to be safe. I wanted her to be away from you. They told me about their attempt to get you back, to have it out with you. To beg you to help them let go, just like you had. I gave them a better idea.'

'You can't do anything, the police—'

'Have no idea where you are. And no one besides your dad will be looking for you. Even if he knows something and goes to the police, as of last week, everyone thinks he has dementia.'

I was stunned. Did Brenda mean my dad was not losing himself? I wanted to believe it but couldn't. They were trying to derail me.

'I don't believe you. He has been forgetting things, misplacing things. He's been leaving ovens on...'

'Neve!' Georgia continued, enjoying herself. 'Who had a set of keys? Who could go in and out of his house whenever they wanted?'

'I – I don't...'

'His cleaner,' she smiled as she jangled a set of keys, her torch light bouncing off them. 'We've been in and out of his house for weeks. Even while you slept.'

'No...'

'And I'm his doctor, Neve.'

'You made it up? What about the oath you took...'

'No, no...' Baz protested, his hands up. 'No, I couldn't do that. I want to help people, and I have helped your dad, I will continue to help your dad, he hasn't done anything wrong. Your dad really does have memory issues. He's had them for months. But...'

'But I saw your dad in with Barry,' Brenda continued, 'and I pushed our dear doctor to tell me what was wrong, so I could use it against you. It was perfect. I knew if we could get you back, we could *keep* you back.' She smiled.

Hearing Baz confirm what Georgia was saying made my head spin once more, and leaning over, I was sick on the hard floor beside me.

'Why...' I managed to say, between heaving.

'We assumed – even as heartless as you are – you'd not leave your poor, unwell dad to fend for himself.'

'The hardest part though,' said Brenda, 'was getting you back here in the first place. We had to be so patient, Neve. We watched, looked closer at your life. I've even been to your café a few times.'

'What?'

'Then we found out Oliver had left you,' Michael continued.

Hearing his name snapped me from the foggy sea I was trying to swim through. It was impossible to process what they were saying, about me, about my dad and being back here. Now they spoke of Oliver. Of someone who none of them knew. I looked at Michael, confused.

'I met your lovely fiancé three months ago. I wanted to buy a house and went to his property agency. Nice guy.'

'No, I don't believe you.'

'We ended up becoming quite good chums really. We spoke of family life. He spoke of you often, and then, one day, he said you'd split.'

'And then we knew… we knew if we pushed you, you'd come home,' Georgia said.

'Neve, we were there when you got drunk and the shop was broken into. That was us. We obviously had no idea the safe was open. We only wanted to trash the place, leave you feeling vulnerable enough to want to help when Holly messaged.'

I thought about the shadow I had seen in London outside the shop. It was one of them. I thought Holly and I connecting when we did was a coincidence. But none of this was coincidence; I saw that now.

'Yes, Neve. We planned this for a very long time,' Brenda said triumphantly, as if reading my mind.

'What are you going to do to me?'

'Oh, fucking hell, Neve, are you that stupid? We're going to leave you down here with my daughter.'

'You can't do this. They will find you.'

'Yes, we intend them to. Once you're dead, we will escape

from down here. We will lead them to where "he" kept us, another part of this godforsaken mine. They will find you, and they will find Chloe, and we will lay her to rest properly. And the Drifter would have vanished again. This place loves a mystery. We'll replace one for another. And my daughter will finally get her rest.'

'The media will love us for a while, but they will quickly move on to bigger stories in other places. And we will get on with our lives. One secret swapped for another.'

'But who was…'

'The Drifter? We don't know. Some poor soul who looked after the mine probably.'

'The man I've been seeing… it was you…'

'Bingo. That night at your café in London, that was me,' Michael said.

'And outside your dad's house. That one was me,' Jamie confessed.

'I was there when you went out with Holly, searching the woods,' Georgia said, smiling menacingly.

'Down the lane. Me again,' Michael said.

'Where have you all been hiding?'

'I took them in,' Brenda said.

I thought about the last time I saw her at her window, when I knew I'd seen a person behind her. And on my first night back, after Brenda and I spoke, someone was watching from her bedroom window. It wasn't my imagination; it wasn't a ghost; it was them.

'Now, Neve, time to get in the hole.'

'No, please. Please don't, I beg you. I'm sorry, I'll go to the police, I'll go to the police right now.'

'And condemn us all to jail. No, Neve.'

'I'll tell them it was all me. I did it all. I promise.'

'It's too late for that. The hole.'

Stepping forward Georgia and Brenda grabbed me under my arms and dragged me the few feet towards the edge. I tried to fight them off. I tried to kick out and scream and bite, but they were too strong, too determined. I thought as they got close, someone would say something. I thought they might pause to tell me another fact about how they manipulated and controlled me. But they didn't, and I was tossed into the darkness.

CHAPTER 54

July 1998
The moment...

The group found Holly as they approached the mouth of the mine. She was covered in black soot from the old coal remains that hung in the air and stuck to the walls. She shook like a small dog.

'Holly, where's Chloe?' Neve asked.

'I – I...' was all Holly could reply.

'Holly, have you seen her?'

Again, Holly was unresponsive until Neve slapped her, snapping her back into the situation. 'Holly, have you seen Chloe?'

'She's still down there. I tried to get her to follow me, but she said I was disorientated, going the wrong way. I tried to get her to follow me, but she wouldn't. She's down there still.'

Baz charged past the group, shouting Chloe's name as he descended into the darkness, Michael close behind, followed by the others who were reluctant to go back. As they traversed the main line wall, calling Chloe's name, Neve felt the darkness was somehow blacker than before. Eventually they came across the tracks where they had seen the Drifter. They hoped he wasn't still down there, waiting for them.

'Which way did she go?' Baz asked, desperation in his voice.

'I told her to follow me up the way we've just come. She didn't – she went that way,' she replied between sobs, pointing in the opposite direction. Baz didn't hesitate and ran on, his zippo lighter's flame barely holding out against the wind he generated running. The others followed as close as they could, stumbling blind in the dark, until they reached a huge cavern that stretched fifty feet away from them, and the same upwards. Baz had stopped and was crouched, looking at the floor.

'What is it?' Michael asked.

'Footprints,' he said quietly, before calling her name.

'Did she have a torch?'

'No,' Holly replied.

'She's blind down here,' he said standing and slowly moving forward, following her footprints in the dirt. Neve didn't know why, but she couldn't follow. Something came over her, something terrible, freezing her to the spot. The others felt it too, and watched Baz take one step in front of the other until he stopped.

'There is something here,' he called back. 'Michael, I need your torch.'

Michael wound his torch and joined Baz's side. Once it had enough charge, he pointed it towards the thing he could also now see. And when the light hit it, it vanished, sucked into a dark hole in the ground. Michael stepped forwards, and just before the light faded out, he could make out the shape of Chloe twenty feet below. Her head split wide open.

Falling backwards he let out a cry and Baz – who had not

seen – shouted to tell him what he could see. Michael couldn't respond. Grabbing the torch Baz wound it up, flicked it on and pointed it down. The beam shook in his hands as the others joined his side to see what had caused Michael to cry.

Everyone but Neve.

CHAPTER 55

2nd December 2019
Night

Falling into the pit seemed to last forever. I knew the ground was approaching as I hurtled towards it, but I couldn't see it until the moment of impact. I heard my ankle snap, and I screamed out in pain. It robbed me of my ability to think, the shock of the injury setting in quickly. Above me, the lights began to fade and over my moaning I heard their footsteps ebb away until they vanished, along with the light they carried. There were no final words spoken. No gasps or cheers – they just left. And for a moment, I did nothing.

Then, I heard my dad's voice in my head. 'Close your eyes, let the light come to you. And you'll see properly.' I did as he said. With my eyes closed, I focused on my breathing. Focused on drawing in enough to exhale. Calming myself with each breath until the pain was under my control, then, opening my eyes, I could make out the walls. I dragged myself towards one and sat against it. I gently placed my hand on my shin. The pain in my whole lower leg was white hot, and I couldn't place the epicentre, so I explored further towards my foot. Before I could reach the ankle joint, my fingers clipped something sharp and I screamed out in pain again. One of my bones had come through the skin. Carefully, I moved over the bone to feel below. My hand came away tacky, covered in blood. I couldn't see how much there was, but it felt like it wasn't stopping. Being a miner's child, I knew I needed to act. There were stories all the time of men being injured down here, miles away from help. I needed to stem the bleeding, and now wished I hadn't dumped my scarf as a signpost to get out. Taking off my top, I wrapped it behind my knee as tightly as I could, hoping it would pinch the artery there and slow the flow. It was painful work and took me several minutes to do. Eventually, I think I secured it.

I told myself to breathe, the heat and dust making it harder to do.

I dragged myself up using the wall behind me and my one working leg. The top of the hole was the same height as a first-floor window – too high up for me to reach – so I tried to climb. I found small cracks in the wall, and using my fingertips I pulled, managing to lift myself from the floor. Reaching higher, I groped and found a small crevice. Jamming my fingers in it, I pulled again. Reaching up again, I found another pebble embedded in the rock and grabbed hold as best I could. Using my left foot, I pressed down on the first small crack and heaved myself higher. If I did this a few more times, I would be able to reach my hand over the top. As I fumbled in the dark to find somewhere further up to place my right hand, the pebble I was holding onto pulled away and I hurtled to the floor. Landing on my left foot, but then falling onto my right. The pain exploded and sent a wave rolling through my entire body. It hurt so much that I had to fight hard not to pass out. I tried to get up, tried to try again, but I couldn't move anything without my right foot screaming at me.

Breathe.

I screamed for help. I shouted as loud as I could. I tried to describe where I was until my throat hurt and lungs ached. And as my voice – bouncing off the walls inside the mine – returned to me for the final time, the panic began to set in. No one would hear me, no one was there. I was going to die down here – die lying on top of my friend. My poor friend.

I rolled onto my side and began to dig. I needed to see her. The others were right. I didn't see her after the fall. I didn't look over and see her dead body. I didn't climb down, using three threaded belts to retrieve her top. I didn't bury her under rocks and dirt. I instructed, and I ran away. And after, I hid in the trees and watched them walk down the lane and past me, broken and terrified. If I was to die down here, I was going to see my friend. Like I should have back then.

That night when we found her, the others gathered around Michael's torch and illuminated her body. They all saw how she lay. But I couldn't look. I couldn't see my friend that way. Holly wanted to call the police, but she didn't move, and as the panic set in, I said something that I didn't mean to say – it was just a thought, a what if, and as soon as it slipped from my mouth I wanted to take it back because I knew I didn't mean it. However, the group latched onto the idea and in my panic, I kept talking. We could hide her, bury her. From that idea came the suggestion to place something of hers somewhere else, and then blame the Drifter. I couldn't do it, I couldn't bury her, I couldn't retrieve something of hers to hide elsewhere. So, they did it for me, and it ruined them.

I kept digging. It didn't take long for me to break through the topsoil, thrown down by the group to filter between the large stones they'd initially dropped down onto Chloe. And until this moment, I hadn't thought about that. How they, under my instruction, dropped heavy boulders and rocks onto Chloe's body. I hated myself for not seeing what I had done until it was too late.

With the soil removed, I then dug under one of the large rocks and using what strength I had, heaved it away. I then was able to reach under the next, and again I moved it, rolling it over and dropping it behind my back. After I cleared the fourth, I felt something soft. An item of clothing, long decayed but still here. I tried to remember what Chloe was wearing that night. Shuffling up, I moved another rock and when I reached under, I felt something thin and hard. A bone.

I had found her.

Fumbling around I worked out it was her forearm, and reaching under another rock, I found a collection of smaller bones, ones that made up her hand. Shuffling onto my back, I kept my arm down the hole, holding onto my best friend and closing my eyes. I waited for what came next.

CHAPTER 56

2nd December 2019
Night

I don't know how long I lay there for, the warm rock under me had the strange effect of being like a heated blanket. Comforting me, numbing me. I knew I was in trouble. For in the darkness, I kept seeing flashes of light, faint and distant. It bounced off the high cavern above me. I assumed it was blood loss, shock, my body shutting down. I had heard that in a person's final moments, lights would appear. Some would say it was heaven, some would say it was electrical impulses in our brains as it began to realise it was dying. I didn't mind either way. I felt like I should want to fight, but the fight had left me and calm washed over me instead. And in that calm, Chloe came. She sat beside me, directly above the broken earth I had dug through to find her, her hair scraped back into a pony-tail like she wore in the summer before she died, her legs crossed. Her knees bounced off the floor as she fidgeted. She looked so young, a child. And she smiled at me. I wanted to smile back, I couldn't. I daren't. Instead a tear escaped from my eye, and as I blinked it away, she was gone.

The lights began to move again on the roof of the cavern.

More intense than before. It almost looked like it had a source. But it couldn't have a source, there was no light down here. 'Just stop it,' I shouted at myself, my words barely audible through the arid space of the inside of my own throat. I knew what was happening, my mind trying to offer hope was only delaying the inevitable. And I didn't want to fight the inevitable anymore. I'd done that for so long, because when I thought about it, how could things have ended any other way? Nobody gets away with it in the end. One way or another, secrets were debts that had to be paid. I almost convinced myself I would be the exception to the rule.

The light above once again moved and I heard something too, a shuffle. I almost shouted again at myself to stop. The shuffle was followed by the sound of my name being called out. I held my breath and waited. It didn't seem like it was in my head. I heard it again, my name being called out from somewhere above.

'I'm here,' I said. My words sharp and dry. I swallowed. 'I'm down here.'

I could barely hear myself. I tried again, and the light moved closer. I begged, *please let this be real, please let it be someone who can help*. But then, what if it wasn't, what if it was Baz or Holly or one of the others, coming back to finish the job? Suddenly, I wanted to hide, to not be seen. I thought I was ready to give up and let the calm take me to oblivion. But I wasn't, I felt myself moving, grabbing stones. I tried to pull them over me, and bury myself, hide myself with Chloe until they left. Then, I would try to pull myself out of this pit and drag myself up through the mine into the world. I didn't think I would manage to, but I would try, and I would die trying. Because trying was something.

I heard my name again, closer now, and I worked faster to hide myself. As I began to cover my legs, the pain once again white hot, the light shone down from above, blinding me.

'Oh my God,' the voice called. And in my state, it took me a moment to realise who the voice belonged to. 'Don't move, Neve, I'm going to get help.'

'Please,' I tried to say, my words inaudible.

'Neve, don't speak, don't move, just stay still, I'll be back soon. I promise.'

The light moved and I heard footsteps running away. I didn't know how, but Thompson had found me. The warm rock that was comforting only minutes ago now became unbearable to lay on. I couldn't escape it. All I could do was wait for Thompson to return, if he was to return, if he was even there at all. I was so convinced that night at university about the ceiling falling in. It felt real, just like this did.

After what felt like an eternity of slipping in and out of consciousness, not knowing if I had hallucinated my saviour, I saw light dance on the cave roof. Then footsteps quickly approached, the light shone down onto my face, blinding me again. He must have seen it hurt my eyes, and angled the torch against the wall in the hole, so the whole space was lit.

'Help is coming Neve, OK? Help is on its way. I need you to stay awake, OK?'

'I'm tired,' I tried to say.

'Neve, open your eyes, come on, open your eyes.'

I did as he asked, and slowly he came into focus above me.

'That's it, well done, Neve. We are going to get you out of here, People, lots of people are coming. People are—'

He stopped and I saw his face drop. Something had stunned

him, and in my state, it took me a moment to place what that was.

'Chloe,' he said quietly. And I began to cry. 'Who did this to you, Neve? We need to find them before they get away from here,' he continued fervently. He was desperate to finally catch whoever was responsible for what had happened. 'We need Hastings to track them down. Who was it, Neve, did you see who they were?'

I nodded towards him.

'Good, that's good. Who was it? Say a name. Tell me a name.'

I almost spoke but stopped. I thought about the damage I had done to the six friends of my childhood and the mother of my best friend. And to the village itself. I thought about Jamie's sadness, Holly's fear, Baz's heartache and Georgia's powerlessness. I thought of Michael and his loneliness. Things I had caused. They had paid their price for what happened in 1998. They had paid for twenty-one years. And if I kept my mouth shut, they could escape the mine, be heroes and victims and have a life once more.

'Neve, who was it?'

'It was the Drifter,' I said.

CHAPTER 57

One year later, 2nd December 2020
Evening

It had been a year to the day since the night at the mine. And as much as everyone around me wanted to make sure I was coping, I wanted nothing more than to be normal. So, for me, it was a regular Wednesday. And I was at work. The day had been as busy as ever and with the last customer gone, I locked The Tea Tree's front door and sighed. Using my one remaining crutch to help me move, I hobbled back towards the till to cash up, but first, I needed a glass of wine. In the aftermath of Thompson finding me down the mine, I spent some time in the media eye, and though I hated the glare I suppose I was lucky. His vigilance saved me. He had spotted me drive by in Michael's car and had gone to his house and found the note. Then, assuming it was something to do with where Chloe's top was found, he headed for the mine, using my clothes to guide him down into the depths. If he had taken a sip of his pint, or stood to get another the moment I passed, I would surely be dead.

The mystery surrounding the Drifter captured the nation's attention again, who he was, where he'd gone. Holly, Jamie and the others returned home, his survivors. They returned a day after I was found. They said they were in another part of the mine, far away from where Thompson found me. The Drifter had kept them there, wanting to have all of those who had seen him in 1998. The world loved them: heroes, survivors, and the village prospered. People flocked to see the mine, the would-be victims of a mysterious, grudge-holding killer. From what I had been told, the pub was thriving. And people were beginning to let go of the past. I hadn't escaped the media either; I was another survivor. It threw our small coffee shop into the spotlight with such force we had to take on new members of staff, just to keep up with demand. I thought that once the story of the Drifter and the mine had slipped from the front pages, business would slow. So far, it hadn't. Business was so good that both Esther and I worked part time, still drawing a proper wage. She could be at home with Tilly more and I could go to my rehabilitation sessions to try and regain mobility in my right leg. I was told it would never fully heal. But, with time and the right exercise, I could walk unaided one day. It wasn't perfect, but it would have to do – this was my punishment, I suppose.

And Chloe, she was found, her body carried out in a small coffin, televised to the world. I never made it to her first funeral, so made a point of being there early to say goodbye. They laid her to rest in the same grave that had been empty for twenty-one years. Dad pushed my wheelchair through the cemetery as people cried and offered reassurances to me, the almost-victim. I felt terrible receiving praise for being so brave, so strong. I felt a crushing guilt every time I thought about how the truth about Chloe was still hidden from the world. And they were all there: Holly, Jamie, Michael, Baz, Georgia and Brenda. They watched me intently. I hugged Holly, hugged Brenda, but only because people were watching. They didn't say anything, and nor did I. When our eyes met it was clear. They would never forget, never forgive, but they would also never speak of what really happened. It was my turn to carry the cross we all had to bear.

And after Chloe's funeral, I left the village, and I vowed never to go back.

Cashing up the till and locking the safe, I sat down to finish my wine before walking to the Tube and home. On the sound system behind me, Kylie played, the song that took me back to where the nightmare began a year ago. Spookily I was doing the very thing moments before seeing Michael's shadow outside, flipping my life upside down. It made me shudder and as panic began to rise, I told myself it was behind me, it was done. The others wouldn't come back because they had their new lives; they had cleansed their guilt from that night, it was now on me. All of it. I doubted they would want to risk anything. Life was a fragile balance. And I knew they would prefer me dead, but killing me now would raise too many questions, pose too many risks for them.

Finishing my wine quickly I double-checked the safe, something I did two or three times a night now, turned off all the lights, locked the door, and stepped into the night. I looked left and right, making sure I was alone. Walking as fast as I could with only one good leg to the station, I boarded the Tube and sighed with relief. I felt safe in a crowd. As I got off at my stop, my phone pinged, a message from Dad, asking how my day was. I messaged back telling him it was long and a good one, then I asked how he was. Since the mine, Dad had been given a clean bill of health. His thyroid condition – which had led to his memory issues – was now under control with simple medication. Baz made sure he took it, just as he promised. He was a good man, a good doctor, just forced into a dark corner by my actions when we were young.

Dad messaged again.

Are you busy next weekend, I was thinking I could come and visit?

I have to work Saturday, but you're more than welcome.

I can help out in the shop if you like?

I'd really like that. Thanks, Dad.

He replied one last time, saying he couldn't wait, saying he loved me, and I couldn't help but well up a little. Those two weeks last year were awful, but Dad and I were close again, like when I was young. Maybe it was worth it all for that.

After a long and painful walk, I made it home and, hobbling through my hallway, I walked into the kitchen and flicked the kettle on before sitting at the kitchen table. My foot throbbed from work and the walk home from the station. But slowly I was beginning to heal. I drank my tea in silence. The events of last year still played heavily on my mind, as did the secrets I could never tell.

Finishing my tea, I showered and got myself ready for bed. Before I could settle, I had to check outside. Stepping into the living room I pulled back the curtain and looked onto the street. It was quiet. Satisfied, I hobbled into the bedroom and did the same to look out back. Behind the flat was a small patch of woodland – which I had once adored. Now I wished they would pull all the trees down. Looking out there always made me feel uneasy. I knew I'd not settle if I didn't. Again, quiet. I let the curtain go, and out of the corner of my eye I saw movement. Grabbing the curtain once more, I looked. Beside one of the tall hazel trees was a shape. At first, I thought my eyes were playing tricks on me, another cracked ceiling moment. But the shape moved, and out stepped a person. A long, dark coat. Heavy boots. They raised a finger to their lips.

Shhhhh.

I panicked, stubbled backwards and fell onto my bed. Cursing, I got up and looked again – there was no one there. Whoever it was, if there had been anyone there at all, had vanished like a ghost.

But I didn't believe in ghosts.

Acknowledgements

First and foremost, I would like to thank my incredible agent, Hayley Steed. Hayley, without your guidance, support and calming influence, I'd be lost at times. This book is the first in our journey together, and because of you, I feel there has been a shift in my writing process. Here's to many, many more! And to the team at Madeleine Milburn Agency, thank you for having me as part of the wonderful family.

I would like to thank my editors, Dominic Wakeford, who worked with me developing *Dark Corners*, for asking the tough questions and helping me open up Neve's story, and to Katie Seaman, who has helped me finalise the journey and bring *Dark Corners* to life as a book. I hope you know how much I value your ideas, suggestions and energy. And thank you to Victoria Moynes and Jon Appleton – your tireless efforts in making *Dark Corners* as good as it can be will never be forgotten. I'm truly honoured to have such support.

Lisa Milton, I'm blessed to be a part of the HQ family, and I'm truly grateful to you.

Another thank you is needed to my lovely writer buddies

who keep me going through the tough times. So, in no particular order: John Marrs, Louise Jensen, Phoebe Morgan, Lisa Hall, Sarah Bennett, Nicci Cloke – thanks guys. You're all blooming legends in my eyes and I feel blessed to be around so many incredibly talented people. Also, thank you to every writer I've spoken with over the past year. I've not worked in an environment where people are so lovely, kind, supportive and nurturing before.

To Tracy Fenton and the team of FaceBook's, The Book Club (TBC), you are champions of so many writers, I feel blessed to be one of them. Thank you.

To Wendy Clarke and The Fiction Café Book Club. Thank you for your support and generosity. You have been such champions of the work I do since I first popped up with *Our Little Secret*, I will always be grateful to the club.

The same thank you needs to be said to the Bertie Arms Book Club. My visits have now become a part of my identity as an author. I cannot wait to share *Dark Corners* with you all.

To my friends, Darren Maddison, John Shields, Babs and Steve Burton, the Futter's, the Kelly's, Richard Taylor, Stephen Gildersleve, Catherine and Tony Mayer and Faye Reeves. Without knowing, your interest, questions and support have helped me not lose sight of the story I really wanted to tell.

A massive thank you needs to be said to the people of New Clipstone. When I visited to research the mine that *Dark Corners* is inspired by, you were gracious with your stories, and shared more than I could have hoped for.

To you, the readers. The support you have shown and kind words you have shared has been overwhelming and wonderful, without the retweets, posts in book clubs and word of mouth discussions I wouldn't be in the place where I am now.

To my family, especially Helen, you ride this roller-coaster with me, and are there for all of the good bits, and all of the challenges. The ride wouldn't be the same without you.

Finally, to Ben. I've said this more than once, but I need to say it again. Without you there would be no motivation, no determination and no inspiration. I will forever try to repay you for this.

**Read more thrillers from Darren O'Sullivan,
the master of the killer twist**

Our Little Secret

A deserted train station: A man waits. A woman watches.

Chris is ready to join his wife. He's planned
this moment for nearly a year. The date. The
time. But he hadn't factored in Sarah.

So when Sarah walks on to the platform and sees a man
swaying at the edge she assumes he's just had too much
to drink. What she doesn't expect is to stop a suicide.

As Sarah becomes obsessed with discovering the
secrets that Chris is clearly hiding, he becomes
obsessed with stopping her, *protecting* her.

But there are some secrets that are meant to stay buried . . .

Close Your Eyes

He doesn't know his name. He doesn't know his secret.

When Daniel woke up from a coma he had no
recollection of the life he lived before. Now, fourteen years later, he's being forced to remember.

A phone call in the middle of the night demands he return
what he stole – but Daniel has no idea what it could be, or
who the person on the other end is. He has been given one
warning, if he doesn't find out his family will be murdered.

Rachael needs to protect her son. Trapped with
no way out she will do anything to ensure they
survive. But sometimes mothers can't save their
children and her only hope is Daniel's memory.

Closer Than You Think

He's watching. She's waiting.

Having barely escaped the clutches of a serial killer,
Claire Moore has struggled to rebuild her life. After her
terrifying encounter with the man the media dubbed
The Black-Out Killer, she became an overnight celeb-
rity: a symbol of hope and survival in the face of
pure evil. And then the killings stopped.

Now ten years have passed, and Claire remains
traumatised by her brush with death. Though she
has a loving and supportive family around her, what
happened that night continues to haunt her still.

Just when things are starting to improve,
there is a power cut; a house fire; another victim
found killed in the same way as before.

*The Black-Out Killer is back. And
he's coming for Claire . . .*

Keep reading for the first chapter . . .

28th August 2018
Bethesda, North Wales

The eighth

He once read somewhere that people become who they are based on their environment and experiences. Their childhood memories, the interactions with friends and profound moments, good and bad, create the building blocks of existence, and once those blocks are set, they are solid, like a castle wall. Some people are kind, some passionate, some victors, some victims. Some are violent. He knew that more than most. And although people couldn't fundamentally change, he knew, from personal experience, they could evolve. Transform. A switch could be thrown, showing a different way to be, without really being any different at all. It happened in nature: the caterpillar doesn't change its DNA when it becomes a butterfly, but unlocks a part of itself that has lain dormant, patiently waiting for the right moment to create a cocoon. He had experienced several evolutions which had altered the direction of his thoughts and actions. But these didn't change who he was. He would always be someone who killed.

And it wouldn't be long before he would kill again. A matter of an hour or so. He wanted to fulfil his purpose now, but knew he had to wait, be patient, and watch. Standing in the shadow of a wide tree, he looked into the eighth's bedroom window, waiting to see her enter, and he thought about when he would be in that room with her just before he ended her life. He knew she would panic and cry and scream before he sedated and killed her, because they always did.

He had planned to be outside her house after dark. But, with it being such a long time since he had done the one thing that made him feel alive, the thing that made him feel like he was flying, he arrived early and took time to enjoy that forgotten sense of anticipation. This also gave him a moment to reflect on the last person he'd failed to kill in this manner. A woman named Claire Moore. She played on his mind more than she should. The one that got away, so to speak.

Before coming to Bethesda, he'd felt compelled to write a letter to Claire. He wanted to explain the reasons for his absence from the world. He revealed to her that after their eventful night a decade before, he needed to regroup, re-evaluate. After her, he never intended to kill in the same manner as he would tonight. But then he discovered she was moving on, leaving that night, their night, in May of 2008 behind. He wrote that he had learnt she was becoming the same person he felt the need to visit before. Which told him she was forgetting him, and he didn't want his last survivor to forget him, because if she did, everyone else would.

He knew, one day, she would read his letter. Perhaps, before then, he would write more. If so, he would let her read them all, right before he ended her life. He could have killed Claire Moore several times in the past few months but decided not to. He wanted to wait, savour the moment. He wanted her to know him as well as he knew her, and to understand his reasons.

He wanted to be able to taste the connection they once shared on the tip of his tongue, as the light in her eyes faded. Claire Moore would die, as she nearly did by his hand all those years ago, but not yet, not until he was in buried in the centre of her soul once more. He wanted every voice to sound like his, every shadow to be one cast by his frame blocking the light. It was the reason he was in Bethesda, and why the woman whose window he looked into would die.

The knowledge of what would happen within the next hour, and what would follow over the coming weeks – the speculation, the fear – coursed through his veins so hard his skin itched. He knew he needed to focus, to contain his excitement, until night staked its claim over the day. He centred on his breathing, regulated his heart rate. He pushed thoughts of what he would do to the woman in the house opposite him out of his head.

Then she, the eighth, walked into her bedroom. He watched her step out of her work clothes, her light skirt falling effortlessly around her ankles. He enjoyed the sight of her slim frame in just her underwear, and the tingle that carried from behind his eyes to his crotch. It was a feeling he hadn't felt in a very long time. There had been plenty of kills since 2008, but not one reignited the fire he remembered from a decade before. For the past ten years, when the itch had been unbearable, he had scratched it discreetly, and taken those no one cared for. The old and alone, the homeless, the migrant. But this one was to be a spectacle, like in those wonderful days in Ireland, putting him back where he belonged, in people's minds, in Claire's mind – a destructive force touching everyone like cancer.

He missed being someone who was feared. In the days when a simple power outage caused widespread terror, he would often kill the electricity to a street, just to watch people panic, thinking they would be next. He especially enjoyed one occasion, three months after that night with Claire Moore, when a storm swept off the Atlantic and cut the power in Shannon. It caused the whole town to descend into terror, thinking he had visited. Police took to the streets, people locked their doors. News helicopters circled, expecting to see a house fire in the aftermath – his other calling card. But there was no fire, no death as he was in Greece on that day, on the island of Rhodes, enjoying the sunshine without a care in the world. He intended that trip to be one in which he learnt to be the man he would become, the man he had evolved into. But, seeing the news, the terror coming out of Ireland, drove the desire to kill once more. It was there, on the sun-bleached Aegean coast, that his metamorphosis began, as he felt a more primal calling. He needed to kill, not because it was his purpose, but for the thrill of it. After a brief search he found his victim, an unaccompanied male who had survived the Mediterranean Sea to start a new life in Europe, and he ended his life, luxuriating in the power he felt while doing so.

But the power didn't last long, because no one cared about this man's death. And upon returning home to Ireland, he could sense he was being forgotten. Over time, only the areas he had visited remembered the horror of those months between April 2006 and May 2008. To try and cling on to his power, he would still toy with their memories, killing the electricity from time to time, just to see the panic unfold. He would walk through the town and watch as whole families squashed together in one candlelit room. But time heals all wounds, and their outright terror diminished to a quiet readiness. Eventually, a power cut became just an annoyance once more.

The eighth hadn't closed her bathroom door and he could see as she unclipped her bra and dropped it on the floor. He glimpsed her breasts, and the tingle intensified. But he didn't want to fuck her; the very idea was repugnant to him. His pleasure came from somewhere else.

He visualised his approach as he waited for the sun to set. Once darkness held, he would go to the single distribution substation. It was less than two hundred metres away, and he knew it supplied the power to her house, along with a few hundred others. The enclosed five-metre wall containing the substation was built in the Nineties, along with the houses it supplied, and was secured with a padlock on its front gates. The bolt cutters that sat heavy in his rucksack would make light work of that. Then it was a case of isolating the switch gear and using a rewired portable generator that would intentionally overheat and blow. This simple and well-practised task would black out the entire street and beyond.

He pictured the walk from the substation to her back door, and then breaking in. He knew he would find her stumbling around upstairs with her phone as a torch. He suspected she would be in her nightwear. He thought about what he would do to her. The fun he would have. The joy he would feel feeding off her fear.

Then, once satisfied, he would place her body in the bathtub, douse her with petrol and ignite her. He would leave before the heat cracked the windows and smoke billowed into the sky. He would go home and cook himself a meal, a pasta dish to replenish the burnt carbohydrates from his evening's work, as he knew from experience work drove his appetite. Then, full and content, he would watch the news, waiting to see what he did featured on it, and the assumptions they would make. And he knew he would get away with it, because he'd gotten away with it before.

His kills in Ireland landed in the lap of a brute of a man named Tommy Kay. Kay was a drug dealer with a reputation for being heavy-handed if a favour or loan hadn't been repaid. He was sent to prison for running down a man in his Range Rover, nearly killing him over a hundred-pound debt. Kay's arrest and that night with Claire Moore were a few months apart, and although Kay was never charged with the murders in Ireland, he was widely believed to be the serial killer that haunted the country, never saying otherwise. Perhaps he enjoyed the notoriety it gave him?

But Kay's motivations for tacitly claiming his kills weren't his concern, because one day they would know how wrong they had been. Until then, he would play on what the media would no doubt suggest: because Kay was now dead, tonight was a copycat.

After ten minutes the eighth came out of her bathroom, a towel around her body, another wrapped around her hair. She turned on her TV, then stepped towards the window, her arm outstretched to close her bedroom curtains. She couldn't see him. He knew it. The fading sun directly behind him was low. The trees tall. She wouldn't be able to see anything beyond the dusty orange skyline. But still he pressed himself further into the tree's shadow. She paused before drawing the curtains, her eyes looking out above his head. The last line of sun painted colours in the evening sky. A perfect disguise for him. Hide the ugly thing that he had become in something equally beautiful.

It was almost time. Another thirty minutes and it would be dark enough to work. He smiled, knowing how tomorrow's newspapers would read.

CHAPTER I

6th May 2018
St Ives, Cambridgeshire

As I lay on my right side, left arm under the pillow that my head rested on, I fiddled with my necklace, counting the keys that hung from the thick silver chain. Four keys. Front door, back door and two smaller window keys, one up, one down. I watched the alarm clock flick from one minute to the next. I had done so for the last hour, waiting for it to say 05:05, then the alarm would sound, and I could get up. I'd wanted to get up at three minutes to four, a dream of fire waking me, but forced myself not to. By doing so, I hoped I could present myself as a woman who wasn't struggling to sleep. Although, I don't know who I was trying to kid. I was struggling to sleep, I always do at this time of year.

I watched the minutes turn into hours and waited for my alarm before rising, because it felt like a victory over myself. It was me telling myself I could be normal if I worked hard at it. And that was important, to be as normal as I could be. This daily victory was one of the few things I liked about the month of May. It seemed small, maybe even pointless, but the small things mattered more than I could have possibly foreseen. I had no choice but to enjoy the little things. Like the morning sunshine and the sound of the breeze in the trees; the buzz of bees in my garden collecting nectar from one of the many flowers I grew. If I focused on these details,

I would get through the month I dreaded. Then June would come, and I would survive another year.

Rolling over to face the window, I looked through the small gap in my curtains to see pale blue sky outside. Not a cloud in sight. It made me smile. A cloudless morning was another victory. Stretching, I uncurled my arms and straightened my legs groaning as my muscles pulled, and blood flowed in my limbs. A feeling I liked. Reaching over, I turned off my bedside light and picked up my phone, checking the date. I didn't know why I did that. I knew exactly what day it was. I had been checking and counting down for weeks now. The date that was the source of my sleepless nights, the date that ruined the month for me was only thirteen days away. Thirteen long days until I could reclaim the night for its intended purpose. I couldn't help but feel a rising trepidation that started just below my belly button and slowly oozed up through my stomach and chest. I sat upright and tricked myself into thinking gravity would stem the flow. With a few deep breaths, it worked.

This year marked ten years since it happened. My mother had somehow convinced me it would be healthy to go back to Ireland, back home. I didn't like flying; I didn't like the idea of going back there again. But Mum stressed it would be good for me. It would cleanse me, and, she said, would help me remove the guilt I was feeling for enjoying the time I was spending with my new friend, Paul. She was right, of course, but it didn't make me feel any better about it.

The red digital display flicked to 05:05, and the buzz made me jump. Gently, I hit the off button with my left hand. I looked at my emails on my phone. There wasn't much going on aside from some spam emails from Groupon, trying to sell me unmissable deals on spa weekends. This was exactly what I needed, and yet another thing I couldn't do.

There was also one unread Facebook message. Sighing, I opened the app and I saw who had sent it. Killian. He had messaged at 03:19. I shouldn't have read it. But I did anyway.

Hi, Claire, how are you? Is everything OK? We keep missing each other. I've been thinking about you, being May and all... I hope you are all right. I am here to talk if you need a friend.

I went to reply but stopped myself. Instead I clicked on his profile, seeing his photo hadn't been changed in all the years I had known him. The same lopsided smile, same thumbs-up gesture. The same mountain range behind him. I scrolled down to see the group page he was an administrator for: the Claire Moore Support Page. Tapping the bold letters, the next image I saw was a picture of me. I couldn't bring myself to read things from the past written there, as kind as the words were. I just wanted to see if there was anything new. The last post was from January.

Claire, on behalf of everyone here at CMSP, we want to wish you a Happy New Year. 2018 will be a good one.

I hadn't responded to the message, but remembered that shortly after a cheque came through the post from the support group, with a note attached saying I should go away somewhere nice.

I didn't spend it, I never did.

I threw the phone on my bed and rolled onto my back. I regretted reading the message. The group have always been supportive, but recently, Killian unnerved me in a way I couldn't put my finger on. To stop myself overthinking and ruining the day before it had begun, I looked towards the window. Lazy dawn light filtered through the thin curtains, casting beams of honey across the ceiling. I focused on the colours, letting myself enjoy the softness for a moment. Owen would have loved me observing this; he would tell me to enjoy the moment for as long as possible, as all things are short-lived. If only he knew how right he had been. I could almost hear him saying it, his voice light and melodic. I stopped myself. Perhaps one day it wouldn't hurt so much.

Lifting myself out of bed I slowly placed my feet on the cool wooden floor and walked quietly into my bathroom, careful not to disrupt Mum and Geoff who were asleep in the room next to me. I hadn't intended to stay the night at Mum's. I'd only wanted to come for a quick cuppa and book the online tickets for our flight to Ireland, tickets she insisted she paid for. But a quick cuppa ended in me staying for dinner and then it was late. Going home by myself was too daunting. Mum knew this, and once it had crept past eight and the daylight had faded, she offered the spare room so I didn't have to ask.

Closing the bathroom door behind me I switched on the light and waited as my eyes adjusted. Then, stretching again, feeling the blood move around my body, I considered how much I hurt. I did most mornings. Sometimes it was excruciating, sometimes tolerable. This morning I was OK. The only part of me that felt discomfort was my right foot – it always seemed to ache more in May than at any other time in the year, suggesting my pain was more psychological than physical. I popped a codeine tablet, just to be safe. Considering the mirror, I noticed that my eyes looked dark and heavy. Age was doing its dance on my face. Not that age really mattered anyway, it was all just borrowed time I would have to give back. I realised that getting older and watching a face wrinkle was a gift some didn't receive.

I heard footsteps in the hallway, followed by my mum's sleepy voice.

'I'm outside.'

'Thanks, Mum.'

She knew I was in the bathroom and had gotten out of bed,

so I knew she had an eye on me. It meant I could have a shower. Something I cannot do unless I know I am safe, even after all this time. Removing my necklace, I hung it on the back of the door before stepping into the shower and turning the water on. After the initial shock of cold water hitting me, it quickly warmed until it was so hot my skin turned pink as I washed the night away. Another night survived. Another night in the countdown completed.

As the hot water poured over my head, I focused on the heat on my scalp. I couldn't help wondering, as with most mornings recently, what I had been doing exactly ten years ago when my life had been so very different. Owen and I were probably still in bed, his heavy arm draped over me, our bedroom windows wide open, letting the cool breeze waft our net curtains, making them float like ghosts. We would get up, shower, maybe together, and then have breakfast before going our separate ways to work. He would kiss me goodbye at the door before jumping into his car and driving down the lane towards Cork. He might have been back that day, or he might have been going off-site for a few days in another part of the country. With his car out of view, I would climb into mine and drive to the pre-school where I worked. The children would arrive, and I would spend the next six hours playing, reading, cooking and helping with toilet breaks, giving gold stars to the little ones who went all by themselves. I would then come home, cook for us both, and go to bed with the windows wide open once more – oblivious to pain, heartbreak. Evil.

I knew it wasn't healthy to reminisce; that wasn't my life anymore and nothing would bring it back. I turned my attention to the torrent of hot water that ran over my forehead and into my eyes, sticking my lashes together. It stung a little, but that was good. It stopped my dark memories pushing forwards. I stayed there, head against the tiles, until thoughts of what my life had been like a decade ago washed down the plughole.

Wrapping myself in my dressing gown that I'd brought round

to Mum's a few months ago and left here, I put my necklace back on, comforted by the weight of the four keys, and walked down the narrow corridor of Mum's bungalow into the kitchen. As I passed her room I could hear Geoff snoring. No sooner had I flicked on the kettle, the cat, Baloo, greeted me. He was named after the bear in *The Jungle Book* because of his colour and the huge paws he'd had as a kitten. He meowed and stared at me, unblinking.

'Are you hungry, little man?'

He rubbed himself up against my shin to tell me yes, and acting on cue I rolled up my dressing gown sleeves and took out a pouch of his food from the cupboard beside the bin. As soon as I'd emptied the pouch into his bowl, he dismissed me. The bloody cat didn't like anyone.

I made a cup of green tea, adding a slice of lemon, and walked to the back door, needing to take some measured breaths before opening it. With my heart beating faster than before, the door creaked open, letting the rousing spring morning flood in. The air was clean and fresh, making goose bumps rise on my exposed forearms.

Dawn was my favourite time of the day. The world was still asleep, and felt somehow different. The air smelt cleaner, richer, as if the lack of cars and noise and bustle of people wrapped up in their own sense of importance allowed the trees to sigh. Dawn brought a sense of peace and magic that didn't exist at any other time in the day and, for a short while every morning, I felt like I had it all to myself. I drank it in, the peace. Again, it was in the small things, things I had only let myself see in recent years.

I stepped barefoot onto the lawn. The morning had not warmed the dew enough to evaporate it. As I walked towards the bench in the middle of the lawn, I felt the cold creep through my feet, soothing them. Broken blades of grass from yesterday's cut stuck to my soles. I couldn't look; the grass cuttings served as a powerful reminder of something I longed to forget.

I looked back towards the bungalow to see if Mum had come into the kitchen to make sure I was all right. The kitchen was empty. But I could see my footprints in the dew, perfect shapes that caught a glimmer from the rising sun. My eye was drawn to the impressions of my right foot. I had to look away. Then, sitting on the bench under a maple tree, I allowed myself to momentarily forget where I was, letting my thoughts and anxieties dissolve like sugar in hot water. This feeling of serenity wouldn't last long, so I let myself be wrapped up in it. Although the sun was weak, I could feel it warm my skin. Undoing my dressing gown, I let it touch my neck and collarbones. I focused on what I had been taught by my doctor a long time ago: enjoy the sunshine on your skin. I took a deep breath and focused on my neck which was gently warming, and drew in the smell of morning dew.

After about five minutes the moment faltered, and without warning my mind drifted back to the thoughts of flying home with Mum in ten days' time. It had been a long time since I'd last travelled any distance, and I wasn't sure how I would cope. I felt the small ice-cold hand I'd housed for a decade pluck my diaphragm like a guitar string, making the next few breaths hard to draw. I didn't want to go, but I knew I needed to. It was the right thing to do. I owed it to him, at the very least. But really, I owed him more than I could ever repay. Sighing, I sipped my now-cool tea and waited for the noise of the day to start. I heard a dog barking a few doors down, then a front door somewhere along the row of houses attached to mine opened and closed.

The world was awake, and it wasn't mine anymore. Going back into the bungalow I tried and failed to not look at my footprints.

CHAPTER 2

6th May 2018
St Ives, Cambridgeshire

I sat quietly in the kitchen for half an hour, thinking about how I hadn't been to see my doctor for a very long time. Dr Porter had been great. She listened. She knew how I felt about most things. But the last few visits, we went around in circles, discussing nothing new. And so, I stopped going to see her. Dr Porter knew most of my secrets. Most. But not all. Some things I couldn't say, and some things I wouldn't ever say. My thoughts were interrupted when I heard Mum and Geoff moving around their room, and wondered when they'd join me in the kitchen. Eventually, Geoff crossed to the bathroom and called out good morning as he did.

'Morning, I'll make you both a brew,' I called back.

'Thanks, love,' he shouted through the door.

As the kettle began to boil, I felt my phone vibrate in my dressing-gown pocket. I couldn't help but smile to see who the message was from.

So, it turns out I'm not needed on site anymore. I'm coming back later today. Do you fancy a takeaway? No pressure to say yes.

Paul wasn't due back till the weekend, and then he was seeing his daughters who lived in Cambridge. With my trip to Ireland in ten days, I wasn't likely to see him again for another few weeks. I guess that was why our ... whatever we were, worked. We were taking things slow, because we had to. Paul was also older than

14

me, quite a few years older. He was divorced and had no intention of having more children, which made things less complicated. At first, knowing his children were adults felt weird. It was one of the first things I had commented on when Mum told me how old they were. But, if we became anything other than two adults getting to know each other, I would cross that bridge when I came to it. With everything else going on – every other bridge I had to cross on a daily basis – it didn't seem that important.

We'd been spending time together for a few months now. We'd met online, which was something I wasn't sure I wanted to do but Mum, the most forward thinking sixty-four-year-old I had ever known, insisted it would do me good to meet new people, get me out and about. She had been trying for years, so, finally I said yes. She crafted my profile, stating I was Claire O'Healy, her new surname after marrying Geoff. If she put my surname it would have undoubtedly drawn the wrong attention. She wrote things in the 'about me' section I wasn't sure were entirely true, things she insisted were accurate but told me I couldn't see. She cropped a photo of me and her in my garden from last year and then hit complete, making me real in the digital world. I didn't want to see what was being said, assuming people would be unkind. And if I was honest, meeting someone was so terrifying I convinced myself I was happy on my own. It had taken me a long time to get to a place where I could manage my own company, and I wasn't sure I was ready to share that with anyone. But still, under the fear, I was also lonely.

Mum told me she would vet the potential 'friends' I would talk to and be discreet in doing so. She told me most were just looking for sex, but this didn't faze her. There were a few who appeared desperate, and only one she had seen who seemed nice. So, on a wet night a few months ago, both of us sat at my kitchen table between a pot of fresh tea and she told me all about him. A man named Paul.

When she stated he was forty-eight, I blew on my tea and raised an eyebrow. He was fourteen years older than me, and only fourteen younger than her. But after she read his profile to me, I understood why he'd made the shortlist. He seemed genuine, kind. Devoted to his children. Hard-working. He was a divorcee, but he didn't seem to have baggage, and I believed it as divorce was so common these days, lots of people didn't have complications after separation. That was the thing I was most drawn to – Paul appeared to be uncomplicated. Something I wasn't. With my curiosity piqued, I asked her to show me his message.

Hello, I'm Paul. I'm new to this so not sure what the right etiquette is. You look nice, and it's nice to be around nice people.

She showed me his photo on the dating website. He looked great. His hair was grey, but in a sexy George Clooney way, and he looked athletic and tall. Mum joked that if I didn't want to meet him she would, stating that Geoff wouldn't mind. We both chuckled at the idea. Mum and Geoff had their difficulties, as all couples did. But they loved one another dearly.

Looking back to the picture, in which he was grinning, standing by a river or lake somewhere, I could feel my hesitation rising. Meeting new people had become nearly impossible for me. With each introduction came a fresh wave of panic about who they were and what motivated them. An online introduction was unchartered territory I didn't feel I could navigate. I didn't know how you could get to know someone without seeing them face to face and reading their eyes?

'I'm not saying you have to shack up with anyone,' Mum said, interrupting my thoughts.

'Shack up? Does anyone say that anymore?' I replied, smiling.

'Claire, stop deflecting. It will be good for you.'

I dropped the smile. She was right; I was trying to sidestep the conversation. 'Mum, it's been a long time.'

'I know, that's why we're doing this. You shouldn't be on your own.'

'I'm not, I've got Penny.'

'A friend who has a family of her own.'

'I've got you and Geoff.'

'And we've got each other, Claire – you know what I mean.'

'I'm not sure I can, you know... be around somebody else.'

'You can.'

'Fine, I'm not sure I want to.'

'That's just your fear talking, Claire. After everything you've been through you deserve to have someone nice in your life.'

'But what about—'

She cut me off by reaching over the table and resting her hand on my forearm, on my scar, and although it had faded and lost its raised texture, it was still there – a permanent reminder of the past. I pulled away awkwardly, and knowing why, she apologised.

'Claire, we both know Owen would be all right with it, it's been long enough.'

'I have no idea how to do this.'

'Do what? All you're doing is saying hello. Getting to know him. The best thing about doing it this way is if it's too much for you, if you decide you don't like him, you close the app and lock your phone. God, I wish they had this when I was in the market after your dad.'

'Mum!'

I'd taken another week to pluck up the courage to say hello. Our chat was slow, both he and I not responding quickly to one another. I half expected him to rush in, overload me with messages. But he seemed as tentative as I was. We kept our conversation light, commenting on the weather and things happening in the local news. Eventually we both opened up a little and spoke of musical interests, our hobbies and our jobs – well, his anyway. I wasn't sure if it was weird or fated that Paul was in a similar line of work to Owen. But while Owen had worked on building sites, installing cables and switches into homes before they were decorated, Paul oversaw the building projects at a more senior level. I wondered, for a moment, if they might have met, but quickly quashed the ridiculous thought. When Paul asked me about what I did, I lied and told him I was taking time away from childcare. Well, part lied. Technically, I *was* taking time out: nearly ten years, in fact.

He spoke of his children often, and I spoke of not having any. We didn't talk about our pasts and I was glad he didn't ask. We exchanged emails, eventually numbers, and when we spoke over the phone, I couldn't hide the nerves. My voice shook as I fumbled for words to say. He commented on my accent, asking where in Ireland I was from and I was surprised he knew the area. Paul had family near Limerick and had visited a few times when he was younger. Then, after a month or so of chatting, we had our first dinner with Mum and Geoff. As weird as it sounds to be going on a double date with my mother, I was glad she suggested it. I couldn't face it alone.

We met at an Italian place in nearby Huntingdon. He made me laugh – made us all laugh, in fact – and appeared to be completely composed despite telling me after, via message, that he was nervous all evening. He was kind, we all could see it. Geoff, who was protective over me, treating me like his own daughter, told me as we drove home that night that he liked Paul a lot. When Mum noticed he didn't drink after he opted for a soda and lime when we had a bottle of red, she was won over. I wasn't so sure; both Mum and Geoff had to convince me I should see him again. Our next date, if you could call it that, was breakfast at a café nearby. I went alone, and for our short but lovely meet, the past didn't matter; the future wasn't real. We were just 'in the moment'. Two people talking and sharing and laughing like nothing else mattered. I almost felt normal again.

What I liked about Paul the most was his patience. We had shared a few kisses, each time becoming more fervent. But no further than that – I wasn't sure how ready I was for anything more. It had taken me years to be comfortable in my own skin.

It was a lovely surprise to know he would be back today. And, although I was still trying to be cautious, I couldn't help feel excited by the idea of us spending time together. He was the first person in a long time I had let myself become close to (other than Penny, of course, but that was different).

Now he knew who I once was, and what I was. He didn't know much, as he hadn't followed the story when it happened, but he knew enough to not need an excuse to head for the hills. But here he was, for now. I wasn't expecting it to be for ever. Not once he knew everything. And over the next few weeks, with the anniversary approaching, it was likely he would know most of the details. Someone, somewhere would dig up the past and force me to relive what happened in some magazine or online blog. Then the messages of support would come back, and my quiet life that I fought so hard to maintain would become noisy once more.

My phone vibrated again, lifting me from my daydream, as another message came through.

Or, if you prefer we could eat out somewhere?

I replied, the smile staying firmly in place.

No, a takeaway would be lovely.

His reply was instant.

Perfect. I'll be leaving the site in a few hours, then another few to get home (if the traffic gods are kind).

Don't rush, I'm not going anywhere.

Watching my screen, I saw the three dots telling me he was messaging back. It seemed to last a lifetime. Eventually he responded.

I hope not.

Regardless of the fact I was older and wiser and more battle-scarred than a teenager, I couldn't help, for a moment, feeling like one. My heart fluttered.

Geoff walked from the bathroom back into his room as Mum came into the kitchen. I turned my back, busying myself with the tea. I hoped she didn't see my cheeks had flushed. When I turned to face her she smiled, still groggy from sleep. She was wrapped in her dressing gown, which was frighteningly similar to mine. Was she young-looking, or was I dressing myself as an older lady? I wasn't sure. She kissed me on the cheek, sat at the kitchen table and asked me what my plans were for the day, expecting the answer to be as it was most days: 'Oh nothing, I'm just going to potter around.' When I sat opposite her and flippantly said Paul was coming over for a takeaway, she couldn't hide the mischievous glint in her eyes.

'Oh.'

'Mum! I know what that smile means, don't be so crude!'

Geoff walked into the kitchen scratching his stomach and yawning, like an old bear waking after a winter's sleep. He noticed I was blushing. It didn't shock me; Geoff was one to notice the small things.

'You two all right?' he asked.

'Oh, more than all right, I'd say,' Mum replied, her tone playful and teasing.

'Oh yeah?'

'Claire is on a promise.'

'I'm not on a promise, Mum! Who even says that anymore? Paul's just coming around for a bite to eat.'

'Yeah, Geoff did the same thing nearly twenty years ago.'

'She's not been able to get rid of me since,' he said, laughing and squeezing Mum's shoulder with his wide calloused hand before sitting at the table beside her.

'You two are hopeless,' I said, smiling at them before getting up to grab the mugs.

'So, what time is he coming over?' Geoff continued, blowing on his tea.

'I don't know, later?'

'Want us to pop out and get a bottle of wine or something?'

'No, I'll go,' I said, and both Mum and Geoff looked at me a little too quickly.

'Claire, shall I come with you?' Mum asked delicately.

'I'll be fine.'

'Are you sure?'

'Yeah, I want to go for myself.'

'Good for you!' Geoff replied, a little too eagerly.

It wasn't every day I had something to look forward to. It wasn't every day I even needed to get dressed. Paul coming back and wanting to see me filled me with an unexpected sense of purpose. I needed to do something before seeing him. I decided I wanted to be out in the world, to get us a bottle of wine and something for dessert; I wanted to be the one to do it.

I had to prepare myself first.

ONE PLACE. MANY STORIES

Bold, innovative and
empowering publishing.

FOLLOW US ON:

@HQStories